Praise for the Children of the Su...

Prince of Swords

"Allow yourself to be swept into a world where good and evil battle, where goddesses and princes fight demons and shape-shifters. This is a world Jones excels at creating, [an] exciting, colorful realm."
—*Romantic Times*

Prince of Fire

"Linda Winstead Jones pens a perfect romance laced with strife, mystery, and an intense passion hot enough to singe your fingers."
—*Romance Junkies*

Prince of Magic

"Punchy battle scenes and steamy lovemaking will please genre fans, but it is Jones's gift for creating complex heroes and villains that lifts this story out of the ordinary."
—*Publishers Weekly*

Praise for the Sisters of the Sun Trilogy

The Star Witch

"Bewitching . . . A fabulous climactic romantic fantasy . . . filled with fascinating twists, beguiling."
—*Midwest Book Review*

". . . done! Very sensual."
—*Booklist*

". . . ntastic denouement . . . For an action-packed and . . . ing romance, *The Star Witch* is just what the doctor . . . ed."
—*Romance Reviews Today*

continued . . .

The Moon Witch

"I can hardly wait to find out how she will [entwine] all the threads she has created! . . . This series is just too good to miss."
            —*The Romance Reader*

"An enjoyable romantic fantasy that grips the audience . . . Action-packed."
            —*The Best Reviews*

"A unique and imaginative realm . . . Prepare to be swept away!"
            —*Rendezvous*

"[W]ill enthrall . . . Lushly imaginative."
            —*Publishers Weekly*

The Sun Witch

"Entertaining and imaginative, with a wonderful blend of worlds and technology and magic. The characters are different and engrossing; the villain is fascinating."
            —*New York Times* bestselling author Linda Howard

"Charming . . . Winsome . . . The perfect choice when you want a lighthearted and fun, yet sensual, romance . . . with all the magic of a fairy tale."
            —*Bookbug on the Web*

"Fabulous . . . The story is spectacular and this author is unforgettable."
            —*Road to Romance*

"She has a special, magical way about her . . . It's Jones at her very magical best. I am very glad to see her back . . . She shines."
            —Deborah MacGillivray

"Amazing adventures unfold . . . Marvelously captivating, sensuous, fast-paced."
            —*Booklist* (starred review)

"Hot."
            —*Affaire de Coeur*

22 Nights

Linda Winstead Jones

BERKLEY SENSATION, NEW YORK

THE BERKLEY PUBLISHING GROUP
Published by the Penguin Group
Penguin Group (USA) Inc.
375 Hudson Street, New York, New York 10014, USA
Penguin Group (Canada), 90 Eglinton Avenue East, Suite 700, Toronto, Ontario M4P 2Y3, Canada
(a division of Pearson Penguin Canada Inc.)
Penguin Books Ltd., 80 Strand, London WC2R 0RL, England
Penguin Group Ireland, 25 St. Stephen's Green, Dublin 2, Ireland (a division of Penguin Books Ltd.)
Penguin Group (Australia), 250 Camberwell Road, Camberwell, Victoria 3124, Australia
(a division of Pearson Australia Group Pty. Ltd.)
Penguin Books India Pvt. Ltd., 11 Community Centre, Panchsheel Park, New Delhi—110 017, India
Penguin Group (NZ), 67 Apollo Drive, Rosedale, North Shore 0632, New Zealand
(a division of Pearson New Zealand Ltd.)
Penguin Books (South Africa) (Pty.) Ltd., 24 Sturdee Avenue, Rosebank, Johannesburg 2196,
South Africa

Penguin Books Ltd., Registered Offices: 80 Strand, London WC2R 0RL, England

This is a work of fiction. Names, characters, places, and incidents either are the product of the author's imagination or are used fictitiously, and any resemblance to actual persons, living or dead, business establishments, events, or locales is entirely coincidental. The publisher does not have any control over and does not assume any responsibility for author or third-party websites or their content.

22 NIGHTS

A Berkley Sensation Book / published by arrangement with the author

PRINTING HISTORY
Berkley Sensation mass-market edition / December 2008

ISBN: 978-0-425-22491-5

BERKLEY® SENSATION
Berkley Sensation Books are published by The Berkley Publishing Group,
a division of Penguin Group (USA) Inc.,
375 Hudson Street, New York, New York 10014.
BERKLEY SENSATION and the "B" design are trademarks of Penguin Group (USA) Inc.

PRINTED IN THE UNITED STATES OF AMERICA

10 9 8 7 6 5 4 3 2 1

For Lisa and April,
the daughters I acquired by marriage.
You have both enriched my life.
Love you.

Prologue

The Columbyanan Palace in the Sixth Year of the
Reign of Emperor Nechtyn Jahn Calcus Sadwyn Beckyt
First Night of the Spring Festival

ALL evening, Merin had tried to avoid the woman who
now literally cornered him on the stairway which led to his
quarters on Level Four. He'd made an appearance at the
palace festivities, as was expected, but once there he'd
found himself the target of many curious and ambitious
women. There was something about the arrival of spring
which made females of a certain age and their mothers
think of weddings and babies. What a disastrous state of
mind.

None of those females had been more dogged than the
woman who'd ambushed him on the stairs as he'd attempted to escape to the quiet comfort of his private quarters.

Cipriana Etain, wife of a highly placed secretary who
was here on this night to celebrate the Spring Festival, blocked his avenue of escape—unless he was willing to appear a coward who would turn and run down
the stairs. If her hips were not so wide, he might think of

rushing around her. No, she obstructed the way quite well, with her hips and her voluminous gown and her glare. Her daughters stood behind her, pink-cheeked and intimidated and not yet so wide. They were actually bone-thin like their father, and seemed to be as reserved as Secretary Etain. All three women were breathless. None of them was accustomed to climbing so many steps.

"I thought I had missed you, General Merin," Lady Cipriana said, trying to hide her breathlessness with a laugh. It didn't work well, as she ended up practically wheezing. "You're a difficult man to claim for an audience." She rested a hand on her heaving bosom. "May I call you Tearlach?"

"No one calls me by my given name," he responded. Not friends, not lovers, certainly not this irritating woman.

"Surely your mother . . ."

"You're not my mother."

Displeasure was evident on her plain, weathered face. "I tried all evening to claim a moment of your time, *General*, but you were always on the move. A dance here, a conversation there, and I swear there were times when it seemed you simply disappeared."

He should be so lucky.

"You never did get the chance to dance with my daughters, Irinia and Ileana." She indicated the girls with a wave of her hand, and they curtseyed, one after the other.

"That's my loss, I'm sure, but it was a very busy evening," he said. "Now, if you'll excuse me . . ."

The older woman's expression changed, her mouth and her eyes hardening. "Not just yet, General. I worked much too hard to claim this time with you to let you get away so easily."

Merin met the woman's glare with his own. If she did

not feel it necessary to be polite, then neither did he. "What do you want?"

The woman placed her hands on those generous hips, her plump and stubby fingers looking pale against her dark gown. "You are three years past thirty, General, only a few years younger than I. It is long past time for you to take a wife. From all I hear, you are next in line for the position of Minister of Defense. A man of power needs a woman to soothe and aid him, to give him children and provide solace and stability and social acceptability." She nodded decisively. "Either of my girls would make you a fine wife. They are both pretty and virtuous. I have taught them well, so you can be assured that no man has ever touched that which is a husband's to take. They are healthy and do not speak much, and they have been well taught in the arts of homemaking."

"That sounds lovely, but . . ."

"Whichever you choose will come with a substantial dowry, including a family house north of Arthes." She grinned tightly. "You made your reputation the hard way, General Merin, with blood and sweat. My family can provide what you lack. Social standing. Respectability. A well-respected family name and all that comes with it."

The woman had managed to praise and insult him in the same breath.

One of the girls looked at the floor and blushed. The other concentrated on a spot on the wall. He could only imagine how humiliating it must be for the sisters to stand there while their mother tried to sell them, using money and virtue to make the deal.

Merin stared at their mother. "Madam, I have had a long day, and this is a discussion for another time."

"No, it is a discussion for now, General. I have waited as long as I can." She pursed her lips tightly and then made an outrageous offer. "If you'd like to assure that one or the other would be to your liking, take one now. Whichever you pick, she will be yours for the night, if you wish."

He had thought nothing more could shock him, but the annoying woman proved him wrong. "Are you offering up one of your daughters for . . ."

"A trial of sorts," Lady Cipriana said sharply, "to see if she suits behind closed doors. Just choose the one who pleases you best, and she is yours."

"That's ludicrous," Merin said beneath his breath, certain that to so much as touch one of these girls with the tip of his little finger would mean an immediate wedding ceremony.

"You must . . ." Lady Cipriana began.

"I *must* do nothing," Merin interrupted. "When the time comes for me to take a wife, I won't make my choice in the stairwell, ambushed and harassed by an overly ambitious mother." He bowed to her without respect, nodded to the girls in sincere sympathy, and then he made his way around them all, coming close to the lady's wide skirts but managing to avoid touching. Once past the women, he ran up the stairs.

General Hydd must've started talking in public about his upcoming retirement. That was the reason so many women had tried to corner him tonight. What they didn't know was that Merin had been offered the post of Minister of Defense years ago, almost immediately after Emperor Jahn had taken control. At the time he'd been battle weary and not all that certain of the new emperor's abilities.

Now he knew that Emperor Jahn—a man he had first known as Devlyn Arndell—was a fine man and a grand emperor. If he was offered the post of Minister of Defense now, he would probably take it.

On Level Four, Merin found another obstacle to his

much-needed seclusion. General Hydd himself waited in the hallway.

If he tried to palm off one of his daughters . . .

"There you are," the general said impatiently. "I looked for you at the ball and you weren't there, so I suspected you'd be here, but no one answered my knock."

"I went for a ride after I left the gathering," Merin explained. A hard ride in the cool night air had felt wonderful, and the bonfire he'd ridden toward had been primal and powerful. Unfortunately, his excursion had given Lady Cipriana a chance to position herself and lie in wait. "I apologize for not being here when you arrived."

General Hydd waved his hand, dismissing the inconvenience. Still, he was tense, and Merin could not help but wonder why.

They stepped into Merin's private quarters, which consisted of four large rooms connected by many doors. Each room was lavishly furnished. He preferred dark, cool colors, so the draperies and upholsteries were in deep shades of blue and green. Housekeepers were here every day, dusting and sweeping, seeing to his clothing if it needed cleaning or mending, scrubbing the floors. This large portion of Level Four was his to call home, his reward for years of service—service which had not yet ended.

These four rooms were larger than the house in which he'd been raised. He had servants ready for his call, night and day. He had more clothes and boots and fine weapons than any one man needed. And when he was made Minister of Defense, *if* he was made Minister of Defense, his station would once again be elevated. Was that why the current minister called upon him so late at night? Had the time come?

"I need your help," the general said when they were behind closed doors. "Emperor Jahn has finally agreed to take a wife."

It was about time. "Who is the new empress to be?" Merin asked.

General Hydd made a sour face. "No one is sure. The emperor has decreed that six suitable women be brought to him by the first night of the Summer Festival, at which time he will choose among them."

Merin laughed. What an absolutely ridiculous plan! And one which reminded him very much of the irreverent soldier Devlyn Arndell had been before he became Emperor Jahn. That young man would find this a sort of revenge on those who commanded that he take a wife, a rebellion of sorts. Merin didn't laugh long, as the general before him obviously didn't think the situation was funny. At all.

Merin poured two mugs of wine and offered one to the older man, who as a proper Minister of Defense had a suitable wife, two sons, and three grown daughters. General Hydd gratefully took the wine, and he looked as if he needed it more than Merin did. He didn't waste much time downing at least half of the strong, sweet drink. "Six women," he said after he wiped the back of his hand across his wine-stained mouth. "Couriers will be dispatched immediately, as some of the ladies live quite a distance from the palace. There is one candidate I thought you might be able to assist us with."

Merin could not imagine how he might be able to help. He didn't know a single unmarried woman in Columbyana he would consider suitable for the position of empress.

"You fought with a small contingent from the Turi Clan during the war," General Hydd said.

Merin's heart sank and sat in his stomach like a boulder. That was a time in his life he preferred not to think about, if at all possible. "They are a rather primitive people, General. Surely there is not a woman among them the emperor would consider taking as his wife."

"I'm afraid there is." General Hydd took another long swig. "It seems that in recent years the miners among the clan have unearthed an excess of gems in the mountains they call home. The find was extraordinary, and as a result the clan has become quite wealthy."

The conversation reminded Merin too much of the one he'd just had on the stairway. Brides for sale! "Is Columbyana in financial difficulty?"

The general sighed. "Always, to some degree."

"Enough so to sell the position of empress?"

Hydd shrugged his shoulders. "Not really, but wealth is certainly a consideration. The Minister of Finance suggested Belavalari Haythorne as a candidate."

"Bela?" Merin wished he was back in the stairwell, trapped by a husband-hunting mother. Recovering quickly, he pretended to cough, then cleared his throat and began again. "Belavalari Haythorne of the Turis?"

"Yes. Her father is chieftain, or some such, and Minister Tomos likes the idea of having an imperial connection by marriage to all that wealth."

Horrors. Bela in the palace. Bela as empress. Bela married to Emperor Jahn. Impossible. "Belavalari Haythorne is just a girl, and if memory serves, she isn't at all suitable for the position of empress."

"She's twenty-three, according to Tomos. That's hardly too young for marriage. If she's truly unsuitable, then she won't be chosen."

"If she comes here and she's not chosen, her family will be insulted and they'll attack the palace."

General Hydd straightened considerably. "They wouldn't dare."

"You'd be surprised," Merin mumbled.

Hydd tossed off his indignation. "In any case, it's done. The decisions have been made. The Haythorne girl has been chosen as a contender, and it is not in my power to undo that fact. Still, I know the Turis are an odd tribe of people, different from other Columbyanans in many ways. Who would you suggest we send to collect Lady Belavalari? We don't want to insult her father or cause an incident. Their customs are so unusual, I'm not sure who would be best."

Lady Belavalari. The girl he remembered was no lady.

"I'll go," Merin said.

"You?" The general was genuinely surprised. "That's a generous offer, but not necessary. I'm sure it will take every bit of the three months allotted to travel to the far corner of the Eastern Province, deliver the news, and return with the bridal candidate and a proper contingent of chaperones and such."

Merin sat in a nearby chair, as his legs did not feel all that steady at the moment. "It is not an act of generosity I offer," he said, "but one of necessity. I know the Haythorne family well. *Lady* Belavalari's brothers fought with me for a time. When I was wounded, I spent some time among the Turis."

"Still, you could instruct a courier . . ."

"If you send a stranger to Chieftain Valeron Haythorne to suggest that his only daughter travel to Arthes to be inspected to see if she's good enough to be empress, that poor courier's head will very likely come back with a note of regrets."

"They wouldn't!"

"They would," Merin said softly, knowing the Turis would consider such an act justified. "Besides, I have been thinking of getting away from Arthes for a while. The trip will do me good." He stood and downed what was left of his wine, and it was settled.

Merin wondered what kind of reception he would get from the Haythorne family and the Turi Clan who loved and looked up to them. If Bela had told her family everything that had happened, it was entirely possible that *his* head would be delivered back to the palace. He doubted anyone would bother with a note of regrets in his case.

Chapter One

✴

AMONG the Turis, marriage was a simple thing. A man and woman promised themselves to one another with their actions more than with formal words. There was an exchange of gifts, a simple dance, a kiss, and then it was done. The clan gathered to celebrate their union with food and drink and general merriment.

Bela did not feel particularly merry at the moment. She watched with sullen and openly acknowledged self-pity as her friend Jocylen offered Rab Quentyn a bowl of stew she had made with her own hands. He took it and drank some of the broth, and then he placed a ring of brightly colored spring flowers upon her head. They joined hands, and while simple, slow music played on a single lute filled the night air, they took a turn, skipped in unison, and spun about. Jocylen laughed, and because he was so pleased with her joyous response, Rab laughed, too. They kissed, a joyous cry from families and friends filled the air, and it was done.

Bela did not shout or laugh, but she did move forward to offer Jocylen her congratulations. She wanted her friend to be happy, she truly did, and she knew how very much Jocylen loved Rab. But no one else understood her, no one else knew all her secrets, and now Jocylen would spend her days cooking and making a home, and in short order there would be children to care for and the newlywed would begin to spend her time with other married women who were devoted to their husbands, women who spent their days talking about babies and sewing and how best to cook a tough piece of meat.

Bah! Bela had never cared for any of those things, much to her mother's dismay. She preferred hunting with her brothers to cooking, and she had no intention of taking care of any man. Not ever.

Jocylen smiled at Bela and took her hand. "You dressed well for my special occasion, I see."

Bela glanced down at the plain, drab green gown which draped simply and ended just short of her best sandals, sandals adorned with gemstones from the mountains which surrounded the village of the Turis. Unhappy as she was at the turn of events, she would not attend her beloved friend's marriage ceremony in her usual male-style clothing. Heaven above, she had even washed her hair! "Did you expect any less?" Bela asked, as if her efforts meant nothing.

"With you I never know what to expect," Jocylen responded.

The circlet of gold which adorned Bela's brow was heavier and less comfortable than her usual cloth or leather circlet. Yes, she had gone to great lengths to make herself presentable. Perhaps she was displeased to see her friend marry and join the ranks of the wives of the clan, but she also wanted to see Jocylen happy. Which she was. Blast!

"If he hurts you, I will gut him."

Jocylen's eyes widened. "Rab would never hurt me."

"Well, if he does . . ."

"He won't!" Jocylen rose up on her toes, as she was a good half-foot shorter than Bela, and kissed a reluctant cheek. "Don't worry so, Bela. We will still be friends. Forever, no matter what."

And then Jocylen was whisked away by new relations. Food and drink for all would follow, and then the newlyweds would retire to their home and do what newly wed couples did. Poor Jocylen. Bela had tried to warn her friend, but the warnings had been dismissed. Somehow the new bride expected bliss in her husband's bed.

She'd think differently in short order.

Alert as always, Bela was among the first to hear the quick hoofbeats approaching. She and a number of the men rushed to meet one of a pair of guards who had been posted at the western edge of the village, on this side of the river. Since so many riches had been discovered in the nearby mountains, mountains owned and protected by the Turis, they'd had to take measures to secure the safety of the people.

Some men would do anything for wealth.

Byrnard Pyrl leaped from his horse with a grace Bela admired. "A rider approaches. He wears an imperial uniform and his horse is clad in a soldier's imperial green as well, but of course that doesn't mean he's who he appears to be."

Bela's heart gave a nasty flip at the mention of imperial green. They did not see many soldiers out so far, not since the end of the war with Ciro, but still—her heart and her stomach reacted fiercely.

A handful of men gathered weapons and torches and collected their horses. The would-be intruder would be met and turned away from the village. None but Turis were welcome here. Strangers were not allowed simply to ride into their midst and be accepted.

Bela quickly collected her own sword and ran to her horse, intent on joining the men who would meet the rider. She was not surprised when her brother Tyman ordered her to remain behind with the other women. No one but she would see the glint of humor in his eyes. She looked to her older brother Clyn, who did not have Tyman's sense of humor. He, too, shook his head in denial.

Just because she was dressed like a woman tonight, that didn't mean she had to be treated like one!

A group of six men, her brothers among them, galloped toward the western edge of the village, their torches burning bright long after the men and the animals had vanished from sight. Bela watched those bits of light for a moment, and then she hiked up the skirt of her long gown and leaped into the saddle. Her sword remained close at hand, tucked into the leather sheath which hung from her saddle.

"Belavalari, don't!" a well-dressed and attractive older woman cried, rushing forward from the group of revelers. Bela knew that her mother would very much like to see her only daughter become a wife, as Jocylen had. She wanted to see her daughter among those women who cooked and cleaned and sewed and birthed babies.

"Sorry, Mama, I have to go."

"You do not . . ."

Bela set her horse into motion before her mother could finish her protest. Her loose hair whipped behind her as she raced from the village, her mare galloping into the darkness, away from the fires which lit the night celebration. For the first time this evening, Bela smiled. She was more warrior than woman, and when it came to protecting these people from intruders, it was as much her duty as it was her brothers'.

MERIN was not surprised to see the riders approaching with force and mistrust; this was a typical Turi greeting. It was for this reason that he had chosen to make the trip alone. He was sure that Valeron would send a chaperone, and perhaps a warrior or two, with his daughter when they left the village for Arthes, but on the initial leg of the journey other travelers would've only slowed him down.

And would've made this initial greeting more difficult.

The Turis would not be suspicious of one traveler, especially when he was a soldier with whom many of them had once fought. If Merin had arrived with a contingent of soldiers, that would've been another story entirely.

Merin slowed his horse and held up both hands, so the riders would see that he was unarmed. As they drew close, he was happy to see two familiar faces. Tyman and Clyn, sons of the Turi chieftain, had fought with him for a time, when the threat of Ciro's Own had come near their home. Even though they had not parted on the best of terms—he had wished for an army of Turis to fight with his sentinels well beyond the clan's lands, and they had refused—he trusted them. They were good, if somewhat primal, men.

The chieftain's sons were not happy to see him, but they wouldn't kill him—not right away, in any case. Not unless their sister had said too much after Merin had left their village.

"I bring a message from the emperor," Merin called out. His hands remained visible, but even so three of the riders drew their swords. Tyman and Clyn did not draw arms.

"What do you want?" It was the fair-haired Clyn who moved closest to Merin. The elder Haythorne son was extraordinarily large. Clyn was probably Merin's age, or thereabouts. He was a full head taller and was wide in the shoulders. A long, blond braid fell over one of those shoulders. His chest and arms were unusually muscled, but those muscles did not impede him in swordplay, as they might with some men. Clyn was an intense and gifted swordsman. In any fight, Merin definitely wanted Clyn on his side.

The big man did not look like an ally at the moment.

"As I said, I have a message . . ."

Tyman, the more hotheaded brother, rode forward and almost ran into Merin's horse. The animals danced on graceful hooves. Tyman's loose, long hair—reddish brown and wavy like Bela's—danced around his angry face and rigid shoulders. "Give me one reason why I shouldn't kill you here and now."

Judging by the expressions before him, Bela had talked. What had she told her brothers? The truth or her twisted version of the truth? Anything was possible. "One reason?" Merin looked Tyman in the eye. "Kill me, and an entire army will come down on your head. The Turi have many fierce warriors, I will give you that, but Emperor Jahn has you in numbers. Kill me, and they will crush you all."

It was true, and surely they knew that; yet Tyman still gripped the handle of his undrawn sword.

"And if you are killed by a woman?" an unexpectedly soft voice asked.

Merin's head snapped around. He had been so intent on Clyn and Tyman he had not seen or heard the seventh rider arrive. She moved into the light of their torches, the gold circlet across her brow glinting in the firelight, her wild chestnut hair shimmering. Her dress had been hiked up to allow her to ride astride, and so her long, strong legs were exposed to the night air. She simply did not have the reservations that others of her age and gender possessed.

"Lady Belavalari," he said.

She drew her sword, and something on the handle of her weapon caught the light in a strange way. He didn't have time to study the weapon's grip; he was more focused on the blade and the woman who wielded it. She could kill him, and at the moment she looked as if she had killing on her mind.

"General Merin," she responded, "I did not think ever to see you again. I did not think you would be so foolish as to come anywhere near the Turis."

Bela was older, leaner of face, more confident than he remembered. The shape of her body was a bit different: softer, a bit rounder, but maybe it was the unexpected dress. No matter what she wore, she was more strength than gentleness.

"I have a . . ."

"Message," she interrupted sharply. "I heard. Are you still a general, or have you been demoted to courier?"

"I am still a general," he said calmly.

"What foolish mission would lead you here, where your life is all but worthless? I would think a general would be smarter, though in my experience you're not known for your vast intelligence."

A couple of the men laughed, but not Bela's brothers.

"I need to speak to your father," Merin said, ignoring her gibes. Was she trying to provoke a fight so she'd have an excuse to cut him down? That was certainly possible.

"First you have to get past me," she said.

He had heard tales of female warriors who'd lived in the past, and he imagined they might've looked very much like this. Bela Haythorne was stubborn, strong, willful, skilled, and fearless. She was in many ways everything Merin had ever wanted in a soldier.

Unfortunately, she was also deceptive, manipulative, and determined to have her own way in every situation, no matter what the cost.

She was very close to him now, and she held her sword steady and thrust it forward so that the tip of the blade came near his heart. Not threateningly close, not yet. Again the exposed portion of the grip caught the light from a torch and glinted brightly. Bela's arm did not seem to be strained, as she continued to hold the weapon steady.

"It is your decision, Bela," Tyman said in a low voice. "Kill him, and we will gladly fight the war that follows. You have every right to take his head, and any other part of him that strikes your fancy."

Only one man laughed that time, and the harsh sound was strained and short-lived.

Thanks to the darkness of night and the way she'd narrowed her calculating eyes, he could not see the warm, mossy green he remembered. After all this time he should not remember that particular detail, but he did. Narrowed or not, night or not, he *could* see the anger and the hurt in her eyes. "Is that what you want, Bela?" he asked. "Do you want my head?"

"Yes," she whispered.

"Then take it." Hands out, defenseless, he looked into her eyes without fear.

For a moment he thought she might take him up on the offer, but eventually the sword fell and she looked to Clyn. "Take General Merin to Papa, let him deliver his message, and when that is done, have him escorted to the other side of the River Hysey." Her gaze returned to him. "Consider my generosity a parting gift, General. If I see you again I *will* take your head."

BELA spun her horse about and urged the mare to a full run, not looking back, not acknowledging to anyone that her heart was pounding too hard and her mouth was dry.

Tearlach Merin, here after all this time. She'd never admitted to anyone, not even Jocylen, that she'd spent the better part of a year foolishly waiting for him to return. It would have been a ridiculous confession, considering the circumstances. She'd never admitted to anyone that she dreamed about General Merin now and then. Well, he'd had plenty of time to come back, and he hadn't. Now it was too late. Much too late!

Just when she had her life settled as she pleased, just when she was happy with her lot, he came waltzing back, looking just as pretty as ever with that dark curly hair that did not hang even to his shoulders, and those deep, dark brown eyes and that perfect nose and the lovely full mouth. She knew men did not like to be called pretty, but Tearlach Merin was.

Too bad looks were deceiving.

Bela held on tight and let the horse run free in the night. With every hoofbeat against the ground her worry eased. Merin wouldn't be here for very long. He'd deliver his message and then he'd be gone long before sunup. Maybe this time he'd know better than to come back. It wasn't as if he had returned for her.

And if he had . . . ?

Many villagers were standing about, waiting to learn who had come calling at such a late hour. Bela dismounted, withdrew her sword from its sheath, and then, for her mother's benefit, she smoothed her wrinkled skirt and ran the fingers of one hand through her hair. "The man who entered our territory is a messenger from the emperor," she said simply. No reason to tell them all that it was General Merin, come back to taunt her. They'd find out soon enough. "He'll need to speak to Papa before he leaves." She glanced around, but saw no sign of Jocylen. The poor girl had probably already retired, not knowing what awaited her in her marriage bed. Really, women should be told the truth, instead of being fed pretty lies about love and pleasure.

Bela found her mother in the crowd. "I'm exhausted," she said. "It's been such a long day."

Gayene Haythorne narrowed her eyes suspiciously. Bela was never the first to bed. She preferred staying up late and sleeping long past sunrise when possible. "Are you ill?"

Did heartsick count? Bela wondered. "No, I'm fine." She looked toward the narrow lane that led to Jocylen's new home. "I'm just a bit worried about Jocylen. Poor girl. You know how I feel about marriage, Mama. It is a horrid and unnatural state for women."

"It is not," her mother said genially. They'd had this argument many times, and had finally come to an understanding: they would never agree.

"In any case, I have worried about Jocylen all day, and worrying is exhausting."

"As I well know," Gayene replied, not even attempting to hide her true meaning.

Bela did not respond to that. She had given her mother no reason to worry. Not today.

"I'm off to bed." Bela gave her mama, an attractive woman who was almost as tall as she, a kiss on the cheek.

Bela's progress was stalled by a warm hand on her arm. She did not pull away, but stopped to look directly at her mother. "You look beautiful in a dress," Gayene said, "with your hair down and your face clean." Her eyes flitted briefly but with evident displeasure to the sword Bela carried. "You should pretend to be a lady more often."

Then they both smiled. Differences aside, there was an abundance of love in the Haythorne family.

When Bela heard the approaching riders, who moved at a much slower pace than she had, she said a quick good night to her mother and hurried toward home. She did not look back. She would not give Tearlach Merin the pleasure. Oh, she felt like such a girl, with her heart pounding and her hands trembling, all on account of a *man*. The crystal grip of her sword vibrated, and she held on tight. "No need to worry about him, Kitty," Bela said softly. "He won't be here long."

Did Kitty vibrate because she wanted to take Merin's head? Did she long for battle in this time of peace?

The Turi village was laid out like a wheel, with the town square at the center, essential businesses around that square, and houses extending from that center like spokes. Beyond the houses were farms, small and large, and a couple of ranches. Even farther to the west ran the River Hysey, and to the east lay the gem-filled mountains where so many of the Turi males worked, where some even chose to live.

The Haythorne house was one of the finest in town, which was natural since Valeron Haythorne was chieftain. Still, the building, which was made of wood and stone, was simple. The long, single-story house was clean, large, well built, and plain. There were sturdy furnishings and a few adornments, but for the most part it was a functional home. The Turis were not a frivolous people.

Bela's room was located at the rear of a short hallway. As the only daughter she had always had the luxury of her own bedchamber. Her father was Turi chieftain, and that meant she was all but a princess. Still, she did not fill her room with fripperies. There was no lace, no frills. The only concession to her femininity was a wooden rack built onto the wall where she stored her small selection of jewelry and headbands. Though she would not admit it aloud for fear of sounding frivolous, she liked the sparkle of the gems found in the mountains nearby, she liked the glitter of gold and the sheen of silver.

Bela placed Kitty upon another rack, one which had been built just for that purpose. Like the few feminine adornments Bela possessed, Kitty sparkled. The special crystal from the mountains nearby was alive in a way that was difficult to explain.

Sometimes Kitty spoke to her. Not in a voice that could be heard with the ears, but with a whisper in the soul. For weeks on end Kitty would be silent, and then she would begin to speak again, spreading wonder into Bela's life. Bela reached out and touched her fingertips to the crystal grip. Even though Kitty's existence had been known of for less than three years, she was already legend among the Turis. Every warrior wanted her, and some wondered aloud why Bela Haythorne, a mere woman, possessed such a gift. Many thought that her father had allowed her to keep it, a special gift for a spoiled daughter. What they didn't know, what very few understood, was that Bela had not chosen Kitty.

Kitty, a sword which was as alive as any person Bela knew, had chosen her. The village seer, a grumpy old man named Rafal Fiers, said that one day Kitty would choose another. But not today.

Bela heard the front door open and close several times. She heard raised voices that held a tenor of excitement. Kitty's grip shone bright, as if she were excited, too. Could a sword feel exhilaration? Could it crave and want and feel? Kitty could, Bela knew it.

Her bed chamber door opened swiftly, without the courtesy of a knock.

"The main room," her mother said briskly. "Hurry."

Bela left Kitty upon her rack and followed her mother from the chamber. She should've expected what she found in the main room of her family home, but she had not. The sight took her breath away.

General Merin, better lit here than he had been when she'd seen him on the road, was on his knees, head down, hands tied behind his back. She could not see his face for the fall of dark curls which were surely the envy of many a vain woman. Tyman stood behind the general, the tip of his sword at Merin's neck.

"Stop!" Bela cried.

Her brother lifted his head but not his sword. "We know what he did to you, Bela. He was foolish enough to come back here, and he will pay the price. As soon as he delivers his message to Papa, the general is going to die."

Merin tried to lift his head, but Tyman forced it back down with a tap of his blade.

"You don't understand," Bela began. There went her heart again, pounding too hard and too fast. Why was she alarmed? Maybe it would be best if Merin was dead. Hadn't she just threatened to take his head herself?

But not like this, and not for something that wasn't his fault.

"I do not need to understand!" Clyn bellowed. "He took a husband's rights, and then he rode away and did not look back."

"It was my fault," Bela said, the words hurting a little. She hated to admit that anything was her fault. "I insisted . . ."

"You were seventeen!" Tyman shouted. "He was a grown man who should've known better."

Even from this distance, Bela heard Kitty's urgent whisper as clearly as if the words were being shouted. *Tell all.*

Bela took a deep breath and exhaled slowly. Her mother tried to calm her boys. They would not kill Merin right away, not until her father arrived and the message which had brought him here was delivered. There had to be another way. How could she tell her family what had really happened that night? It was mortifying.

Tell all.

"Fine," Bela snapped. "Since it appears that you *must* know, I drugged the general until he was nonsensical, told him I was twenty years of age and a widow looking for physical comfort, and then I took off all my clothes and his and . . ."

"You didn't," Clyn said in a low voice which was much more frightening than his roar.

"I did," Bela said, lifting her chin in defiance.

"She did," Merin echoed.

"Why?" her mother wailed. "Belavalari, how incredibly imprudent!"

Bela sighed. Tyman still hadn't moved his sword into a less threatening position. "I couldn't do anything!" she said with evident annoyance. "Papa and you two said I was a maid who could not put myself in danger, that I could not fight or ride or wear the trousers you outgrew." She rolled her eyes. "You all wanted me to become something I was not, to wear dresses and be coy with suitable boys who might become husbands. I lied to General Merin so he would take my bothersome virginity and I would no longer be a maid."

"That is nonsense," Tyman said. His sword shifted slightly to the side.

Bela looked her brother in the eye. "Is it? I don't think it's nonsense at all. In fact, I believe my plan worked quite well. Merin left, so I was not saddled with a man I did not want, and once you knew what had happened, you two felt so guilty for not protecting me more diligently that you allowed me to do whatever I wanted. By the time your guilt faded, it was too late to turn back." Her trick had been childish, she could see that now, but it *had* worked.

Tyman's expression hardened. "You do share some blame, in that case, but the fact is, the general took your virginity and did not marry you. For that alone he deserves to die."

Bela pursed her lips. She had hoped it would not come to this, but she couldn't let them kill Merin under false pretenses. If anyone killed him, it would be her. "That's not entirely true."

"You said he took a husband's rights!"

Bela shuddered. That was a memory she could not forget no matter how she tried. "He did. He also married me, *before* the act was done, if you must know all the details."

Tyman's sword dropped away, and Merin lifted his head and looked at her. On his knees, bound, angrier than she had ever seen any man. He was still pretty, far prettier than her, but in this light she could see the years that had passed written on his face. A crease here, a toughness there.

"I did not marry you," he said tightly.

Idiot man! Such lies would lead to his death, if he were not careful.

Bela remembered that night much too clearly, and there was no denying it now. "According to Turi custom, we are very much married, General." It was the perfect marriage, in her mind, even though she had managed to keep her wedded state a secret until now. Merin was an absent spouse and she had her freedom. If her parents ever insisted that she needed to marry, if they ever tired of waiting for her to choose a mate and tried to force one upon her, she could inform them that she already had a husband. The marriage could be undone if there were no children, but not without both husband and wife present and participating in a ceremony not quite as simple as the marriage.

Her plan had been perfect. Until now.

There was stunned silence in the room, and her mother had gone so pale Bela was afraid the older woman might faint. Bela looked down at Merin, who seemed more angry than afraid. His eyes were so dark they looked more black than brown, so deep they seemed to be a bottomless pool of vitriol. She stared into them for a long moment before saying, "Welcome home, husband."

Chapter Two

MERIN glared at Bela. As if it wasn't humiliating enough to be in this position, bound and on his knees, inches from death, she had to complicate matters by lying. Why? Since she'd threatened to kill him already, he doubted her efforts were meant to spare his life.

He could've fought back long before now, taking down at least two or three of the Turis before they got him into this position, but he hadn't wanted to kill or even wound anyone. His job here was one of peace, and it would be a bad start to take his sword or his fists to one of the chieftain's sons.

That did not mean he would let Bela lie to save him.

"I believe I would remember marrying you," he said.

She sighed and lifted her hands, palms up. Yes, she had grown up very nicely, filling out just a little in the breasts and hips. Her face was slightly more angular than he remembered, but was still perfectly proportioned and remarkably striking. That thick brown hair should be ordi-

nary, but thanks to a glint of dark red it was not. Her mouth
was a bit wider than was considered perfect, he supposed,
but it suited her face, as did those perfectly arched dark
eyebrows and the calculating eyes beneath. The gown she
wore was simple, and it hugged her curves with a softness
that was unlike the dresses of those women who lived and
partied in the imperial palace.

She had given him a night he would never forget. And
he had tried to forget.

"Do you remember that I brought you a bowl of warm
cider and you drank it from my hands?" she asked, speaking to him as if he were mentally impaired.

"Yes," he answered through clenched teeth.

"Do you remember placing the wreath of leaves upon
my head?"

"Yes."

"Then there was a kiss and a short and very clumsy
dance." Though she did not exactly demonstrate, she did
stick out one long, slender foot and wag it gently.

"You drugged me. But yes, I remember."

Bela's mother rushed forward, taking command in spite
of the tension in the air. "Untie him immediately," she
commanded.

Clyn and Tyman likely didn't obey many orders—they
were more accustomed to giving them—but they listened
to their mother. In short order Merin found himself released and on his feet. Bela's brothers were still not genial,
not in the least, but they no longer threatened to kill him.

"There's been a terrible misunderstanding," Merin said,
directing his words to the wife of the chieftain, since she
seemed to be the only reasonable person in the room. "I'm
not sure what happened when I was last here . . ."

Oddly, the older woman smiled. "It sounds as if my
daughter tricked you into marrying her. The ceremony
should've been witnessed, but it's no less valid for its se-

crecy. You two would not be the first couple who sought privacy for reasons of pleasure and came back man and wife."

Merin glanced at Bela for a moment, and then back to her mother. He had not imagined that night could be any more disastrous, but here they were, six years later, and it was most definitely worse. "Allowing that somehow we are indeed married, is there any way the marriage can be undone?"

Bela pursed her lips. Clyn might've growled.

"Of course," Gayene said. "Dissolving a marital union isn't as easy as creating one, however. There are certain steps that must be taken."

"Even if one party was not willing or well informed when the marriage took place?" Merin asked.

"Even so, I'm afraid." The chieftain's wife did not look particularly upset by this turn of events. In fact, he could swear she was pleased. She fought the smile that tugged at her lips, but she did not fight very well.

"How long does it take to perform these steps of dissolution?" Merin asked.

"I was certain you'd be killed in the war," Bela said sharply. "I would've been very happy to be a widow."

Merin glared at her. "Sorry to disappoint you."

"Why didn't you tell us?" Tyman all but shouted, directing his anger at his sister.

Bela rolled her eyes and threw up her hands. "I would've told you all when word of the general's death reached the village, and I could've made it a great and sad story, too. I might even have shed a few tears."

"Thank you so much," Merin mumbled.

Bela pinned smart moss green eyes on him, unafraid and unashamed when she should be cowering in humiliation for what she'd done. "But the stubborn man survived. I should've known he would not cooperate." She turned back to her brothers. "If I'd let you two know that we were actually married, you would've tracked him down and brought him back. I didn't want that, so I just told you that he'd taken my virginity and you could no longer treat me like an innocent maid. That was all I wanted anyway, though to be a widow would've been more acceptable in your eyes, I know."

"What if there had been a child?" Clyn asked. "Then would you have told us the truth?"

Merin laughed. "Trust me when I tell you there was no chance of a child to result from this ill-advised *marriage*."

"But Bela said . . ."

Merin raised a hand to silence the lot of them. This was a conversation he didn't want to have with anyone, least of all Bela's brothers. He looked to Gayene Haythorne. "When will your husband return?"

"Ah, yes, you have come to us with a message," she said. "I expect my husband to return soon, but he's often delayed by one sort of business or another, particularly after a celebration such as the marriage which took place tonight. Can you not tell us here and now what brings you back to our humble village?"

Nothing about the Turis was humble! They were maddeningly superior and prideful. "The emperor is in the market for a bride, and some ill-advised minister suggested that Belavalari might make a fine empress."

In an abrupt change of mood, Bela's brothers laughed. Bela herself paled considerably. Her mother only blinked. "Well, that won't do, as she already has a husband in you, General Merin."

"But that mockery can be undone, correct?" he asked.

"If that is what both of you wish," the older woman said, sounding decidedly disappointed.

"Yes," Merin said decisively. His answer and tone were echoed by Bela.

"What, exactly, is involved in dissolving this unwise

union?" Merin asked. Knowing the Turis, anything was possible. Where else in the known world could he have found himself tricked into marriage?

Gayene Haythorne smiled at him, and he felt a chill. Maybe she was gentler than her children, but she was certainly not soft. "We will discuss the matter in the morning. It will be necessary for my husband and the Turi seer, Rafal, to be present when the dissolution begins."

"How long will it take to have this done? A full day? A few hours? We must be on our way very soon if we're to arrive at the palace in Arthes by the first night of the Summer Festival. I did take a few days to prepare, but once I was on the road, I traveled hard, and I can only assume that Bela and her chaperones will need more time than I did on my own."

"I can travel as fast and efficiently as you, General," Bela insisted.

"I'm sure you can." He gave her a curt and dismissive bow.

"The dissolution process will take twenty-two days," Gayene Haythorne said calmly.

Impossible. "That's more than three weeks! I cannot wait here three weeks!"

Again there was that chilling smile. "Then you will escort a married woman to your emperor."

IT was near dawn before Bela was able to drift off to sleep, and not long after when she heard an insistent tapping at her window. She came awake and alert quickly, and was ready to reach for Kitty when she saw the face framed in the window.

Jocylen, poor girl, had no doubt escaped from her new home and come to tell Bela that she'd been right and a wife's duty was a painful and horrid one. Maybe she wanted to hide here.

So why was the new bride smiling so widely?

Bela threw open the big window, and Jocylen leaned inside. "You were so wrong!" she said with a grin.

"I was not," Bela responded with indignation.

"Well, the sex did hurt at first, like you said, and for a few minutes I thought I wouldn't like it at all. But the pain soon passed, and it was wonderful." Jocylen rolled her blue eyes in what looked to be sheer delight. "I have never felt anything like having Rab inside me."

"That's true enough," Bela mumbled.

"Sex is beautiful and it felt good, and it was *fun.*"

"You're jesting."

"Not at all."

Bela grimaced. Maybe Merin hadn't done it right. Just one more failing to hold against him. "He's back," she said sourly.

"Who's back?"

"General Merin. He arrived last night with some sort of ridiculous message from the emperor."

"Your first love," Jocylen said dreamily.

Bela glared at her friend. "The man who took my virginity. It was hardly love." She sighed. Soon enough everyone would know, so she might as well tell her friend first. Jocylen would be so annoyed not to know all that had happened that night. "We're married."

Jocylen's face lit up. "Last night?"

"Six years ago."

The bride's pretty smile faded. "That's not possible."

"Merin was not familiar with the Turi wedding ceremony, so he had no idea what we were doing." Bela sucked in her bottom lip and then let it go. "And I had given him a little something to make him less than clear-headed, so he did whatever I asked without question."

Jocylen's normally wide eyes went wider. "You tricked him? Why? And more important, why didn't you tell me?"

Bela shrugged her shoulders and looked away from Jocylen's accusing expression. "It seemed like a good idea at the time."

Jocylen's heart-shaped face was gentle and childlike and perfect in shape and symmetry. When she smiled, it was coy and knowing. "You did love him."

"I did not! I simply wanted to get my annoying virginity out of the way. I was tired of being a maid, tired of being protected as if I might shatter if a man touched me."

Jocylen leaned a bit more into Bela's room. "If that's true, then why did you choose him?"

Did it matter that she'd been young and naive and foolish? Probably not. "No male from the village would've done. I have no desire to become a wife, and a local man would've insisted upon marriage."

"Yes, I know."

"So it seemed only logical to choose one of the soldiers, and Merin was the most highly placed and therefore most suitable for the daughter of a chieftain."

"He was also the most beautiful, if I remember correctly," Jocylen said.

"You remember correctly."

Why on earth had she gone through the steps that made her Merin's *wife*? She'd known he didn't have any idea what the simple gestures meant, as she'd led him through them step by step. It had just seemed right, for reasons other than her desire to be a widow.

"I suppose I got carried away," Bela admitted. "He was handsome and brave." And likely to die very soon, since he was already wounded and refused to spend more than a few necessary days tending to his injuries. "He was nice enough to me, and I guess I thought if I was going to offer my body to a man, there should be something more than just that one painful poke." A poke and some blood and a startling sensation of invasion. She could not believe Jocylen said her wife's duties were wonderful. And fun!

"One?" Jocylen asked.

"I certainly wasn't going to allow it to happen more than once!" Bela insisted.

Jocylen laughed. "Oh, Bela, on most subjects you know so much more than I, but when it comes to wifely duties, I think you could use some tutoring from me."

"No, thank you," Bela muttered.

"I have to go before Rab misses me. I just had to tell you that for once you were wrong!" With that Jocylen was gone, all but skipping away.

Bela propped herself on the windowsill and watched the morning come alive. The gentle hills where she had played all her life were green thanks to spring's rains and warmth. Beyond those hills the mountains rose majestically, cold and powerful and filled with riches and dangers. To the north the mountains were friendly and filled with gems of many sizes and colors. Those mountains were friendly, habitable, almost entirely covered with lovely and majestic green trees. Just to the south was a less friendly mountain, one as much of stone and harshness as of greenery, one where no man dared to live. It was from that mountain that Kitty had come.

Between the hills and the mountains there were many Turi farms and ranches. All those who lived here were Turi by birth or by marriage, and all looked to her father for leadership and guidance. One day Clyn would take their father's place, but with any luck that would not happen for a long time. As a people, the Turis were quite healthy and long-lived.

This was home, and she loved it here. Perhaps she did not fit in, perhaps she was not the daughter her parents wanted her to be. But she was Turi, and this land was in her blood, as it had been in the blood of her ancestors.

Going back to bed would be a waste, since she knew she would not be able to sleep. There would be no more rest for her, not today. Merin was ignorant of the steps which would be necessary to dissolve the marriage, but she knew very well what was in store for them. Torture. Sheer torture.

Bela bathed well and combed her hair, then braided the long brown strands so they would be held away from her face. She donned a pair of comfortable trousers which had once been Tyman's, and a once-white shirt which had seen better days. She wore sturdy brown boots instead of the pretty bejeweled sandals she had endured last night.

Two girls worked in the kitchen. They were accustomed to seeing Bela dressed as she was when she entered the kitchen each morning for cider and an oatcake. The girls greeted their employer's daughter with a warm good morning, and if they knew what had transpired last night, they did not show it in any way. Not in a glance, not in a smile. Soon everyone would know, much to Bela's shame.

Still, she had no one to blame but herself for this situation, and she would do what had to be done to get herself out of it. She was determined and stoic and ready to take her punishment like a man, without tears or regret.

Bela took her morning meal to the dining hall, which was large enough for a family gathering or even a meeting of elders. She sat and picked at her oatcake, silent and unusually pensive. Her father was there, drinking hot tea and eating a stack of oatcakes with yar nectar and saying not a word. Having been informed of the events that had led them to this point, he was none too pleased. The Turi chieftain was a quiet man whose few words were law. Still, Bela did not like to see him displeased.

It wasn't long before Merin arrived, looking as if he had slept no better than she. One of the kitchen maids served him cider and a stack of oatcakes, and he ate sullenly.

Bela, her father, and Merin—all were quiet and unhappy, and none made any effort to hide their displeasure.

Gayene Haythorne was the odd one this morning. Bela could not help but notice that her mother seemed almost giddy, as if she were quite happy with the turn of events. Did she think the dissolution ceremony would change Bela's mind about marriage? Unlikely. No, impossible!

Last to arrive was the seer. Rafal Fiers was a creepy man of indeterminate age. He'd been an old man for as long as Bela could remember. He'd made it clear on more than one occasion that he did not approve of Bela's less-than-feminine ways, and he sometimes seemed annoyed that Kitty had chosen her. The old man probably wished to possess Kitty for himself, but what he apparently didn't realize was that no one *possessed* Kitty. The magical sword chose a partner, and she had chosen Bela.

Fiers refused his hostess's offer of oatcakes and directed them all into the main room, where last night Tyman had nearly taken Merin's head. When everyone was positioned as he directed, the seer removed a length of braided cloth from his bulging leather bag. Red, white, and black cloth had been plaited together to make a sturdy rope of sorts. The rope might've been twice as long as Clyn was tall, and the colors which swirled together symbolized aspects of marriage.

Poor Merin, he watched the seer closely, but he had no idea what was coming. He wasn't going to be happy about this.

Neither was she.

Rafal chanted in an ancient language only a handful of Turis remembered. Bela understood not a word. As the seer chanted, he gradually herded Bela and Merin closer together. He flicked his fingers, which were wet with some fragrant substance, at them both. One drop caught Merin on the lip and he sputtered, making Bela smile for a brief moment.

Rafal shouted one curt, ugly word at the unhappily married couple and did an unpleasant shimmy. His eyes rolled back in his head. Then he took one end of the rope and wrapped it around Merin's waist. Rafal skipped once, he hopped and turned around, and then he tied a sturdy knot. He then presented himself to Bela, who sullenly but obediently raised her arms. The other end of the braided rope was tied loosely to her waist. About half the rope was used in circling her and Merin's waists and forming the knots, which meant a mere six or seven feet separated her and Merin.

Great.

Then the little old man, who was significantly shorter than Bela and much shorter than Merin, planted himself before them and tilted his head back so he could look them in the eye. His arms rose slowly, palms up.

"A husband and a wife sometimes grow apart. They drift. They become strangers. They forget to appreciate all that the other does in the name of their union, day after day."

Merin pursed his lips but remained silent. A muscle in his jaw clenched.

"For the next twenty-two days and twenty-two nights, you two will be linked by this cord, which symbolizes all that marriage is. When one toils, the other will assist. If one becomes ill, the other will tend. Every burden will be shared, as will every joy."

"I'm supposed to stay bound to Bela for *twenty-two days*?" Merin shouted.

"Yes," Rafal said calmly. "If either of you removes the rope I have used to bind you, there will be no dissolution of the marriage."

"Traveling like this is going to be a nightmare," Merin said under his breath.

Rafal shook a bony finger at the general. "Oh, no, you may not travel. The termination proceedings must be well supervised, and when the time is done, those who witnessed the knotting of this rope will also witness the severing of it. Until that time arrives, you will remain bound together."

The general did not look so pretty at this moment. There was a mighty crease between his dark eyes, and a grimace on his fine lips. "Are you telling me that if we untie ourselves for any reason, we have to start the twenty-two days all over again?" he asked, obviously annoyed and bordering on horrified.

"No," Rafal answered. "If the link is undone, you cannot attempt to dissolve the marriage for another three years. Then, as long as there are no children of the union, you will be free to try again."

Village of Childers
Southern Province

LEYLA had checked the contents of her two large bags twice, and she'd said her good-byes to most of the servants in her employ. She'd had her last argument with her grown stepson, Wybert. She would miss the servants much more than she'd miss Wybert Hagan, who was her only family. She had no close friends in Childers, but she'd said farewell to those few acquaintances who might miss her now and then. It had not been her imagination that many of them were eager to be rid of her. Some were openly relieved.

Coming to Childers nearly fifteen years ago had been a horrible mistake. Marrying a wealthy man old enough to be her father, enduring a loveless marriage, and then watching him die slowly had been a mistake. If she mentally listed all her mistakes, she'd be here all day, and the traveling party was set to begin their journey after the midday meal.

She hadn't had a choice then, not unless she'd been prepared to run from it all and make her own way. Was accepting this ridiculous offer from the emperor yet another mistake? Should she run as she had not fifteen years ago? She didn't know, not yet, but she did know that it was time for her to make a few changes in her life. Some changes would be easier to make than others.

Lady Leyla Hagan was no fool; she knew very well why she was being considered for the position of empress. She would not be the youngest candidate, nor would she be the prettiest. She did not possess great wealth. The control of her late husband's estate had passed to his only son, a child of his first marriage, and while he would not toss her out to starve or make her own way, he also gave her nothing which was not necessary. No, she was being taken to Arthes because of her abilities.

Some called her a witch, but Leyla did not call herself so. She had a gift, she was cursed, she was different.

"My Lady, I have repaired the carriage wheel as you requested. Would you like to inspect it before you get under way?"

Leyla turned toward Savyn's deep, smooth voice. He was smiling gently, which surprised her. Lately he had always looked so gruff, so unhappy, in spite of the beauty of his face. As usual he was clean-shaven, and looked not so much as a year older than the twenty-five he had lived. His body still had the hard leanness of youth and looked elegant even in the simplest workingman's clothes. His face was unmarred by wrinkles or scars, his dark brown eyes were warm and often laughing—though not of late. His longish dark brown hair curled to his shoulders and had the shine of youth.

"I'm sure the wheel is fine," she said. "You always do good work."

"I would feel better if you inspected it yourself, My Lady." He gave her a belated and graceful bow, planting one heel in the dirt and bending low, sweeping one hand out slowly before righting himself.

Leyla sighed and turned toward the carriage house, where her conveyance sat sheltered from the elements. Riding in such a way would make the trip to Arthes much longer, but she would not ride on horseback for weeks. She'd never been fond of riding, and was too old and too spoiled to make the sacrifice now. Besides, the sooner she left Childers, the better all would be, for everyone.

Savyn circled the carriage so that he was hidden from her view. Leyla sighed softly and followed in his footsteps.

"I also repaired the door handle on this far side. It was quite loose," he said as she rounded the coach.

"That was very kind of you." No one was near, not that she could see, but one could never be too careful.

Caution was not a trait she and Savyn shared.

He grabbed her wrist and pulled her body against his, holding her against him so tightly she could barely breathe. "It's not too late to change your mind," he whispered. "Don't go." He pressed his mouth to her throat and let it linger there. "Don't go, please."

Her relationship with Savyn was also a mistake, perhaps the most egregious one. Leyla allowed her eyes to close for a moment, as she enjoyed the way his mouth felt on her throat. She did not have much time for savoring. "I have no choice."

"You always have a choice, Leyla," Savyn argued. "You can use your gift on Bragg and convince him you are not suitable. Send him away. Stay with me."

"I can't." She'd been trying to end this two-year relationship for the past six months. No, longer than that. She'd never intended to make Savyn such a permanent part of her life, such an *important* part. Her leaving was, in many ways, a blessing for both of them. "You know I don't use my abilities recklessly."

"No one else will love you as much as I do," he argued. "It would be impossible."

"You do not love me," she commanded.

"I do. When will you say those words to me, Leyla? When will you admit that what I see in your eyes is the truth?"

"I can't love you," she argued. For so many reasons, she could not love Savyn.

Soon Savyn argued without words. He lifted the skirt of her drab gray traveling outfit and slid his hands up her thighs to the apex. He had the rough hands of a man who worked hard, who labored and had never known a day of leisure, and yet he was surprisingly gentle. His fingers danced with great skill, until she forgot all her arguments. Her legs parted, and she forgot everything but the way he made her feel.

Savyn always did this to her. Every time she went to him intent on ending their ill-advised relationship, every time she argued that they had nothing in common, he touched her and the argument was over. All the arguments in the world didn't matter when he held her. She was a monied widow and he was a wheelwright and swordmaker. If people knew they were involved in any way they would laugh or, worse, think Savyn was involved with her for her position and her power. She was nine years older than he. Nine years! No one ever questioned a marriage or a relationship where the man was older than the woman, but when the woman was older, people whispered. People could be cruel.

She did not want children, and took a potion to make sure she never found herself with one. Savyn was young and happy and wanted babies. He wanted a wife and family and all that came with them. He should have what he wanted, and she could not give it to him.

"Take me with you," he said as he aroused her with hands that knew her too well.

"I can't."

"You can do anything you wish, Leyla. If you won't stay, if I am not enough to keep you here, then take me with you."

And make him an empress's plaything? Never. She would not degrade him that way.

Leyla was confident she would be chosen, even though Minister Bragg had made it clear there were five other women in this odd competition. Yes, the other women would have their own merits, she was sure, but no other could offer a leader the benefits of a wife who had the power to persuade those around him to do as she directed. No other could magically and instantly sway another's mind.

If she could get close enough, she could make certain the emperor chose her. Perhaps that was unfair, but something would have to be done. She could not come back here, not ever.

Savyn slipped a finger inside her, and she stopped thinking of anything but the end of this encounter. Their last. She'd thought last night would be their last time together, and the night before that, and even the night before that . . . but she could not stay away from Savyn, and he could not stay away from her. That was reason enough for her to leave Childers and not look back.

She fumbled with the drawstring at Savyn's trouser opening, loosened his britches and pulled at them, then freed his shaft and wrapped her fingers around it, stroking as she brought him closer. Closer. She wanted to wrap herself around him in every way possible.

He threw open the carriage door and laid her down. Her back was against the narrow floor, while Savyn was more out of the carriage than in. Her legs wrapped around his hips and pulled him closer, and he pushed deep and hard to fill her.

There was no finesse in this joining, no laughter or sweet words. They'd had those things in the past, but this was a fierce and final fuck, a primal and sweaty urge they could not deny. Savyn moved within her fast and hard and deep, wonderfully deep. Leyla climaxed quickly, and so hard there were tears in her eyes. She almost screamed, even though not so far away there were sentinels and one pompous deputy minister preparing for departure, and a scream would surely bring them running. Since she could not scream, she cried, and when Savyn found release, he was crying, too.

They were still joined. Wet, sweaty, disheveled, and weeping.

He was crying because she was leaving him; she was crying because she'd ruined his life.

Leyla had vowed long ago not to use her abilities lightly. She did not call upon her gifts to make her life easier, to get what she wanted, to make others do her bidding. It seemed evil to take a God-given gift and use it for her own comforts. And yet, what else could she do now?

They parted slowly, and Savyn straightened his clothes and smoothed his hair. Heaven above, she loved his dark curls. Her own hair was midnight black and much too curly, but Savyn's curls were soft and warm, like his eyes.

Leyla raised her head from the carriage floor. "I need something to clean myself."

Savyn shook his head, and he did not smile. "No, I think you should leave here with something of me on you and in you, so perhaps you will remember me for a while."

She could tell him, honestly, that she would always remember him, that she would always have something of him with her, but that would not make his life any easier. Best that he think she did not care for anything but his talents as a lover.

Not that he would remember.

After she had straightened her clothing and smoothed her hair, which was easy enough since the mass of black curls was always in disarray, she left the carriage and stood before Savyn. She could see the hurt in his warm brown eyes, she could see the tremble of his lips. It had always been so easy to convince herself that he did not love her, even though he said the words easily. At this moment, she could see that she had broken his heart.

Without hesitation, she reached up and touched his forehead. "Forget us," she whispered. "Forget everything that happened between us in the past two years and three months. Forget words of love, forget whispered plans for a life we should've known we could never have. Live your life without me, Savyn, and be happy."

He slapped her hand away. "What are you doing? How dare you . . ."

But it was too late. The deed was done. She watched as his eyes clouded for a moment, and he backed away from her. Savyn stumbled once, turned around in confusion, and then faced her again. "My Lady Hagan," he said. "I'm . . . I'm . . ."

She did not make him fumble with his words any longer. "The wheel looks fine," she said in an emotionless voice. "And I do appreciate you repairing that door handle. We can't have it falling off halfway to Arthes." She gave him a cool smile. "I'll see that you're paid before I leave."

Savyn still looked a bit confused, but he would remember repairing the wheel and the handle, and though he would realize for a while that there were blank spots in his memory, eventually even that would fade. "Thank you, My Lady."

Leyla turned away so he would not see the tears in her eyes.

"Safe journey, My Lady," Savyn called after her.

She did not respond. As she headed for the house, where

she would make sure someone paid Savyn for his work before she made a last visit to her bedchamber to clean herself and perhaps even change clothes, she wished she could use her ability on herself. She wished with all her heart that she could make herself forget.

Chapter Three

GENERAL Tearlach Merin had marched through downpours of rain and sleet. He had battled soulless monsters that fought without fear or mercy. He had gone days without sleep and fought while blood poured down his forehead and into his eyes, all but blinding him.

He could bear three weeks and a day bound to Belavalari Haythorne.

His "wife" was dressed like a man but looked nothing like one. Her gentle curves were plain enough to see under the trousers and simple shirt she wore. A leather band had taken the place of the gold that had circled her brow last night, and she wore no womanly adornments. She had aged well—she had turned from a girl to a fine woman—and she was oddly appealing. She wasn't traditionally beautiful, but there was—and always had been—something remarkable and commanding about her. Something undeniably interesting. That did not mean he would forgive her for lying to him, for deceiving him in so many ways he could not begin to list them all.

When he looked past his anger, he could see the wisdom of the Turi custom, if the couple in question were actually man and wife. He'd seen many a broken couple in his life in the palace. He'd seen men and women who had once been close grow apart until they were all but strangers. A few of them would benefit from being forced to spend time with their spouses.

But he and Bela had never truly been wed! She'd deceived him, and he had not even realized . . .

"I suppose we must speak, on occasion," she said, interrupting his reflection. "How have you been these past six years?" She sounded very cordial.

"Fine," he answered sharply. "You?"

They sat on a large, flat rock in front of the Haythorne home. It was oddly shaped, fat and curving rather like a bean, and had probably been here much longer than the house. It was too large to move, and too beautiful to destroy. The flat top of the rock was littered with sparkling fissures in crimson and a deep shade of blue.

"Very fine," Bela said decisively. "My days are full and as I like them. I hunt, I take a turn at guarding the village, and I help to train the young ones, as they come of age, to use a sword. I've even done a bit of mining, though I found it not to my taste. My father has sought my counsel on more than one occasion, and I've assisted him in settling more than one dispute between the miners."

"And you got all this by losing your virginity," he said with more than a hint of bitterness.

She pursed her lips slightly. "In a way. I realize now that it was wrong of me to use you as I did, but I was so weary of being shopped about as a bride, bargained over and put on display and dressed each morning to flaunt my wares and try to attract the highest bidder, as if a woman's bosom and the strength of her teeth were proper selling points. Losing my virginity made me less attractive to the men of the village. Men are very odd in that respect," she said, as if the idea puzzled her.

"Yes, I suppose they are," Merin mumbled.

"I declared my distaste for the state of marriage and all that came with it, and after a short while my family . . . gave in, if you will. They found it easiest to let me have my way, and as men were no longer beating down our door asking for my hand, it worked out well enough." She looked much too pleased with herself, even though she was now paying for her scheme. As was he.

"You came about none too soon, I must say," she added. "My mother had even taken to trying to teach me how to *smile* properly. Can you imagine? Not too wide, not too shyly, please don't show so many teeth . . . it was maddening."

Odd that she would say he had come along at the right time, when by her own admission any man with a penis would've sufficed. He did not ask her why she'd chosen him. "Should I apologize for ruining your plan and not making you a widow?" Merin asked, surprised that he not only heard but felt a hint of humor.

"You really should," Bela said, and then she smiled. It was the first real smile he had seen from her this time around, and it was as enchanting as ever, if wider than her mother would've preferred. "It was very thoughtless of you not to die a hero and leave me a grieving widow."

"If only I had known of your ploy. As in all other matters where you are concerned, I was ignorant."

Bela didn't like the turn the discussion had taken. These matters of the past did not flatter her in any way. Still, apparently there were things she wished to know of him. She gave him a sideways glance and narrowed her eyes, like a hawk homing in on its prey. "You said there was no chance of a child. I worried about the possibility for months, and yet you seem so certain that it could not have happened. How could you know there was no baby? Are you broken and unable to make babies? I have heard of such men. How very sad that must be for you."

Merin shook his head. "Bela, how can you be so worldly in some ways and so innocent in others?"

"I am not innocent." She sounded quite insulted.

"There's nothing wrong with innocence," he said. "Most men prefer it in their women, at least to some degree."

"I care not what men prefer."

"That does not surprise me."

Tyman interrupted them, which was just as well. No good could come of this discussion.

"There you are, you laggards." The middle Haythorne sibling smiled widely, enjoying this debacle much too much. It was hard to believe this grinning young man had just last night held a sword to the back of Merin's neck. "Do you think you'll spend the next few weeks sitting about chatting? No! You must work together to prove that you can. You must help one another in one arduous task after another."

"What kind of arduous task?" Merin asked testily.

"We'll make it easy today. You two can weed Mama's garden."

It didn't sound too arduous to Merin, but Bela groaned. Her brother laughed and gave her a shove, and grudgingly she led Merin around the large house she called home. The walls were alternately gray stone and wooden plank, as if it had been built piecemeal and with whatever supplies were available at the time. It was a nice enough house, a warm enough home. He supposed it was his home, too, for the next twenty-two days.

When they arrived at their destination, he understood why Bela had groaned. Mama's "garden" spread as far as the eye could see, and thanks to spring rains it was dotted with more weeds than he could count.

Bela rolled up her sleeves and smiled. "What's the matter, General? Afraid to get your hands dirty?"

*   *   *

LEYLA made them all wait. Deputy Minister Bragg and the three sentinels who would serve as escorts were standing beside her carriage, waiting impatiently for her to join them so the journey could get under way. The carriage driver, who was necessary as she refused to travel on horseback, also stood waiting. She did not care that others had to wait. It had taken some time, but her eyes were dry and her body was clean. Her heart was hardened, as it needed to be.

Her chaperone, Wybert's elder cousin so many times removed it was a gift of charity to call her a relation, followed Leyla with a labored step. The busty Mistress Hilde was already breathing heavily, overexerted from the trip down the stairs. Deputy Bragg had insisted that a chaperone was not necessary, but in the world Leyla had made her own, a female companion—even one she did not like—was necessary. A lady did not travel with none but five men for company. It simply wasn't done.

Leyla was surprised to see Savyn standing with the others. When she'd first exited the house, she hadn't seen him, because he stood more behind Bragg than beside him. Her heart skipped a beat. Had her ability not worked properly? Was her lover here to make a scene in front of everyone? He should remember nothing!

But as she drew near, Savyn simply bowed as all the others did. He didn't even look her in the eye.

He'd come to check the newly repaired carriage wheel, that was all. Leyla convinced herself of that fact as Bragg took her hand and assisted her into the coach. He then took Hilde's chubby hand and held it until she was seated. Hilde huffed and moaned with the exertion. Yes, it was going to be a long trip.

Through the window, Leyla was horrified to see Savyn speak to a sentinel and then mount his own horse.

"Deputy," she snapped.

Bragg turned to face her, visibly weary and more than ready to begin the long journey. "Yes, M'Lady?"

"The wheelwright." She pointed discreetly. "It looks as if he's joining us." Her mouth went so dry she was afraid her words had been affected.

Bragg glanced over his shoulder. "Yes, he is."

Leyla felt as if her heart climbed into her throat. "May I ask why?"

"If you have any objection to the boy traveling with us . . ."

"No," Leyla said quickly. Her objection would only cause a scene, which she did not want to do. "I'm merely curious."

Bragg shrugged his shoulders. "Savyn approached me last week and said that he'd like to go to Arthes and study with some of the blacksmiths there. The most skilled swordmakers in the world reside in the capital city, and he wishes to learn. He's a bright young man, and I was impressed by what he showed me of his work. I'm sure he'll do well in Arthes."

"That's very ambitious of him," Leyla said as she moved away from the window and leaned back.

"Very," Bragg agreed, before tipping his hat and moving to his own horse.

Savyn had asked to join the party before she'd used her gift to make him forget. He knew her too well, and even though he had argued with her on several occasions, he'd realized all along that she would not stay here. He knew she did not change her mind. Often.

"I don't like him," Hilde said bitterly.

"Who is that?" Leyla asked absently. She couldn't be sure, since in her experience Hilde didn't like anyone.

"Deputy Minister Bragg. He has small eyes and a thin mouth. Such people are not to be trusted."

The carriage jerked and was under way as Leyla looked to her stepson's cousin. "I did not know you could judge who to trust and who not to trust by the shape of the mouth or the size of the eyes."

Hilde's own small eyes narrowed. "Don't be insolent."

Leyla considered reaching over and touching the unpleasant woman on the forehead. And then what? She could influence decisions, she could make people forget, she could sway them to her way of thinking. But could she change who a person was at the pit of their soul? She didn't think so. Hilde was bitter deep down, and there was nothing to be done for that. Wybert had surely suggested his cousin for this chore as one last punishment for his stepmother.

"Your outfit is not entirely proper," Hilde said sharply. "You should wear only black or gray. That blue is disgraceful. It's much too bright a shade for a widow."

Leyla thought of the more respectable gray traveling ensemble she had left lying across her bed, still smelling of Savyn. "I have been a widow for five years. I am no longer required to mourn."

Hilde harrumphed. "Most women don't have to be instructed to mourn their deceased husbands."

Leyla wondered if she could reach out, touch Hilde's forehead, and convince the surly chaperone that she could no longer speak.

No, this was her punishment for making so many mistakes. She should've run away long ago instead of allowing herself to enter into a marriage which was strictly trade. She should've insisted on love. She never should've taken a younger man as a lover, or believed that she could have one wonderful thing of beauty for herself. For all those mistakes, she was being punished.

BELA didn't mind weeding, though it was not her favorite chore and there was an abundance of weeds in her mother's garden. Still, being so close to General Merin was true torture. She felt as if she should apologize to him for all she'd done, but in truth she was not sorry and she never apologized. Merin was in a terrible situation, and it was all her fault. He had done nothing but believe her lies.

Odd thoughts, since just last night she had been prepared to take his head because he'd hurt her. He'd hurt her by leaving six years ago, which was silly, because she'd wanted him to leave and they had been caught up in a war that had demanded he leave. And still she'd felt abandoned. She was usually not so indecisive!

Her mother had brought them wine and meat and dried figs at midday, along with a large ewer of water. Starving by that time, she and Merin had both eaten ravenously before continuing with their chore. The rope made it necessary for them to work side by side, but it gave them enough room to work independently. Just enough. They didn't speak much, which was awkward but likely not as awkward as trying to carry on a conversation would've been.

Even though Merin was a general, he didn't seem appalled to be asked to participate in something so common as weeding a garden. In fact, he looked as if he had done this before. He gripped the unwanted growths just so, and always pulled the root as well as the greenery above ground. He never pulled at one of the small young plants, confusing them with weeds. Yes, he had definitely done this before, which she found odd. She supposed that before this, she'd imagined he'd been born with a sword in his hand and a command on his lips.

Born a leader, just as she had been born a misfit.

Toward the end of the day he stood and stretched his long, large body, raising his arms over his head and working out the knotted muscles. Bela did the same. Sufficiently stretched, she looked down at her hands and noted the dirt beneath her fingernails and the mud that was dotted here and there to the elbow.

"There's a creek just beyond that hill." She pointed. "We can wash our hands there."

"Great." Merin headed in that direction. "I haven't been this filthy in years." Bela had to rush to keep the rope that joined them from pulling taut and possibly yanking her to the ground. She was tall for a woman, but was nowhere near as tall as her "husband." His legs were long and strong, and he did not seem inclined to slow his pace on her account.

Bela had convinced herself that she'd chosen Merin to take her virginity because he was the most powerful and the most likely to die, in her opinion. After all, he'd already been injured, and had a number of scars which marked him as . . . well . . . careless or unlucky or both. But in truth, she had admired his physical form from the start. He was a fine example of manhood, from his curly hair to his pretty face to his long body to the large appendage with which he had made her squeal.

When Merin reached the edge of the water, he removed his boots. She suspected that he might want to step into the creek to cool off. She expected he'd roll up his pants legs next, but instead he yanked his dirty shirt over his head and dropped it to the ground, then readjusted the braided rope at his waist so he could unfasten his trousers.

"What are you doing?"

"I'm going to take a piss, and then I'm going to take a bath, of sorts, in this creek."

She could turn her back while he relieved himself, and in truth she would have to do something very soon. She'd been suppressing her own natural urges all afternoon, and would soon have to pee. But if Merin walked into the creek to bathe, he would drag her along, and she was *not* taking off her clothes in front of him! Could she remain dressed for twenty-two days? Yes, she could!

He whipped off his trousers, apparently not caring that she watched. And though she was slightly mortified, she did watch. His entire body was hard, totally masculine, and it seemed there were a few more scars than she remembered. He'd lived a hard life, and the harshness was written on his skin. Even his butt was hard and nicely shaped. There were no scars there, she noted.

With his back to her, Merin relieved himself by the creek. She ordered him not to look and did the same, as quickly as possible. She might consider remaining unbathed and in these same clothes for twenty-two days, but she could not go long without taking care of her body's natural functions. The task was easier for him, thanks to his male anatomy, but she was accustomed to managing quickly and efficiently. When she was done and her trousers were in place, she advised him that she was done.

And then he turned to her.

The appendage between his legs was not as she remembered. Not at all. It was soft and just hung there, not at all threatening or intimidating. That thing wouldn't hurt her, or anyone else. She relaxed a bit.

"Are you taking off your clothes?" he asked.

"No!"

"Not planning to bathe or change clothing for the next twenty-two days?"

Bela pursed her lips. "Twenty-two days is not so very long."

He smiled, and she noticed that his manhood twitched and grew a little. Oh, no! She was not putting herself through that agony again!

She drew the small knife she always wore at her waist and wagged it in his direction. "This is ridiculous. We'll just have to stay married. I don't mind so much, since you're not around to bother me. I'll cut the rope"—she grabbed a section and placed the sharp side of the blade there—"and you can leave. Go tell you emperor I'm not interested in his offer, and we'll continue on as we have, married but separate."

Merin moved very quickly and efficiently. He grabbed the knife from her hand and snatched it well away from the rope. "No. I can't continue as we have because I'm no longer ignorant of the situation. We will dissolve this marriage, Bela, and you will present yourself to the emperor. When he chooses someone else and sends you home, you can return to your people and find yourself another husband to torture."

"I do not torture you!" she protested. Belatedly, her feelings were hurt. "Why are you so sure the emperor would not choose me, given the chance?"

He smiled. "Just be yourself, Bela, and you'll be safe. The emperor will prefer a *female* as his bride, I'm quite sure."

Perhaps she did prefer manly pursuits, perhaps she did not want to be a wife and mother, as it seemed every other female she knew did, but that did not mean she would take such an insult without response. "I am very much a female, and can even appear so when it suits me. Many men have desired me," she said, moving slightly closer to him. She wished she had her knife back. If she did, she might threaten him just a little.

"The empress will have to wear pretty gowns every day. She will have to obey the orders of the emperor and give him children. I imagine he'll want many. She'll have to entertain dignitaries and such every night, and smile at people she does not like."

"I can do that. See?" She smiled widely at *him*.

"As empress, you would be required to bathe every day."

Suddenly she realized that his manly appendage was hard and long and threatening, not at all as it had been moments ago. They were so close it was almost touching her. She took a single step back, moving quickly. "There is no need for you to be difficult!" she protested, without getting specific about *how* he was being difficult.

"Like it or not, you owe me whatever pain and embarrassment this next twenty-two days costs you," Merin said without shame. "You lied to me on more than one occasion, you tricked me, you used me, and thanks to your scheming we're literally bound together for twenty-two very long days. And so you will pay." He looked her up and down. "Taking anything off before we go into the water?"

She shook her head.

"Fine." Merin turned and tugged on the rope as he walked into the creek. Bela stumbled along, her eyes on his bare ass and a scar on his back, not too far from his spine.

She cried "Stop!" as she reached the edge of the water. Merin was already in the creek, the water almost up to his knees.

"Let me take off my boots. I don't want to get them wet."

He nodded once, and she quickly removed her footwear. When that was done, Merin stepped toward the center of the creek and Bela followed. As if she had a choice! Her feet got wet. The cool water did feel wonderful, though she would never tell him so. When the water hit the hem of her pants, she called out, "Isn't this far enough? You can bathe there and I'll stay mostly dry."

Merin turned to face her. The water came to his thighs now. Not deep enough to suit her, but still, since he was not quite as close as he had been on the bank, she didn't mind looking. Somehow he was . . . interesting. "No," he said simply, and then he yanked on the rope that connected them and she was pulled into the creek deeper than she desired. Cool water splashed up and around her, droplets hitting her face and dampening her clothes. Still, Merin pulled on the rope until she was in the water as deep as he was . . . only she still wore all her clothing.

"You're not really going to go the whole time without a bath, are you?" he asked, more amused than she liked.

"I'll work something out." There had to be a way!

"I've seen you naked before."

"And look where that got us!" she protested.

He grinned. "You threw yourself at me," he said softly. "You said you were a widowed woman dying for a man's companionship. You stripped me naked and jumped on as if you could not wait."

"That's how it's done," she protested. "I have seen animals mate, and I walked in on Clyn and his wife, once, so I know full well how a man and a woman are supposed to work."

"Trust me, you didn't get the whole story." He tugged on the rope and pulled her closer to him. She tried to protest, but he was stronger than she was. "If I had known you were an untried maid, things would've been different that night."

"Different how?"

He looked at her strangely. "This is not a discussion we can have, *wife*. I'm really not . . . capable."

"I thought you were capable of anything and everything," she said, giving her voice a sarcastic edge.

"Don't test me."

"I just wonder at what task the mighty General Merin might fail."

She knew in a heartbeat that she had pushed too far. He grabbed the rope and yanked it until her body was fully against his. His shaft poked at her, and it should've been disgusting—but was not.

"There is much more to sexual union than jumping on," he said in a decidedly testy voice. "There is preparation, anticipation, desire. While it is true that at times a man and a woman can sometimes come together quickly and with a joyous outcome, that happens only when they are prepared. If in their minds they have imagined the moment of joining until they cannot wait, if they are lovers who have been too long apart, then it works very well." He moved his hand between her legs, and he was holding her so close and so tightly she could not move. "In other instances, physical preparation is preferred." He found and massaged a very sensitive place between her legs, pressing against her damp trousers and making a circle with his thumb. The touching made her twitch and then quiver, and she could not say it was entirely unwelcome. "Some like kissing, others prefer a more direct method of arousal." He pressed harder and she gasped, and though she wanted to tell him to stop, the words would not come. "And then, when neither the man nor the woman can wait a moment longer . . ."

"Stop," she managed to say, her voice croaking and weak.

"Don't push me, Bela," Merin said as he dropped the rope and backed away from her.

This time she took the warning to heart.

Her heart was beating oddly, and the back of her neck tingled, and between her legs she quivered. A part of her wanted to grab his hand and put it back where it had been so very briefly, but she would not. She knew where that would lead.

She had never seen Merin look just this way. He looked decidedly dangerous, decidedly hungry. Best to leave it alone, for now.

"You already need a bath," he said. With that he picked her up and threw her down so that she went fully into the creek and was soaked from head to foot.

SAVYN did not feel quite himself as he rode away from home. He wasn't even quite certain why he'd asked to make the trip to Arthes when he was perfectly happy in Childers, where he'd been born and raised and had lived his entire life. Hadn't he been perfectly happy there? Hadn't he had a good life? Something didn't feel quite right, and yet he was not compelled to turn back, even though he felt very much alone as the journey continued.

The sentinels and the deputy minister and the man who drove the carriage knew one another well. They conversed often, even laughing as the day grew long. The two ladies were hidden from view in their coach, but they had one another for companionship and conversation. Only Savyn was separate. He did not fit in here, and yet he did not want to turn back, now when it was not too late to do so.

When the party stopped for the evening, his eyes were instinctively drawn to Lady Leyla as she was assisted from her carriage, and somehow he no longer felt entirely alone.

He had always thought her beautiful, as did everyone who laid eyes on her. When she'd arrived in town, she'd been nineteen and newly married to the powerful man who owned everything and everyone in town, and he'd been ten years old and a wheelwright's apprentice. Fifteen years had passed since then, and still he remembered his first sight of her as if it had been yesterday. He'd never known anyone who had hair like Lady Leyla, black as night and wildly curling. She'd smiled at him that day, and he'd been captivated. Even now he remembered that the smile had been a little sad, a little lost.

Now that he was a man, he noticed more than her hair and her smile. Yes, she was older than he, but you'd never know it to look at her. Her face was pale, like milk, and her eyes were a remarkable blue. Truly remarkable. She didn't look much different than she had fifteen years ago. Perhaps her face was a bit leaner; perhaps there were fine lines at the corners of her dark eyes, but somehow those small changes only made her look more lovely. She had a nice womanly shape, and a delicate way of moving, and a perfect face with a slightly pointed chin and an adorable little nose. Her hips swayed a little when she walked, and he had never seen hands more delicate and pale than hers. She put every young woman in Childers to shame. None could compare to her. Watching her stretch her legs after being in the carriage for hours, he could almost imagine what soft hands like hers would feel like on his rough, overly warm face.

Lady Leyla Hagan was more than beautiful, she was also kind. How often had she secretly helped villagers who were sick or had fallen on hard times? She did so quietly, delivering food and medicines on the sly, afraid that her stepson, the less kind Wybert Hagan, would not approve of her actions.

How did he know this? Savyn could not recall where he'd heard the tales, but he knew. The knowing made him long to take her hands in his own and cradle them, just for a while. Even now, when she was answering the emperor's very flattering command, she looked sad. Could he make her smile?

Savyn laughed at himself as he turned to care for his horse. "I am a fool, Albin. A fine woman like Lady Leyla would never so much as look at a man like me, much less touch me or allow me to touch her." She would soon be empress, he supposed. How could the emperor not choose Lady Leyla as his bride, no matter who the other women in the contest might be? She would make a fine empress.

Savyn was certain that with his brother's help, he would find work in Arthes. Maybe he should've gone to the capital city years ago, after their mother had died. Settled there as a solid citizen of Arthes, he would surely catch a glimpse of Empress Leyla now and then, as she was traveling down the city streets or making an appearance with her husband. His stomach knotted. An empress would definitely not smile at a craftsman, much less touch him. Lady Leyla surely did not even remember that long-ago kind smile that had made a child fall in love.

The sentinels had chores to do, and they rushed about setting up camp for the night. The carriage driver saw to the horses, all except Savyn's Albin. There were small tents for the ladies and for Deputy Bragg, lightweight shelters which would do no more than keep the wind from their sleeping bodies. But like the other men in the party, Savyn would sleep under the stars tonight, as he would for all the nights to come until they reached their destination.

Again his eyes were drawn to Lady Leyla, and he watched her out of the corner of his eye as he pretended to give his attention to Albin. She stood alone, not talking to her companion, Mistress Hilde, or with Minister Bragg. Not only did she stand alone, she wore a cool expression that would keep others from approaching. To others she might appear cold, but to Savyn she simply looked lonely.

Traveling could be dangerous. There were wild animals about, as well as thieves who would be drawn to a woman like her, a woman of quality and wealth and delicacy and incredible beauty. Lady Leyla had three sentinels, a driver, and a deputy minister to look out for her, but if necessary he would take care of her, too. He would keep an eye on the lady; he would make sure she was always safe. Something inside him commanded that it was his duty and his right to do so.

After making that decision, after deciding to commit himself to Lady Leyla for the remainder of the journey, Savyn suddenly felt better. He felt more himself, more *whole*, less isolated than he had at any other time during this long, strange day.

Chapter Four

AS if it wasn't bad enough that he and Bela were tied together like a team of horses, they were assigned their own
small cottage, in which they were expected to live, cook,
sleep, and clean. Together. Alone. The cottage was nothing
special, but it was clean and solidly built. Bela had informed him that the cottage was used for infrequent visi-
tors, and for the occasional marriage dissolution ceremony
for a couple who lived too far from the village to be moni-
tored in their home.

The first evening had not been so bad thus far, Merin
mused. He was comfortable enough, clean and dressed in
dry clothes. It wasn't his fault that Bela refused to take off
her wet clothing. It wasn't his fault that she preferred to let
them dry on her body, it wasn't his fault that she preferred
to be miserable than to be naked in his presence.

He could be patient. He could be *very* patient. She wasn't
going to spend the next twenty-one and a half days in those
same clothes.

For the short amount of time they were to remain married, they wouldn't have much, as luxuries went. The rough cottage they'd been assigned was situated not far from Bela's family home, with two smaller and one larger home between them. It consisted of one main room which was furnished with a table and two chairs, a small hearth for warmth and cooking, flint and steel for starting a fire, and a sagging bed that looked much too small for the two of them to share without things getting interesting in the night. There were two plates, a couple of mugs, a pot, and the basic utensils. He had a change of clothes and his weapons, and Bela had brought the same with her—one set of clothes much like the wet ones she currently wore and a fine-looking sword which she stored on a weapons rack on the wall. She handled the sword with reverence, she looked at the weapon as if it were made of solid gold. The grip of that sword gave Merin a bit of a chill at first glance. The stone there looked oddly like the crystal dagger which had dispatched Ciro and ended the war. He dismissed that thought as fancy and concentrated on helping Bela cook their stew for supper.

Merin knew how to cook and was not afraid or ashamed of the chore, even though some found it unmanly. Not knowing how to prepare a decent meal would've made him helpless, dependent on others, and he refused to fall into that trap. The small kitchen area of their marital cottage was well stocked with common herbs, and he flavored the stew with them. Bela watched with some sign of interest. Heaven above, he knew more about cooking than she did. Why was he surprised? She seemed to shun all womanly attributes.

While the stew simmered, they sat side by side in two small chairs and watched the flame lick at the pot that hung over the fire. Now and then Merin glanced at Bela. Yes, he was still angry with her, as angry as he had ever been with any living being who wasn't an enemy, and yet he could not deny that she was tempting, in an odd way.

Not that he would give in to such temptation, but still—it was perplexing.

And entirely physical. She might swear that his attraction was one-sided, but he had felt her response when he touched her as they'd argued in the creek. If he wanted to seduce her—properly this time—he could do it. But he would not. Getting more involved with her than he already was would be a disaster. Bela was likely to be more trouble than she was worth.

If he ever did marry, he'd be better off with one of Lady Cipriana's simpering daughters than with this difficult woman. Bela was everything he did not want in a woman: she was difficult and demanding, and it was impossible to predict how she would react to any given situation. So why did he look at her and get hard? Why had he responded to her so fully this afternoon by the creek, when she was filthy and stubborn and insulting?

He didn't have to worry about anything happening. If he was so foolish as to try anything, she'd probably use her precious sword on him and make herself the widow she desired to be.

"What are you smiling at?" she snapped.

"Am I smiling?" he asked.

"Yes. You look like an addle-headed fool, sitting there with that senseless grin on your face. Do you find me amusing?"

He did, but didn't think it would be wise to tell her so. "No, of course not. I'm simply spending this quiet time remembering better days, that's all."

She snorted. "Remembering other women, I suppose."

"Naturally." He leaned toward her and lowered his voice. "Makes the time pass more quickly as I wait for the stew to be done. Should I share my intimate thoughts with you?" he asked, knowing she would refuse.

Bela wrinkled her nose at the pot and ignored the question. "I'm starving. Isn't the stew done enough?"

"No. The meat will be tough if we don't wait a bit."

"Fine." She slumped back in her chair, eyes on the pot.

The silence was heavy and uncomfortable. Bela's clothes were slowly drying, but remained damp here and there. It was easy enough for Merin's eyes to rake over her body. Her breasts were nicely shaped, even as she wilted in her chair. Her hips were nicely rounded, a woman's finely shaped hips not at all disguised by the manly trousers. Her hair was matted and the braid was less than flattering, but the poor hairstyle only accentuated the fact that her face was strongly feminine and flawless, the cheekbones high, the eyes nicely shaped—not wide and childlike like so many girls—the mouth . . . that wide mouth was near perfect.

Merin found he could not stand the silence—or his own perusal—for very long. "So, tell me about your sword," he said. "It's unique."

"You have no idea," Bela said softly.

"The grip is unusual."

She looked at him and narrowed her eyes. "You'd best know now that you're to keep your hands off Kitty."

Surprised, Merin blinked twice, and then he laughed. "Kitty? You named your sword? And if that's not bad enough, you named it *Kitty*?" He laughed again. "I'm so glad to hear that, Bela, really I am. It proves to me that, like it or not, you really are a girl."

She was incensed, as he'd imagined she would be. "If you must know," she snapped, "Kitty named herself."

Merin's smile faded. He didn't think Bela was teasing him, not with that intense expression on her face. The way she handled the sword, the familiar glimmer of the grip . . . His wife was in possession of a magical sword, and if he wasn't mistaken, the grip was made of a crystal he well recognized. A living crystal, a crystal capable of sucking the very soul out of a man, or a demon.

"Where and how did you come by this sword?" he asked.

"I don't intend to tell you . . . ," she began hotly.

"No more games," he interrupted. "This is serious business. Tell me about Kitty."

WHEN Merin declared the stew had simmered long enough, they filled their bowls and took them to the table. Hungry as Bela was, she was well aware that the food was still too hot to eat. They would have to wait a few moments longer. They sat. The rope that connected them was long enough to allow some freedom of movement, but was not long enough to allow one to sit while the other stood by the fireplace, not even in this small cottage.

"So," Merin said as he stirred the cooling stew in his bowl, "Kitty chose you."

"Yes. Clyn found her in the mountains, nearly three years ago, and he was not pleased when he learned that he couldn't keep her. But it was not his choice to make. It was hers."

He was intrigued by Kitty, as was everyone who learned of her existence. "You call the sword 'she,' and the name is certainly female. Why?"

"She speaks to me in a female voice."

Merin shook his head and took a small bite to test the stew. Apparently it was fine, as his next bite was much larger. It had been a long day, so he must be as hungry as she. "This is fascinating," he said between bites. "What is her purpose? Has she told you?"

"Purpose?"

Merin wagged his spoon in her direction. "Kitty is obviously a magical sword, and in my experience such weapons do not present themselves without reason. Such weapons exist for a purpose. It could not have been chance that Clyn found the sword, and it certainly wasn't chance that she chose you. Why? Have you never wondered?"

"No," Bela admitted. "I accept that I have her keeping, for now. If there is a purpose to her presence here, she hasn't revealed it to me."

Merin grunted softly, then lost himself in the meal for a time. His mind was busy, she could tell by the expression in his dark eyes. And his hair—she had always loved his soft, dark curls, and wished they might've been her own. He'd worked all day and wet his head in the creek, and it had dried as pretty as if he had spent hours arranging it just so. She wanted to touch the curls to see if they were soft . . .

No, it was best to concentrate on other features. Those she did not long to touch. Merin did have smart eyes, and she liked that in a man. Some of her brother's friends were less than intelligent. They might be fine miners or farmers or swordsmen, but they did not question everything the way the general did. They did not ponder the questions of life, they simply existed from day to day. She liked his eyes, not only for their intelligence but also for their depth and darkness. The lashes were long, too, almost like a woman's. Not that anything about Merin was womanly.

Bela quickly convinced herself that it was possible to admire him as a fine specimen of a man and not want him—or anyone else—as a husband.

When they had finished eating, Merin sat back in his chair and pinned those eyes on her. "Show me," he commanded. "Show me what Kitty can do."

Kitty did not always respond to commands, but immediately the grip of the sword glowed bright, indicating that she was awake and prepared.

"All right," Bela said, standing slowly and turning toward the sword. She moved away from the table, choosing the largest clear space available. Merin came with her, and stood beside and just behind her. Bela lifted her right hand. "Here, Kitty," she said softly.

The sword, grip glowing, rose slowly and spun in place. Bela did not take her eyes from the weapon, not even when Merin uttered a vile and interesting combination of curse words. She'd have to remember that one. Such a curse would shock even Clyn!

Kitty flew across the room, quick and precise, planting her crystal grip in the palm of Bela's hand. It was warm to the touch, as was normal when Kitty was awake. Awake, alive, stimulated . . . Bela was never sure what to call it, but there was a significant difference when the sword glowed and spoke.

And she did speak, in a voice only Bela could hear. *We need him.*

"We do not," Bela responded aloud.

"We do not what?" Merin asked. Bela ignored him.

It is no mistake that he is here. We need him.

Bela hated the very idea of needing anyone or anything, most of all a man! "Why?"

Merin spoke again. "You're talking to Kitty, aren't you?"

"Yes!" Bela said impatiently. "Now shush!" He was taken aback. Apparently no one told a general to shush, not in his world.

We need him, Kitty said again, and then she pulled away from Bela's grip and spun about so fast that the shining blade was a blur. The grip glowed brighter than she had ever seen, and the speed increased until there was nothing but a circle of bright light in view. Kitty rose slowly toward the ceiling, spinning all the while. Bela looked up. So did Merin. Kitty turned so that she was spinning against the ceiling, and then she moved to a position directly over their heads. Bela held her breath. Kitty was dangerously close and she was moving dangerously fast.

"What does this mean?" Merin asked softly.

"I don't know. She's never done this before."

"Great," he mumbled, laying his hand at his side, where his own sword should be. Even a general didn't wear a sword for weeding and cooking stew. The light from Kitty's grip grew so bright they could no longer look directly at it. The entire room glowed, as if the sun shone in this one-room cottage.

"That's enough," Bela said, but Kitty didn't respond.

We need him. The voice was louder than usual, more insistent.

Before Bela could respond, Merin looked at her. "We need who?"

Bela's heart skipped a beat. "You heard her?" No one else heard Kitty. No one!

"That was Kitty?"

The light faded, the sword's movements slowed, and then it flew down, tip first, to embed its blade in the wooden floor near Bela's feet. Her feet and Merin's, actually, as if Kitty had purposely placed herself midway between them. Another few inches, and the rope that bound them would have been severed and they'd be married for at least another three years. Bela held her breath.

Merin reached out to touch the crystal of the grip, which was dim, sleeping once more.

"Kitty doesn't allow . . ." Bela began, but she stopped speaking when Merin touched the grip and Kitty didn't awake to move away from his touch or, worse, slap his hand or take a finger for daring to try. Instead, she allowed Merin's long, sun-touched fingers to wrap around the crystal.

"Remarkable," he said in a low voice.

Bela looked at Merin, her mouth thinned and the fingers of both hands clenched into fists. "Do you know what this means?"

He managed a wry half-smile. "It means you are in

possession of a magical sword like no other I have ever heard of."

"Yes," she said sharply, "but that's not what I mean. You heard her speak!"

"Once, yes." He took his hand from Kitty and turned to Bela.

"We *both* heard her."

"And that bothers you?"

"Hell, yes!" Kitty was hers! Bela poked out her lower lip, just a little. No, she had always known that no one owned Kitty. What they had was a partnership, an agreement.

And now they were three, apparently. "She has chosen you," Bela said sullenly. "At the moment, Kitty is as much yours as she is mine."

A decent man would not have smiled so widely.

IN the following days, Merin and Bela found methods of managing the delicacies of life without severing the braided rope that bound them. The cottage was only one room, but there was a front door, and the rope was just long enough for them to separate themselves for bathing, changing clothes, and taking care of other personal matters which were best not shared. They did develop a kind of trust, which was all but unavoidable. In this situation, they were forced to trust one another—to a point.

Each day they were given a chore, and it seemed that each was more arduous than the last. Mining was a hard, dirty job, and climbing steep rocks while attached to a woman wasn't easy. Farming was just as hard and dirty, but there was little if any climbing involved.

But any job they were given was easier than sleeping in the same bed, night after night.

One night they'd tried sleeping on the floor, which had allowed them to lie as far apart as possible, given their restraints. It had been a long and uncomfortable night, and somehow they had drifted toward one another in sleep and ended up with legs entwined and Bela's elbow in his chest, in spite of their efforts. The bed was so small they always ended up all over each other in the night, and it sagged so much it drew them toward the center, night after night. That would've been fine with any woman but Bela.

Merin was hard most of the time these days, and he couldn't do a damn thing about it. Six years ago Bela had told him she'd taken a potion to prevent babies. That had been a lie; one of many. This time around he knew damn well she was taking nothing to keep her from conceiving, as she didn't plan to allow for the possibility.

Neither did he.

In the past he'd gone without sex a lot longer than twenty-two days. He could do so again. It was just difficult when Bela was always right *there*.

Since the night he'd heard Kitty speak, the sword had remained silent. Maybe Bela was mistaken when she said that his hearing the weapon's words meant something. It might've been a fluke, or a mistake. Maybe the power had grown too great to contain, and that was why he'd heard. Still, he hoped he was wrong. What soldier wouldn't want such a weapon? Even though the crystal grip of the sword was too small for his comfort, almost as if it had been made for a woman, a part of him hoped he would be able to keep it.

When he and Bela went their separate ways, whom would Kitty choose?

They left the cottage on this fine morning knowing someone—it was usually Tyman or Clyn—would be waiting with their assignment for the day. Merin was ready. He could use a bit of hard physical labor right about now. He wanted to be exhausted, to be so tired he could not so much as think of sex. He wanted to work himself into a state of sheer exhaustion, so that he wouldn't wake in the night smelling Bela's hair or being aware of the way her body fell against his in the wilting bed.

He was surprised to find Bela's mother waiting outside their door. She wore a smile that spoke of secrets, and she greeted her daughter and that daughter's soon-to-be-ex-husband with a hug. "You two look lovely and well rested on this fine morning," she said.

Merin had no time for niceties. "What's the chore for today?" he asked. "Would you like us to dig a big hole and then fill it in?" Even though his tone was harsh, a little digging wouldn't be a bad thing. He wanted every muscle in his body to ache so he could think of nothing else.

"Not today, General. You'll be glad to know your current task is an easy one."

Great. Just want he didn't want.

"You two are to throw a party."

"A *party*?" Bela said, sounding as horrified as Merin felt.

"Yes," Gayene said in a serene voice. "A party for the people of this village. An evening of merriment for your friends and neighbors. There should be food and drink, as well as music or some other sort of entertainment."

"How are we supposed to provide these things?" Merin asked. "Can I use the currency I carried with me on this journey to buy . . ."

Gayene was shaking her head before he could finish the question. He was not surprised by the negative answer. Nothing about this ordeal was meant to be easy. There was only a little bit of food in the cottage. They could barely fit themselves in the one-room hut, much less the entire village. "And how many days do we have to plan this *party*?"

"Providing all that is necessary is your task, General, and the party will take place tonight."

"Tonight?" Bela screeched. "You take weeks to plan a get together! This isn't fair!"

"Fair," Gayene said thoughtfully. "Why, I'd say you should've thought of that before you tricked General Merin into marriage."

Merin felt a moment of vindication, but since he was stuck in the same hell as Bela, his satisfaction was short-lived.

Gayene departed, leaving Bela with a plain brown package which apparently held the dress she would be required to wear. Merin was told to wear his uniform, which had been stored with his other things and would be delivered before the end of the day. The party would commence at sunset.

When he and Bela were alone and the unopened package had been deposited on their miserably misshapen bed, they stared at one another blankly. Hard physical labor was much easier than this.

"Food first, I suppose," Merin said. "Do you hunt?"

"Of course," Bela said, sounding only slightly insulted by the question. Her eyes lit up. "If we make a few extra kills, we can barter for the other things we'll need. The woman who owns the bakery is always happy to trade for meat. Byrnard Pyrl plays the lute quite well, and so does Pero Nestor. I think we can convince one of them to make a trade, as well."

Merin tried to think as she did. Bartering was a good idea. "I noticed that the pub is in need of repair. The door is almost off its hinges and there's damage to the roof. Think the owner would trade labor for mugs and ale?"

Bela smiled, and it was quite nice. Wide and real and filled with joy. "What a wonderful idea. I think we can make this work!" Without thinking, she stuck out her hand. Without thinking, he took it. They shook hands as if consummating a business deal, but quickly broke the contact. The simple touch of hand to hand had ignited something best left cold.

* * *

THEY had been lucky in their travels thus far, Savyn thought as he watched Lady Leyla step into her carriage to begin the day's ride. There had been a few periods of light rain, but no storms, which were frequent enough in springtime. Savyn didn't mind getting wet, and the sentinels didn't seem to mind, either. As long as Lady Leyla was dry and comfortable, all was well.

The carriage got under way, and as had become his custom, Savyn directed his horse to the right side of the carriage, where on occasion he could glance to the side and catch a glimpse of Lady Leyla through the open windows. He longed to ask her why she always looked so sad, but he didn't dare approach her, much less ask such a personal question. Only Minister Bragg and Mistress Hilde dared speak to her.

And yet, Savyn did watch. Night and day, he kept a close eye on her. Sometimes he imagined himself taking her face in his hands and asking her to smile for him. He might as well imagine challenging the emperor for her hand, for both were equally impossible.

There was a warmth in his heart for her, what was surely no more than an infatuation, and yet . . . it felt like more.

More than once on this long morning he had glanced to the side to see her watching him with an expression of sheer annoyance on her exquisite face. He supposed a gentleman would acknowledge the lady's annoyance and ride elsewhere, but he did not. Once, late in the morning, their eyes met from a great distance and Savyn felt a swelling of his heart—and a swelling of something other than his heart, as well.

He could never have one such as her to call his own, so while they traveled and she was his to protect, he would imagine that she might be his own. Such imaginings were feeding his dreams quite well these days. He gave the lady a smile, and she sharply looked away from him.

There was no logical reason for it, but Savyn was sure that Lady Leyla was not nearly as cold as she appeared to be.

BELA was proud of herself and of Merin as their plans came together. They'd gone to her family home to gather her bow and a quiver of arrows before setting out, and before the sun was directly overhead, they'd each killed one large boar. One they used to trade; the other had been roasting all afternoon and would soon feed the village.

The party would surround their cottage. There were burning torches and a few borrowed tables, and lots of ale and mugs, as the pub owner had been glad to make the trade Merin had suggested. There were wildflowers on the tables, arranged in a hodgepodge of borrowed glasses. Bela had been surprised at how eager people had been to help, to loan things and make trades. Normally she didn't like to ask for help, so she had not known.

She cut her eyes to the side, trying for a nonchalant expression. Merin looked very nice in his uniform. It fit him perfectly, showing off his fine body and impeccable posture. He had shaved for the festivities, and she liked the look of his face when he was clean-shaven. He had a very nice jaw, strong and nicely edged, and his lips should not be hidden under facial hair. They were . . . nice. Yes, he was a fine figure of a man, one any normal woman would be glad to call her own.

Most of the day's chore had progressed very well. Bela's only problem was with the gown she had been ordered to wear. She looked down at the fabric, which was clutched in her hands, and grimaced before ordering Merin to wait outside, on the other side of the door. He obeyed, without comment this time.

She could refuse to wear the stupid dress, she supposed, but that would mean failure, and failure meant Rafal would cut the rope and all their work, a week of torture, would be for nothing. They wouldn't be able to attempt dissolution of the marriage for another three years, and all their suffering to this point would be wasted.

Merin waited on the other side of the door while she changed into the unwanted gown. What was wrong with her green gown? It was good enough for other occasions when she was ordered to dress like the daughter of a chieftain, so why would it not do now? It was difficult to move as much as she should, with the restrictions of the rope that bound her to Merin, and she had to stand near her side of the door and pull the dress over her head, and then work the fabric under the rope that encircled her waist. Like the braided rope which had almost become a part of her, the required gown was red and black and white, and it also seemed to be braided. Strips of gathered fabric swirled and entwined, hugging her body too closely. The V-shaped neckline dipped much too low. No matter how she tugged at the fabric, you could see the swell of her breasts, even though that swell was not as impressive as that of other women. Time and again she attempted to pull the material up and over her relatively small breasts and closer together in the center. No matter how she tried, that soft swell of her bosom was revealed. How embarrassing!

Throwing her hands in the air, she gave up. The dress was not going to cooperate. There were black strappy sandals set with red stones, and her golden headband, but she'd left them on the bed and could not fetch them without Merin coming inside.

How she longed to spend the entire night right here, a solid wooden door between them. Was she required to actually attend the party? Could she not just remain here while Merin, on the other side of the door, watched over the proceedings?

Finally, he called, "Aren't you dressed yet?"

"I am," she said sullenly. As he opened the door slowly, she added, "If you can call this 'dressed.'"

Merin studied her intently, his gaze raking her up and down. She knew that look. It was feral and primal. She had seen it once before, when he'd hurt her. She'd seen hints of it once or twice in the past few days, but never like this.

"Shoes," she said, pointing to the bed and turning away so she didn't have to see that disturbing expression on his face.

He followed her. "And your hair."

She snapped her head around and glared at him. "What's wrong with my hair?"

He smiled at her. "Nothing, but you wear that braid almost all the time, and a gown like this one deserves something special."

Bela tried to sneer. "I'll get my ladies' maid right on that."

She had to sit to put on her shoes, and Merin joined her on the edge of the bed. He began undoing her braid, and with a sigh she allowed him to do as he wished. If it kept him occupied, that would be a good thing, she supposed.

His fingers felt heavy and good in her hair. From where he sat, Merin could easily reach her hairbrush, which had been left on the small bedside table. He began to brush her hair, moving gently and slowly, as if afraid he might hurt her. She closed her eyes and savored the sensations. Since he could not see her face, he would never know that she liked this.

"You look beautiful tonight," he said grudgingly as he brushed her hair.

"So do you," she responded just as reluctantly.

He sighed a little. "The proper response to such a compliment is a simple thank you. And besides, men are not supposed to be beautiful." Now he sounded like he was having fun with her.

"But . . ." she almost said *But you are*, before deciding that was unwise. "I have never been proper, and I don't intend to start now."

He laughed, turned her about, and placed the circlet of gold in her hair. Once again, his eyes raked down her body. "More black, red, and white. Are the colors symbolic in some way?"

"Yes."

"How? Tell me."

Her mouth went dry, and she found she could not discuss love and passion with Merin, especially not now and not here on this bed. "Ask the seer for an explanation, if you wish one."

"I'd rather hear it from you," he said without anger.

Bela stood abruptly. "Perhaps another time, when we have nothing better to discuss. Our guests will be here soon."

Merin stood, and again he gave her that look that chilled her to the bone. It was a look that cut straight through her, a look that she felt to her toes. She'd rather weed a hundred gardens or mine a hundred days than be put in this position again.

Heaven above, at this moment she felt as if Merin actually were a husband. *Her* husband.

Chapter Five

THE social gathering that was their task for the day went very well, all things considered. The villagers were amused by the situation, and though that annoyed Merin, he could not blame them. If this was happening to someone else, he'd find it funny.

A local man played the lute without making too many mistakes, and there was dancing in a grassy square lit by blazing torches. A young lady at the lute player's side occasionally joined in, playing a lilting gemshorn. It was apparent from their skill that they had performed together in the past—and both had been more than happy to trade their musical abilities for meat.

The boar was well done and tasty, and plenty of ale was drunk. Children of all ages ran and played, with endless energy, and those who were not able to dance because of age or infirmity sat on chairs Merin had collected from the pub. Talking and laughing with those around them, they probably passed the evening gossiping about him and Bela, but maybe they were allowed.

Bela's friend Jocylen and her husband were obviously happy with one another. They would likely never find themselves bound together for twenty-two days—not that they would mind such a situation. Bela and Jocylen seemed anxious to share some womanly talk, but thanks to his proximity they could not speak freely. Instead, they exchanged cryptic glances and a few fluttery hand signals he had no chance of deciphering, and more than once Bela leaned over to whisper in her friend's ear. Merin tried not to listen. If she was talking about him, the words were probably not flattering.

Bela swore she did not care for womanly things, and then she acted very much like a woman. She was perplexing.

Though he did not attempt to listen, did not move closer to catch an occasional word, Merin did wonder what Bela would tell her friend about him, if he were the topic of conversation. Would she list all his faults, or were there a few virtues she would discuss? They didn't get along well at all, and neither of them wished to be in this untenable situation, but she did think he was "beautiful."

No one was more beautiful than Bela, not tonight. Odd that he should even think the word in regard to her, since she was not pretty in any traditional sense. Her features were too strong, too sharp, to be called beautiful. It was the hair and that revealing dress, he supposed, that made his mind turn to admiration of beauty. She should wear the thick chestnut tresses down more often, rather than always catching them up in that staid plait. Tonight her hair waved very nicely, full and silky as it rippled over her shoulders and down her back. The golden band she'd been wearing on his arrival was her only adornment. It was simple, and added just a touch of shine and sparkle to a woman who needed no adornment at all.

She should also wear dresses more often. The one which had been provided for her was striking. Bela looked like a goddess in that dress, tall and curvaceous and strong. She looked as if she could tempt any man to long for things he should not. It wasn't as if she wasn't tempting enough in britches and manly shirts, but in that revealing gown which made it so clear she was a woman . . . she was amazingly tempting and utterly female.

Merin's brow furrowed. Was it his fault that Bela hid her femininity behind manly clothes and pursuits? Had their one time together been so traumatic that she shunned all womanly things so she would not be subjected to such an ordeal again? That night had been a disaster. Drugged and close to senseless though he had been, he remembered that much.

He'd thought she was ready as she stripped away his clothes and climbed atop him. No, more than ready—she'd been anxious, or at least she'd pretended to be. She hadn't been able to undress herself or him fast enough. She'd known what went where and had been eager to begin. Well, he'd thought she'd been eager. Knowing her better now than he had then, he realized that what he'd seen as eagerness had instead been impatience.

She'd jumped on his erection and lost her maidenhead, squealing in surprise and pain before making a hasty escape. Thanks to the potion she had used to take half his senses, he'd been unable to chase after her. Even though he'd been confused and frustrated at being abandoned so early in the act, he could do nothing but lie there, unsatisfied and befuddled.

He had never before considered that she'd been almost entirely ignorant when it came to matters of sex. Ignorant and impatient—not a good combination, not at all.

Apparently their brief and unfinished encounter had been a harrowing experience for her, one that made her wary of a natural relationship between a woman and a man. He could fix her ignorance, though, if he had a notion. He could fix it very easily.

Merin was not altogether surprised when the seer Rafal Fiers ordered him and Bela to dance. She was openly annoyed by the command, but Merin found he did not care. They slept in the same bed, they worked side by side, they lived unrelentingly in one another's shadow. One dance wouldn't change anything.

Bela had to teach him the steps of the Turi Calchas Dance, which was slow and sensuous and often demanded that their bodies be very close. Only a handful of couples participated in this particular dance, he noticed, so he had to ask, "Is this some sort of secret ceremonial dance that's going to pledge me to something or someone?"

"No," Bela said tersely. "this dance is reserved for men and their wives. Like it or not, we qualify."

"For the next fifteen days," he clarified.

"For the next fourteen and a half days."

"Of course."

The steps were simple, their bodies brushed now and then. The dance was not so primitive as to mimic the act of sex, but it was definitely arousing. The tempo, the way their bodies came together and then moved apart, the soft and rhythmic sound of the lute and the trilling gemshorn— yes, this was a dance not of joy or celebration but of passion.

"What do the colors mean?" he asked, anxious to change the subject. "Red, black, and white. What do they symbolize?"

Bela sighed. "Later."

"I could ask someone else."

"Go right ahead," she said, but in the wash of firelight he could see her blush. "You are so annoyingly impatient."

She thought *he* was impatient? No one was more impatient than Bela. "Later, then," he said. The dance called for him to lift her off her feet and spin her around, and he did so easily. Bela was tall, she was muscled, but she seemed light as a feather at the moment, as if she almost floated from the ground. The wind caught her skirt and her hair and whipped them gently around, right before he placed her on her feet.

The music ended, and the party was over. Couples collected their children, if they had them, and headed for home. Others simply walked away arm in arm. Many said good night to Bela and Merin and thanked them for the meal and the entertainment, as if the host and hostess had had a choice in the matter. Clyn and Tyman glared at Merin before they left, Clyn with his wife, Tyman with a young girl he had been courting. Gayene Haythorne and her chieftain husband looked pleased with themselves as they said their good nights.

"We should clean . . ." Bela began.

Merin grabbed her wrist and pulled her toward him. "Tomorrow morning will be soon enough. You shouldn't be cleaning anything in that dress."

"It's not as if I'll ever wear it again," she protested.

Merin raked one finger down a length of black fabric. "You never know. Maybe your next husband will want to dissolve your marriage," he teased.

"There will be no next husband," Bela said sharply.

It made him sad to think that she would never have what her friend Jocylen had found. It made him angry to realize that she would close herself from all things womanly because of one bad night.

"Anything is possible," he said.

She looked aghast in the fading torchlight. Soon the flames would burn out and all would be dark, as was right at this time of night. "I suppose you will marry one day," she said, more than a hint of accusation in her voice.

"I suppose I will," he said.

"You'll likely pick some brainless, childlike woman who will expect you to take care of her." Bela almost sneered. "Why bother?"

"I would like to have children one day."

"Why?" she sounded horrified.

Merin found himself smiling. "You don't like children?"

"Once they're of an age they're all right, I suppose, but babies stink and they require constant care. They can be uncommonly loud and demanding, considering their small size, and they expect to *drink* from their mother's breasts as if she were a sow."

Merin brushed a thumb against Bela's nipple, and she gasped. He felt it harden instantly, as her body unwillingly responded to his touch.

"I did not ask for a demonstration," she said primly. "I know very well where my breasts are located."

They stood there for a while, and the light of one torch died. Another soon followed.

"We should go inside," Merin said.

"We should, I suppose. I'm very tired." She glanced toward the door to their small cottage as if there might be a monstrous beast hiding behind it. "Nothing has changed," she insisted.

He disagreed. Somehow, everything had changed.

MERIN lit a single lamp inside the cottage. Bela tried very hard not to look at him as he began to remove his uniform without bothering to ask her to stand outside or turn her back. Maybe he just planned to sleep in his trousers, as he sometimes did.

But like it or not, she had to get out of this blasted dress, and she did not want him watching while she shed it.

Merin stripped down to plain, dark green trousers and then stopped to fold the rest of his uniform. It was easy to forget that he was a general of high station in other parts of Columbyana, given all they'd done in the past few days. He had never complained about the menial labors which had been required of him. He had never once tried to use his position to weasel out of this untenable situation.

He sat on the side of the bed and removed his boots.

"Would you stand outside while I put on my night-gown?" she asked, thinking her voice was amazingly sweet and serene and reasonable.

"No," Merin said. "I don't think I will."

Bela placed her hands on her hips and glared at him. So much for reason! "We have an arrangement, and it has worked quite well until now. Why become obstinate now?"

"I'm tired, just as you are," he said, and in truth he did sound weary enough. "I don't want to step outside and stand there while you wrestle with that gown and your nightdress, when it would be so much easier if I helped you take it off."

Bela took a step back. "No! Just because we danced, just because I let you brush my hair, just because . . . just because . . ."

"Don't you ever wonder, Bela, why all these other women of your village are so happy with their husbands? You are curious about other aspects of life, and yet you don't seem to wonder why you are the only woman who runs from a man's attentions as if he plans to slit your pretty throat at the first opportunity."

She pursed her lips. "Perhaps I am different from other women in some ways."

"You are different in many ways, Bela, some very good and some very bad. I feel rather responsible for your dis-taste for men, even though what happened six years ago was not entirely my fault."

"Let's not discuss . . ."

"Let's," he said. "I have a proposition for you. You let me show you what you're missing, and if I'm wrong, if you still want nothing to do with men when I'm finished, then tomorrow I will do your work as well as my own. You can sit and watch, if you'd like, sipping water or wine and resting as comfortably as is possible, given the situation, while I labor away."

She smiled. "You will begin the day cleaning up the mess from tonight's party."

He nodded his head, and still Bela felt a rush of panic. "This is a bad idea. I don't want to be hurt, and we can't take the chance of making a child. If there's a baby, we can never dissolve this marriage. *Never.*"

"There will be no baby," Merin said confidently, "and I can and will stop what I'm doing at any time. All you have to do is tell me to stop, and it is done. I'm not a monster, Bela. I don't plan to attack you and I won't hurt you."

"You can't know . . ."

"I promise." His voice was smooth as silk, and the sound caused her blood to do a little dance, and a little something somewhere tugged and fluttered. It was quite unusual.

Bela could not say she was not curious. Jocylen was delighted with her marriage and her husband, and other brides seemed more than happy enough. Still, she could not help but remember the pain and invasion and horror of their first encounter. Was she hopelessly broken? Could Merin fix her? Was it possible that she was *wrong*? "If I say stop . . ."

"I stop."

"You swear." She took a step closer to the bed.

"On my honor."

A man like Tearlach Merin didn't swear on his honor lightly. "What am I supposed to do?"

He smiled at her. "Nothing." He scooted over and made a place for her on the bed, beside him. She'd been attached to him for many days, and still it made her nervous to sit beside him now. They seemed so *close.*

"Lie back."

"Turn out the lamp first," she said. Their oil lamp didn't cast a lot of light, but it would be enough for him to see her. Not that she was shy, but . . .

"No." Merin hovered over her for a moment. She expected a kiss would come next, so she closed her eyes and puckered her lips a little. He lowered his mouth to her throat instead of her mouth, and lingered there.

Yes, it did feel good as his lips danced across her throat. Soft and warm and tingly good. She felt as if she were unraveling, as if she were melting beneath the attentions of those fine lips. Merin's mouth dropped lower and he kissed the valley between her breasts, moving slowly, languidly. He stole her breath, and just like that it seemed her very blood changed. He raked his lips and his tongue there, seeming to be in no hurry. The tip of his tongue touched the swell of one breast and then slipped just inside the fabric to taste skin which had been hidden from view.

Bela closed her eyes, as it seemed she could better enjoy the unexpected sensations this way, when all she had to do was feel.

Then Merin, stubborn Merin, lifted his head. "Tell me about the colors. His fingers raked down a length of gathered fabric that just happened to cover a sensitive nipple. She jumped when his fingers brushed over it and then came back again to test the shape and hardness. "Black?"

To refuse again would only delay his return to his proper work. "Dark times," she said, surprised by how very dry her mouth was.

"The sort of dark times that might lead a woman and a man to think of ending their marriage?"

"Yes."

Merin scooted her back on the bed and very gently pushed her onto her back with insistent but tender hands. When she was laid out on the bed like a goose at a family feast, he moved the black fabric aside to expose her nipple, and then he took that nipple into his warm mouth.

Shocked, Bela started to protest. She was no goose, and she would not be spread out as if she were General Merin's own personal feast! But what he was doing to her felt too good, it felt wonderfully good in a way she had not expected. She was languid and edgy, both at once. Protest was unnecessary. Her body rose off the bed, ever so slightly, to move closer to his. He responded by sucking her nipple deeper into his mouth. She gasped, grabbing a handful of dark curls to pull him closer, tighter.

She had felt nothing like this before. The last time, she'd been in such a hurry to have the chore done and over with that she hadn't allowed for such luxuries as touching and licking and sucking. And this was a luxury, a luxury of sensation and decadence. A moment ago she had felt as if she were unraveling, and now she felt as if everything in her body was growing tighter, more tightly wound.

Eventually Merin lifted his head from her breast. She was all but panting, and her body screamed for more. Between her legs she ached, and her heart was pounding so hard she could feel it.

"White," Merin said, raking his fingers down a section of white fabric that draped across her hip.

"It's silly . . . ," Bela began, wishing he would simply get back to what he'd been doing. Why did he insist on speaking when he had more important things to do?

His hand became more urgent, his thumb traveling down her hip to her thigh. One caress of his hand and a new kind of sensation was set into play. "White," he said again.

"Fine, if you insist on being difficult . . ."

"I do," he said with a smile.

"Pure love," she whispered, and the two words roused a wave of discomfort inside her. She should not be speaking of love with Tearlach Merin. He might get the wrong idea and think she believed in such fantasies. She tried to give her voice a practical tone. "Love given and blessed by the powers above, love precious and untainted, that sort of nonsense."

Merin's hand continued down her thigh, and then he began to pull her skirt up, exposing her legs. His fingers brushed her bare skin as he worked slowly, ever so slowly. Her mouth went dry again, and it seemed that her body wanted to seize and push him away. He'd said he would stop if she asked, and she decided to test that promise. "Stop," she whispered.

He did. His hand stilled, but he did not rise up and leave her. It was as if he knew what she was doing, as if he knew she was testing him.

Bela relaxed, as much as relaxation was possible at this moment. Her wave of reservations receded. She was in control here; he would not hurt her. "Proceed," she said softly, and with a smile he did.

"I'm not sure that I believe in pure love," he said as he continued to push her skirt high. "Commitment to another, yes. Devotion and affection particular to two people who have been drawn to one another definitely exists. I have seen it with my own eyes. But nothing in life is entirely untainted. Nothing is pure."

She would love to say that she agreed with him entirely, but damn if he hadn't stolen her power of speech with his hands.

Again he kissed her throat, which she had found to be strangely sensitive and receptive to the attentions of his mouth. He even took her earlobe between his lips and sucked it. Bela closed her eyes and listened to the demands of her body. She'd been so sure when they'd begun this exercise that she'd make him stop long before this, as soon as she found his attentions unpleasant. But now she wanted more. In the past there had been nothing but pain and disappointment, and still she wanted more.

Hope was a frightening and debilitating thing.

"Red." His fingers crawled up a section of crimson fabric which draped from just beneath her breasts to midbelly. His hand started low and traveled under the rope that circled her waist, the rope that bound them. She felt the warmth of that hand to her very core.

"P-p-p-passion," she said, embarrassed that she couldn't say the word without stuttering.

"I suspect you are more afraid of the passion than you are of the dark times," he said as he continued to caress her body.

"I am," she whispered.

"You should not be afraid of passion," he said. "It's a beautiful and natural thing."

"Not in my experience," she said, even though at the moment she did feel beautiful and natural.

His hand found her bare thigh again and began to caress there. "We're going to forget that one bad night and start over. No lies, no manipulations, and no desperation. Just touch and pleasure, Bela. Just passion."

Once again he took her nipple in his mouth. His hand climbed higher, and in response her center grew damp and anxious. There was an insistent tugging sensation there. She wanted him to touch her. She wanted him to keep going. She wanted him to *hurry up!* A part of her wanted to tell him again to stop, but she didn't.

Merin touched her in a place so sensitive, so intimate, she gasped. She hadn't known her body was capable of producing these sensations, of jerking and writhing as she tried to bring him closer. He massaged the nub at her entrance, and she held on to him as new sensations were born. He sucked her nipple deeper, and she balled her hands into fists as she gasped loudly.

She was hot and so was he; she was washed in a new and unusual type of desperation. She wanted something, but she didn't know exactly what. Just more. More Merin, more of this delicious marvel. She made a funny sound. She didn't mean to, it just happened. How embarrassing! She didn't care, as she made another sound and rocked her hips.

Merin slipped a finger inside her, and she shattered. Ribbons of pleasure so intense they made her weep whipped through her. She gasped and cried out sharply. She came up off the bed, holding on to Merin tightly so the sensations wouldn't carry her away. Her head fell back and her thighs parted, and she was aware of nothing but the pleasure whipping through her body.

Too soon it was done. Bela collapsed to the mattress, boneless and breathless, completely unwound. Her mouth was dry, she could not breathe, her heart was pounding, and oh, she wanted to do that again. Why did married women ever leave their beds?

When her brain began to function once more, she raised her head and looked at Merin, who still had on his trousers, trousers which were mightily strained at the moment.

She was not a complete fool, in spite of the mistakes which had led them to this point. He was hurting; he had not shared any of the pleasure he had given her. "What about you?" she asked. She still did not wish a repeat of their first encounter, but she had jumped on him without preparation at that time, and apparently preparation was a large part of the act.

He shook his head. "Much as it pains me, this is as far as we can go. No babies, remember?"

"I remember." If there was a baby, they would never be able to undo the deceitful marriage. She fell back against the bed and smiled. "That was fun. When can we do it again?"

Merin laughed hoarsely. "When you want me to die. I wanted to do this for you, I truly did, but I can't continue to pleasure you and stop."

"You made this wonderful sacrifice for me, and all along I thought you didn't even like me much."

"I don't," he said.

That hurt more than it should've, but she shouldn't be surprised.

"But that doesn't mean I don't want you." Once again Merin's hands moved to her dress and his fingers danced. "We've had the black, and I suspect we could handle the red quite well. It's the white we lack, Bela."

"You don't believe in pure love."

"No, but red and black alone would make for a sad marriage, don't you think?"

"I don't know," Bela said thoughtfully. "If there was enough of the red . . ." She stopped speaking before her rambling led them to a place they wouldn't be able to escape. At this moment she was warm and satisfied and oddly happy, but Merin was right, and that knowledge stole some of her happiness.

MERIN wasn't at all surprised when the following day's chore was to dig a big hole and then fill it again. That's what he deserved for mentioning the senseless chore to Bela's mother. They didn't get started until after they'd cleaned up the mess the villagers had made at their celebration, which took some time.

He and Bela had hardly spoken all day. Instead of making things better between them, last night he'd apparently made them worse. There was a new tension in the air.

The area where they'd been told to dig was beyond the edge of town. It was a warm day, and soon they were both sweating from their labors. What a contrast they were to the washed and well-dressed couple they had been last night. What a contrast to the man and woman—man and wife—who had tumbled about in their bed after all their guests had left.

He should've allowed her to suffer delusions about sex and remain unattached for the rest of her days. Perhaps it was harsh punishment for the mistakes of a mere child, but could he bear to remain bound to her for the next fourteen days and not touch her again? And if he touched her again . . .

"I've been thinking," Bela began.

"Don't," Merin said brusquely. "No good can come of it."

She actually laughed. "Your mood is obviously not as bright as mine is on this fine spring day."

He might've laughed, but was in too much pain.

"You're grouchy. Perhaps we should talk later," she said sensibly.

"Perhaps we should." He threw himself into the job of digging, glad for the aching muscles and the sweat and the exertion that helped him to forget he was not in this hole in the ground alone. A short while later he and Bela climbed out of the hole and began to fill it in, one shovel of dirt at a time.

They were alone, and yet not entirely unsupervised. Now and then someone would show up to check on them, to make sure the senseless hole was sufficiently deep and wide to qualify for a chore, to make sure they did not attempt to undo their bonds.

More than once, Merin considered cutting the rope that bound him to Bela and riding away, conceding to a marriage that would never be a marriage, condemning them both to a life bound to a spouse they did not love, a spouse who lived a great distance away.

Maybe it would be a worthwhile sacrifice. This was torture.

When the hole was filled in, they decided to walk to the creek to bathe off the worst of the dirt before going home. They were so dirty a cloth, some soap, and a ewer of water would not suffice.

He hoped the water was cold.

They had become accustomed to the rope between them and no longer stumbled with it, as they had in early days.

Neither of them could be called clumsy, and they'd adjusted to the restraint very well. Merin whipped off his shirt and kicked off his boots, and then he stepped into the creek with his trousers on. He did not want Bela to realize that he was aroused just because she was near.

Bela did the same—she took off her boots and her shirt, and gratefully splashed water onto her body. He tried not to look too closely, but he could not help but note, as he had last night, that she had nice breasts of just the right size. They were rounded and shapely and high, not too large and not too small. The nipples were dark and, as he remembered, responsive.

Apparently she had recovered from her extreme shyness which required a door between them when she bared her womanly attributes.

"Is it all right to tell you now what I've been thinking?" she asked.

"I suppose." Anything to take his mind in a different direction.

"Last night . . ."

"Let's not talk about last night," he said harshly.

She grinned widely, and wearing that smile, she was fetching, pretty even with the smudges of dirt on her face. No simpering maid could compare. No traditional beauty could hold a candle to this woman.

"I promise to be quick about it, but please allow me to talk. If you find you cannot bear it, tell me to stop, and I will. I promise."

"Fine." How much worse could it be?

"Last night you taught me something," she said, wonder in her smooth voice. "You showed me a pleasure I had never before imagined."

"Stop," he said, pain in his voice.

Bela obeyed him. She stopped speaking, but her wide smile said too much.

"Proceed," he said grudgingly.

"You introduced me to sexual pleasures without risking the possibility of a child, which was considerate of you, especially as I'm quite sure I would've agreed to just about anything at one point or another. When you had your mouth on my breast and your hand . . ."

He was wrong; she *could* make it worse. "Stop," he said again.

"Sorry," she said, wise enough to realize what she was doing. "To put it simply, I wondered if it was possible for me to do the same for you."

Merin was so stunned, he said nothing.

"I know you are frustrated," she said. "I see it in you, in your eyes and the set of your shoulders"—she grinned—"and in your trousers. Sorry to be blunt, but it is true, and I am not afraid to learn how I might take away that frustration without condemning us both to a red and black marriage. Pleasure shared without the risk of a child. It's possible for me, but is it possible for you?"

"Yes," he said, his voice hoarse.

"We could approach Odella Bydeen about obtaining a potion to keep me from conceiving, but I hear it takes some days for the potion to be effective, and besides, Odella talks too much and everyone would know we'd asked. It's hardly in the spirit of ending a marriage, and I don't think my brothers would agree, so that potential solution is not feasible. That leaves one other possibility. So, tonight will you show me what I can do?"

There was no other like Bela, that was certain. She was not shy; she did not hesitate to grab life and all it offered. "Tonight?"

"If you would prefer to wait . . ."

Merin pulled Bela close and led her hand to his strained trousers. "Here. Now. In the name of all that is good . . ."

She laughed and stroked, and Merin closed his eyes. Bela had hands that were gentle but not shy, a stroke that was tentative but not afraid, and when she moved her hands to the laces that held his trousers closed, his hand found her breast and he caressed her there as he bent his head to kiss the side of her neck. Sweating, dirty, she still tasted good. She smelled like heaven. His own personal heaven.

He took her face in his hands and looked into her moss-green eyes, eyes which were alive with passion and curiosity and life. Bela did not hesitate to look fully into his eyes, even though her fingers closed around his erect penis, even though she stroked him slowly, up and down the length. Maybe it was the light, maybe it was the way she stroked, but at this moment she was beautiful, beautiful like no other woman he had ever seen.

That was as far as they got before they heard hoofbeats approaching at a fast rate of speed.

Merin cursed. So did Bela, as she dropped her hands and backed away. He did his best to straighten his trousers, not an easy task at the moment.

They rushed for the creek bank and Bela pulled on her shirt. Merin stepped into his boots just as Tyman crested the hill. Good God, how could he have known? And how had he gotten here so quickly? Judging by the expression on his face, Bela's brother was not happy.

"Trouble's come calling," Tyman said. "You two get dressed and get back to the village. We need every sword." He gave his sister an annoyed and brotherly look. "You're becoming more trouble than you're worth, Bela."

THEY'D been traveling for days and had weeks left to journey, and already Leyla was bone weary. She could bear the bumps of the carriage and the stifling heat and the less than adequate food and the unpleasant company of a disapproving relative by marriage and crude sentinels. She could bear sleeping on the ground—or more often lying awake on the hard ground, trying to claim a bit of sleep.

What she could not stand was Savyn's presence. If he

were not here, she would be able to forget, at least to some degree. If he had stayed behind in Childers, he might already be courting a proper young girl by now. At the very least, she could imagine it was so. Instead, he was ever present, silent and distant and achingly handsome, and a constant reminder of what she could never have again.

Perhaps she deserved to be tortured.

Blessedly, Hilde was taking a late afternoon nap. The old woman's snores filled the confines of the carriage, but the snorting and sawing were preferable to her constant words of criticism. How would she bear the remaining days of this journey without touching her companion's head and convincing her she was mute?

The carriage jerked to a stop, waking Hilde, who snorted and slurped and grabbed about for something to hold on to. At first Leyla was not concerned. They might've come to an obstacle in the road, or perhaps there was a problem with the horses.

And then one of the sentinels screamed, and the hairs on the back of Leyla's neck rose up and tingled.

Bravely, she poked her head out of the window to her left, to see what was going on. From this vantage point she could see all. A silver-haired man dressed all in black rode among the others with a sword in one hand and a hatchet in the other. Two men had already fallen and lay dead: one sentinel as well as the carriage driver, who had obviously jumped from his post to do battle. The attacker was fighting the other two sentinels while Deputy Bragg hung back, placing himself between the battle and the carriage. He would likely be fighting the attacker soon, since the man in black was a superior swordsman to the sentinels. In fact, he moved like no other she had ever seen, with speed and accuracy which should not have been possible. Long silver hair, unnatural in its brightness, danced in the wind, and the way his weapons moved was uncanny. Another sentinel fell, the victim of a single swipe of the silver-haired man's sword.

The door to her right opened, startling Leyla, and she snapped her head about as Savyn offered his hand. "This way, M'Lady," he said in a low but insistent voice.

She did not hesitate, but jumped across the carriage and took the hand he offered. The attacker would not be able to see them from here, at this particular moment. If he moved closer or more to the side, however, he might witness their escape.

Tempting as it was to leave her unpleasant chaperone where she sat, she could not. "Come, Hilde. Hurry!"

The woman shook her head. "I won't put my life in the hands of an untrained boy who knows nothing of warfare. Don't be foolish. The sentinels will save us. Get back in this carriage, where it's safe!"

Leyla shook her head. She knew in the pit of her soul that this carriage was no longer safe, and she trusted Savyn with her life much more than she'd trust an army of sentinels. And they did not have an army of sentinels. All that remained was one sentinel and one diplomat, and soon there would be no one to protect them. "Come with us," Leyla insisted. This time Hilde simply shook her head.

"We cannot wait for her," Savyn insisted. "We must make our escape."

"We cannot leave her here." She had seen the silver-haired attacker move. Even though he was outnumbered, he would not lose. Would he show mercy to an old, helpless woman?

Savyn did not ask again. He lifted Leyla from her feet and tossed her over his shoulder, and then he ran away from the carriage, away from the fighting. He carried her into the woods lining the rough road.

He did not pause, did not seem to be burdened by her weight as he rushed into the deepest part of the woodland.

He ducked often, and still low-lying limbs sometimes brushed their heads or Savyn's arms. Low growth occasionally slowed his progress, but he fought through, staying in the thickest part of the wood, where they would be well hidden from a horseman. In the distance, they heard a woman's bloodcurdling scream, and Savyn's step faltered.

Leyla's heart almost stopped. That could've been her scream, if Savyn had not rescued her. "Put me down," she said.

"We cannot go back," Savyn said without pausing.

"I know," Leyla conceded. They would be able to move faster if he did not have her weight.

Savyn whipped her down and set her on her feet. He took her hand, and they began to run side by side.

Chapter Six

✳

TYMAN had not thought to bring an extra horse with him—not that mounting while bound to Merin wouldn't have been a challenge—so Bela and Merin ran toward the village. It wasn't far, yet Bela felt as if she couldn't move fast enough. She and Merin ran at a steady and comfortable pace. Neither had to slow or shorten their stride for the other.

Her sometimes irritable brother had not waited for them. What had he meant by that comment about her being too much trouble? How could a crisis that would put an expression like the one on Tyman's face be *her* fault?

Once the village was in sight, she and Merin cut sharply to the side and headed for their cottage to retrieve their weapons. There was no question, no *Should we?* or *Might we?* They both needed to be armed before facing whatever trouble had come to the Turis. Once they were safely inside the cottage, Bela called for Kitty, and Kitty came. Merin strapped on a sheath and sword with the ease and speed of one who had done just that many times. He was efficient but not panicked, ready for whatever might be waiting. They briefly looked one another in the eye before heading out of the cottage to see what kind of trouble had arrived.

Their movements were cautious and quick as they headed for the village square. They did not have to go quite that far to find the trouble. It was easy enough to spot the crowd of villagers that had gathered at her father's house.

As soon as Bela could see through the crowd well enough to recognize the spotted horse and the red-haired man standing beside it, she groaned. Nobel Andyrs was Turi himself, or once had been, but Bela's father—acting as chieftain—had banished the brash man from the village months ago. Nobel had gotten into a dispute over a mine claim more than once, and on the last occasion he had killed the other party. He was greedy and unpleasant and unrelenting.

Nobel was also one of the foolish men who had pursued her at one time, even though he knew very well she was no maid and had no desire to be anyone's wife. She'd refused his attentions vehemently, and when he'd finally realized she was not being coy, he'd been angry—not heartbroken. He'd wanted an alliance with the chieftain, not a bride. Their last encounter had not ended well for Nobel.

As she and Merin approached, making their way through the crowd of women and children and older Turis—most of the younger men of the village were working in the fields or in the mountains—the red-haired outcast turned his head to look at her. Perhaps he had heard their approach or seen the wave of the crowd that made way. He smiled and then, as Bela and Merin made their way to the front of the crowd, Nobel's gaze fell to Kitty. That was when she saw the flash of lust in his pale eyes.

When Merin revealed that kind of deep desire in a glance, at least he was looking at *her.*

"Here to sacrifice more fingers?" she asked, her grip on Kitty tightening very slightly.

Nobel raised his left hand, displaying the three fingers which remained there. "If that thing you carry dares to so much as scratch me again, my man will gut your mother."

It was then that Bela saw the other men, those who stood beyond Nobel and his spotted horse. They looked as rough as their leader and were all well armed, and one of them clasped Gayene Haythorne too closely to his filthy body. He also held a very large knife that touched her slender throat.

"What do you want?" Bela snapped, trying not to show her fear—and failing. That was her *mother*.

"What I have always wanted, Belavalari Haythorne. You as my wife, of course." He glanced pointedly at the telling rope which bound her to Merin. "I understand you will be available in a short while."

"She will not be available for you," Merin said calmly, his voice deep and even. How could he stay so calm when a madman held a knife to her mother's throat?

A few weeks ago she'd been blissfully unattached—for all intents and purposes. Now an emperor wanted to inspect her for bridal consideration; she'd had to reveal the secret marriage to Merin in order to save his neck; and now Nobel was back. This was just too much for any woman to bear. And others wondered why she shunned marriage!

Nobel looked at Merin, unafraid. "I would make her a widow and have the deed done now, but I'm not foolish enough to kill a general of your standing and suffer the consequences. My bride and I will not wish to spend our lives running from an army."

"In that case, I demand that you release the Lady Gayene," Merin said. He added a curt "Now," when his order was not immediately obeyed.

Bela cast a glance at her husband. What seemed like moments ago, he'd been caught up in need and lust and, well, her. Now he was every bit the general, displaying no weaknesses, no needs at all. He was, in fact, quite impressive. Any woman would be proud to call this man husband, even if temporarily.

"Before I order that done," Nobel said, "I must inform you that I have a large number of loyal men waiting not far away. If I and my companions don't return to them very soon, they will fall upon this village like a plague. They will spare no one." His eyes flitted over the villagers who watched, and he smiled, not at all shamed to threaten bodily harm to the weakest among them.

"We have fought the likes of you before," Bela's father said with anger.

"And you lost many of your clan in the process," Nobel reminded him. "Do you want that for your people again? Do you want to see the funeral pyres burn night after night after night?"

He did not. None of them did.

"How do we know you're not lying?" Clyn asked.

"See for yourselves." Nobel pointed in the direction of the river, where a constant Turi guard watched for invaders. In the distance, a gentle hill that looked over the village was lined with mounted men. Nobel's men. Bela could not help but wonder what had happened to the guard who had been stationed there. Even the best among them couldn't defeat so many armed men.

Nobel raised a hand and Bela's mother was released. Gayene fell into her husband's arms, unharmed but obviously terrified.

"Here is my proposition," Nobel said. "I will wait for Bela's current marriage to be dissolved, and then we will be wed." He looked at Merin, bolder than he should've been. "Don't look at me with such disapproval, General. It's obvious you don't want her. I do. You should not complain that I will be waiting for your departure."

"Well, you're out of luck," Bela said, intent on telling Nobel of Emperor Jahn's plans.

Merin reached out and snagged her hand, squeezing it

too tightly. "Don't argue with the man, you exasperating woman. Be still, for once."

She turned to glare at him. Exasperating woman? Be *still*? And how dare he stop her from . . . His eyes caught hers and she instantly understood. For some reason Merin did not want Nobel to know that she was to make a trip to Arthes to be introduced to the bride-seeking emperor.

Nobel turned away with a smile on his face, and he reached for a bulging sack which hung from his horse's saddle. He tossed the bag carelessly; it landed at Bela's feet. The unbound sack hit the ground hard, and from the opening a few colorful stones spilled out. Most of them were red and dark blue, like the stones found in the Turi Mountains, but many were a pale yellow, almost clear in color. "My first payment for my bride," he said. "It's quite generous, don't you think? The rest will be delivered on our wedding night, sweetheart." He had the audacity to wink at her.

Bela surged forward. "I will never marry you, Nobel Andyrs! If there was no other man on this earth, life as we know it would end because I would not allow you anywhere near me! Try to purchase me as if I were a horse—*try*—and I will send Kitty toward another part of your body. You'll wish she'd aimed higher and taken another finger when I'm . . ."

She stopped speaking when Merin yanked on the rope that bound them and she fell back so hard she ended up on her ass in the dirt. Nobel and all his men laughed, and then Nobel looked down at her with something besides lust in his pale blue eyes. She could not help but shiver.

"You *will* marry me, Bela, because if you don't, my men will raze this village to the ground. No one will be spared. Not your family, not the women, not the children. No building will remain standing. No sow or dog will live when we are done. Every field will burn."

A chill ran down her spine. This was beyond madness.

Why? Why would he wish to wed her when with his new-found wealth he could have any other woman . . . as long as the woman in question was not too discriminating about the man she called husband.

"Say nothing," Merin commanded softly, before turning his attentions to the red-haired interloper. "The marriage will be done fourteen days from tomorrow morning. Don't show your face here before then. Is that understood?"

"Of course, General," Nobel said with a touch of humor. "I'll see you then."

Nobel and his men rode toward the waiting riders—the waiting army. Bela and her family stood there in stunned silence and watched them go.

None dared to challenge the Turis, but Nobel dared. None should want her, but Nobel did. Nobel Andyrs should not be capable of raising an army of men willing to listen to him, but apparently he was.

Merin offered her a hand to assist her from the dirt, a hand she refused as she struggled to her feet. "I don't care what he says, I won't marry him. I'd rather stay married to Merin, if I must!" It was intended as an insult, but didn't come out sounding at all insulting.

She tried to imagine Nobel touching her as Merin had last night, and she immediately felt weak and queasy, as if she'd eaten something bad. "You got it wrong, you know," she said in a calmer voice. "The marriage will be done in thirteen days, come tomorrow morning. Thirteen, not fourteen."

"I know," Merin said in a low voice.

"Then why?"

Merin pinned his eyes on her. "I bought us another day, that is all." Then he turned to Bela's father, general to chieftain. "I suggest we discuss this situation in the privacy of your home. Now."

"There is no need for privacy," the chieftain said. "We

must devise a plan, and I need the men of this village with me in order to do what must be done. We will defend our homes and our people from Nobel and his men."

Merin moved closer to the chieftain, all but dragging Bela with him. "There is a spy in your village," he said in a lowered voice. "Until we know who that traitor is, we cannot involve anyone beyond the immediate family."

Bela's father stubbornly lifted his chin. "None of my people would dare . . ."

"Then how did Nobel know that Bela and I were in the process of undoing this marriage? He was not surprised to see the rope that binds us. Someone told him."

CAYSE Trinity stared at the woman he had just killed. As with the others who littered this battlefield, he had taken her life quickly, as painlessly as possible, and without regret. He did not intend for anyone to suffer at his hands, least of all a woman.

Something was wrong here. This pudgy hag could not possibly be the potential bride he'd been sent to kill. She was an old woman, not fit to be empress for a ruler who was barely past his thirtieth year. It did not take long for him to discern what had happened. The opposite door of the carriage, the one he had not been able to see while fighting the sentinels, stood open.

Did the woman he had been hired to kill think she could escape? And what kind of lady fled and left her companion behind? A selfish one, he imagined. Or a smart one. There was no way the hag could've kept pace with a younger woman fleeing for her life.

He was not overly concerned by this turn of events. He'd find Lady Leyla, and he'd finish the job he'd been well paid to do. In fact, he was a little bit pleased that this mission wasn't as easy as he'd first thought it would be. Everything was so easy for him these days that he welcomed a little challenge.

Not that chasing down a pretty woman would be so hard.

Trinity exited the carriage, leaving the body of the old woman where it lay. He patted the silky black neck of his fine and faithful stallion Gano, an animal who had served him well, and surveyed the scene before him. This was an almost peaceful little valley, or had been before he'd ambushed the party. Now it was littered with bodies and would be peaceful no more.

Before entering the woods to give chase, Trinity made sure all those he had killed were well and completely dead. Magic was not unheard of in this part of the world, and he knew too well that sometimes death was not the end. Sometimes death was a trick, an illusion. Trinity pushed at one man after another with the toe of his black boot. He looked deeply into their blank, lifeless eyes. The sentinels and the one official were all good and dead, much to Trinity's relief.

He'd expected sentinels to provide him with a more vigorous battle, but these young men had not put up much of a fight. They'd been surprised by the attack, and none could match his speed. None was as good at killing as he was. It had all been over too soon, much too soon.

Trinity had been dead once. His own death hadn't lasted long, however. His inept witch of a mother had worked a spell to bring her beloved son back to life, but she'd made a miscalculation along the way.

She had saved him, but he could not die again.

He had lived on this earth for nearly five hundred and forty years, most of that time hidden away on a mountaintop in the far north part of the world, half mad and wishing for the death he could never have. He'd tried to find death at his own hand many times, but he always lived. He could feel pain, however, which made the attempts at ending his own life quickly lose their appeal.

Eventually he had left the ice and snow of the north and moved toward civilization. Eventually someone had found him, someone who had discovered what he was. That someone had taught him that he did have a purpose to serve. Perhaps he could not die, but he could send others to the afterlife, when it was their time.

It was Lady Leyla Hagan's time.

Just as he was about to lead his stallion into the forest, Trinity studied the battlefield and frowned. There was an extra horse, and the saddle upon it was not of imperial issue. Perhaps the lady of the party had ridden on occasion, but he didn't think so. A man's saddle was strapped to the horse's back, not a sidesaddle which a proper lady would've insisted upon. It was a decent enough saddle, but not one which a fine lady might possess.

Lady Leyla had not made her escape alone.

Trinity smiled as he turned toward the thick woods, giving the twosome who had escaped his initial attack a bit of a head start. He might as well take a few moments and grab a bite to eat before giving chase. He always carried food in his saddlebags. Perhaps he could not starve to death, but being hungry was truly uncomfortable, and killing always gave him a fierce appetite.

Rare moments of anticipation were among the few joys he had left in his unbearably long life, and as he chewed on a hard biscuit, he imagined tracking down the fleeing couple through the night.

This might be fun. Cayse Trinity hadn't had fun in a very long time.

CHIEFTAIN Valeron had not been easy to sway, but finally Merin had what he wanted: the Haythorne family in a closed room. No outsiders were allowed, and the doors to this main hall were closed even against their trusted servants.

The guard at the entrance to the village had been found wounded and bound, but very much alive. Nobel was being very careful not to harm anyone, not yet. He did not want war, not if it could be helped. He wanted Bela.

"I still cannot believe that anyone in the village would betray us to one such as Nobel," Lady Gayene said.

It was Clyn who looked his mother in the eye and said, "The general is correct. Nobel knew too much."

"Perhaps he bought his information from someone who is in dire need. It's apparent he's amassed quite a lot of gems since he left us." Gayene's eyes lit up. "Maybe the person who told him about Bela and the general didn't know Nobel's intentions."

They began to discuss and submit and deny possible traitors, all of them talking at once. Names Merin knew and names he did not know were bandied about. Everyone was passionate about who among them might become a betrayer, for riches or out of ignorance.

"It doesn't matter who the traitor is," he interrupted when the names and voices began to blur. "Not yet, at least. It might actually turn out to be a good thing, as Nobel's appearance today warned us of his intentions. He might've simply ridden in with his men, slaughtered anyone in his way, and taken Bela by force."

"He could try," Bela said softly.

Her words and her tone were tough, but he had seen the fear in her eyes when her mother had been threatened. "Has he always had an interest in you?" Merin asked, his eyes on Bela.

"For a time," she said, sounding as much puzzled as angry. "But I made it clear that I was not interested and he turned his attentions to others. He always flirted with the

prettiest girls with the frilliest dresses and the silliest gig-
gles after he recovered from our last encounter." She wrinkled her nose.

"You took his fingers?" he asked.

"That was Kitty. He had the audacity to make a grab for
her, not knowing that she has the ability to move and even to
fight on her own." Bela grimaced a little. "I did not know that
she could be so harsh, but she did not like Nobel at all."

It surely had not been pleasant to watch Kitty defend
herself and send Nobel's fingers to the ground in the process. Merin had seen worse. All who'd fought in the war
against Ciro had seen worse, but no matter how manly Bela
tried to be, she was still a woman, and women should not
be subjected to such bloody sights.

It was necessary.

Merin knew the words he heard came from Kitty and
were for him alone. Even Bela seemed not to hear.

Apparently the magical weapon could read his thoughts.
That was disturbing.

"He wants Kitty," Merin said, still feeling slightly ridiculous referring to the sword by name. "Even if he can
have her only through you."

"Yes, but why?" Bela asked. "He cannot touch her; she
won't allow it. Even if I was his wife, he would not be able
to touch her."

"Are you so sure?" Merin asked. "I can hear her. Perhaps any man who is your husband . . ."

"What?" Tyman, who had been sitting silent and sulking,
shot to his feet. "You heard Kitty? She has chosen you?"

"I still hear her, too," Bela said defensively.

"But the general hears her, too, now," Clyn said, remaining calmer than either of his siblings. "Does anyone
else know this? Could our spy have told Nobel that being
married to Bela gives a man rights to the weapon he craves?
Is that why he's back now?"

"No one knows I heard Kitty's voice," Merin said with certainty.

Bela sighed, and all eyes turned to her. "That's not entirely true. I told Jocylen." She looked around the room. "But she would never tell anyone. I told her it was a secret."

One of the whispers last night, perhaps, Merin thought. Word had traveled quickly, if that was the case.

Tyman sighed. "She likely told her husband, who might've told the men he farms with or drinks with or . . ."

"No," Bela said. "She would not tell."

Merin looked down at Bela, his wife for the moment. A wife he craved but could not entirely have, a woman who was an unusual and tempting mix of innocence and brashness. At the moment she was hurt, but did not want anyone to know that she was in pain.

If Nobel was here because he knew that Bela's husband had also heard Kitty speak, then Jocylen was their traitor. Perhaps unintentionally, but still a traitor.

SAVYN held on to Lady Leyla's hand and pulled her along as he made a path into a deeper part of the forest where the trees grew close together and there was thick, green growth at their feet. They were headed for a small mountain, a collection of rocky hills. If they climbed a bit to an area where no horse could travel, maybe they'd be safe. Maybe. Branches whipped at his skin and scratched his cheek, but he did not slow down. The only way he could save Lady Leyla was to get her far, far away from the attacker. He would hide her; he would keep her safe.

He had never seen such violence in his life. The most recent war had been brutal, he'd heard, but it had never come so far south, not in any significant way. Their village of Childers had been sheltered. He did not feel sheltered now. The attacker had moved with speed and ruthlessness, and he had killed without hesitation. So much blood had been spilled, and all Savyn had been able to think of was getting Lady Leyla away from it all.

Fortune had been with him. He'd been riding away from the others, on the opposite side of the carriage, where on occasion he might peek through the window and see that all was well with the women. If he had been riding with the sentinels, he'd be dead now, too, and then who would save the lady?

Savyn broke through a section of thick growth and found himself running up a grassy hill. He was breathing hard and so was the lady, but he could not stop. They could not slow down. Would there be a place in these hills where they could hide? A cave, a deserted lean-to, a hole in the ground . . . anything would do.

"Please, stop," the lady called breathlessly.

Savyn turned to look at her, and he immediately felt guilty. There were leaves and sticks caught in her hair, and her face was flushed, and her fine dress was torn in several places. The hem of her gown was generously dusted with dirt, and her breathing was labored. She was beautiful, still, though it would not be wise for him to take such notice.

"I need to take a deep breath," she said. "Just a moment."

"I'll carry you," he offered.

She shook her head. "No, I can't let you do that. We'd move too slowly and the journey would be too arduous for you." Her eyes met his, and he felt an immediate and improper reaction. "Maybe he's not following us. Maybe he only wanted to rob the sentinels and Deputy Bragg, and he's headed in the other direction with whatever he took from them."

"I hope that is true, My Lady, but we cannot know. As soon as you are ready, we'll climb."

She studied the grassy hill before them. It was oddly

shaped but not horribly steep. It would be a hard climb but not an impossible one.

Savyn realized that while they'd been resting, neither had bothered to drop the other's hand. They stood there, frightened and sweating and red-faced and disheveled, and held hands as they readied themselves for the climb to come. It felt oddly natural, perhaps because he had begun to imagine himself in love with her.

He squeezed her hand lightly and nodded his head, and she nodded hers. They began to climb, and Savyn had almost convinced himself that no one was following, when in the distance they heard a voice filled with dark humor shout, "You cannot hide from me, Lady Leyla. I'm coming for you. Death is coming for you both."

THE mood that had made Bela offer to—and even long to—give Merin the same pleasure he had offered her last night had disappeared along with Nobel's ridiculous ultimatum. No, it was the very idea that Jocylen might've been the cause of this disturbing state of affairs that made her pout. She trusted Jocylen with her secrets.

The newlywed had been coerced by her husband to tell all, that was the only explanation. Rab had forced his wife to reveal what she knew, and that made him the traitor. She could only imagine the sort of torture Rab might've used to make Jocylen talk. Men had quite an arsenal of weapons of which she had been ignorant until sharing a bed with Tearlach Merin.

They had not bothered with a door between them as they undressed, not tonight. After eating a simple supper of cold oatcakes and cabbage stew, they had both silently shed their clothes, bathed with a bowl of tepid water and a few soft rags, and then fallen into bed, Merin still in his trousers, Bela in her plainest nightgown.

They lay side by side, comfortable enough but not touching. Tonight there was no laughter and no anger, no teasing and no bantering, no pleasure at all. Neither of them was anywhere near sleep, and even when the lamp had been doused and the only light in the room was the moonlight through one small window, they did not sleep.

After a long while of restless silence, Merin asked, "What is she? Do you know?"

"What is who? Kitty?"

"Yes, Kitty."

"A magical sword, you know that."

"Yes, but how and why?" He sounded only slightly perturbed. There was more curiosity in his deep voice than anything else. "Someone made her, but who, and for what purpose? How long had she been waiting in the mountains before she was found? Was it an accident that she was discovered by your brother, or was that a part of her plan?"

"I don't know, and I'm not sure how we *can* know. Rafal claims to see very little where Kitty is concerned. Clyn did try to find out more, but the seer could tell him nothing. He was so annoyed when Kitty spoke to me and no one else could hear."

"Yet he did accept that you heard her."

"Eventually." Bela smiled in the dark. Her eldest brother had been very stubborn where Kitty was concerned, at least for a while. "When Kitty started telling me things I should not know, and when she revealed some of what she could do, others had no choice but to believe. Even Clyn."

"Where, precisely, did he find her?"

Bela hesitated, wondering if it was a betrayal of any kind to tell Merin too much about Kitty. But she quickly realized that she trusted him, even with this. How odd, when she had never given her trust easily. "He found her on Forbidden Mountain, even though he should not have been there. No one is allowed there, but he'd been searching for a new mine and got lost. Clyn never gets lost, but there you have it."

Merin laughed harshly. "Forbidden Mountain? The Turis are not a subtle people, are they?"

"I suppose not," she conceded.

"Why is this mountain forbidden?"

She mulled over the question for a few minutes, and Merin did not push her to hurry with her explanation. "I'm not entirely sure. The mountain is pretty and harmless enough from a distance, and there's water and growth which should make it habitable, but nothing lives there, not even animals."

"And yet your brother found himself on it."

"Yes. Later he said he should've realized when he moved onto Forbidden Mountain, because he began to feel uncomfortable. Unsettled. He said the place really did feel as if it were forbidden, bone deep. Once he realized how far he had traveled, he was moving down the mountain, coming home, when a windstorm whipped up and he crawled into a shallow cave for shelter. Something sparkled there, he said, and for a moment he thought he'd found an area rich with gems."

"But he found Kitty instead," Merin whispered.

"Yes. He brought her home, intending to make her his own, naturally, but normally agile Clyn was clumsy with Kitty in his hands. He practiced with her often but he kept dropping her—or else she was trying to escape from him and he just thought he'd dropped her."

"The crystal handle is small," Merin said, "as if it were made for a woman."

"Perhaps that is so," Bela said softly. Had Kitty been made for her? "One night I woke up to see an odd glow in my room, and it was Kitty, lying on the floor beside my bed. The next morning I tried to return her to Clyn, wondering how the weapon had come to be in my room. He was furious, and accused me of taking her." She snorted. "As if I would stoop to stealing anything." Her cheeks grew warm. "Well, except a husband."

"Let's not discuss that at this moment, if you please." Merin's voice was curt, and she knew he was probably thinking that it was her fault he had been dragged into this mess with Nobel. And he was right.

"I was able to handle Kitty quite well and Clyn was annoyed by that, but I did give her back. She followed me home."

Merin laughed harshly and briefly.

"Seriously! Everywhere I turned, there she was. I kept trying to return her to Clyn, and she kept turning up in my path or in my bedchamber. This went on for months. And then she began to speak to me, and to move on her own in my presence, and . . . and she was mine."

"And until I came along, no one else heard her voice?"

"No one." Bela turned her head. Even in the dark she could see the fierce lines of Merin's hard face, the gentle curl of his hair, the very nice shape of his strong chest and arms. She did not admire men, not in this way, but she did admire Merin. She admired him too much. "Why you?" The question was too vague, too powerful, so she decided to be more specific. "After all this time, why did Kitty choose you?"

As she finished the question, Kitty answered, and Bela knew these words were for her alone. Apparently Merin did not hear, even though the voice was louder and more clear than ever before.

I am as much in Tearlach Merin's keeping as I am in yours.

But why?

We need him.

I need no one. The thought was painful and a little lonely, Bela decided. Maybe it wasn't a terrible curse to need something or someone.

Kitty grew silent, almost sullenly so, and once again Bela turned her gaze to Merin. His eyes were closed, but she didn't think he was asleep. Not yet. Should she give him a shove and make him look at her? Should she touch him and try to regain what they'd almost found in the creek that afternoon?

Last night he had shown her great pleasure, and today she had been more than willing to do the same for him. She still wanted him . . . something in her wanted to wrap her arms around him right now and see where the kissing and the touching would take them.

But even though Merin was attracted to her physically, he did not truly want her. He did not love her. All he wanted from her was physical, and if they were not literally connected, he would not want even that from her. Silly girl, she had never even dreamed of love, and yet here she was, lying in the dark, longing for it. She had only recently discovered passion, and already she knew that lovely as it was, powerful as it could be . . . it was not enough, not for her.

Bela covered her face with her hands and choked back the urge to scream. She was turning into a sentimental woman, no better than the worthless girls who dreamed of nothing more than marriage and men and the motherhood which always followed. Tonight she wanted something she had never before desired. If Merin loved her, if he wished to remain with her, if what they had found could turn into something more . . .

But as long as he wanted only to be rid of her, it could not be done. She would not debase herself that way, taking only the physical from him. Red and black, was that all they could have?

In the dark Bela cursed the Turi tradition which had her bound to a man who made her question everything about her life. Was she wrong to wish for the love she had so recently denounced as impossible?

Kitty's words were almost gentle. *No, you are not wrong.*

Can I make Merin love me?

I do not know. His heart is hidden from me.

It's hidden from me, too.

With a sigh, Bela instinctively cuddled closer to a warm, sleeping Merin. He was her husband, at least for now. He was the only man who had ever made her dream of love. Could she make him love her? Could she uncover his hidden heart and make it her own?

Chapter Seven

MERIN was awakened by sunlight pouring through the window. Sunrise fell upon his face, as it did every morning. Today he was surprised to find Bela already awake and dressed. She must've gone about the task with great care not to wake him during the process. He did not normally sleep so deeply that she could jostle the bed and the rope that bound them without awakening him. He was not normally comfortable enough with any woman to sleep when she was in his bed, but he had, by necessity, learned to sleep well enough in Bela's company.

"We will not take on any worthless assigned task today," he said as he sat up. "There's too much to be done."

Amazingly, Bela smiled at him. "Good morning to you, too."

He found himself studying her face for a moment. She was very pretty in the morning, fresh from sleep and bright-eyed. "Good morning. There's too much to be done for us to spend the day digging a useless hole or helping a farmer prepare his fields."

"Of course you are correct," she said. "I thought today we might travel to the place on Forbidden Mountain where Clyn found Kitty. He took me there once, and I'm certain I can find it again."

Merin shook his head. "There are plans of defense to be made, weapons to be readied, a traitor to find . . ."

"My father and my brothers are capable of handling those tasks," Bela interrupted, a tone of conviction in her voice. "Some of the questions you had last night made me think, and I decided that perhaps if we knew more of Kitty's making and purpose, we might learn why Nobel desires her so much. There are a number of caves near the place where she was found, and one in particular where Clyn found her. There might be clues to all we need to know in one of those caves."

"Or there might be no clues at all, and we will waste a lot of time when we need to be here, readying the village for attack. Besides, didn't you say that no one is allowed to travel on that mountain?" Even though apparently she had been there, and so had her brother. Twice. "Hence the ominous name," he added harshly.

Bela shook her head gently, and strands of fine, unbound hair swayed across her cheek and her shoulder. Before they left the cottage, she would braid it with swiftness and precision, but he liked it this way, loose and soft. "That is a valid point, but I still think we should at least try to learn what we can. Nobel would not go to so much trouble just for me, I assure you."

Yes, go. Go now.

They both heard Kitty's voice, and Merin turned his attention to the sword, which hung upon the wall. It glowed dimly and seemed to throb with excitement. "Kitty, can you not simply tell us what we need to know? Who is your maker? Does Nobel wish to possess you, or is it truly Bela he desires?"

He took the resounding silence as a negative response.

After a few moments Bela said, "I tried to ask while you were sleeping, but either she does not remember or she simply won't tell."

"What if there's nothing to find?" he asked, frustrated at the possibility. "We could waste days on that mountain and come away with nothing of consequence."

"We won't know if we don't try."

"Fine." Merin rolled up and swung his legs over the side of the bed so he was sitting beside Bela. It was strange to feel so comfortable there, half-naked and bound together. Unwillingly married. Unwillingly attracted. He would have to fight the attraction, which was surely so strong only because they had been physically close for such a long time. "How far?"

"A three-day walk, if we do not tarry along the way."

Merin nodded his head. That was longer than he'd like but was acceptable, given their time constraints. It would take six days to travel—three to the site and three back to the village—and if he allowed two days for searching the caves in the area, that would put them back in the village six days before Nobel's scheduled arrival. He would still have time to help with the defense of the village. "We'll pack supplies and rations and leave here as soon as possible."

"All right."

He looked into Bela's eyes. That was a mistake, one he quickly corrected by glancing away. "If we do not find answers which will help us, we'll leave Kitty there."

The only response he received was a screeching whine which cut through his brain. Kitty did not like that idea at all. Judging by the expression on Bela's face, she was no happier than the sword about that suggestion.

"We cannot risk such a treasure falling into Nobel's hands, can we?" Merin asked logically.

The screech stopped abruptly. Was that Kitty's way of agreeing with him? It was impossible to tell.

Merin looked again at Bela, expecting an argument. Surprisingly, she nodded in compliance, though she was clearly not pleased with the idea. She knew as well as he did that Kitty could not fall into the wrong hands. He had a feeling they had seen only a small sampling of Kitty's capabilities. They had seen only what the sword wished them to see. What an odd and potentially frightening thought.

Yesterday afternoon Bela had stood before him in the creek and touched him. She had been very close to offering more. He had looked into her eyes and seen more than he'd wanted to see. Beauty. Depth. Promise. He longed to touch her again, to feel her writhe and hear her scream. He wanted, so much, to be inside her. But suddenly those longed-for pleasures seemed like a very bad idea. Bela was a sweet trap he might never escape, and neither of them wished to remain married. She wanted to return to her life of freedom, and he wanted nothing more than to return to the palace at Arthes to resume his position and perhaps take his time choosing a suitable bride, as the emperor was attempting to do in his own ridiculous way.

"I've been thinking," he said.

Bela's eyes seemed to brighten. "Have you?"

"When Nobel has been taken care of and the marriage is officially dissolved, we'll still have to make our way to Arthes so you can be presented to the emperor."

Her face fell, and Merin tried to comfort her by taking her hand.

"But I know the emperor well," he said, "and I know what he likes in a woman and, more important, what he does not like. Along the way I can instruct you on what to say and do and how to dress, and in that way we can assure that he will not choose you. When that is done, you can return home with a clear conscience and resume your life as you wish to lead it."

She looked a little stunned, and then a little hurt.

"I will of course provide a proper escort," Merin added quickly. "I wouldn't expect you to travel home alone."

"Of course not," she said coldly.

"And if you'd prefer, one of your brothers can travel with us. Clyn has a family and Tyman has responsibilities of his own, so I thought that might be impractical. But if it is what you'd like, we'll make it happen."

"Impractical," she said shortly.

"Yes. Most other chaperones I could think of would slow us down, and I don't wish to arrive late. Once the marriage is dissolved, we'll have to travel hard to make the Summer Festival deadline." What had he said wrong? Something, obviously.

"Get dressed," Bela snapped, her mood suddenly darker as she reached up and began to braid her hair. "We have a long day ahead of us."

Merin had the unpleasant suspicion that it would be *very* long.

WHEN they'd run across this place last night, Leyla had been very glad of the shelter the shallow cave provided, and even more, she was now grateful for the few hours of sleep she had managed to take. It was hard to sleep with Savyn so near. It was impossible not to be physically close in the confines of the small cave, even though he tried very hard not to touch her any more than was necessary. But her body and her mind remembered what it had been like to press her body to his, in search of pleasure and comfort. She remembered having her lover inside her, screaming his name, making him shudder and shout and whisper sweet words of impossible love.

He remembered nothing.

She'd hated to stop, but they both needed rest, and they hoped the attacker might've gone in the wrong direction.

The silver-haired killer could not have followed their trail, not on horseback, and if he'd remained on his horse, he would've had to go a much longer way around before intersecting their path. She could not imagine any horse making the climb up this slope without falling. It was too steep in places, too unpredictable.

Maybe they were safe, for now. Maybe.

"Good morning, My Lady," Savyn said as he came awake. He worked diligently to keep his body away from hers as much as possible. It was not an easy task.

"Good morning, Savyn." She tried to swallow, but her mouth was too dry. "Perhaps you should call me Leyla."

His eyes grew wide. "I could not. It would not be proper."

Because she was older and of another station. Because they could not, should not, have any relationship other than lady to craftsman. "Perhaps it is not proper, but if we run into strangers along the way, we will draw too much attention to ourselves if you call me My Lady. I will call you Savyn, and you will call me Leyla, and if we do run into other travelers, we will not rouse any suspicion. And if the killer asks about us . . . perhaps we will not be memorable to those we have passed."

"You are always memorable, My . . . Leyla." Savyn blushed a little, as he was prone to do on occasion.

His face was rough with stubble, which was odd, since he was usually so meticulous about his grooming. Leyla wanted so badly to reach out and touch Savyn's face, to soothe him, then to kiss him. She wanted what they'd had before she'd set him free from their memories. But her reasons for making him forget were still valid. He deserved a young wife who would have his babies, a girl who would love him without condition, a woman who could give herself to him entirely. Leyla was not capable of giving all of herself, not to Savyn, not to anyone. He deserved to have a normal and loving relationship, one which would not cause nasty whispers among his friends and neighbors, one that did not need to be concealed. She could not give him that, either.

"We need a plan," she said softly.

"Beyond escape?"

"Yes. I think we should make our way to a village or a large farm and then"—she almost swallowed her words—"and then we can split up. You can go home. I will change my name and try to hide among strangers." With her gift, she could make that work very well. She could convince the others that she was their sister or their aunt, a long lost relative come home to stay. She could make them believe they had known her for years, even forever. And when a killer came looking for a stranger, he would not find one.

"Do you think that's wise?" Savyn asked, openly concerned.

"I do."

Leyla was still determined to set her lover free. She would release him so he could have a good life. Nothing else mattered. She might live out her days as a housekeeper in a small village, but Savyn would have more. Savyn would be free of her.

THEY traveled in silence, which gave Bela time to think. Thinking was horrid. Absolutely horrid.

She had given in to a previously undiscovered and totally feminine need for love. How embarrassing. She knew that there were many men who sought the company of women for nothing more than physical gratification. Why could she not do the same? Why could she not be satisfied with the pleasures Merin could show her? No, she had to moon over him and wish for more, which was absolutely mortifying.

He did not want more. He did not lie awake at night wondering if he could make *her* love *him*.

Given how quickly and entirely he reacted to her when it came to sexual desire, she knew she could seduce him, if she pleased. Could the physical interaction lead to all she desired? Could she seduce him time and again and *make* him love her? Would a man so loyal and good willingly take that which he believed belonged to his precious emperor? She could not be sure. Loyalty had not stopped him from touching her thus far.

Bela realized she did not have much time to make Merin love her. Time was crucial. She suspected he would fight giving in to temptation even more as they came closer to her presentation to that emperor. She could not wait much longer, if she decided to try.

Kitty whispered to her. *We need him.*

"Why must you make things difficult?" she said softly. She still did not wish to need anyone!

Merin did not turn to face her as he spoke. "I apologize. Should I slow down?"

"No, you're fine," she said as she followed in his footsteps. Getting on and off a horse would be difficult, bound as they were, and a good part of the trip would take them into jagged landscape not suitable for animals—as if they could coerce even the most loyal animal onto this mountain. Their entire trip would be made on foot. "I was talking to Kitty. I don't see why she can't tell us more."

"As you said earlier, perhaps she does not remember, or else she simply does not know." He took a few more steps upward, and Bela could not help but admire the view from behind. "I certainly don't remember my conception or my birth. Perhaps it is the same for magical objects which are made."

"Perhaps so," she agreed. Obviously Merin had not heard Kitty's latest words, which was just as well. She might want and desire him, but she would never admit that she needed anything or anyone. It was not in her nature to display that sort of weakness.

Still, she was starting to care for this stubborn, handsome, dedicated man much more than she should. Perhaps this was love, the elusive thing Jocylen spoke of with such joy. If that was the case, why didn't she feel joy? Why didn't she bubble and giggle like her friend?

Because Merin did not return that love—or whatever it was that she suffered—she supposed. Because he was not, and could never be, a permanent fixture in her life. He was not Turi, and she would never leave her home to live elsewhere. This was all she knew. If she could convince Merin to love her, and he did concede to stay, what would he do? She could not see him as a farmer or a miner or a tender of animals. Her father was chieftain, and after his death or withdrawal it would be Clyn's time to serve in that position.

We must have him.

Bela stumbled, and her heart stuttered in time with her clumsy feet. Kitty was so doggedly insistent!

Merin slowed down and offered her a hand, thinking she'd lost her balance on this steep and rocky slope. She took that hand and regained her balance, mumbling softly spoken thanks as she held on to his strong hand longer than was necessary. Up ahead there was a less steep and greener section of the mountain, where they could travel less strenuously and refill their waterskins before moving onto a harsher path once again, but for now the path was arduous.

Bela had chosen not to pursue a traditional female role. She had chosen to learn to fight and ride and hunt and dress as a man would. She wasn't sorry for the choices she'd made; they had been her choices. This unconventional life was hers by design. What if Merin desired to take a wife like Jocylen and the other young women of the village?

What if he wanted a sweet and gentle woman who would wait for him endlessly, preparing his meals and mending his clothes and offering her body when he wished it and giving him a baby every year? That was not the life Bela had chosen. She could not be that woman! Could she change for a man? Did she want to?

Would he take her as she was, different and occasionally difficult and often mule-headed?

Like Merin, Bela herself was sometimes stubborn to a fault. "I am who I am," she whispered.

"What did you say?" Merin reached a small plateau and turned to face her. Behind him to the right, the rocky face of the mountain loomed. To the left, the gentler tree line was thick and green and alive. Her husband looked right and proper there, a part of this land he did not call his own, but he was not Turi. He would never call this land she loved home.

If through some bizarre circumstance he fell in love with her, he'd probably expect her to return with him to Arthes, where she would fit in even less well than she did here. She could not be a wife of the court. She could not live a palace life, restrained and proper, a general's bride.

There was no need to worry, as he had not asked her to, and certainly would not.

"Nothing," she responded. "I said nothing at all."

TRINITY scanned the ground around the cave, noting the dust and pebbles which had been disturbed. It was now midday, the sun hanging high in the sky. He knew that his prey had slept here last night. He inhaled deeply, closing his eyes to sharpen his keen sense of smell. There were two of them, one man and one woman, and they had left early this morning, headed east.

He led Gano and had for some time, now, not expecting

the fine, loyal animal to carry his weight on this hill which some might call a mountain. Since those he sought were on foot, walking was not a disadvantage, and in truth he was not in a hurry. He had all the time in the world.

Still, Trinity was a little surprised that the two had eluded him for so long. He'd expected to find them last night and end this job, but they had traveled in a bit of a circle, making illogical choices and leading him around and around. Were they that smart, or did they travel so inconsistently and oddly because they were lost and afraid? Lost and afraid was more likely than smart.

They had no food, so he expected that when they'd left this cave, they'd headed in a direction that would take them to the nearest town or house. There were a few settlers on the other side of the hill, he knew from his travels. He would certainly find those he sought there. It would be a shame to kill them too quickly, especially as they had proven to be more fun than he'd imagined they would.

The woman was probably pretty, as she was being considered as a potential empress. Trinity hadn't been with a pretty woman for a long time, and he did not think he had ever lain with a real lady. Maybe he could separate those he sought and kill the man, then devise a plan to present himself as the woman's protector. As a lady she would need one, he imagined. Had she seen him from her coach before she'd run? A disguise of sorts might be necessary, just in case. He could pretend to be someone else for a while; he had done so before. Maybe he could even seduce her. He was a generous lover. She would die happy.

Trinity bent down and placed his head in the cave where his prey had slept last night. Again, he closed his eyes and breathed deeply. The scent that filled him was heady and sweet and unique. Yes, he would know Lady Leyla when he found her.

* * *

LEYLA'S legs ached from the constant walking, but she did not ask Savyn to slow down or to carry her again. She did hold his hand, as much for comfort as for assistance. He steadied her. He had steadied her for the past two years, just not quite so literally.

The sight of the thatched-roof house in the distance was so welcome she almost cried out in joy. Smoke rose from the stone chimney, and well-tended farmland surrounded the small house. Leyla's step increased in spite of the pain, but before she'd gone very far, Savyn stopped her. He planted his feet and drew her back so she stood close by his side.

"Why have you stopped?" she asked, anxious for shelter, food, rest, and the sight of people who did not wish to kill her.

"I'm going to find a safe place for you to wait while I go to the farmhouse and ask for food."

"No!" She did not want to be alone . . . and she saw no reason why she couldn't go with him.

Savyn reached out and placed both hands on her cheeks, and he gazed down at her with intense eyes she knew too well. She noticed, as she had that very morning, that his beard was coming in, rough and untended. He was usually so well-kept and clean, so meticulously pretty. Not today. He was also always willing to listen to her commands. Again, not today. He was determined and commanding, unwilling to offer her all that she wanted. "We do not know what might await us there, My Lady. The man who ambushed our party might've visited this farm. He might still be there, waiting for us."

Leyla's heart leaped at the idea. "Then you should not go there either," she said insistently. "If it's not safe for me, then it's not safe for you."

He gave her an impossible smile. "My life is of no consequence, but I will not allow anything to happen to you, My . . . Leyla." He stumbled over the words, as he started to call her My Lady once more and then remembered her request. In the past he had often called her My Leyla, and as he said the words, a kind of dulled recognition flitted into his eyes and then was gone.

Savyn dropped his hands as if he had finally realized the impropriety of the intimate gesture. "I will find a comfortable and safe spot for you to wait, and I will go to the farmhouse and beg for food. I believe I can pass for a beggar on this day."

Leyla studied her ragged, dirty dress. She could only imagine what her always unmanageable hair looked like. "So could I."

Savyn shook his head and smiled gently. "Never."

She felt a rush of anger and fear. "If the man who seeks us is there, waiting, and you don't come back, what am I supposed to do?"

"You run," Savyn said softly. "Run, and don't look back. Hide. Steal. Beg if you must. Don't let him find you, no matter what. You have a gift. Don't be afraid to use it."

"I rarely use my gift," she said, "and when I do, I must be close enough to touch. That isn't always possible."

"If I don't come back . . ."

Leyla grabbed his hand and held on tight. "You will come back to me," she insisted. "You must." She looked into his eyes, and her heart broke for what she'd given up and could never reclaim. If she'd believed love was enough, she never would've made him forget what they'd had. It had been selfish of her to believe that they could have even a small bit of what they wanted without pain. "I need you, Savyn." He could never know how much meaning those words had for her.

Savyn instinctively leaned forward, as if moving to her for a kiss, but he stopped himself long before their lips met. He looked confused for a moment, and then he glanced away from her and began to study their surroundings. "That thick group of trees over there will offer you shelter and cover," he said, trying to be stoic but revealing too much with the emotion in his voice. Somehow, some way, he had suffered a flash of memory he should not, *could not*, have.

As they headed toward the place where Savyn intended to leave her, he did not take her hand.

Chapter Eight

MERIN had not bothered to pack a small tent, and on this first night on Forbidden Mountain he had not even sought out a small cave for shelter. The night was mild. Erecting even the most primitive shelter would take time they did not have, and besides, he did not mind sleeping beneath the clear skies. They each carried a small blanket to cover the ground, and that would suffice.

He had built a fire just before darkness fell, using fallen limbs, dried brush, and the flint and steel he carried in his pack. Their food—which for the duration of this journey would consist of oatcake and a goodly supply of a mix of oats, dried fruits, and nuts—did not need to be warmed, and apparently there were no animals on the mountain, so predatory cats would not be a problem. Still, the fire did offer them some comfort. He suspected they would need the fire more tomorrow and the next night, as they moved higher, where the air would be cooler this time of year. Perhaps they would even have to search for shelter, but he hoped not. He did not want to take the time for even the smallest of comforts.

Traveling would've been much easier if he and Bela had untied the rope that bound them and stored it in one of the packs, as long as they were out of sight of the village. But they had given their word before leaving. Bela's father and the seer, Fiers, had both insisted. Merin had known more than one wizard in his lifetime, and he suspected the Turi seer would know if they did not keep their promise. The little old man possessed a goodly amount of power. Besides, Merin did not break his word, certainly not to make his own days easier.

And yes, being apart from Bela would make his life much easier.

Tonight something was wrong with his *wife*. Something was always wrong with her, but tonight there was something new. He could feel it and he could see it on her face, a face he was coming to know so well. She was bothered by something, and she was not telling him what or why. Usually she was quite comfortable when it came to voicing her complaints, but tonight she kept secrets, as she had all day.

Maybe she was afraid he would wish to resume their physical interactions, now that they were once again alone. He could put her fears to rest where that was concerned.

While Merin was certainly not averse to the pleasures of a woman's hands or her mouth, he knew he would not be satisfied with anything less than everything where Bela was concerned. Everything; all of her. If they touched as a man and wife might, he would end up inside her and then they would never be unwed. They'd make a baby, if not tonight, then in the nights to come, and if there was a child of the union, they would be forever married, at least under Turi law.

He studied her pensive face, which was striking with

the flickering fire to illuminate the features. When had she become beautiful? When had the sight of that face begun to make his stomach and his heart clench?

"I expect nothing of you," he said sharply and without emotion.

Her head snapped up. "What?"

"What began in the creek before Nobel's arrival, I do not expect you to finish it. Now that I'm thinking clearly, I realize such a physical liaison would not be wise, not for us."

She studied him for a moment, and though he studied her closely, he could not tell what she was thinking. Was she relieved or insulted? Usually Bela's emotions were very clear on her face, but at the moment she was unreadable.

"Does that mean you have no interest in touching me as you once did?"

No interest was not the right phrase, but it would do. "That is correct."

"Pity," she said softly. "Now that you have enlightened me, I find myself rather intrigued by the physical interactions of a man and a woman."

Her words cut through him and seemed to grab at his insides, deep and with surprising strength. He tried to ignore that grabbing. "When we are no longer wed, other men can intrigue you."

She was silent for a moment, and then she said, "I don't think so."

Merin felt a surge of anger. He did not want Bela to be afraid of men. That's why he'd tortured himself to show her the truth of sex properly—if only partially—done. "It would be preposterous for you to live without such physical pleasures. If you don't want children, there are precautions which can be taken, with time and planning. There's no need for you to take a husband if that is your concern . . ."

"Do you think I am a loose woman who will search for such pleasures with just anyone?" Her voice rose slightly and reverberated among the rocks.

Apparently he could say nothing right tonight. "I did not say . . ."

"Do you think I should become the village prostitute?"

"Good heavens, no!" His patience was gone. "I don't understand you at all, Bela. I can never entirely grasp what you want and what you don't want. You shun all things womanly, but by God, you are acting very much like a woman tonight. Why can't you just tell me what you want? Why can't you just be straightforward?"

"Fine." The word was a sharp, stinging snap. "I want love," she said honestly and without stammering. "Until you returned to us, I did not think I desired love at all, but you have taught me differently and it is quite maddening. I'm not sure I can forgive you for that, for turning my life upside down and inside out and making me want what I never before cared about." Her eyes met his, and he saw the anger and confusion there. "I am a straightforward person in all matters," she said. "I do not keep secrets and dwell upon my thoughts in private."

Merin laughed bitterly. "*You* do not keep secrets?"

Her expression was contrite, even sheepish. The anger seemed to fly away, leaving her more confused. "Long ago I did what was necessary, but I did not enjoy lying to you and my family. I merely did what I believed had to be done. Six years ago I had the body of a woman, but my mind was still very much that of a child."

"A spoiled child willing to do anything to get what she wanted."

"Yes," she whispered.

There had been nothing childlike about the woman he remembered, and seventeen was a marriageable age for many. But she was right—her thinking at that time had not been right. Merin found it wise not to recall too clearly that night when she'd thrown herself at him. It wasn't just the unpleasant finish that dismayed him, but the memory of her bare body pressed to his, all too briefly.

"My thinking is no longer muddled by childish desires and stubborn plans of defiance and deception," she continued. "I leave all that behind me now, Tearlach Merin, and speak only the truth. I think I might love you. No, that is a cowardly way to say what's in my heart. I *do* love you. I'm certain of it."

Again, she surprised him. "You say that only because I'm the first man to make you . . ."

"That's not why," she interrupted without anger. "You are handsome and gallant and strong, and you're a powerful man in many ways. You have a fine body and a pretty face. I would be lying if I said that I do not admire all that in you, and I do not wish another lie to come between us. There is more than power to admire, of course. You care about people and you're willing to sacrifice much of yourself for others." She cocked her head and studied his face too closely. "But more than that, I am drawn to you in a way I cannot entirely explain, as if something inside me craves you to the pit of my soul. That was true six years ago, though I did not recognize it at the time, and it's true now. I might tell others and myself that I chose you because I thought you would die in battle and leave me a convenient widow, but I was inexplicably drawn to you even then. I might've said that any man would do, but that's not the truth. Only you would do, then and now."

No other woman would share her feelings so openly, so evenly, and without demand. He could only do the same. "You are intended for the emperor."

"Do you never defy your Emperor Jahn?"

"Never."

She sighed. "Do you love me, even a little?"

He hesitated, and in the moment of absolute silence he wished for an interruption of some kind. The caw of a bird or the howl of an animal would suffice, in this place where there was neither. There was only the crackle of the fire, which accentuated the deep silence between them. Finally he said, "I do care for you, Bela."

"That's not the same as love," she responded quickly. "I care for many people, but I love very few. My family. My friend Jocylen. And you. My love for you is different from all the rest. I'm not sure I can explain it."

"You should not love me."

"I know," she whispered. "You have not answered my question properly, Merin. Do you love me?"

In truth he didn't know, but the answer had to be no.

Bela looked a little disappointed, but she was not surprised, and she did not cry or rail against him. "I hope that one day you might, because until you do, I can't allow you to lie with me as a husband lies with his wife. It would be wrong."

He had just told Bela that they could not touch in that way, so why was his first instinct to argue with her?

She did not flirt or plead or bat her eyelashes, as other women might've. There was not a single tear, not a sniffle. Bela wasn't playing with him. No, she was deadly serious. "I'm going to get some sleep," she said, grabbing a nearby blanket and placing it on the hard ground between them. "It's been a long day, and we have much to do tomorrow."

Bela remained close, thanks to the braided rope that bound them, and Merin found himself watching her as she closed her eyes and seemed to find sleep quickly.

No, he did not, could not, love Bela, but he had to admit she was like no other woman in the world, and he wanted her to distraction.

* * *

SAVYN returned to Leyla as quickly as he could, but in his absence she'd been crying. Her eyes were red and her face was puffy. She was probably worried about what would happen if she found herself on her own, without his protection.

"I have bread," he said, smiling and ignoring the fact that she was upset. "And a small amount of fatty meat. I also have a tin cup of water. I think it'll taste better than what we drank from the creek this morning." He had tried so hard not to spill even a drop. "It isn't much, but it'll do for now. According to the farmer's wife, there's a village only a day and a half walk from here. We will head in that direction in the morning. I can find a job there and earn enough to buy some real food, and then we will decide what to do." It was almost dark, so it made sense for them to remain here, in this thick copse of trees, for the night.

As he'd walked back from the farmhouse, Savyn had been trying to think of the fastest way to get Lady Leyla to safety. Since she was destined for the emperor, emperor's men would be best. But how, and who could he trust? He only knew he had to get rid of her as soon as possible.

He had started having vivid fantasies about the woman in his care. Realistic, bone-shattering, mouth-watering sexual fantasies, as if he knew what it felt like to hold her naked body against his. As if he knew what she sounded like when she whispered his name with passion. As if he knew what it was like to push into her wet heat and find a pleasure like no other.

She was so glad to see him that she threw her arms around his neck, which caused him to spill a few drops of the water. But she quickly realized the impropriety of her reaction and pulled away, dropping her arms to her sides. Everything in him wanted to drop what he carried and pull her back to him, but he did not. They weren't right, these fantasies. She was intended for another, and was of a class he could not dream of touching.

They ate in silence, and then, as darkness fell, he made a bed of sorts from the large leaves of a pollux tree. The leaves would not be soft, but they would keep the dirt from the lady's back. When the bed was prepared, she lay upon the ground and pulled her knees up to her chest, drawing herself into a tight ball of terror.

Painful as it was, he lay down beside her and comforted her as best he could, without going too far, without revealing how he felt. Why did the words *I love you* play at his lips? He barely knew Lady Leyla. Perhaps he had admired her from afar for many years, but that did not mean he had the right to dream of loving her.

The image of her smiling at him flashed in his mind, and he shook it away. She was a kind woman, that was all. She smiled at many people, those she knew well and those she did not know at all.

He rubbed a hand along her arm and whispered to her that all would be well. Leyla did not agree, but neither did she argue. She eventually fell asleep, and when she did, she unwound slowly and drifted toward him. Soon her body was resting against his, and Savyn was so hard and needful that the pain kept him from sleep.

Her arm circled his waist and she sighed. Her head fell against his shoulder, and a mass of black curls tickled his cheek. Soon one of her fine legs was draped over his, and they were entangled as lovers might be.

While she slept, he kissed her pale and perfect cheek, being very careful not to wake her. His arms wrapped around her. His swollen cock was so close to her entrance that with a shift of clothing and a swaying of his body, he could be inside her.

But fantasies or no, he could not even dream of such a joy. And yet, when he did finally sleep, that is exactly where his dreams took him.

* * *

TRINITY came across the sleeping couple not long after the sun rose. They'd left a trail a child could follow, and he had not been a child for a very long time.

The two slept entangled, clinging to one another, no doubt in search of safety and comfort. The woman was, as he had imagined, beautiful. Even though he could see only a mass of black hair and the curve of a pale cheek, he could tell. She was fine, in that way wealthy and pampered women were, but she also had an earthy and real beauty which would've shone through no matter what her class.

The man who held her was more common in his manner of dress. It was easy to judge a person's station by their shoes, he had found. The lady wore finely crafted boots which were adorned with fancy stitching. The man wore sturdy but plain boots which marked him as a craftsman or a shopkeeper. He was not a poor beggar, but neither was he a lordly gentleman.

And yet they held on to one another as if they were very well acquainted. Fear did strange things to people.

He could kill them both while they slept. It would be quick and easy, and with his speed and accuracy they would never suffer. They would never know what had happened, if he dispatched them in that way. But Trinity had gone far beyond quick and easy where this job was concerned. The next few days could be very entertaining.

He cared nothing about the man, and would be glad to kill him outright and take the woman for himself, but if he killed the man now, Lady Leyla would know and despise him for it, and that was not the game Trinity had planned.

When the couple woke, they might be startled to see him here, but they would not recognize him. Trinity wore a fine suit of clothes very much unlike his normal simple attire, and thanks to a strong batch of black tea brewed with the leaves of a yar bush and carefully applied, his long hair was now more brown than gray. Most of his weapons were concealed in his saddlebags, one of which was a long, sturdy case capable of carrying and concealing his sword. He wore a small dagger at his waist, something any well-to-do traveler might carry. He had plastered a smile on his face miles back and practiced a vapid expression until it felt natural to him.

If they had seen him at all during the attack, it had been at a distance, and he had been moving very quickly. His gray hair was his most memorable feature, except for his pale eyes, and neither of them had been close enough to see his eyes.

"Hello," Trinity called in a friendly voice as he approached the sleeping couple. He led his horse behind him, and together they made much noise. If he had wished to do so, he could've moved toward the sleeping couple without making a sound, but that was not the game.

Trinity loved the game.

The couple on the ground came awake quickly and as one, remaining entwined as they sat up and turned to the intruder. Trinity took a deep breath. Yes, this was her, and she was more attractive awake than sleeping. Her eyes were a remarkable blue, and she had the even and perfect features of a woman who had always been, and would always be, exquisitely beautiful. Men had fought for such beautiful women for centuries.

The man scrambled to his feet, placing himself protectively in front of Lady Leyla. "Who are you, and what do you want?" Now that he got a good look at the man, Trinity realized the lady's protector was not much more than a boy, scruffy beard aside. Surely he had not seen his thirtieth birthday.

Nor would he.

"I'm just a traveler, like yourselves," Trinity said, his smile remaining in place. "Trinity. Cayse Trinity is the name." He might've give them a false name, but for what purpose? They would both soon be dead, and he rather longed to hear a pretty woman speak his name again. It had been a long time. When they did not offer names, he continued. "And you are?"

The boy offered a hand to Lady Leyla and assisted her to her feet. "My name is Savyn Leone, and this is my wife, Leyla."

Even if he had not known who they were, he would've known this simple boy was not married to the fine woman who stood beside and behind him. They were not of a class, for one thing. She outshone him. Still, it would not be wise to reveal his knowledge. "Pleasure to meet you," Trinity said with an outstretched hand to show that he wielded no weapon. "Where are you headed?"

Savyn offered his own hand, but the woman did not. She cowered. "We travel to a village to the east," he said. "We have family there."

"I am headed in that direction myself," Trinity said, as if he were pleasantly surprised. "I do not see a horse nearby. Are you afoot?"

"Yes, we are."

"Perhaps your wife would like to ride."

Lady Leyla shook her head. She had not recognized him, but neither did she trust him. The boy was less certain.

Savyn turned to her. "You should ride while you can. The trip will be much easier for you."

She was easy enough to convince. Of course she was. Lady Leyla was not accustomed to walking for hours on end, or running from danger.

Trinity allowed Savyn to assist Leyla onto the horse. Gano accepted the unfamiliar rider with ease. The glance the two who had run from him exchanged made him wonder if there wasn't more going on here than was obvious. The boy was infatuated, that was certain. But what of Lady

Leyla? Why did she look at the boy so? She was frightened and this boy was her protector, the one she relied on to keep her safe. That was it, surely.

Once properly seated, Leyla smoothed her wild black curls and straightened her once-fine blue skirt. Yes, she was definitely a lady, poised and accustomed to the saddle and elegant, even in her current disheveled condition.

"I've been traveling alone for quite some time," Trinity said as they set out at a leisurely pace. It was necessary to walk single file as they left the copse of trees, and he remained at the rear, where he could watch his prey. "I long for friendly conversation." As he said the words, he realized they were true, at least in part. He had no friends. Friends always died, and that was painful, so he had given them up long ago. He worked alone. Whom could he trust but himself? "How long have you two been married?"

"We are newly wed," Savyn said, lying so smoothly that Trinity was impressed.

"How very sweet," Trinity said as they finally left the thick growth and made their way toward the rough road in the near distance. As they no longer had to walk in single file, Trinity made his way forward so he could see Leyla's face. Her chin was lifted, and she kept her eyes straight ahead. She possessed an air of superiority, but there was a deep sadness in her eyes that made her more real than other women of her station. He wondered why she looked as sad as she did scared. Maybe he would find out before he took her life. Maybe not.

Leyla was much more real and appealing than the lady who had hired him to kill her, that was certain.

BELA found herself humming a gentle tune as they climbed. She was happy, and why shouldn't she be? She loved the majestic beauty of the mountains, and she loved to tread on this ground where so few had been. Even the physical exertion of climbing was exhilarating. Her body ached, but it was a good sort of ache. Not many women could make this climb, but she could.

Had this forbidden mountain accepted them? She did not feel as anxious as she had the last time she walked this path. She did not feel as if she did not belong, as she had then. Maybe they were welcomed here because they had Kitty in their keeping—or, rather, Kitty had them.

As they had yesterday, they took turns leading the way, Bela directing Merin when he was in the lead. They came upon a fork in the path. She was following him, and the view was very nice. Since he was often above her as well as ahead, she had a good view of his ass. Until recently she had never found a man's rear appealing, but Merin's was nicely tight and, like the rest of him, perfectly shaped.

While the truth had been hard to accept, she no longer fought. She loved Tearlach Merin, and it was possible that he loved her, at least a little. Otherwise, he would not have hesitated last night when she'd asked him if he loved her. A man who felt no love at all would've uttered a quick denial. Merin had needed a moment to think.

Bela had been drawn to this man from the moment she'd seen him, so many years ago. She'd wanted him, used him, hated him, and deceived him. She'd threatened him with bodily harm and, yes, shed a few silent and secret tears because of him. Had she always loved him? Had she been fighting these inconvenient and strong and fabulous and heartbreaking emotions for *years*?

It was so unlike her to long for anything and not simply *take* it.

The journey was not easy, but it was pleasant enough and they were as prepared as possible. It would be impossible to carry their swords as they usually did, hanging from their belts, so Kitty hung against Bela's back, where she could not swing and catch stone. Merin's sword was carried in much the same way. Against those leather-encased swords they each carried a pack of supplies. Food. Waterskins. Blankets. A small and serviceable knife. Flint and steel for fire, when they had access to wood. All that they needed for this journey was in these packs.

Kitty had been silent all day, and that was just as well. Bela felt as if she needed time to think about what might come next without being constantly reminded that she needed Merin, which seemed to be Kitty's only contribution of late.

As they climbed, her mind took her to terrifying and impossible places. Her thoughts spun, disjointed and uncertain. How could she proceed? How could she make her husband love her?

Love. She'd never thought she'd desire it for herself, not in this way. Bela did not want to be beholden to a man, or anyone else. She did not want obligations or commitments. And yet now, after a relatively short time bound to Merin, she wanted very much to commit herself to him. Just as strongly, she wanted him to commit himself to her.

"It's beautiful here, isn't it?" she asked as she took a few quick steps to bring herself to Merin's side. They were on a wide, flat patch of stone where it was possible to walk side by side.

"Yes," he answered without looking at her. He had not bothered with shaving implements for this journey, and already his beard was coming in. He looked rather rough, with all that dark stubble. He looked very manly and fierce.

"The Turis began in these mountains," she said, attempting to start a genial conversation. "Perhaps not here on Forbidden Mountain, but farther to the north, we began." She pointed. "According to legend, the first Turis were born of stone, snow, and sunlight."

"Hard, cold, and hot," Merin muttered. "Sounds right to me."

Bela found herself smiling. "General Tearlach Merin, are you trying to pick a fight with me?"

"Of course not."

"You *are*."

"You're usually quite eager to argue," he said almost bitterly.

"I suppose that's true, but I don't feel like arguing today." Bela took a deep breath of the fine mountain air. Perhaps nothing grew here, perhaps this was not a livable or comfortable mountain, but it did have its own beauty. "It's odd, since Nobel's demands are so annoying, and it looks as if we'll end up at war with him and his men, and an emperor I have never seen wishes to inspect me and perhaps make me an empress, which would be agony, and you refuse to admit that you love me a little, and . . ."

"You're turning into a woman," Merin said sharply, obviously still trying to get a rise out of her. Did he think constant argument would make her want him less?

"You have taught me that there are worse curses in life than womanhood," she said sweetly. "Perhaps it is even a blessing, in some respects."

He turned to glare at her with exquisite dark eyes that made her heart do strange things. She had never realized that eyes could be so sensual, so alluring . . . so telling.

"Blast it all," Merin snapped, "I want the old Bela back. Threaten to take my head. Tell me you wish to be a widow. Let me hear your anger echo through the hills. Torture me, but not like this!"

"Do I misunderstand you?" Bela asked in a rational voice. "When I'm nice to you, it's torture?"

"Yes!"

That was a good sign, she decided. "Then I shall do my best to be unpleasant for the remainder of the day. Just for you, Merin. It's my turn to lead." She rushed ahead of him, making it imperative that he run to keep up with her, since the rope that bound them together was not so very long. Soon they were in a shaded, narrow passage where the sun did not touch them. As she climbed upward, stepping onto and over jagged stone, Bela smiled and wondered if Merin was admiring *her* ass.

Chapter Nine

✳

LEYLA did not trust the stranger who traveled with them all day, chattering about the weather and his potmaking business and how he'd disliked his life as a farmer's son. The man who called himself Trinity said nothing alarming, and his words sounded sincere enough, and heaven knows she was glad to be able to ride for this leg of the journey.

But she did not trust him, not at all. At the moment she trusted no one but Savyn. The man said he was a potmaker, but he had no pots. He explained that he'd sold all of his supply and was headed home to make more, before setting out to travel the countryside and sell them once again. That could very well be true, she supposed.

She and Savyn both looked behind them often during the day, trying to be surreptitious so their companion would not realize they were worried about who might be behind them. Were they still being followed, or had the killer taken a wrong turn? One wrong turn, and he would no longer be a problem, not unless he decided to backtrack and found himself on this road. Maybe they were safer as a party of three, no matter if she trusted Cayse Trinity or not.

Clouds had been rolling in all day, and in the late afternoon sprinkles fell from the sky. The light rainfall felt good, and Leyla lifted her face to catch the drops on her skin. Judging by the dark clouds, they would soon have much more than a sprinkle to contend with. When they rounded a bend in the road and saw the hut which had been partially built into a small, rolling hill, it seemed like a godsend. There was no sign of life around the place, other than the wildflowers and weeds which grew tall. One side of the hut and a portion of the roof had fallen in. The hut looked deserted and was perhaps home to rodents or other small animals. But most of the roof remained, and they would soon be in need of that shelter.

"Perhaps we should wait out the coming storm there," Trinity suggested.

Savyn looked up at Leyla, a silent question in his eyes. They would have to spend the night somewhere, and if there was a storm headed their way, this crumbling haven would be better than any campsite. She nodded once, and then Savyn agreed with Trinity and they headed in that direction.

Before they reached the shelter, the rain began to fall harder than before. It fell in Leyla's eyes and quickly soaked her dress, and her hair stuck to her skin. Rain soaked into the ground and released the scent of grass and dirt and spring storms. Leyla was doubly glad of their rough sanctuary when she heard thunder rumble in the distance. She did not care for storms, and lighting made her blood dance in strange ways.

Savyn assisted her from the saddle, and the two of them ran to the door of the hut, which hung crookedly, more off its hinges than on. Trinity took charge of his horse and led the stallion to an overhang on one side of the hut—the side that had not fallen in—an overhang perhaps intended for such a purpose. He spoke softly to the horse he lovingly called Gano, and that eased some of Leyla's fears. A man who loved animals could not be all bad.

It took all of Savyn's strength to lift the wooden door and slide it aside so they could slip into the hut, which at first sight Leyla realized had indeed been long abandoned, except for the small animals which had sometimes nested here—though not today. The furnishings consisted of one broken chair and a few pieces of what had once been a table. There was a stone fireplace which was crumbling but looked functional. Dirt and dust spoke of years of abandonment, but the fact that some of the filth and cobwebs had been disturbed revealed that other travelers had stopped here for rest or shelter, though not very often.

While Trinity was seeing to his horse and they were alone, Leyla turned to Savyn. There was just a bit of light coming through the broken wall and the off-kilter door. Savyn was scruffy and dirty and wet, just as she was, and the only thing that soothed her was looking into his eyes. He had forgotten everything; she had forgotten nothing.

She was about to tell Savyn that she didn't trust Trinity when the man who had joined them this morning entered the hut and shook off his wet hat with a laugh. "Good fortune, finding this shelter. We can stay here until the storm passes. Looking at the sky, I'd say we might be here all night." He walked to the fireplace. "Perhaps we could build a fire, if we can find a bit of dry wood." He eyed the chair and what was left of the table. "Wet as we are, I'd prefer to sit on the floor and have a warm fire, given the choice. What about you, Leyla?"

"A fire would be nice," she said.

Trinity set about breaking apart the chair. They would need a tool of some sort—an ax, perhaps—to cut the thick wood of the table into small pieces which would fit in the hearth. Leyla shuddered as she thought of the last ax she'd seen, remembering the attacker and the way he had wielded his weapon in such a deadly manner.

Savyn offered to help, but Trinity smiled and with a wink told them to rest. He was quite talented at starting a fire, using bits of straw from the floor as kindling and building up the smaller pieces of the chair before taking a flint from his pocket and making a spark which lit the kindling. Now and then his hands moved so fast they were almost a blur, and Leyla shuddered. The killer had moved just so, unnaturally fast.

Was it possible that they had not eluded the man who pursued them? Was it possible that he was here with them, in this cabin? The clothing and the hair were wrong, and he could've easily killed them many times during the day. But the way he moved . . . it was uncanny.

"Where did you say you were from, Trinity?" Leyla asked.

"A small town north of Arthes. I grew up a farmer's son but never had any love for the land."

"So you learned to make pots," she said.

"Yes, everyone needs pots," he said in a jovial tone. "Even the poorest household must have porridge. My pots are the finest." He droned on about pots, repeating what he'd said earlier in the day, almost word for word.

Soon a fire was blazing, and as they were all wet, the heat was a comfort. The light was also welcome, as she could see Savyn's face more clearly. The sight of him was always a comfort.

She could also see Trinity. The hat he wore had protected most of his hair from the rain, but the very tip of his brown braid had been soaked by the rain, and by the light of the fire she could see that the end of the braid was no longer brown.

It was a silver gray, almost white.

She gripped Savyn's arm tightly. Did he see? Did he

know that the man who had offered her a ride, chattered all day, and built them a roaring fire was the same man who had promised to kill them? Yes, she knew by the way his muscles tensed that he saw and realized as she did.

Savyn stood slowly and offered Leyla his arm. She took it, and together they edged toward the door, Savyn keeping his body between her and Trinity as much as possible. Trinity still had his back to them, and from their vantage point the end of his braid was bright silver and unmistakable.

He could not see them, and yet the room was too small for them to move without his knowledge. "It's still raining very hard," he said without turning about. "Surely you two aren't going outside in this storm."

"I need a private moment with my wife," Savyn said, his voice amazingly calm.

Smoothly and with grace, Trinity spun and stood to face them. His smile was cold. His pale gray eyes were colder. "I know you two are newly wed, but your private moment can surely wait until the storm passes."

"I just need a word," Savyn said.

"In that case, allow *me* to step outside so you can have your privacy. We cannot ask the lady to stand in the rain, now can we?" He walked toward them, the remaining leg of the chair he'd dismantled resting easily in his hand.

Savyn made sure Leyla was at the door. "Run," he whispered.

She clung to his shirt. "Not without you."

"Dammit, Leyla . . ."

"What gave me away?" Trinity asked. His face was hard; it was no longer the face of a friendly, tedious potmaker. "Pity, I did not want the game to end so soon."

Leyla saw the chair leg come up, and she pulled at the back of Savyn's shirt, trying to urge him through the narrow opening in the doorway. Instead of coming with her, he surged forward to meet Trinity's swing. The chair leg smacked into Savyn's head, and he went instantly limp and dropped to the floor.

She stared down at Savyn's bloody face and the gash in his scalp. This was her fault. All her fault. Her body was numb and she could not move, could not even breathe. Trinity raised his weapon to finish the job of killing a man whose only crime had been to love a woman he could not have, and Leyla forced herself to act. She threw herself between Savyn and the chair leg, taking the blow on her shoulder. Pain radiated from her shoulder down her arm and her back, and she screamed. Then she turned to slip through the opening and run with all her might, praying that Trinity would chase her instead of taking the time to finish killing Savyn.

BELA was surely doing this to him on purpose: being agreeable, smiling often, looking much too pretty for a woman who had spent two full days climbing a mountain. Merin was positive he did not look so good.

Tomorrow they should reach the site where Clyn had found Kitty. With any luck they would find clues to her purpose in the area. He needed to think about that chore, he needed to dedicate himself to it in order to take his mind off the woman who had moved close to him in sleep, as if her body was now so accustomed to sleeping beside him that she needed his warmth, even though the night was again mild and the fire he had built was just now dying down.

She was intended for Emperor Jahn, and he was a general who obeyed orders as well as gave them. He did not take that which was not his.

The only problem was that Bela felt like she was his. Gut deep, he was sometimes certain she belonged to him. She was his wife, emperor be damned. It wasn't as if Bela was Jahn's type, in any case. No, she was Merin's type, he just had never realized it, not until recently.

He was accustomed to depriving himself of things he wanted. In times of war, in times of sacrifice, he had denied himself. So why was it so hard to deny himself now?

In her sleep, Bela sighed and wiggled and moved her head to his stomach, which she used as if it were her personal pillow. Eventually her hand settled between his legs, which almost caused him to shout and throw her off. He did not. Instead, he lay there suffering and confused. He had not been so confused since he'd been a child.

Eventually Merin did sleep, and when he did, he dreamed of Bela and sex. He dreamed of her strong thighs wrapped around his hips as she took him in. He dreamed of pleasure that only she could give him.

TRINITY squeezed through the doorway and chased Lady Leyla into the rain. Savyn was down and would be down for a while, and Trinity realized that if he let his target get away again, she'd be more careful from here on out. She knew his face and it would be difficult to sneak up on her next time. No, he had to catch her now, and since it was dark, with only flashes of lightning to illuminate her, he could not allow her to get ahead of him.

He could finish the man after he was done with the woman. The blow to Savyn's head had brought him down, and would keep him down for a while. Rain washed over Trinity, and he soon realized what had given him away. The rain rinsed away the brown color in his hair. The mixture of tea and yar leaves stained his shirt, and that meant the gray of his hair would be revealed. But for the rain, the game might've continued for a while. Too bad it had to end so soon.

A lightning flash revealed the fleeing woman. She had

run to the road and was making her way toward town, as if she could outrun him, as if she could escape. Most of his weapons were still stored with the horse, but he had a small knife on his belt and a sturdy stick of wood in his hand. That would suffice for one small woman.

Trinity ran. With his speed and strength, and unencumbered by skirts and fancy boots, he was soon upon his prey. He grabbed Lady Leyla by the neck and she tripped, and then they both went tumbling to the ground. They landed hard and mud splattered up, covering her face and much of his. She screamed and she fought against his hold, but she could not escape. He pinned her arms to the ground, and held her so she could barely move.

"Shhhh," he said calmly, his lips near her ear. "Don't make this worse than it has to be."

Trinity had planned to seduce Lady Leyla properly, but that was no longer an option. He still wanted her, but he would not force himself upon her. He was not that sort of low man. His mother would've been horrified at the very thought. Still, he might not have to give up all that he desired. "Do you wish to live awhile longer?" he whispered in her ear.

"Yes," she shouted.

Again lightning flashed, and she was illuminated for him. Lady Leyla was soaking wet and covered in mud, and yet she was still stunning. She remained a lady, fine and elegant.

"Do you know what I want from you, for those extra minutes of life?" Surely she knew, as he was aroused and pressing against her.

"Yes," she said, not so loudly as before. Her voice shook.

Moving efficiently, he rolled Leyla onto her back. Not being a fool, he kept her hands immobile and pressed into the mud. Rain washed some of the mud from her face, and he could see the terror in her eyes and in the set of her mouth. He did not want to see terror, not now. He wanted passion; he wanted softness. In the mud and the rain and with her blood soon to be on his hands, he wanted it all.

"Does Savyn live?" Leyla asked, and Trinity saw the ardor he wished for himself.

"For now."

An unexpected strength was added to her terror. The lady was tougher than she appeared to be. "Promise me that you will allow him to live. There is no reason for Savyn to die."

"Your Savyn has caused me a lot of trouble," Trinity said truthfully.

"He is a good man," she whispered. "He deserves better than this end."

Trinity was very good at reading people's faces, and he was surprised by what he saw on Lady Leyla's face. "You love him."

"I do," she said passionately. "Promise me that you will let him live, and I will allow you to have all that you want from me. I will not fight you, I will not cry, I will not lie here motionless as if I despise your touch. All that you wish for in this last moment of my life will be yours, if you swear to me that Savyn will live."

Lady Leyla was terrified but sincere. She would do anything for the man she loved, and that touched Trinity. No one had ever loved him in that way. No one ever would. "All right," he said. "Please me well, and after I send you on, I will walk away without revisiting the hut and finishing off your lover. He is your lover, isn't he?"

"Yes, he is." She fought against his grip but was unable to move. "I cannot please you without the use of my hands. Release me, please. It's not as if I can fight one such as you."

That was true enough. "Fight me, and after I see to you, your Savyn will die slowly and in incredible pain," Trinity promised before he released Leyla's hands.

Lying against this woman he had been paid to kill, Trinity felt a surge of loneliness. He wished for softness in his life, but it was not meant to be. If he dared to care for anyone, he would have to watch that person grow old and die. He had done so many times, and it was so painful that he did not care to go through the agony again. Turning his back on that pain meant he turned his back on the pleasure of a woman's touch. He could—and did—pay for sex when the urge struck, but that was not the same as love given freely. Not that Leyla offered herself freely. No, there was a price. But it was not cold, hard coin.

With his fingers, Trinity gently wiped away the rest of the mud on Leyla's face. He wanted her to be pretty for him. She remained very still while he saw to her, while he wiped away the muck that should never touch a lady like this one.

She would die very quickly, without any pain. He would see to it.

He lowered his head and kissed her, while rain washed over them and lightning flashed. Though Leyla was not a passionate kisser, she did not spit at him or bite or push him away, and it seemed that eventually her mouth did move against his, a little. It had been a long time since a woman he had not paid had kissed him, and he liked it, even though he could taste her fear. For a moment he regretted what he had to do, but it was his duty, his calling, to send on those whose time had come.

Part of him wanted to kiss her for a long while, to simply enjoy the softness and the promise and the simple ecstasy of touch. But Leyla tasted so fine, he could not wait much longer. His mind wanted this to last, but his body was impatient.

While they still kissed, his hand pulled at Leyla's wet skirt, lifting it high as the rain pelted their bodies. She kept her word and participated in their liaison. Her hands touched his shoulders, and then his neck, with a woman's gentleness. Those fine, gentle hands skirted softly up his face to touch his head, and then she gently pulled his lips from hers and she smiled.

His heart nearly stopped from the sheer joy.

"You do not wish to hurt me," she whispered.

Trinity felt a sharp pain in his temple, and he realized she was right. He did not wish to hurt her, not at all.

"You do not want to harm Savyn, either," she said, her hands pressing harder against the sides of his head. "You *will not* harm either of us. To do so would bring you great pain. To even *think* of taking our lives would bring you to your knees with agony."

Her words were strange, but yes, she was correct.

Leyla's soft voice whispered, "When you touch me, the pain is astonishing."

His hand, which had been resting so wonderfully against her thigh, began to burn as if he had thrust it into a raging fire. Soon his whole body burned, and when he looked into Leyla's eyes, he no longer saw fear or helplessness or even beauty.

He saw the witch.

"You cannot move," she said in a strong voice. Lightning crackled overhead, and in the flash of light he saw the face of a strong woman who was in command of herself, and of him. "Not until I tell you that you are allowed." She cocked her head to the side, and one hand moved to his forehead. "It hurts, doesn't it?"

"Yes," he rasped, burning and unable to move.

"Soon I will allow you to go, but not yet," Leyla said, and he saw and heard the savage in her. The *witch*. "Why did you once wish to kill me?"

"I was paid to do so," he answered quickly, hoping to finish this as fast as possible so the pain would end.

"By whom?"

"A lady like yourself, a woman who did not wish you to reach Arthes and perhaps win the position of empress."

"Political intrigue," she said with a humorless laugh. "I should've expected as much. Does this lady have a name?"

He gave her the name she asked for, could not have stopped himself without biting off his tongue. She did not seem to recognize the name, as she repeated it softly.

The rain did not stop. It poured down on them, cold and relentless. Trinity wanted to escape but could not. He was trapped here, he was prisoner to this woman who held him immobile with the touch of a seemingly gentle hand.

"You have killed many people," Leyla said tenderly.

"Yes."

Her fingers danced on his forehead, tender and yet somehow afire. "In your soul you must know that what you have become is wrong," she said. "In your heart and soul and mind you must know that to take the lives of others is wrong."

"Not wrong," he said in a raspy voice, desperate to defend himself. "It was their time . . ."

She pressed the palm of her small hand to his forehead, and when she did, he felt the grief and horror of all that he had done. He felt the pain as if it were his own. "Yes!" he shouted. "It was wrong."

So wrong, and yet all he could do. All he knew was killing, and he tried to deliver death quickly, he did his best to make his victims depart easily and without pain. And yet—it did hurt. There was pain for them as they departed this life.

"You must pay for your sins, Trinity," Leyla said, and her voice was gentle. "From this day forward, until the day you die . . ."

"No!" he shouted.

"You will feel the pain of those you killed," she continued. "You will see their faces and hear their voices, waking and sleeping. They will haunt you."

"Not until I die," he said hoarsely. The witch who cursed him didn't know what a *very long time* that was.

"Yes, until you die," she said. "Until God takes you or rejects you, you will feel the weight of every soul you took from this world. You will pay for what you have done, and you will never again take the life of an innocent. Never again!"

His head hurt, it felt as if it were about to burst, it felt as if the lightning above was in his head, bouncing around in his skull, trying to escape. Before his eyes the woman beneath him appeared to be not a beautiful witch but one of the young soldiers he had killed when he'd attacked their party. He heard the scream as if it were in his ears. The rain turned to blood and fell upon him, warm and sticky. It fell upon her, too, bright red and abundant. There was so much blood.

"Redeem yourself, if you can," the witch added, and then she removed her hand from his throbbing head. "Now, *run!*"

Trinity leaped to his feet and began to sprint away. He did not even think of retrieving his beloved horse, for that would mean facing the witch again. He ran from her and her magic, he ran from what she had done to him, even though he knew it could not be undone. No one had told him she was a witch!

Her curse was already at work. As he ran through the storm, the narrow, muddy road was lined with ghostly figures of those he had killed. He had killed many in his life as an assassin, and it seemed they stretched forever. They screamed at him, and together their screams were louder than the thunder, brighter than the lightning. Again the rain turned to blood, and the ghosts moved closer to him until they were so near he could not breathe as he fought his way through them.

What had he done?

* * *

LEYLA ran toward the hut, praying that Savyn wasn't dead. The blow Trinity had delivered could've been a killing blow, but maybe it had just rendered Savyn senseless. Maybe he was alive.

She slipped through the doorway. Savyn was lying on the floor just inside. He was in the exact same position he'd been in when she'd made her escape. Judging by the way his head was positioned and the single bleeding gash there, Trinity had not delivered a second blow. He had not lied about that, at least.

"Savyn," Leyla whispered as she dropped to her knees beside him. She was shaking, as much from fear for Savyn as from the strain of using so much of her gift at one time. Her shoulder hurt where the stick which had injured Savyn had fallen so hard. She felt very close to dropping into a deep sleep herself, but could not until she knew Savyn was all right.

She had no dry cloth—even her underskirt was soaked— and she needed something to bandage Savyn's head. She carefully unbuttoned his shirt and worked it off of him, then folded it into a thick length which would wrap around his head and stem the flow of blood. It wasn't much, but it would have to do until morning. "I love you," she said as she bandaged his wound. "I love you so much. I'm wrong for you and I know it, but that doesn't matter, not now. In all my life, I have never loved anyone the way I love you. Even before we became intimate, before I realized what true passion was like, I loved you. You made me laugh," she said softly. "You made me feel like a woman, not a frightening freak of nature."

When his head was bandaged and it seemed the bleeding had stopped, she ripped strips from her underskirt and laid them near the fire to dry. Perhaps by morning she would have a more suitable bandage. When that was done, she placed her head on Savyn's chest. He was much too heavy for her to move—just taking off his shirt had been a struggle—and now and then a bit of rain came through the door and landed upon them. But they had the light of the fire, and Trinity was gone, and they were both alive.

The strain of using so much of her power had sapped Leyla's strength, and even though her heart and her shoulder were in agony, she passed out with her cheek pressed to Savyn's heart.

BELA woke with the sun, as usual. Her head rested on Merin's chest, and her hand was nestled between his thighs. It was only fair, since his hand was resting quite comfortably on her right breast. He slept on, and she did not disturb him. Not yet.

In was in Bela's nature to take what she wanted. Whether it was sneaking into Tyman's room at night and borrowing his practice sword or lying to a handsome general in order to lose her bothersome virginity, Bela was like a bull when it came to getting what she desired.

She was twenty-three years old and just now learning that some things could not be taken. Some valuable things had to be earned, they had to be won in a gentle battle. Merin would have to be won. Love would come only at the end of an ardent, persistent battle.

Was she prepared to fight? Was she prepared to risk anything and everything?

More important, was she willing to be *patient*? She could, given the current state of affairs, wake Merin most agreeably and take the pleasures of their bodies entwined. He fought the concept of love, but his body wanted hers. He wanted her very much. But if she did that, if she tricked him again, he might never forgive her.

Belavalari Haythorne had never been known for her abundance of patience.

No, she was rightly Belavalari Merin at the moment, was she not? Wife of Tearlach, daughter of the chieftain Valeron, potential mother of the children of a hero. Together she and Merin would make fine, strong sons and daughters.

If she could make him love her.

Merin awoke not long after her, and his hand flew from her breast as if her skin were on fire. "Sorry," he muttered, sleep still in his morning-hoarse voice.

"No need to apologize," she said as she removed her hand from between his thighs.

"We should arrive at our destination this afternoon," he said, turning directly to business, trying to dismiss their closeness. Perhaps trying to dismiss his own desires.

"Yes, we should." Bela sat beside him and admired the view from their place so high in the world. "I'm anxious to explore that area where Kitty was found. Would you kiss me?"

"What?" He was surprised by the bold and unexpected question.

"Kiss me," she said. "If you wouldn't mind. I've never been kissed, except for last time you were here, and I've almost forgotten what it was like. Besides, I had lied to you then, so it was not a true and righteous kiss. I do remember it as being pleasant, and I thought while we are still married and there's no one around to see . . ."

"It's not a good idea," Merin said gruffly.

"I know," she said, looking him in the eye. "But after you've left us, I do not want to regret not taking a proper kiss when the opportunity presented itself."

"Fine," he said, not at all in the mood for a kiss by her reckoning. He grabbed the back of her head and pulled her toward him and coolly pressed his mouth to hers very briefly before pulling away.

It was not enough.

"That is not as I remembered," she said.

With a sound very much like a grunt, Merin pulled her mouth to his again and delivered a much more proper kiss. His wonderfully full mouth was warm and tender, and it lingered against hers. His beard was rough, but she liked the feel of it brushing against her tender skin. Bela found her lips parting of their own accord, as if inviting more. In response, Merin gave her more. A tip of the tongue, a nip of the lower lip, a movement she felt to her bones.

Her body instinctively swayed toward his, and she rested her hand on his thigh, where it seemed to fall quite naturally. She tilted her head, inviting more, and for an all too brief moment, Merin gave her more.

And then it was done.

"I felt that kiss everywhere," she said honestly. "Still do." She rested a hand on her chest. "Kissing was not nearly so pleasant last time, perhaps because I was so ignorant of what might come next."

"We must go," Merin said gruffly, rolling to his feet and grabbing for his blanket.

"Yes, I suppose we must." Standing languidly, Bela stretched her muscles and faced the morning with a smile. "What a lovely day it's going to be."

Chapter Ten

※

FORBIDDEN Mountain was alternately rocky and forested, with periods of hard climbing combined with easier hours of crossing shallow creeks and walking gentle natural paths beneath ancient trees. As Merin had been told, there were no animals here, neither large nor small. That alone gave the mountain an unnatural feel, though he could not say he felt any trepidation or unease on this mountain that was said to be so unwelcoming.

Other than the occasional possibility of a nasty fall, there was not much to reckon with in the way of danger, he thought as he climbed, unless he could count kissing Bela. That had definitely been dangerous. Too bad there wasn't more peril along this journey. He was sure a good sword fight or tussle with a mountain lion would make him feel much better. It would, at least, take his mind off a more immediate problem.

Bela. Bela was his problem. He'd been more comfortable when she'd threatened to take his head, when she'd seemed to hate him for not dying six years ago, as she'd

planned. Now she smiled at him often, and she asked for
kisses and she talked about love as any other woman
might.

No, not as any other woman. Bela presented all she
thought and felt without pretense, without a put-on shyness
or uncertainty. She said what she felt and asked the same of
him.

He could not tell her that her very presence was driving
him to the brink of insanity, that the braided rope which
bound them seemed to grow shorter and more binding every day. He could not tell her that he had suffered fantasies
of keeping her as his wife, even though he knew he could
not, should not . . . no, *could* not.

Emperor Jahn had become a much better emperor than
Merin had thought he could be in those early days. The
man who had once seemed to be practically worthless had
become a fair and kind ruler. Jahn had his quirks. This ridiculous bridal contest proved that well enough. Still, he
was emperor, and if Merin returned and informed Jahn
that the woman he'd been sent to fetch was his wife . . . he
would not be pleased.

*Why do you care about pleasing an emperor more than
you care about pleasing yourself?* Kitty whispered.

Merin sighed. He did wish whatever power gave the
sword life would get out of his head. Was nothing private?

*Nothing. Hope, fear, desire, love, hate, shame—it
bounces about the universe like wildfire. Those emotions
and the actions that follow them create the world you live
in, the world I live in for now.*

Merin glanced back at Bela, and she smiled. If she heard
Kitty's words, she gave no sign. It was damned odd that the
power in the sword could choose to speak to both of them
or only to one. Merin did not much like being so closely
connected to a magic he could not entirely explain—a
force which might be much more powerful than he or Bela
or any among the Turis realized.

Kitty went silent. Was she sulking? And when had he started thinking of the weapon as "she" instead of "it"? He had lost control of his life in so many ways . . .

A clatter of rocks not far behind them alerted Merin that someone or something else was nearby. A muffled curse told him it was a man—or men—who followed. Miners? There were not supposed to be any Turi miners this far to the south, but perhaps they were lost or exploring, searching for another plot of rich land on this forbidden mountain. Nobel or his men? Probably not. Dishonest and greedy as the man who wished to wed Bela was, he'd seemed pleased enough with their agreement. Still, he was not a man to be trusted, so anything was possible. Who else would dare to follow them here?

Merin scrambled to a flat expanse of rock and unsheathed the sword he wore against his back. He dropped his pack to the ground, and Bela, who had surely heard the sounds, smoothly did the same. She dropped her sack of supplies and drew Kitty, whose grip shone brightly—perhaps brighter than before. The sword also emitted a keening noise, a sharp sound of excitement and preparation.

Moments earlier Merin had wished for trouble to distract him. It appeared that trouble was coming.

WHEN Leyla woke, it was late afternoon, she could tell, by the slant of sunlight coming through the broken door and the fallen wall. The fire had died, the rain had stopped, and Savyn's heart continued to beat, strong and steady.

She rose and placed her hand on his face, rubbing gently against his rough beard. There had been many times in her life when she'd wished she had no powers, no gifts which made her different. This moment was the only time she had ever wished to have a different gift. If she were a healer, she could take away Savyn's wound, she could undo what Trinity had done.

As she caressed his face, Savyn stirred and opened his eyes. He did not look at her, but shifted his gaze to the side. He had never been afraid to look her in the eye. Did he blame her for what had happened? Did he hate her for bringing him into this situation which had almost killed him?

"Where is he?" Savyn asked, sitting up sharply, then gasping in pain as he placed a hand against his bandaged head.

"Gone," Leyla whispered.

Savyn wrapped his arms around her and pulled her close, all but crushing her to his body. "Did he hurt you?"

"No."

"Are you certain he's gone?" Savyn held her too tightly, but she didn't mind. In fact, she reveled in the sensation of his arms around her. She stroked the back of his head as he said, "I won't let him hurt you. I swear on my honor, I will die before I let him hurt you."

Leyla's heart skipped a beat. Thanks to her, Savyn could not remember what they'd once had. He should not be so intent on protecting her. He should not say these words which spoke so clearly of love and possession.

She rested her head against his shoulder. "You know I have a gift," she said.

"Yes." His answer was soft, as if he were reluctant to admit that he knew. Perhaps now that he did not remember their intimacy, he was afraid of her and what she could do, as so many others were.

"I used my ability to make Trinity go away." Leyla stroked Savyn's thick, unwieldy bandage, even though she knew she should move away from him. "He won't come back. We are no longer in danger. He even left his horse and all that was with it, so when we leave here, we can ride to town. No more walking for us," she said, trying to lighten her voice.

"We can set out in the morning," Savyn said. "You will ride and I will walk, so we don't put too much strain on the animal."

"You will ride alone or we will both ride," she said, her voice leaving no room for argument. "You've been hurt. I will have it no other way." She tried to move away, but he was holding her too close. "Why wait here all day?" she asked. "I hate this place." Trinity had revealed himself here; Savyn had been injured and almost killed here. She wanted only to escape.

"We need only wait until after the sun rises," Savyn said, and as she had done for him, he ran his strong hands against the back of her head in a comforting gesture. "We cannot very well travel down the road in the pitch-black of night."

A chill walked down Leyla's spine. The hut was dimly lit, but there was plenty of sunlight coming through the fallen wall and the door and the holes in the roof; there was more than enough to light the interior of their rough shelter. Pitch black? She pulled away and took Savyn's face in her hands, being careful of the wound on the side of his head. His eyes were unfocused. He was looking at her, and yet—he was not.

"Savyn, can you see me at all?"

"No," he said. "It's much too dark. I can't see anything at all."

Leyla closed her eyes tight and fought back tears. Crying would not help the situation. "Savyn," she said gently, "my dear Savyn, it is no longer night. The sun shines. I fear the blow to your head . . ."

"Do not tease me, Lady Leyla."

She took his hand, a hand she knew so well, and moved it into the warm sunlight that shone through the partially opened door. "Do you feel that?" she asked. "Do you feel the warmth of the sun?"

Savyn was very still for a long moment, and then he said, "I feel it. Why is everything so dark? Why can't I see?"

Once again, Leyla wrapped her arms around Savyn, and this time it was she who held too tight. Perhaps this was a temporary effect of the injury, but it might also be permanent. They would not know for quite some time. "The blow to your head has taken your sight."

She wondered if the pain she'd inflicted on Trinity was enough to make him pay for what he'd done. At the moment, she suspected not.

THREE men came around a sharp turn in the path and were surprised to see Bela and Merin waiting for them; armed and ready. Bela's mind worked quickly. The three rough-looking men were not Turi, and they were not dressed like the miners who worked on the mountains north of Turi lands. They were armed, but had stored their knives and swords for the climb, as she and Merin had done.

Merin did not presume to force her to stand behind him as though she were a defenseless female, though he did manage to place himself a bit more in the forefront. And it was he who asked, "Who are you, and what do you want?"

For a moment the three men were very still, and then one of them, the one in the middle, said in a lowered voice, "That's her."

Bela sighed. They were here for her. What now? Merin, an emperor, Nobel, and now this.

The men were obviously heartened by the odds—three men against one man and one woman—but they were ignorant to be comforted by their greater numbers. Bela was no ordinary woman, and Tearlach Merin was no ordinary man.

The three who had been following rushed forward,
drawing their weapons as they ran, screaming a coarse sort
of war cry that might've been meant to strike terror into the
hearts of their intended victims. This section of the mountain was rough and rocky, but was also blessed with occasional large expanses of fairly flat ground. The landscape
was sufficient for fighting, though Bela made a mental note
not to move too far to her left as she fought, as there was a
sharp drop just a few feet away.

And if she went over that edge, Merin would fall with
her. They remained bound, and to undo the rope would
mean remaining married. She had no problem with that,
but she wasn't sure about Merin. She had tricked him
enough, in the name of what she wanted. She would not do
so again; they would have to remain attached as they
fought.

Merin stepped forward and took on the man in the lead,
sword to sword. The second and third men came toward
Bela. She was their intended target, so it made sense, she
supposed, to send the greater number to her. Kitty shone
brightly as metal met metal, and the men seemed to be
surprised yet again. That surprise made her certain they
were not Nobel's men, nor were they here for the magical
sword. For some reason, they wanted to kill her.

She was quick and well trained, and Kitty was remarkable in battle. Sparks flew, the tip of the sword moved with
precision to cut flesh, the strength of the blade kept metal
from finding and cutting Bela's skin.

Merin quickly dispatched the man who had been foolish
enough to take him on, and then the second man who
fought Bela moved his attention to Merin, as the other, the
man who was so obviously in charge, remained before
Bela, his sword swinging and thrusting with some measure
of skill.

Joined, and careful in their movements because of that
restriction, Merin and Bela soon stood back to back, fight-

ing without words, without hesitation. The men they battled were skilled swordsmen. Otherwise the fight would've ended very quickly. These were not common highwaymen who were lost, but were well-trained combatants. They were also very determined.

Merin killed his opponent with an impressive and well-placed swing of his sword, and Bela was momentarily distracted. The man who seemed determined to kill her took that moment to swing mightily and knock Kitty out of Bela's hand. The magical sword soared, her grip shining brightly as she flew. As Kitty hit the ground and spun out of Bela's reach, the potential killer's sword came up, and the blade touched Bela's throat.

At that same moment, Merin turned and placed the tip of his sword at the remaining attacker's side. "Move, and I'll gut you," he said.

The response was quick. "Move, and this blade goes through her pretty throat."

The three of them stood very still for a long moment. A breeze wafted through, cool and refreshing, whipping Merin's curls and the strands of hair that had come loose from Bela's braid.

"You cannot escape this," Merin said, his voice rock solid and calm. "Walk away, and you can live."

The man who held a sword at Bela's throat shook his head. "No, I must finish this job."

"Job?" Merin said. "This ill-advised attack is a *job*?"

The man was losing his patience. He glanced at the bodies on the ground, and Bela could feel the increased pressure at her throat. The one remaining assailant was close to panic. A moment more, and she'd be dead.

There was no time. A shock might slow him down. She held out her hand. "Here, Kitty!" In an instant, the sword streaked through the air and the shining grip smacked into Bela's palm. She grabbed it, spun her head aside so her throat was no longer in immediate danger, and ran the blade of the sword through the adversary's side, just as Merin did the same.

The last of the assailants fell, not quite dead but quickly headed in that direction.

Merin looked to Bela first and studied her quickly and efficiently, making sure she was unharmed. She nodded, and he dropped to his haunches to confront the wounded man. "Who hired you, and why? Was it Nobel?"

"I would not call my profession a noble one . . ."

"No, Nobel Andyrs," Merin said impatiently. "Do not play games with me in the short time you have left."

"Why should I tell you anything?" the man asked angrily. "You have killed me."

Kitty whispered, and Bela could tell by the expression on Merin's face, and by the words that followed, that they both heard.

"You are concerned about the fate of your soul," Merin said. "You've killed before. You've done murder for money, and it has tainted your spirit. Confession at the end of your life might make amends for some of your sins. Perhaps you won't burn, if you confess."

The terror on the man's face was real enough. "Fine. I was hired by the Lady Rikka to kill Belavalari Haythorne before she reached Arthes. If I could make it look like an accident, all the better. She did not tell me you would delay so long before beginning the return journey, or that it would be so damned difficult to get onto Turi land." He coughed, and a trickle of blood ran out the side of his mouth. "During the commotion of a few days past, we were able to sneak onto the land and wait, and since you two headed into the mountains, we have been following."

"Why?" Merin asked. "Why would Lady Rikka want Bela dead?"

"Didn't ask," the man on the ground said. "Don't care." He looked Bela in the eye, and she saw death there. Death and fear. "If you do not die, she will take her anger out on my family. I have a wife. I have children. I'm sorry," he said weakly. "I'm very . . ."

With the last of his strength, the dying man burst up and grabbed Bela's shirtfront. He yanked at her, and he screamed as he ran toward the rock's edge.

And then he jumped. Bela's feet came out from under her, and she felt only air and a heart-stopping fear.

THE failed assassin's final act took Merin by surprise. In a split second, the man went over the edge, taking Bela with him.

Merin was pulled along just as she was, thanks to the rope that bound them, but he dug in his feet and held on to the braided rope with both hands, dropping his sword to the ground. Near the precipice he latched onto a protruding rock, waiting for the force of Bela's fall to pull at him, to try to yank him with her as she dropped. The sharp edge of the rock cut his hand, but he held on.

He was not pulled over the edge; the pressure that had dragged him this far ceased abruptly. Merin had a horrific vision of the rope that connected them coming undone so that Bela dropped to her death. After all, it was made of nothing more than fabric. Red, black, and white. It was not meant to hold the weight of a woman who dangled over the side of a mountain.

Bela deserved better than such an end. She should live to be an old woman surrounded by children and grandchildren, she deserved to live her life happy and wonderfully different and defiant. She deserved happiness.

He was heartened by the curses which reached his ears, and by the fact that while he was supporting Bela's weight, she was obviously not free-falling down the mountain.

Sitting up carefully and keeping one arm around the rock for support, Merin glanced over the edge. Bela hung there, just a few feet away, holding onto a small protrusion in the side of the mountain. The man who had pulled her to the ledge and beyond lay far below, dead and broken. Merin tried not to look at that body and imagine Bela lying there, but it was difficult. It could've been her. It might still be her, if he was not careful.

She looked up and caught his eye. "Cut the rope."

"I will not," he said, holding on with all he had.

"If I fall, you might be pulled down with me!" she argued.

"Then don't fall," he said almost calmly.

Bela was stubborn, as usual. "Kitty!" she screamed. "Cut the rope that binds me to this stubborn man. Now!"

The sword, lying behind him where it had fallen when the attacker had pulled Bela to the edge, remained silent.

Merin turned all of his attention to getting Bela up and out of danger. If she could continue to support some of her weight by holding on to the side of the rock wall, he could pull her up and over the edge in short order. He dug in his feet and pulled. Out of the corner of his eye, he could see that Kitty's grip shone bright.

Save her.

"I'm trying," Merin said anxiously.

We need her. You need her. The world needs her.

That was taking things a bit too far. Maybe Kitty needed Bela—maybe he did, too. But the world?

There is much you do not yet know.

Of course there was. What else was new?

Merin ignored the interfering sword and gave all his attention to pulling Bela up to him. He drew her up a short way, and she was able to grab on to another protrusion in the rock. Bela was not very far down—the length of the rope prevented a distance of more than a few feet—and she had a hold on the mountain and would not let go. He pulled, she climbed. In a matter of minutes that seemed like hours, she was hauling herself over the edge and onto solid ground.

Merin pulled her the rest of the way and drew her into his arms, yanking her close and holding her so that their beating hearts pounded against one another. So close. He had come so damn close to watching her die.

Eventually Bela spoke. "Blast, Merin, why didn't you cut the damn rope?"

"You don't know me at all, if you think I could do that."

"But . . ."

"Would you?" he interrupted harshly. "If I had been dangling over the side of the mountain and you were up here, would you have cut the rope?"

She sighed in evident resignation. "Never."

"Then you should not expect less of me."

They sat there for a long while, panting and clinging to one another, both of them fighting off the images of what might have been. It was Bela who spoke first.

"I knew there was a good reason I didn't want to go to Arthes." She was slightly breathless. "People there want to kill me. Who the hell is Lady Rikka?"

Merin drew away slightly, but he did not let Bela go. "She was once married to Emperor Sebestyen, the current emperor's father."

"What does that have to do with me?"

"I don't know." He smoothed away a strand of misbehaving red-brown hair.

Bela grabbed on to the rope that bound them together— the rope that had saved her life—and ran her fingers along a frayed portion where the rope had scraped against rock.

"Thank goodness the cord didn't break," Merin said, trying to hide the absolute terror that washed through him at the very thought.

"It is a strong rope, as the bonds of marriage are meant to be strong. Everlasting," she added. "Indestructible."

She lifted her head and looked him in the eye. "I'm

sorry I tricked you," she said. "I never should've lied to you, I never should've forced you into a marriage you didn't even understand just so I could have what I wanted. What I did was terribly selfish and childish, and if I had it to do over again . . ."

Merin silenced Bela with a kiss which quickly turned deep and desperate. He wasn't sorry she'd tricked him; he wasn't sorry they were bound together. If he could do it all over again, he would do very little differently.

When the kiss ended, they were both breathless again.

"We still have a short way to travel before we reach the place where Clyn found Kitty," Bela said, in an obvious attempt to divert Merin and dismiss the kiss. Something about the power of the moment made her nervous. Was she afraid to get what she said she most wanted?

"Are you ready to resume the journey?" he asked.

She nodded, and together they rose to their feet. Merin glanced at the bodies. There was no way to bury the men who had died, not here where there was no dirt to be dug. He did not have the time nor the supplies to build a proper funeral pyre. They had died in an act of violence and evil, and so he had few qualms about leaving them to rot where they lay.

Bela retrieved Kitty and stored her properly. Merin did the same with his weapon, and they resumed their expedition. No, their *quest*. He had no idea what awaited them at the site of Kitty's discovery. Perhaps answers to all their questions were waiting to be found. Perhaps they would find nothing at all. No, Kitty's words hinted at something momentous. *The world needs her.*

Merin suspected he would find more than answers on this journey. Perhaps he would find a wife. A true wife, a woman he could keep forever. Such a discovery would change everything in his life, if not in the world. He couldn't very well choose to keep a woman intended for the emperor and then expect to retain his position in Arthes. And did he want to retain his position? Had he truly been content for the past six years?

As they turned onto another rocky trail, he wondered if he would still feel this way when the shock and horror of seeing Bela hanging from a mountain ledge faded.

SAVYN lay on his back, eyes open to see nothing but darkness before him.

They had decided to remain in this hut until he was at least somewhat recovered. No, that was not right. Lady Leyla had decided that they would remain here. It was right that she make the important decisions, he supposed, as she was a lady intended for the emperor and he was a lowly craftsman.

Still, something in him rebelled at the way she was taking care of him, the way she dribbled water into his mouth, the way she tended and fussed over him. She had changed the bandage on his head, she'd clucked over him like a mother hen. It was not right. He had intended to care for her, to protect her, and yet she had been the one to get rid of Trinity and now she was caring for him.

He was useless, and would forever be so if his sight did not return.

Savyn could smell Leyla as she neared him, and the scent was sweet and arousing and familiar. He could hear the rustle of her skirt as she knelt beside him, and the sound was comforting and wonderfully near. "I found some dried meat in Trinity's saddlebag," she said, her whispering voice soft as a spring breeze and just as welcome.

Unbidden, he had a startlingly clear vision of Leyla naked and spread before him. In this mental picture she smiled and beckoned him to come to her. She smelled just as sweet as she did at this moment. Her voice was just as welcome.

He shook off the fantasy before he gave himself away with the natural reaction of his body.

"Have you eaten?" he asked.

"Not yet."

"I will not eat until you do."

She sighed and settled more comfortably beside him. "You are so stubborn," she said, but he heard her take a bite. He smelled the meat, and it made his empty stomach rumble. "There are quite a few supplies in Trinity's bags," she said between the first bite and the second one. She placed a broken bit of the meat to his lips, and he opened his mouth to accept it. "Weapons, of course, but also coins and a change of clothing and a razor and a goodly supply of a traveler's food. Meat and biscuits, mostly, but there are also a few apples. He left his flint behind, too."

The food that hit Savyn's stomach was welcome, but he found he could not eat very much. Neither could Leyla, apparently. She sat beside him and talked, but she didn't eat much.

"We could stay here for a while," she said. "Until you're better, at least. Once your sight returns . . ."

"What if it doesn't?" he asked sharply. "I have never heard of a blind wheelwright or a sightless swordmaker. The only blind man I ever saw was a beggar. Is that what I will become if the world stays dark?"

Leyla placed a soft hand on his rough cheek, and he almost buckled with the pleasure of that simple touch. "You will not become a beggar. Not only is it not in your nature, I will not allow it to happen."

"Am I supposed to allow you to take care of me for the rest of my days?"

"If necessary, yes," she responded.

Savyn reached up and found Leyla's delicate wrist with his fumbling hand. He held on to her and guided her palm to his mouth, where he kissed it as if he had that right. She tasted as familiar as she smelled. "I will not allow you to care for me," he whispered. "I would prefer to beg, or to die."

"Don't say that," she whispered, and she did not jerk her hand away, as he had thought she might.

"This is wrong," he said darkly.

"Yes, it is," she agreed too calmly. "But I have faith that your sight will return. I heard of such a case years ago. A man fell from the roof and hit his temple, much as Trinity hit yours. This man lost his sight for a time, but it eventually returned. Yours will, too." Finally he heard a hint of uncertainty in her voice. "I will have it no other way."

He had not been talking about his injury or his lost eyesight, but it was just as well that she believed that had been his meaning.

Savyn realized with a thump of his heart and a soaring of something bitter in his stomach that he loved Lady Leyla. He did not only admire her beauty and her kindness, he did not wish to protect her because she was of a powerful family from his village and had smiled at him when he'd been a child. Wrong as it was, impossible as it was, he loved her.

Would she laugh at him if he told her how he felt? No, he didn't think she would. She was not the kind of woman who would be cruel.

Not that it mattered. Savyn would not burden the woman he loved with the affections of a worthless blind man. Until and unless his sight returned, he would keep what he felt to himself.

Chapter Eleven

MERIN seemed to feel the energy as they approached the site where Clyn had found Kitty, just as Bela did. The sun shone a bit brighter, even though it was now hanging low in the western sky. The air that filled their lungs was cleaner. Crisper. And Kitty was happier. Her glow was bright; her hum, content.

Not long after leaving the site of the battle, they had come across a cold, rushing creek. It would be their last chance to bathe and to collect water before stopping here, on their way down the mountain. From that point on, the way was rocky and rough, so they had no choice but to stop for a short while and take advantage of the water source. They had bathed, accomplishing the chore quickly, as the water was so cold. They had drunk greedily and filled their waterskins, and then they had collected what wood they could carry. There were no trees, no fuel for a fire near their destination. They could not carry enough for more than a small fire, but perhaps that was all they'd need before they headed down the mountain again.

Bela led the way as they took their final steps toward their destination. She had been here once before, with Clyn, but at that time she had not felt this brilliant energy, shimmering and palpable. She had not felt Kitty's joy.

She came to a halt on a flat expanse of rock, her eyes on the low entrance to a cave that was little more than a hole in the rock wall. The cave was tiny; she had explored it briefly on her last visit and had not been comfortable in the dark confines for more than a few seconds. She wondered how Clyn had fit in there when he'd retrieved Kitty.

Bela pointed, and Merin nodded. They dropped their armloads of wood and Merin took a step toward the cave, but Bela delayed him with a tug on the rope which bound them. The braided rope was no longer crisply colored. The black was gray and frayed, the red was faded, and the white was turning an ugly gray, like muddy snow. And yet the meanings of those colors remained unchanged.

"Maybe we should wait until morning," she said. "It will soon be dark, and I really don't want to be in that tiny cave when the sun sets. Besides, it's colder this high on the mountain, and I think it would be a good idea to get the fire going before the sun is gone."

Merin looked dismayed. "We've come all this way, and you want to wait until morning?"

Bela shrugged her shoulders. "After we build a fire we can explore the immediate area, if you'd like, but I suggest that we save the actual exploration of the cave for morning, yes." She felt rather like a coward, which was odd for her. Kitty was too bright, too excited, as if she expected something momentous to happen here. Bela knew that once they found what they were looking for, her time with Merin would change. She liked having him all to herself, and wanted that to continue for a while longer. One more night. Just one.

"Did you and Clyn search far beyond this area when you were here?"

Bela shook her head. "No. He showed me where he'd found Kitty, I poked my head into the cave, and the next morning we left before the sun had fully risen."

Merin was obviously impatient, so Bela pointed upward. "There are more caves there. If we can get the fire going well before the daylight is gone, we can always search there."

"Yes," he said, sounding relieved to have a plan that would keep them both busy until night fell.

And when night fell . . . what then?

TRINITY had regained some of his senses when he ran across the family traveling in the opposite direction. He actually had no direction in mind. He stumbled along the road mindlessly, afraid of the sleep which brought such realistic nightmares. Afraid of the waking moments which were filled with hallucinations. No, not hallucinations. Memories. Memories so vivid they made him scream and weep.

He could not remember shedding a tear since he'd been a small boy, even though he had certainly had opportunity and reason since his mother both had saved and ruined him. Since the witch had cursed him, he'd shed many. How long had it been? A day? Two? A week? Time had no meaning, not for him, not anymore.

The family he passed had a wagon and two horses to pull it, and suddenly Trinity wanted to ride. His feet hurt. He was tired of walking. The family paid him little mind as he stepped into the grass to allow them to pass on the narrow road, but the woman did eye him suspiciously. He likely looked a mite rough at the moment, not at all his usual charming self.

After they passed, Trinity turned, and with the grace and skill he still possessed, he jumped into the moving wagon, sprinted past the three small, frightened children in the rear of the wagon, and pulled his knife, the only weapon he had left. It was soon at the throat of the man who held the reins.

"I need one of your horses," Trinity said, his voice rough and shaking, his eyes on the sharp blade which rested at the man's throat.

"Please, don't hurt us," the man said as he pulled on the reins and brought the team to a halt.

Trinity's hand began to shake. Behind him, children were crying. The woman who sat so close shook with fear. Her face had gone snow white. Trinity's trembling hand began to move away from the throat he had threatened, and there was nothing he could do to stop it. The pain that shot through his body was intense, it was bone deep and shattering, and unless he moved away, it would not stop.

"I don't want to hurt any of you," Trinity said, wondering if that statement would stop the pain. It did not. "I just need a horse!"

The woman seemed to sense his trepidation. Her fear faded; he could see the change on her face and in her calculating eyes, now that the blade was no longer near her husband's throat. "One horse alone cannot pull this wagon and all of us," she said. "We have a very long way to go." Her lips thinned. "Get out," she said. "Get out of our wagon and leave us alone."

Trinity turned his attention to the woman. He wanted to threaten her, but could not. She was harmless. She was a mother. She had never hurt anyone; somehow he knew it. The witch had made it clear that he could never again harm one such as her.

The husband and father, a smallish man who should have been of no concern, grabbed the back of Trinity's shirt. He stood abruptly, and with a grunt and a heave tossed the interloper over the side of the wagon. Trinity, knife still in hand, flew through the air for a moment and then landed on his back with a thud. The wagon took off, moving much faster than it had before, leaving him behind.

Before he'd been cursed—for the second time in his too-long life—he might've given chase, taken the wagon, and left the annoying family sitting on the side of the road, a bit worse for wear. But now he lay in the road with tears in his eyes, as past victims haunted and taunted him. It was as if they were with him, even though Trinity knew that if the people in the wagon turned, they would only see him on the road. No longer a threat. No longer a man. He was nothing more than a pathetic lump of muscles and skin, good for nothing. If he could kill himself, he would do so, but he had tried before and he knew he would be no more successful now than he'd been then.

With a flash of hope, Trinity wondered if the witch's curse had changed him somehow, if it had affected the original curse. He retrieved the knife which lay in the road nearby and sat tall, and without hesitation he swung the knife up and plunged the blade into his chest. It hurt, and he screamed as the sharp metal cut into his body, into his *heart*, and the blood poured. He yanked the blade out, and the deadly steel hurt as much leaving his body as it had entering.

The blood flow stopped too soon, and his body healed itself. He saw the broken skin come together, he felt the broken heart repair. No, he still could not die. The witch would not give him even that.

Since being shown his purpose, Trinity had dedicated himself to killing those whose time had come. If he were not paid to do the job, someone else would be. He could not save those who were meant to die, he could only send them on properly and quickly. He did not needlessly hurt people, not usually, but delivered quick and painless deaths. That was his reason for living; his purpose in life. And now that was gone.

All because he'd suffered a moment of weakness. He

had wanted softness in his life, even if it was not freely and lovingly given. He had craved the touch of a beautiful woman, and it had cost him all he valued in his pathetic life. Where was he to go now? What could he do?

Lying in the road stained with his own blood, watching the sun set, Trinity had a revelation. The witch had said he could never again harm an innocent, and he now knew that to be true. The most recent disastrous encounter had shown him that the curse was a strong one. He could never again take the life of, or even scratch, an innocent. Lucky for him, the world was filled with people who were not at all innocent.

And that class of people included the woman who had hired him, the woman who had sent him to kill Lady Leyla without informing him that his target was a witch.

MERIN lay as far from Bela as the rope would allow, which meant he was more off the blanket than on it. Neither of them slept; neither of them spoke. There was a new tension in the air, one he recognized too well. Did she? Did she know it was passion that danced between them and made this night unbearable?

Seeing her go over the edge of a cliff had made him look at everything in a new light. He had been willing to let her go, to hand her over to Jahn and then to watch her return to her people. He did not fear that the emperor would choose Bela for his bride. He'd spent enough time around the new emperor to know what kind of woman appealed. Simpering. Silent. Dressed in frills and feathers and too many jewels. Proper smiles. Ample curves. Soft whispers, when she did dare to speak.

Bela seemed to Merin to be the perfect woman in many ways, but she possessed none of the attributes Emperor Jahn desired.

Perfect woman. Ha! She was stubborn, she had lied to

him—in the past, he conceded—she would not be an obedient wife, would not be content to stay at home and cook
fine meals and tend babies and . . .

He had never wanted a wife like that. If he had, he
could've married years ago. Bela was who she was, and
could not be changed. He realized with unusual clarity that
he did not want her to change.

"You are too far away," she said. "Come closer."

"I should not."

"It's cold, even with the fire."

"It's not so cold," he said, ignoring the chill on his face
and hands.

"I can't sleep with you so far away," Bela continued.
"Our sagging bed always brings you close, whether you
wish to be close or not." There was a hint of humor in her
voice. "And now I cannot sleep without you near. I am cold
and I need your warmth. You have given it before, why not
now?"

"Things have changed."

"Have they?" Since he had made no move to slide closer
to Bela, she slipped across the blanket to be close to him.

"You know damn well they have."

"You have always wanted me," she said softly. "That
has not changed."

"No," Merin confessed through gritted teeth.

"Is it your resolve that has changed? Do you still intend
to present me to your emperor so that he might take what
you want?"

"Bela . . ."

"That word, the whisper of my name, it sounds very
much like a warning."

"Perhaps because it is a warning. If you don't stop
this . . ."

"What?" She came a tiny bit closer. Her foot slipped
slowly and decisively between his calves. "We'll end up
making love?"

"We'll end up having sex," he corrected. "There's no need to make it sound pretty, Bela." Was he feeling proprietary about Bela because he wanted her physically? Was that all this was? He had never been in such agony, but then it had been a long time since he'd been forced to deny himself what he wanted.

"You know I want more," she said. She lifted the rope that bound them and slowly ran her hand along the length. That did not help matters at all. "I could take my knife right now and cut this rope. I could call to Kitty and have her do it for me. And once that was done, you'd be stuck with me."

"For another three years," Merin added.

"Do you really think we could remain wed for another three years and not produce a child?" she asked.

"If you're here and I'm in Arthes, that will not be a problem."

"I would follow you, this time," Bela said sincerely. "I would follow you anywhere."

She would, too, just to be difficult.

"I will admit to having just a bit of worry about how this will work," she confessed.

Good. Worry was good.

"You gave me joy with your hands and it was very nice and made me want more, but I know very well how large you are, and I do wonder if you and I will fit properly without undue difficulty." She gave a soft sigh that almost undid him. "Yes, you are very large and I am not, so . . ."

Merin groaned. Bela could not have picked a more unfortunate statement at this point in the evening.

"Would it work properly?" she asked in a lowered voice.

"You know damn well that it would," he responded, more sharply than he had intended. "But, Bela, we are not . . ."

"If you could love me, we could have a good marriage," she said, ignoring him and slipping a bit closer. He felt her heat now, she was so near. "If you could love me, we could take on Nobel and the emperor and anyone or anything else that gets in our way. Nothing could defeat us, Tearlach Merin. Together we could be magnificent."

If she touched him, this would be over. He already felt as if he were about to break, about to fly into a thousand pieces. But she did not touch him, and he knew why.

The next move was his to make. It all began or ended here and now, and the choice was his.

BELA'S mouth was dry, and her heart was beating so hard she was amazed Merin didn't seem to hear it. She was tempted to jump on his body, but she was attempting to show a bit of finesse about this. Besides, she had jumped on him once before, and he was bound to remember that night if she did so again. What happened next was entirely up to him. *Love me*, she thought, trying to send a message to him without spoken words. *Love me the way I love you.*

Merin rolled over to face her, and she'd come so close, his move put them nose to nose. She ran her foot along his leg, just a little. "I don't want to lose you," he said, sounding only slightly reluctant. "Not to a mountain, not to an emperor . . . not to any other man. I didn't plan for this to happen."

"Nor did I." She smoothed back a strand of curling hair so she could see his face more clearly in the moonlight and the flicker of what was left of the fire.

"I will lose my position in Arthes, most likely. Whether you're his choice or not, Emperor Jahn will not take kindly to me marrying one of his potential brides."

"We are already married," she reminded him.

"Not properly," he said.

"We're married enough for me," she said with a smile. Merin was not going to disappoint her. He was not going to turn his back on her, not tonight. "Will you suffer greatly if you are no longer a great general to the emperor of Columbyana?"

"No," he answered quickly and surely. "It's time for me to leave Arthes. Past time, to be honest. There's nothing for me there."

"There is everything for you here," she whispered.

"I know," he answered, his voice even softer than hers.

"I love you," she said. "Do you love me?"

"I believe I do." Merin sounded bemused and befuddled by the confession, as if he had never before thought himself capable of love.

"That is not a very convincing declaration of love," she teased.

"How about this, then?" He took her hand and guided it to his trousers, where she could feel the incredible hardness of his very large penis. She had not been lying to him when she'd revealed her doubts about their physical compatibility.

And yet : . . he said it would work just fine, and she believed him. She had come to trust him as she trusted no one else. "That is a sign of your physical desire, not love," she said as she stroked lightly.

"You know me not at all," he said, moving his mouth to her throat.

Lovely. "I want to know you," she said, her eyes drifting closed. "What do I need to know of you now?"

"If I did not love you, I would've seduced you long ago to assuage my physical desire, then I would've cut the rope and left. I would've told the emperor that you were already married, without bothering to tell him that your absent husband was his own general and next in line for Minister of Defense."

Bela laughed. "You would not have done such a thing. You might've wanted to, the thought might've crossed your mind, but you are a good man, Merin. You do not take that which is not yours to take."

"Are you mine to take?"

"I am," she breathed.

Hard as he was, willing as she was, she rather expected he'd loosen a few bits of clothing and fill her aching body quickly. But as usual, he surprised her. Taking his time, he undressed them both. They lay upon one blanket and covered themselves with the other, blocking out the chill of the night as they created their own heat. Now and then he stopped to kiss or stroke a newly exposed bit of her flesh, or to introduce her hand to a bit of his flesh. Oh, what fine control he must have! If she had taken charge, they'd be finished by now!

How lovely that she had not taken charge. What pleasure she would've missed.

The covering blanket fell and cool air washed over her bare body, but Bela felt decidedly hot. Her body trembled gently, and she ached. Her breasts and her loins were heavy, and she literally hurt for Merin. With every caress of his hand, with every kiss, she was more frantic, and yet she also appreciated the beauty of anticipation. There was pleasure in this intense wanting, especially knowing that soon she could have all she wanted from him.

Soon she would have everything.

Merin spread her legs and stroked her, and she felt herself grow wet and even more ready than before. The ache became more intense, more centered, until she almost could not breathe. He hovered above her, blocking her view of the moon with a mass of dark curls and a face she could not see well.

And then he filled her, slowly and carefully, and Bela found a new bliss. It took a moment, it took great care, but yes, he gave and she accepted, and he fit quite well inside her. *Quite* well. He moved slowly and carefully, in and out. She gasped and grabbed at his shoulders, startled at the sensations he aroused. Her hips lifted off the ground to bring him deeper, more fully inside her.

His movements were careful and steady, thrusting and withdrawing, stroking her inner muscles until she thought she would scream. Soon his movements quickened and so did hers, and then she broke, and a scream was torn from her throat.

Pleasure; heat; passion; love. She had it all. Merin found his own release, and she felt it. She felt his shudder, and deep inside she felt the spurting release of his seed. Would it catch so soon? She did not know and did not care. Tonight there was only pleasure and love and a future of endless possibilities.

"So," she said dreamily. "We are truly man and wife now."

"We are," Merin responded, his voice as strained as hers. Strained in a lovely way.

"I will take your name, I suppose," she said, wrapping her arms around his sated, bare body. "Belavalari Merin. Bela Merin. Mrs. General Merin. I suppose I should call you Tearlach, in that case."

"You may call me anything you wish."

"You're very agreeable at the moment," she teased.

"I am."

"So, which of us will cut this cord which binds us?" She reached for her knife, which lay with her clothes not so far away.

Merin lifted his head and looked down at her as he clamped his hand over her wrist. It was too dark for her to see his expression well, as the fire had died down considerably, but she could see that he did not smile, and Bela suffered a moment's horror. Now that his body was satisfied, did Merin no longer want her? Did he wish the undoing of their marriage to continue? If there was no child, then the marriage could still be dissolved.

"We both gave our word that we would not cut this rope while away from the village," he said, sounding annoyingly sensible.

"But everything has changed since we made that promise," she argued.

"Tired of having me so close?"

Bela sighed before answering. "No, of course not."

"We will cut the cord together," Merin said in a firm voice, "and we will do it in front of your family so they know there was no deception this time. There will be no whispers among the clan, no speculations on how the cutting came about or which of us did the deed."

It was true that if they descended from the mountain unbound, some would say she'd done the cutting herself in order to get what she wanted. Again. Or they'd say that there had been an accident, and poor General Merin was only making the best of a sad situation. People would talk. They always did. "I don't care what people say."

"I do," Merin whispered. "I care very much."

He did love her. In years to come he would love her more. She'd make it be so.

He didn't move away from her, nor did he reach for their clothes. He did pull the blanket over them to catch and hold their heat. In a little while he began to kiss her again, to run his tongue along her sensitive nipples and to kiss her throat and her mouth. His tongue was lovely. His hands were bold and certain. They made love again, more slowly this time, and again Bela's scream of pleasure shook the mountain.

MERIN slept so deeply, he did not dream. He did not wake constantly to look at the woman beside him. The sky was gray with creeping morning light when he woke to find Bela's hands on his body. Soon she was atop him, wrapped around him, riding him slowly and with an open and joyous passion that only made him love her more. There was no other woman on the earth like this one. She did not rush impatiently to the end, but rode him slowly and with an unexpected languidness, as if she did not want this to end. The day came alive, and she closed her eyes against the light. Her rhythm did not change, but remained slow and sensuous. Was she truly as flawless as he believed her to be, or did he see her through love-clouded eyes?

Soon he forgot everything but her body and his, her need and his. He closed his eyes, too, and gave everything he was over to physical sensation, to his pleasure and hers.

Bela's wide smile, as she dropped onto him sated and happy, was catching. Merin found himself smiling as he ran his fingers through her hair, as he possessively caressed her bare hip. She did not lie there long, however, but soon jumped from him and reached for their clothes. When she ran across a piece of his clothing which had been mixed with her own, she tossed it to him.

Dressing while attached to another person wasn't easy, but they had learned how to make it work. In a matter of moments they were fully clad, shirts to boots.

Clothed and ready to meet the day, they turned toward the small cave. They left their packs at the rugged campsite, piled atop their blankets, as they did not intend to remain in the small crevice very long and there was nothing among their supplies they were likely to need. Still, since yesterday's attack Merin did not want to be too far from his weapon. He strapped his sword onto his back, and Bela carried Kitty.

Kitty's grip began to glow as they neared the cave, as if the sword was anxious, as if there was something here. Something important.

Merin knelt down and peeked inside the cave, shifting his body aside so the light could enter and he could see more clearly. The cave was low, and it was impossible to tell how deep it might be, as it was shadowed at this time of day. Early afternoon would be the best time to see deep into the cave, he imagined. That was when the sunlight would shine directly inside.

But they did not need the sun. They had Kitty.

Merin moved forward on his belly. Bela and Kitty were right behind him. Just when he was certain he had reached the far end of the crevice, another segment was revealed. The small cave was much deeper than he'd thought was possible. They continued to scoot forward. Farther back, the cave actually got larger, higher, and a bit wider.

"I think this might be the wrong cave," Bela said nervously. "The one where Clyn found Kitty was not this deep, I'm sure of it."

Who could be sure of anything where Kitty was concerned?

Finally, Merin saw the end of the cave. Kitty's grip glowed brightly, and when her illumination hit the rear wall, Merin caught a glimpse of what looked to be a crude drawing. No, not a drawing, he decided as he slipped forward and looked more closely. A carving, one that appeared to be very old.

"There's something here," he said as he scooted closer. Bela was right behind him; necessarily so, as they remained tied together. Not for long, perhaps, but still physically bound. "I'd like a closer look." He moved up onto his knees. His body occasionally blocked the light, and without the light from Kitty's grip the images that had caught his attention disappeared completely. "Did you see these the last time you were here?" he asked, turning about to look at Bela.

"No," she whispered. "I don't think this is the right cave. Maybe I remembered wrong."

"I doubt that," Merin muttered.

Bela craned her neck to look around him. "What is it, exactly?"

"I can't tell." It was frustrating. The closer he moved, the more he blocked the light. Just when he was about to make sense of the cave drawing, it disappeared. He was close enough to touch the back wall now, and yet he could see nothing. He rubbed his hand against the wall and felt nothing: no indentions in the rock, no crevices in the stone, even though he knew they were there.

Suddenly the cave was filled with brilliant light. The burst of illumination came from Kitty's crystal, he knew, but he did not have time to dwell upon the why for long, as he became lost in the image before him.

The people in the carving were crudely drawn. There was a man with curling hair, and a woman dressed in men's clothing. They were connected by a string from one waist to the other, and by a sword which hovered in the air between them. Merin studied the carving closely. There was discoloration around the cuts in the stone, and the carving had been dulled and softened by time. Lots of time, if his estimation was correct.

And yet . . .

"That's *us*," Bela said.

"I believe it is."

"How is that possible?"

"It's not," he whispered.

The cave was ominously silent, as was all of Forbidden Mountain, and Merin suddenly realized how far he and Bela had traveled into the mountain to find this impossible carving. Backing out, which was their only choice, would take some time. He'd thought the situation could get no worse when Kitty's light went out, the mountain rumbled ominously, and pebbles began to fall all around them.

Chapter Twelve

SAVYN knew it was morning because the warmth of the sun touched his face as he felt his way to the door of the hut where Trinity had attacked and blinded him. Sunlight came through the fallen side of the shelter, as well as through the door. The room was warm, and would be warmer late in the day, after the sun had been shining on the roof for many hours.

He knew Lady Leyla was here because he could smell her sweet scent, he could hear the soft swish of her skirt as she moved.

In their days here he had memorized the dimensions of and obstacles in the very small hut enough so that he no longer tripped and fell with every other step. He could make his way from their improvised bed to the door in four steps. His hand found the rusted door handle. He had to pull hard to make the ill-fitting door move, and when he did so, he felt the wash of warm spring air on his face. There was no hint of light, however. He wished every morning for that light to be there, he prayed for a sign that he would heal and recover his sight.

Every morning he was disappointed.

His head hurt all the time, sometimes sharply, at other times dully. He always felt as if his skull was not large enough to contain what was inside it. The blow to his head had done more than draw blood and leave him senseless for a while. It had damaged him deeply, in places he could not see or even imagine. When the pain left, would his sight return? Would the pain ever leave?

In their days here Leyla had kept herself busy making the place habitable and taking care of him. She'd even shaved his face with the razor she'd found in Trinity's supplies. They had several days' worth of food still, thanks to the assassin's saddlebags, so that was not a worry. Not yet. There was a creek a short walk from the hut, just inside the forest on the other side of the road, so they had water for cleaning and for drinking. He was sorry—deeply sorry— that Lady Leyla had to be the one to fetch that water, day after day.

Savyn felt as if he were caught in a vicious cycle he did not quite understand. This was not home, and yet it felt as if it could be. His sight was gone, and he kept hoping that Leyla was right and it would soon return, but so far he had been disappointed in that respect.

At night he and Leyla shared a bed of blankets—blankets taken from Trinity's supplies—on a rough floor. The blankets were laid out in the part of the hut that was built into the hill, where the occasional rains that came at night could not touch them. The accommodations were much more common and rough than a lady of her station was accustomed to, and yet Leyla seemed to sleep well enough. He did not. It wasn't just the pain that kept him awake. When he slept, he was plagued with dreams he should not have. Even in his waking hours, his mind went to places it should not go.

Savyn heard Leyla approaching long before she placed her soft hand on his back. "I have been thinking," she said softly. "If someone sent Trinity to kill me, as he said, then I am not safe. I can't return to Childers. Someone might be waiting for me there."

"I'm sorry," he mumbled.

"I'm not." Her hand felt so comfortable against his back, so right and comforting. "That place was never home for me. Well, I won't say never, but rarely. I was only occasionally happy there."

"Yours was not a marriage of love," he said, somehow knowing the words were true.

"No, it was not," she said flatly. "I was sold to the highest bidder, bargained for as one might bargain for a fine horse."

The wrongness of it cut to Savyn's heart. "I did not know."

"No one did, until now."

His own mother had not been perfect, God rest her soul, but she would never have allowed such an offense. "Surely your family objected to such an arrangement. Your mother and father, were they living when this injustice occurred?"

"Who do you think did the selling?" Leyla asked sharply. Then her hand rubbed against his spine, her fingers tracing and dancing there. "I'm sorry. I did not mean to lose my temper and get into a subject best left to lie. How did we get to this conversation? Oh, yes, I do not want to return to Childers." Again her hand settled against the small of his back, where it remained still and wonderfully soft. "I could change my name and settle elsewhere, anywhere. No one there would ever have to know of my gift, and I could make my way . . . somehow."

"You could marry again," Savyn said bitterly. "You could choose your own rich man this time, and . . ."

"No," she said sharply, dropping her hand. "I won't. I'll

beg, if I have to. To marry for comfort would be no better than to sell myself all over again. I am a decent cook, you know, and I'm handy with a thread and needle, and I would make a very decent governess."

Leyla would be wonderful with children, a thought which made Savyn wonder why she'd never had any of her own. She was a witch, after all. Perhaps she had made use of a potion to keep from catching the child of a man who had purchased her. He had heard of such concoctions, though they were not commonly used.

"In any case, I don't know where to go just yet," she said, her voice calmer. "A small village, perhaps. Someplace where I can . . . can . . ."

"Hide," Savyn supplied sharply.

"Yes," she whispered. "A place where I can hide."

She made the prospect sound lovely, not at all frightening. He would love to go with her, to hide from the world in her company, but what good would a blind man do Leyla in her new life? Then again, how could he find his way home? Search as he might, he could not find many of his own happy memories from home. There were confusing snippets of something he could not quite grasp, as if his happiness there had been elusive. Secret. Clandestine.

Again an image of Leyla, naked and smiling with her mass of dark hair curling behind her, came to his mind. Just as quickly, it was gone.

"For now we will stay here," she said. "You need time to heal, and I need time to decide what comes next for me, where I might go. The hut is not the best of lodgings in Columbyana, but I have cleaned it thoroughly, and until winter arrives, it will offer sufficient shelter. I believe I have scared away the rodents that used to live here." There was a hint of humor in her voice. "We know there's a village not far away. As soon as you're better, I'll take

some of Trinity's coin there and buy supplies. There was
quite a lot of coin in his saddlebags," she added, sounding
pleased.

"What if I don't heal?" Savyn asked. He closed his eyes
and drank in the warmth of the sun, if not the light.

"You will." Leyla sounded determined. She was confident, even if he was not.

Savyn turned to face her. She was so near, it was as if he
could feel her skin almost touching his. Almost. With one
hand he found her face without fumbling, as if he knew
exactly how and where to reach. He cupped her cheek in
that hand and lowered his head to kiss her.

He had no right, but he wanted the kiss more than he'd
ever wanted anything in his life. Her mouth met his softly
and willingly, and oh, it was like coming home. It was like
claiming the warmth and love of the home neither of them
possessed, with a touch of their lips. They touched nowhere
else, but she did not pull away, she did not move back. Not
even when their tongues danced so well, as if they searched
for one another after a long time apart.

She should be surprised and shocked by his boldness,
but did not seem to be anything more than welcoming.

He ended the kiss and threaded his fingers through her
hair. "Leyla, why do I feel so certain we have kissed before?"

BELA held her breath. It seemed that her heart stopped,
and then restarted with a vengeance. The earth shook, the
walls crumbled, and the image of her and Merin and Kitty
fell to dust, revealing an opening which had long been
closed.

Merin wasted no time scurrying forward, as the passage
behind them closed in. The mountain shifted, and rock
cracked and fell. Thanks to Kitty they were not lost in

darkness, and it soon seemed that the way before them opened wider and longer as if by magic. Behind them, the cave continued to fall in. Bela felt the dust and pebbles at her feet, and she did not dare to look back.

They were well trapped, unless there was another way out.

The farther they scurried into the mountain, the harder Bela's heart pounded. How would they escape this? And what if they didn't? What if there was no way out? Had she just found love only to lose it? Would she and Merin be buried under a mountain of rock?

Eventually the rumbling stopped, and pebbles and dust stopped raining down upon them. The passageway ahead grew wider and higher. And sturdier, thank the heavens. Soon they were both standing tall, walking toward the center of the mountain, since there was no walking back.

It took several minutes for Bela to realize that Kitty no longer glowed. No, the light that illuminated their way came from the walls around them, walls which glistened with streaks of crystal like that from which Kitty's grip was made.

Merin took her hand, and she clasped it tight. There was a brighter light at the end of the tunnel, as if daylight awaited them there. No, not daylight. The glow was more like moonlight: softer than the sun, more blue and crisp than yellow and warming. There was no warmth in this glow. Soon Bela heard the rush of what sounded like water. Flowing, strong, abundant water.

"An underground river," Merin said, relief in his voice. "That's good news; the water must leave here somehow."

"I would imagine so."

"We're safe, for now," he said with confidence, "and we will find a way out, I promise you."

"Merin," Bela said, not yet entirely accustomed to calling him Tearlach, given name or not, truly married or not, "if I must be trapped inside a mountain with anyone, I'm glad it's you."

He squeezed her hand but kept his gaze straight ahead, focused on the glow that pulled them forward.

"Well, Kitty," Bela whispered, "What do you have to say for yourself now?"

Home.

They stepped from the stone corridor into a cavern aglow with the stone which had lined the walls on their pathway to this place. Even the river which ran through the cavern in a twisting S-shape glimmered, thanks to the crystals beneath the surface. The grotto was vast, and it sparkled as if it were the mountain's personal jewel. The ceiling was high above, much higher than she'd thought possible, and larger crystals grew there, seeming to drip from the rock that made up the walls, the floor, and the ceiling.

"It's beautiful," Bela whispered.

"Yes," Merin agreed absently, and then he walked toward the nearest section of wall to his left, where more carvings drew the eye.

Bela held her breath. The figures which had been carved into the cavern walls looked ancient—worn and faded and even chipped away here and there—and judging by the number of them in this chamber, they had taken many years to complete. The crude depictions wrapped around the cavern, filling the walls.

Like the carving they had seen before the cave-in, the first image depicted her and Merin, side by side and connected by a string that spanned waist to waist. Kitty hovered above their heads. The images that followed had Bela holding her breath, much as she had when the mountain had rumbled.

The carvings primitively depicted the two of them on their knees surrounded by plants, perhaps weeding. There was more. Much more. They were sleeping side by side in a ridiculously exaggerated sagging bed. Kissing. Fighting . . . climbing a mountain. *This* mountain. There was a scene depicting a fight with three men, men who were obviously unimportant because they were little more than stick figures, and then one of Bela going over the side of the mountain and hanging by a thread, saved only by Merin's strength and her own determination.

Then there was a crude depiction of what had happened last night and this morning . . .

Merin did not speak for a while, as he studied the images. His face grew stonier and stonier. His lips thinned. "Bela, tell me you didn't see these carvings when you were here before."

"I did not!"

He looked at her with disbelieving eyes. "How is this possible?"

"I don't know," she said. "How is Kitty possible? How is any magic possible?"

Merin knew of enchantment. He had fought demons in years past, with the power of good magic on his side.

Bela's eyes lingered on the depiction of this morning's encounter—a crude depiction of her astride him. She almost recoiled. Her breasts were not that large, and they did not sag! Merin's softly curling hair did not stick out in all directions, either, and neither of them had legs quite so long in proportion to their bodies. His penis was more than large enough, but it was not *that* large. A few things were exaggerated, and that was as annoying as the impossible accuracy of the carvings.

"It seemed like an impulsive choice," she whispered. "To wake and climb upon you, to make love while the sun rose. And yet here . . . It looks as if neither of us had any choice when it comes to what brought us here." A crushing sadness fell upon her. Did this mean her love for

Merin wasn't real? That his love for her was somehow fabricated?

"Well, we do have a choice when it comes to where we go and what we do now," Merin said, his voice as hard as the stone which surrounded them.

He pointed, and Bela followed his direction. The next carving depicted them inside a crumbling cave, and from there the string of images went crooked; it drifted high and low and it curled. At first glance it looked as if they had three choices, and each choice would bring them to a different end.

LEYLA wanted, very badly, to lay Savyn upon the blankets which had become their bed and make love to him. She wanted to comfort him the only way she knew how, with her body, but to do so would undo all that she had sacrificed for him. She wanted Savyn to have a good life, free of his commitment to her, and for that to happen, she had to be willing to walk away, to let him go.

Most of all, she wanted him to see. She wanted him to smile again, to laugh, to *look* at her with eyes that smoldered.

Instead, she led him to the bed and told him to sit while she put together a crude and tasteless breakfast from what she'd found in Trinity's saddlebags. Hard biscuits, dried meat. The apples were already gone.

"I thought today I'd explore a bit and see if I can find some wild berries," she said, trying to inject a carefree tone in her voice. "It is the right season for redberries, and soon there should be blue, as well. It will be nice to have something to eat besides hard, dried food." All of it taken from an assassin's possessions. She did not add that point aloud, but the thought crossed her mind, and she imagined it crossed Savyn's as well.

"You said you were going to town to make some purchases when we found ourselves low on supplies." Savyn leaned against the wall and drew one long leg in, making himself as comfortable as possible in the small hut.

Leyla hesitated. She could not tell him that she wasn't ready to leave him alone or that she didn't think she could manage getting him to town. He had become comfortable enough in this small place, but to be out in the open, to travel, to be among strangers in his condition, would be confusing and frightening.

"I don't feel like going to the village today," Leyla said. "Maybe tomorrow, or the next day. There is no hurry."

"Are you afraid?" Savyn asked, his voice soft and kind.

"No," she said truthfully. She was not afraid for herself, at least.

"What if he's there? What if Trinity comes back for you? For us." It was evident in Savyn's voice that his concern was not for himself.

"He won't. Trinity is far from this place by now, I guarantee. And if by some chance he were to see me . . . he would not dare to harm me." In fact, he would likely run from her in terror.

If she'd known what the assassin had done to Savyn, she might've killed him on the road. She might've instructed him to take his own life. But she had not known, and perhaps that was just as well. A quick death was too good for one such as Trinity.

She sat beside Savyn, took his hand, and placed a bit of biscuit upon it. "Eat this first." The hard biscuit was followed by water from the dented tin cup he had been given by a farmer's wife so many days ago, then by dried meat and more water. She made him feed himself, this time she even made him lead the cup to his lips. There were a few missteps along the way, but eventually he did well. She hated the way his eyes remained dull and unfocused. She hated that he did not, could not, look at her.

Even after he was finished, Leyla remained sitting beside him, the plate and empty tin cup in her lap. Savyn breathed deeply once, then reached out and very accurately found and gripped her wrist. One sun-bronzed finger rocked against her pale skin, and she wondered if he could feel the increase in her pulse.

"The blow to my head did more than take my sight," he said, agony in his voice. "In my head I see things I should not see. Scents, sensations, visions—and they seem so real, even though they could not be. There were moments before I was hurt, I will admit, when I had thoughts I should not have had, but they were not like this. Those thoughts were not so real, so vivid. I think I must be going mad, Leyla. I think . . ." He dropped her wrist and withdrew, as much as was possible in the small space. "Never mind. My head aches all the time and I'm not thinking clearly. I'm confused and angry and reaching for something which could not possibly be real."

Leyla held her breath. He could not remember them! It was impossible. "What makes you say such a thing?" she asked, needing more information in order to know what he was seeing and sensing in his mind.

"It is unimportant. Berries," he said, the tone of his voice taking a sharp and oddly happy turn. "I would love to have a handful of redberries, if you can find some."

MERIN walked near the wall as he studied the carvings there. Thanks to the light given off by the crystals which filled the cavern, he could see the details well enough. *More* than well enough.

Had a powerful seer long ago seen the choices he and Bela would make, or had their choices been made for them? Had they been led to this point, or was this simply destiny?

No, not entirely destiny, not according to the stories on the cavern walls.

At least three outcomes were possible, from what he'd seen so far. One: He and Bela would die here. They'd confront one another in anger, sever the rope that bound them, and never find their way out of this mountain. Two: Still joined, they'd find their way out, following the river, and once they were back in the village, he'd cut the rope and ride away. Bela would remain behind. She would be taken by a man he assumed must be Nobel, though it was difficult to tell for sure. That man would take Kitty from Bela and kill her with her own sword.

The third scenario was more complex, more detailed. This was obviously where the artist who'd done this work had intended for them to go. The images were more detailed, and the string of depictions was longer than the other two sadly presented possibilities—which might be warnings as much as predictions, he decided.

Merin occasionally reached out to touch the images, wondering if they would disappear. He had seen much in his lifetime, so he should not be surprised by this turn of events. There were gaps, passages of time in the story where there was no clue as to what would happen, but the basics were clear, easy to read.

If they survived the challenges set for them, he and Bela would make a baby, and it was that child who would wield Kitty. It was that child, that *daughter*, for whom Kitty had been made. He had been right all along. The crystal grip had been fashioned for a woman. That woman was not Bela.

The story ended with the image of that girl, that woman, standing on a mountain with Kitty raised above her head. She was much like Bela in shape and size, but possessed a head of curling hair much like Merin's. The depiction was unsophisticated, but she was drawn as a strong woman, a warrior . . . a woman headed into battle.

Merin turned to Bela in anger. "You knew."

"I did not!"

"You've had Kitty in your possession for more than two years. Are you telling me she never told you that she was intended for your daughter? Our daughter?" The words tried to stick in his throat.

"Yes, I'm telling you exactly that," she said. "Really, Merin, do you think I want a daughter who's destined for battle? Do you think I want to make a child who will *need* Kitty? That means war, and war means suffering, and no mother wants that for her child, especially not a girl."

Merin narrowed his eyes. Bela would love to be a warrior, if the opportunity presented itself. She turned her back on all traditional female roles and embraced manly things. Would she not want the same for her daughter? "Do not lie to me."

"I'm not!"

He wanted to believe her, he wished to believe her, but their past history interfered. She had deceived him once before to get what she wanted. "Are you already with child? Is that why you seduced me last night and this morning, to make sure you caught the child before I saw all this?"

She gave him an incredulous look. "I seduced you?"

"Yes."

"Well, if I did, it was an incredibly easy seduction," she said sharply. "It's not as though you were not willing."

"I never said I was not willing."

"But you did say . . ."

They were playing out the most deadly scene on the cavern wall. "We cannot argue," Merin interrupted, taking the warning to heart. "Not now."

"You started it," Bela said sullenly.

"I apologize." Once they were out of here, they would finish the discussion. "Right now we need to concentrate on finding our way out of here. According to the drawing on the wall, we need to follow the river."

"How do you know the drawing is correct?" Bela sounded a bit panicked. "Do you truly believe our future is written in stone?"

Merin gave a wave of his hand. "Apparently so."

Bela pursed her lips and barely glanced at the cavern drawings.

"It will be all right," Merin said, not feeling the comforting words to the pit of his soul, as he should've. "Perhaps what's depicted on the wall has been right so far, to a point, but there are three possible futures awaiting us. Every choice we make changes what's to come, for better or for worse. We make our own future, Bela."

She looked him in the eye, and he saw fear and strength, determination and uncertainty. "I do love you," she said. "I believe what I feel is real, not . . . not magically thrust upon me so I can give birth to a little girl who will grow up to be a warrior." She shuddered. "But how can I know? How can either of us know that we've not been manipulated?"

"By Kitty?" Merin asked.

"By whatever makes Kitty live, yes," Bela said. "She speaks to us, she reads our minds. What if she also influences our thoughts and emotions in order to get what she wants? Our child?"

We need you both.

The declaration was for both of them, for Merin and for Bela, and both reacted to it strongly.

"Oh," Bela said flatly.

"What?" Merin asked.

"All this time, Kitty has been telling me that we need you. I thought that *we* included me, but I think all along she must've meant her and our daughter. They are the *we*."

"I once heard something similar from Kitty," Merin confessed, "and I suffered the same misinterpretation." When Bela had almost fallen to her death, Kitty had been frantic. *We need her. The world needs her*, Kitty had said.

Apparently the world needed Bela so she could give birth to a warrior who would one day take Kitty into battle.

He almost snorted as he studied the vast, beautiful, and potentially deadly cavern. "We have been led here. Every step, every seemingly random decision, they have all brought us here." Merin instinctively pulled Bela into his arms, as the crystals around them pulsed and whispered. They emitted not words, but instead gave off a harmonious, rhythmic chant that seemed to be in time with his heartbeat.

"We can change our destiny, Bela," he said with conviction. "We do not have to be led any longer. We can search inside ourselves for what's real and what's not."

"How?" she asked, sounding heartbroken and uncertain. "After seeing all this, after knowing what they want from us, how do we make our own future?"

Merin took a deep breath. "To start, we leave Kitty here."

Chapter Thirteen

✳

SAVYN stood in the doorway and listened as Leyla crossed the road and stepped into the woods to search for berries. He used all his functioning senses to determine which way she was walking, and how fast. He heard her stop once, and surmised that she had turned to look at him before she stepped so deep into the forest that she could no longer see him. Just in case she was watching, he lifted his hand and waved, assuring her that he would be fine alone.

Even when he could no longer hear her movements, he continued to stand in the doorway for a while longer, listening to the sounds of the day: to the flutter and caw of birds, the buzz of insects, the chirping and rustling of small critters which scurried in the forest. The sun warmed his face, and Savyn was glad that he could feel something to remind him that it was daytime, that the sun shone and the world moved on.

When he was certain Leyla no longer watched, Savyn patted the biscuits he'd slipped into his pocket earlier and he stepped outside, taking care with the first uneven step.

He hadn't taken four steps away from the hut before he fell, stumbling over his own two feet, and landed facedown in the dirt. Since the stormy night when he'd been hurt, Leyla had always assisted him when he'd left the shelter, but he could not rely on her to lead him forever. Could not and would not.

The mishap made him angry, but he'd been angry with himself a lot in the past few days. Angry for not dying, angry for not seeing, angry most of all for having ridiculous fantasies about a woman he could never possess.

If he wasn't near Leyla, if he could not smell her scent and hear her voice, maybe the fantasies would stop. The imagining became more vivid with every passing day, and the dreams . . . the dreams were remarkable and torturous. In his dreams he could see. Most wonderfully of all, he could see her. The dreams were so blasted real, and he could not shake them as long as he lived in her presence, as long as he could smell and hear and touch her.

Besides, Leyla would not move on as she should while she was burdened with a blind man. She needed to leave this godforsaken hut, she needed to change her name and start again in a place where no one knew her, where no one wanted to hurt her. Where he could not find her, if he ever suffered the foolish notion to try.

Eventually Savyn found his way to the road. He stumbled a time or two but did not fall again. With every step the trek became a bit less strenuous. He did not turn toward town, but made a sharp right so that he was backtracking, heading back the way he and Leyla had come. He did not remember every small detail of their journey along this road, but he knew that the thick growth of ancient trees to his left continued for quite a distance, and if he heard anyone coming, he could hide there.

Savyn shuffled his feet along the road for a while, afraid of falling again even though he was finding his stride and balance. By the slant of the warmth on his face he knew where the sun was, and he oriented himself toward it. When he drifted too far to one side, as he occasionally did, he could tell by the change in the texture beneath his feet and quickly righted himself, sometimes holding his hand out to feel the feathery tops of the tall grass.

It wasn't long before he questioned his decision to run. He'd never felt so isolated in his life, and there had been times when he'd known he'd had no one but himself to rely on in this harsh world. He was twenty-five years old, and yet except for his fanciful infatuation with Leyla, he could not recall ever being in love. That was not normal, he was quite sure. There were many pretty, unattached women in Childers, and several of them had made themselves all but available to him. For some reason they paled in his memory, as they had paled when they'd approached him. They did not have much appeal for him, and he could not understand why.

For Savyn, sex was a subject of fantasy, not a reality. He had not lain with any of those women, not even the boldest among them. And yet in his dreams of Leyla, in his fantasies, he could well imagine every sensation, every joy, as if it were real, as if he had somehow known those pleasures in reality.

He sometimes imagined himself in love with Lady Leyla, when he allowed his mind free rein. She was perfect, in his eyes—in his mind. What woman could compare to her? None, he was sure, but what good did that do him? Fantasies were all he was allowed. Fantasies should not be enough for any man.

Frightened as he was, uncertain as he was, he did not once seriously think of turning back. He did not know how he would live, or even *if* he would live, but he was certain to the pit of his soul that he had to leave Leyla behind. For her sake and for his.

*   *   *

BELA was certain Kitty would put up a fuss at Merin's suggestion, but that did not happen. The enchanted sword remained oddly silent as Merin proposed that she be left here in the cavern as they made their escape. Of course, Bela had seen what Kitty could do, and for all she knew, the magical weapon was capable of making her way out of this cavern and down the mountain on her own, just as she had made her way from Clyn's house to Bela's bed-chamber.

But if that was the case, why hadn't the sword appeared at Bela's side years ago? Why had it been necessary for Clyn to find the weapon and carry it down the mountain before Bela heard the crystal voice which had become so familiar to her? Her fingers wrapped possessively around Kitty's crystal grip.

My power comes not just from the stone and metal which form the substance of me, but from the one who possesses me. I was impatient. Perhaps I should've waited, but as you can see from the story on the walls, it was not meant for me to wait.

"You're right. It's best that we leave Kitty here," Bela agreed with a shiver.

She will find me, when the time comes. Until then, I will be content to wait. I will be patient.

The sword yanked itself forcefully from Bela's hand. Kitty spun away, she whipped up and around, her blade moving so fast a whirring sound filled the cavern and her steel and crystal became nothing more than a blur. Her grip glowed, and in response the crystal in the walls all around them shone brighter. The glow became so bright Bela had to close her eyes. Merin took Bela into his arms and held her close, shielding her as much as he could. Bela hid her face against his shoulder, glad for his presence and his protection, even if that protection was nothing more than his strong arms around her. If Kitty came near them, if she was truly unhappy at the prospect of being left behind, they could die here, cut to ribbons in an instant. There could be no defense against an angry Kitty.

Bela had never before thought to be afraid of Kitty. Never. Were her instincts so wrong? She had always felt only good from the sword she so proudly called her own, she had never been frightened by what the sword could do.

Perhaps her instincts were not wrong at all. Kitty did not come near. Bela didn't fool herself into thinking loyalty or fondness had anything to do with that fact. The sword still needed her, and needed Merin, too. The weapon which was more than a weapon wanted her warrior.

After several long moments an ear-splitting crack shook the cavern, and soon the bright light dimmed so that Bela no longer felt compelled to hold her eyes so tightly shut. She opened her eyes cautiously and glanced around the cavern, which was once again awash in a soft glow.

That light throbbed gently, much as a beating heart might.

At first Bela saw no sign of the sword, but then her eyes were drawn slightly up, as were Merin's. A good two feet of Kitty's blade was buried in stone. The tip of the blade had pierced a particularly graphic depiction of last night's encounter and cut through the wall to its resting place. The grip extended from the cavern wall, and after a moment the glow of the grip died. Kitty was sleeping. Kitty was waiting.

Merin took Bela's hand and squeezed it. "We follow the river," he said hoarsely.

"We can't know that the drawing is correct," she argued. "What if it's only leading us deeper into the mountain?"

"The river has to dump out somewhere," Merin said sensibly, "probably on the other side of the mountain from the Turi holdings."

Her heart skipped a beat. Of course he was correct, it only made sense, but still—she did not like the picture he painted. "It will take us forever to get home!" If they exited on the other side of the mountain, it could take *weeks* to get back to the village, depending on how far down the mountain they found themselves and the pathways they might—or might not—find. By then, what would Nobel have done? To her family, to her friends. She and Merin had to be there to fight! Bela increased her pace. "We must hurry."

LEYLA practically ran back to the hut. Her skirt was filled with redberries, and she held it high to capture the luscious berries securely. She didn't want to lose even one. She'd already eaten a handful, but would eat no more until Savyn had enjoyed some. She had no sugar, no honey, no flour or seasonings to make a cobbler or a pie. But the berries alone were sweet, and Savyn would find them a wonderful change after days of dried meat and biscuits.

"Savyn?" she called as she pushed open the heavy, crooked door. Immediately she knew he was not here. She did not see him. He was not waiting silently in a shadowy corner. The hut was empty.

She rushed outside, still gripping her skirt in one hand so the berries would not fall. He must've walked outside to relieve himself, that was all. Maybe he was simply tired of the musty hut. She'd cleaned as best she could, and the place got more than its share of fresh air through the holes in the roof and the walls, but it still smelled of years of neglect.

Leyla looked around the side of the hut, which was easy to do as the back was built into the steep, grassy hill. Could Savyn have climbed that hill? Blind?

Frantic, she turned around and screamed his name. He was lost! Somehow Savyn had stumbled away and gotten turned around. Why hadn't he waited for her, if he needed to get out of the hut for a while? She tried to calm herself. He couldn't have gone far, and was sure to hear her scream. She'd call, he'd yell in response, and she'd follow the sound of his voice and lead him back here. Oh, he must be so afraid!

She never should've left him alone. They should've continued to exist on what little food they had until it was gone and they had no other choice. Leyla stood there and listened carefully, expecting an immediate response, a frantic "I'm here!" that she could follow.

Silence.

Her heart thudded loudly as she screamed again, "Savyn!" She held her breath as she listened for an answer.

He was hurt, he'd fallen, he'd . . . Leyla's hands went numb and she allowed the berries to fall to the ground as she dropped her skirt. No, Savyn hadn't gotten lost or hurt. He had run from her. She knew it. Should've expected as much after this morning's confession and the way he had taken her wrist in his hand. Somehow he had begun to remember their past, and it was torturing him. He'd run, blind and helpless, because he could not bear her company any longer. He'd rather stumble about, alone and lost, than remain here with her.

She had never intended to hurt him so much; she had never intended to make him suffer for loving her.

Leyla took a step toward the road Savyn had surely taken when he'd escaped. Her dusty boots squished a few redberries which were scattered on the ground around her, but she barely noticed.

Her heart hurt in a way she had thought impossible. Her heart was hardened after a life which had never been easy. There should be no pain, not for her, but knowing Savyn was gone ripped her apart.

For years it had been easy for her to dismiss her relationship with Savyn as strictly physical. The physical had brought them together, and heaven knows it had been pleasurable enough. She'd never allowed herself to believe that what she felt for Savyn was anything more than fondness

for a talented sexual partner, not even when he spoke words
of love.

But deep down she knew their relationship was much
more than simply physical. In all her life, no one had ever
wanted her just for herself. Her parents had feared and sold
her. Her husband had purchased her for her beauty and her
magical gifts. Her new family had despised her. Only
Savyn had wanted her for herself. Only Savyn had brought
love and pleasure into her dismal life. All these years she'd
convinced herself that she had used the younger man for
his hard cock and his pretty face and his ability to make
her forget, for a while, who she was—who she had become.
But now that he was gone, she longed for nothing other
than his arms around her, his voice to assure her she was
safe.

She loved Savyn. Until he'd gone, she had not realized
how much.

Making him forget had been a mistake, perhaps the big-
gest of her mistake-filled life.

BELA followed Merin's lead as they walked along the
rocky bank of the river, which was in her estimation more
of a creek than a river, though in the cavern drawings it had
looked much more fierce. The water ran through the cavern, beginning at a wide and crooked crack in the wall—
probably fed by a massive underground spring—and
flowing quickly through the glimmering cavern.

They left Kitty and the cave carvings behind, and yes,
she did suffer more than one moment of doubt. Kitty was
hers! The weapon was special and powerful, an ally like no
other. And the sword was intended for her daughter, apparently. Hers and Merin's.

Nobel would be pissed. Bela supposed that was one advantage of hiding Kitty in a place where she would not be

found. The precious sword would not fall into Nobel's hands.

As they walked, bound by the braided rope and often hand in hand, the water which ran through the cavern grew wider and a bit deeper. It sparkled with radiant crystals which shone beneath the surface, sometimes creating rainbows deep in the water and all around, sometimes throwing colored patterns onto the walls. Bela tried not to look at the water too much. Something about it was enchanting, and not in a good way. She could get caught up in the glow and the life there; she could easily sit down and run her fingers through it and just . . . stay.

She and Merin moved deeper and deeper into the mountain, not speaking as they searched for a way out. Did his mind go to the same places hers had gone?

Bela was terrified. What she felt for Merin was so deep, and it seemed so real—but what if it was not? What if her love for Merin was false, what if it had been created by the magical sword which directed that her warrior be made? Made of unconventional woman and heroic man, made for battle but conceived in love. But what if the love faded as they left Kitty behind? When Kitty no longer had the power to reach into her mind, would the love which had grown so strong fade away?

Now that she knew love, she did not want to lose it. She wanted what she felt to be real . . . she wanted it to last. She wanted more nights like last night, more sunrises like the one she had seen such a short time ago. Heaven help her, she even wanted babies. Babies who would be safe, babies who would not be called to fight in battles so fierce they required a magical sword and a destined warrior.

It was true that Bela herself would've been pleased enough to be called to fight, but her unusual life, her sometimes shocking choices—they were hers. She had made them *on her own*. Would her daughter have those same choices, or was the unborn child doomed to fight whether she wished to or not?

The cavern began to narrow, and soon there was barely room for the water which rushed through, much less a path beside the water. Merin's booted feet slipped into the water, and he recoiled and uttered a sharp curse as he jumped back.

"What is it?" Bela asked.

Merin turned and looked her in the eye. "You know the way Kitty could get into our heads and talk?"

Bela nodded.

"Imagine a hundred or more Kittys talking at once," he said, and then he glanced down. "The crystal that makes the water glow is alive the same way Kitty is alive."

"Great." Bela glanced ahead, noticing that the path narrowed considerably. They would have no choice but to walk in the water.

Merin turned his back to her. "Hop on," he said.

"That's not . . ." Bela had been about to say "necessary" when Merin grabbed her arm, jerked her to the side, and in doing so forced her to step into the river.

As soon as the rushing water touched her boots, the voices invaded her mind. She could not make sense of any of it because, as Merin had said, they all spoke at once. They screamed, they chattered . . . they even laughed. Bela leaped from the water, and this time she gratefully jumped on Merin's back, throwing her arms around his neck and wrapping her thighs around his waist. "Just for a while," she said, feeling cowardly but not particularly caring about that at the moment. "It's horrible and grating and loud," she said. "How will you be able to stand it?"

Merin looked ahead at the sparkling river that seemed to stretch forever, throwing rainbows and unnatural light onto the walls and the ceiling so far above. "What choice do I have?"

* * *

FOR all her well-shaped muscle, Bela didn't weigh much at all, particularly positioned as she was on his back. Just as well that she not have to listen to this. It was all Merin could do not to turn back and run from the water and the voices.

He knew what lay behind him, so he would not go there. Death waited if he retreated. Death from starvation, most likely, or perhaps he and Bela would die from thirst. He could not imagine taking a drink from this water. No, life lay ahead, life for him and for Bela. All he had to do was survive the cacophony in his head.

The voices spoke in many different languages. Some were soft and some were insistent. Some screamed, some whispered. The whispers were hardest to ignore.

Soon all the languages Merin did not know faded away, and the crystals spoke to him in the language he could understand. Some laughed at him, others urged him on. Some thanked him, a few expressed their disapproval of his methods. It wasn't long before he began to mutter responses, answers which were angry and confused, for the most part.

After a short while, Bela began to hum what sounded like a lullaby. Even though the tune was soft, her lips were near his ear and Merin heard her well. He concentrated on that sound, on the harmonious humming, on the soothing melody, and while the voices didn't go away, they did fade somewhat, slipping into the back of his mind. The maddening sounds remained, but he did not listen to them. Instead he listened to Bela.

As if the voices knew he was no longer paying proper attention, they stilled for a moment and then began again, differently this time. There were many voices, but they spoke as one. Even Bela's lullaby couldn't keep them out of his head.

You are ours, Tearlach Merin. Body and soul, you are destined to serve us.

"I serve only the emperor," Merin responded.

Do you? Do you truly serve your emperor?

Merin did not have an immediate answer for that. He had not served Jahn well, not of late. He'd failed in a simple task; he'd lain with a woman who was meant to be presented to the emperor.

Our child will be strong and smart, she will serve us well.

The very idea made Merin's skin crawl, and then it made him angry. "You won't have my child." If there was a child. Was it already done? Did Bela carry the daughter who was meant to wield Kitty?

The lullaby stopped. "Are you talking to them?" Bela asked.

"Yes."

"What do they want?"

Surely she knew. "They want our daughter."

Those last two words were whispered in a hundred—no, a *thousand*—voices that resounded in Merin's head. *Our daughter. Our daughter.*

"Sing," he ordered gruffly. "For the sake of my sanity, Bela, sing."

She no longer hummed, but instead sang the tune. Her voice was surprisingly clear and pleasant. What she had hummed was indeed a lullaby, a soothing song of sweet dreams and full moons and white dancing flowers. The words were as soothing as the melody alone had been. They were soothing because they were delivered to him in a pleasing voice he loved to hear.

The song was short, as lullabies often were, and when it was done, Bela immediately began again. She did not stop, she did not leave him alone with the voices. Gradually the unwanted voices in his mind faded away, even though he moved into deeper water.

But all was not well. Merin was afraid that too soon Bela's feet would touch the cursed river, and when that happened, there would be nothing more he could do to save her from the voices.

LEYLA sat upon the bed she and Savyn had shared, her legs drawn to her chest, her head down so that she rested in a tight ball of agony. What now? What should she do? Her life had not been easy, and she had made many mistakes along the way. She had made many decisions she wished could be undone. She'd been hated, desired, and feared. She'd been bought and sold. But she had never been alone.

Was that why she thought she loved Savyn, so she would not have to be alone? How weak was she that she would hold onto a man who was better off without her, just so she wouldn't have to exist without companionship? She had always been different, she had always been separate, but she had never before felt as if her world was as black as Savyn's had become when Trinity had hit him on the head and taken his sight.

She began to rock back and forth, uncertain, uneasy. All her life, important decisions had been made for her. Where to live; whom to marry. As a child her parents had instructed her when and how to use her magical abilities; as an adult her husband had taken on that job. Savyn was the only decision she had ever made on her own, the only decision more important than what gown to wear or whether they should have chicken or beef for supper, and she had ruined his life in the process.

Blind and every bit as alone as she was, was Savyn still better off without her?

Chapter Fourteen

MERIN trudged through the fast-flowing but shallow water for what felt like an endless period of time. With each
step he focused on the next step. He took one step and then
another, refusing to think too far ahead. Though they came
close a time or two, Bela's slim, tall boots never touched
the water, as he had feared they might. He slogged on. The
voices spoke, Bela sang, time stopped. Finally the shape of
the passage changed: widening, sprawling, opening into
yet another grotto which was as large as, or larger than, the
one they'd left behind. He walked faster, came close to
running, when he saw dry land—dry rock—once again.

When Merin was well out of the river, he was glad to
put Bela on her feet and stand tall for a moment, free of the
river's enchanted water and strange influence. He stretched
tired, tight muscles. For a while, at least, they would be
able to walk alongside the river rather than through it. The
quiet that had come to his mind the moment he'd left the
river was as stunningly shocking as the original assault of
voices. Along the way he had become accustomed to the

noise the crystals made, as if they were becoming a part of him.

He had never thought to see anything like the caverns they traveled through, and though he was drained and more worried than he would allow Bela to see, he could not help but be awestruck by the beauty of this unnatural place. The walls and the water sparkled like something out of a dream. They glimmered like a lady's jewel, eye-catching and beautiful. And yet the background for that enchanted gleam was cold, hard rock which was jagged in many places and downright dangerous in others.

The rainbows thrown off by the river and the crystals were softer here than they had been a short way back, but they were no less startling or stunning. The place was vivid color and stark gray, plain stone and sparkling crystal, beauty and stark terror.

Without the sun to guide them, he could not say what time of day it might be. It seemed as if they had been traveling for many hours, but time was odd and he couldn't be certain. No matter how long it had been, he was unusually tired, exhausted after the trek through the water. He was also hungry. He should've put a few of those hard Turi oatcakes in his pocket before entering the cave, but he had not expected . . . he had not expected any of this.

"Sit for a moment," Bela said kindly, and Merin wondered how bad he must look for her to sound so concerned.

"I'm fine."

"You're not fine," she said, taking his hand and sitting on a wide, flat section of stone. He had no choice but to sit with her, and she was right. He needed the rest. It felt good to sit and watch the water rather than to be trudging through it.

A part of him wondered if they would ever get out of here. Perhaps this enchanted river ran through the mountain endlessly, twisting and turning back on itself. Would

they step from this cavern, round a corner, and find themselves back in the original chamber, where carvings marked
his life—and perhaps his life to come—and Kitty was buried in stone?

It was such a relief to be out of the water, to hear nothing in his own head but silence. "We can rest here for a
while," he said, leaning back on his hands. Bela leaned
back, too. Fatigue washed through Merin, and he soon
gave in to the tiredness and lay back on the stone. It was not
a soft bed by any means, but felt good all the same. Bela
did not hesitate to lie beside him, as she had on so many
nights. Above their heads the crystals sparkled like count-
less stars. Gemstones streaked the rock far above, beautiful and bewitching.

Merin closed his eyes and quickly fell into a deep sleep,
exhaustion overtaking him. Bela's warm, soft body rested
against his, and she slept, too. He woke once to hear her
even breathing, to take comfort in the fact that she was
there, still connected, still his. When he returned to sleep,
with crystals sparkling all around—above and beneath
him—he dreamed briefly of a daughter who looked like
Bela but had his dark, curly hair. She was tall and had her
mother's wide smile, and she held a sword as well as any
warrior he had ever trained. She was unafraid; she was
beautiful. And he was comforted by the unshakable knowledge that she was going to be all right.

IT wasn't as though she had not dreamed of this before,
Bela thought as Merin removed her clothes and kissed
her body and aroused her with his hands. From that night
when he'd shown her what sexual pleasure could be, she
had experienced many different versions of this particular
dream.

This one was different. It was more real than the others,
more wonderfully vivid, and the dancing lights around

them were like their personal rainbows. Yes, Merin was making love to her in a rainbow.

His face was as comely as ever, if more colorful than usual as the bright hues of the rainbow cut across his face. He took his time in preparation. In past encounters she had been anxious to get to the end, to take the shattering pleasure, but he was right in insisting that the preparation was important. She had come to love this part, when Merin kissed and aroused her so patiently, when she knew in her heart he was not at all patient.

As in the way of dreams, one minute he was dressed in clothing damp with water from the enchanted river, and the next they were both undressed. She liked him this way, naked and pressed against her, wonderfully bare and entirely hers. Bela had never thought of herself as being soft in any way, but when she and Merin held one another this way, the softness of her body and the hardness of his were in stark and wonderful contrast, and for the first time in her life she was glad of the softness of her body. It was right for this. For them.

When she was more than ready, he thrust inside her and she cried out in relief and pleasure. Her cries echoed, they reverberated and turned into what sounded like a laugh. Had she ever thought they would not fit properly? Had she ever thought this would not be achingly wonderful? She was his, and he filled her very nicely. He filled her perfectly, stretching and pushing and thrusting and claiming. Too soon they found completion together, their bodies arching and trembling as one.

It was hot. So hot. They created an intense warmth that rose from their bodies in waves. Sweat beaded on her flesh, it made her and Merin slick with the heat they made.

And then the rain came, gentle and cooling, and Merin's body drifted down to cover hers for a moment before he rolled away. They lay on their backs, naked and sated, as the gentle rain washed over them. She had never felt anything like it before, and she had been out in the rain many times. This rain felt like gentle fingers, it cooled and caressed.

This rain was like the rainbow that danced around them, that colored their bare bodies red and blue and yellow and green. It was tender, and it was theirs. When the rain stopped, Bela rolled onto her side and draped one leg over Merin's body. What a wonderful dream.

THOUGH it was hard for him to know how much time passed as he walked, Savyn realized when the day began to fade. The warmth on his face had gradually disappeared, and the temperatures had begun to cool. The day had not been a waste. Throughout the day, which had seemed unbearably long, he'd learned a thing or two. A fallen tree branch, sturdy but slender, helped him make his way along the road without tripping again, as he swept the ground before him. He could also tap it along the grassy edge of the road to make certain he was moving straight ahead and not listing or weaving to one side. He'd had to trip over the damn branch in order to find it, but it had been a good enough trade.

His hearing was quite good. In fact, he heard everything. Insects, the wind in the trees, small animals in the forest, Leyla's voice.

For a long while after he'd heard her frantic cry, he'd waited to hear her step or the horse's hooves on the road. She was likely to feel responsible for him and his infirmity, so she'd probably try to collect him as one might a wayward dog. If he heard her coming, he would slip into the forest and hide there. He would not be led about like a wounded and faithful dog, no matter how noble Leyla's intentions might be.

Savyn realized that he had gotten too accustomed to calling the woman of his fantasies Leyla, in the short time they'd been on the run. He should revert to the more proper Lady Leyla, or simply Lady. He had no right to call her or to *think* of her by her given name. No right at all.

He waited for quite some time, listening closely, but she did not come. There were no footsteps or clopping hooves on this lonely path.

Lady Leyla would be fine without him, Savyn assured himself as he trudged forward. In fact, she would be much better off. If she had decided to search for him, perhaps she had gone toward the village which had been their original destination days ago, a lifetime ago. She would find help there. Maybe she would even make her life there, with a new name.

When darkness fell, Savyn continued to walk along the road. He had his stick, his hearing, his memory of this path. What difference did it make if there was light to illuminate his way or not? He was lost in darkness. But even without his sight, the night was ominous. In the distance a wolf howled. Night birds cawed. Something in the forest hissed, and insects attacked his exposed skin, taking particular delight in his neck. He swatted them away, determined to keep moving as long as possible. He needed to put some distance between him and Lady Leyla. He needed to escape.

Still, before morning arrived, he was compelled to rest, even to sleep. He found a soft patch of grass on the side of the road away from the forest, and he lay there for a while, sleeping in spurts, waking often to a noise or a breeze. Maybe some wild animal would attack him in the night and take his life, such as it was. It was a risk he would gladly take if it meant the torturous fantasies would stop.

Savyn felt some relief when morning came. He was still alive and Lady Leyla had not found him. Maybe she had not searched for him at all. Maybe she was glad to be rid of her burden; maybe she was already in the village, where she could start a new life.

And still, he was not surprised a short while later when he heard Lady Leyla call his name again, much as she had the day before. He also heard the gentle clop of a horse's hooves. Perhaps she had gone toward the village at first when she searched for him, or perhaps she had remained at the hut for a while, awaiting his return. Whatever had delayed her, she had not given up, as he had hoped. She was coming for him.

Savyn considered moving into the woods and finding a sheltered spot to hide, but now that the time was upon him, something inside refused to take that step. He could imagine too well thinking himself hidden while he was exposed in some silly or pathetic way. He could imagine Lady Leyla seeing him too easily and taking pity on a man who could not even conceal himself properly in the woods. So he kept walking. Even when he knew she was close enough to see him, he did not turn about. What would be the use? He could not see her.

When she was close and the horse slowed, he half expected her to start haranguing him. She should. He had caused her a great deal of trouble by running. But instead of attacking him, she remained silent. It was a few minutes before he heard the horse stop. A moment later Lady Leyla's feet hit the road, and soon her steps trailed his. She kept a distance, and did not try to run to catch up with him. Instead, she continued to follow, her footsteps in time with his, a soft echo of his own tread.

Finally she asked, "Where are we going?"

Savyn sighed. She was going to make this difficult. She was going to make him say it. "We're not going anywhere, not together. You can go on to the village. I half expected you'd be there already. Have you decided upon your new name?" He did not stop or even slow down.

"I'm not going anywhere without you," she said, her voice even, but a little thick. Maybe she had been crying.

"There's no need to be afraid," he said. "You'll be fine."

"I'm not worried about myself!" she said, finally showing a hint of anger.

"I certainly don't want you to worry about me," Savyn said. "I'll be all right. If my sight returns, I'll go home and take up where I left off, mending and building wheels and making swords."

"And if it does not?" she asked sharply.

"Then I will go where God takes me, I suppose."

Her pace increased; it almost sounded like she was running. When she grabbed his arm and yanked, shifting him off balance, he almost fell. Instead, he righted himself clumsily and turned to face her, wishing he could see her angry eyes and her wild hair and her luscious lips. Yes, he had to get away from her. This had to stop, or he would go mad.

"There is something you do not know," she said softly, even though there was no one around for miles to hear her words.

"I imagine there is much I do not know."

"I lied to you," she said more harshly.

"A fine lady such as yourself owes me nothing, not even the truth."

"Stop it," she whispered.

"Stop what?"

"Stop being so damned gallant and calm. I lied to you! Because of me, an assassin took your sight and nearly killed you. You should despise me!"

"And yet I do not," Savyn said. "I do not despise you at all. Could not, even if I wished to do so. Why is that, Lady Leyla?"

He did wonder what lie she had told him, but in truth he did not care. He still wanted her. He still loved her. What a ridiculous notion, that he might be allowed to love one such as her.

"We were lovers," she said, her voice even lower than a whisper.

For the first time in a long while, Savyn laughed. "I believe I would remember if that were true."

He heard Lady Leyla take a deep breath and hold it for a moment before she said, "I took the memories from you."

Savyn felt as if she had kicked him in the gut. What she suggested was a ridiculous notion, and yet it explained much. His fantasies were, at least in part, lost memories fighting to come back. His love for her, his need to protect her, they were not new at all. Everything fell into place, and he felt a rush of fury and regret. "Why? Why would you make me forget?"

She spoke softly and quickly, spitting out the words. "I was leaving, and I had no choice in the matter. More than anything, I wanted you to be happy, to have a wonderful life, and I could not give that to you. All I could do was let you go, and I did so the only way I knew how."

"By using your witchcraft on me and erasing a part of my past?"

"Yes."

He did not know whether to be angry or relieved. In truth he was both. "Can you put the memories back?"

"I don't know," she said, and she reached out to touch his forehead. "I have never tried. I suspect the memories are simply gone and cannot be retrieved."

Savyn wished again that he could see her eyes at this moment. Was she sorry she'd ravaged his mind to clear her own conscience? Did she regret using witchcraft on her lover?

"Someone's coming," he said, sensing the rumble of the road, hearing the distant creak of a wheel. "A wagon," he added. "Two horses, I believe."

"We should hide in the woods until they pass," Lady Leyla said, taking his arm and guiding him and the horse in that direction. He wanted to shake off her hold, but did not. With his stick he could find his way to and into the forest, but locating a proper trail and a hiding place was another matter. He had become a pathetic creature.

When they were a short distance from the road, he asked, "What was I to you, Lady Leyla, a stud? A convenience when your husband could not satisfy you? Did you pay me for my services?"

"No!" she said, softly but insistently. "It was not like that, not at all."

"Then what was it like?" he asked.

Lady Leyla came to a halt and said, "We can wait here. We're far enough from the road and the growth here is thick enough that those passing should not see us."

Using her voice as a guide, he found and grabbed her face. "What was it like?" he whispered.

"We should talk about this later," she said, her voice as soft as his own.

"No, we will talk about it now. I want to know what you did to me, and I want to know why. Did your husband pay me to do what he could not?"

Lady Leyla sighed. "You and I were not together until long after my husband died."

"Did you love him, then?"

"No," she answered sharply. "I was a spouse bought and paid for, a slave as much as a wife. There could be no love in such a relationship."

"Did you love me?" He could hear the wagon on the road as it passed them without pausing. Children laughed and talked quickly, making so much noise there was little chance anyone would hear the words in the forest above the creak of wheels, the clop of hooves, and the voices of children. And if anything was heard, it would be dismissed as the whispers of animals or the scurrying of forest dwellers.

"Love would not have been wise," Lady Leyla said, her voice trembling just slightly. "Not then and not now."

"Of course not. The fine lady and the poor craftsman would not make a proper couple, not at all, not even when I could see. My, how people would talk."

"I never cared for any of that," she insisted. "People have talked about me all my life, and I learned a long time ago to dismiss whispers, to ignore the hate and the fear. But you, Savyn, I suspect you trouble yourself more than I do over what people say."

"Did you ever ask me if I cared about such things?"

"I am nine years older than you!" she said sharply, ignoring his question. "It would not be at all fair for me to bind myself to you when a future was impossible."

Savyn placed his hand on her cheek. Yes, the curve of her cheek felt familiar, just as her scent and her voice and his fantasies were so sharply and torturously familiar. Nine years seemed nothing to him, so unimportant that he was angry she would even think of it as a problem. "If all this is true, then why do you tell me now? Why didn't you just let me go?"

"You need me," she whispered, though the wagon had passed and the time for whispering had passed as well. "You can't go out into the world alone, not like this."

He didn't want her to feel sorry for him. She could hate him, she could want him, she could be bored with him, or angry or frustrated—but he would not have her pity. "I've been having fantasies about you," he said. "Vivid dreams so real I thought they would drive me insane."

"You should remember nothing," she said softly.

"And yet, I do. I have always had a gnawing need to protect you, and there are moments when my hands itch to touch you, and I have to clench them into fists to keep from reaching out. Since I've been injured, it's become more intense, more real, but from the moment we left Childers, there was . . . something. Something maddening. I knew long before I stole a kiss what your lips taste like," he whispered, lowering his head slightly, "and I know very well what it feels like to slide into your heat, how you gasp when you find release, how your fine sheets sometimes smell of us. If you took all that away, why is it still with me? I swear, the bits and pieces that flit through my mind are enough to steal the last of my reason."

It was Leyla—Lady Leyla—who closed the distance between them and kissed him. Her lips met his and it was, as before, like coming home. Like finding himself again, after being lost for so long. It no longer mattered that he could not see. He could feel. He could feel very well.

She tasted as he knew she should, and when his hand caressed her breast, the gentle swell filled his hand, as was right. As the kiss grew deeper, Leyla made an agreeable sound that spoke of need and passion and the love she denied. Trinity's horse ran from them; they did not care. Leyla—just Leyla, not Lady Leyla, not when he held her this way—wrapped her arms around his waist and held on. She was so warm and soft, so right in his arms.

Savyn dropped to his knees, still entangled with Leyla as they fell. The kiss turned frantic; they were lost in each other, for the moment. He sucked her lower lip into his mouth and held it there, then deepened the kiss and thrust his tongue into her mouth, devouring her, taking what he had only dreamed of.

This was his dream come true, and it was good. He did not need to see in order to kiss Leyla, in order to arouse her. He had held her in the dark many times and he knew her body well, just as she knew his. It was such a relief to know that there was a reason for his love, for his fantasies. He was not mad, and his aching need to protect her, to be with her, to have her, it was all natural and right. Leyla had tried to take this from him, but in spite of her magic he remembered. Perhaps he remembered with his heart, not his head. Perhaps her magic could not touch him there.

He pushed her skirt high, his fingers brushing her bare thighs, and she whispered, "Yes." She was ready for him, wet and hot, and he teased her with hands that knew her body very well. He did not think, he simply followed instinct as he aroused her.

Leyla fumbled frantically with the ties of his trousers and released his swollen penis. She rolled onto the ground and brought him with her, her thighs wrapping around him. Her gasp and her hands spurred him on as she guided him to her damp center.

He thrust deep, and when he did, everything he was, all he had ever been, was inside Leyla.

Savyn forgot that he was blind as he made love to Leyla hard and fast. It might've been nighttime in the confines of her bedchamber, with the drapes shut tight so no one would be able to see. They were upon hard ground instead of her soft mattress, but he did not care. All he cared about was being inside her, making her shake and scream.

She did shake and scream, and as her inner muscles quaked, he found his own release deep inside her. How could something so pleasurable be wrong? He did not care that she was older than he was, he did not care that people would talk. She was like no other woman in the world, and she was his. He could not remember details, she had taken them from him, but the feelings of possession remained. Leyla was his.

No, she had been his, but no more. He could get lost in her body, and he was glad to have this encounter to remember, since she had taken his other memories from him. He could not trust a woman who had used her magic on him, and he would not be a burden to her as she started her new life.

Leyla kissed him sweetly, and he was tempted to tell her

that he loved her, one last time. He was certain he had told her before, perhaps many times. But if he said those words to her now, she would never let him walk away. She would follow him no matter where he went, obligated and forever bound.

"I needed that," Savyn said casually as he withdrew and moved away from Leyla to right his trousers. "It's been a while—I think," he added sourly, "and I was sorely in need of relief. So were you, judging by your reaction. It's nice to know that one skill remains, sight or no."

"What?" He could hear the pain in Leyla's voice, and was sorry for it, but the truth was impossible.

"You heard me. I am blind, but you are not deaf, Lady Leyla."

He heard the rustle of her gown as she straightened her skirts.

"So, what now?" he asked sharply. "The horse is gone."

"I never wanted to keep Trinity's horse in any case," Leyla said, her voice slightly thick. "Everything I took from the saddlebags is well hidden back at the hut."

Savyn tried to keep his expression impassive. He did not smile or frown. "I suspect you are not going to allow me to keep walking away from you."

"I can't," she whispered.

"Then we will travel to the village up the road together, and there we will part. I suppose it would be best if we separate before we see the villagers. I will pass myself off as a traveling beggar, and you can make up whatever tale you wish to start your new life."

"I would like to stay with you," Leyla said. "I can take care of you, at least until we know if your sight will return or not. It's still too soon to say for certain."

"No," Savyn said sharply. He knew she would argue with him, he knew she would be hard to shake, if she wished to remain with him. "You lied to me, Lady Leyla. You took my memories with your damned magic, you nearly drove me insane."

"I thought it was for the best," she whispered.

"Well, you did a good job, My Lady. I have forgotten. I thank you for the fucking, but if I ever loved you, that love is gone."

MERIN opened his eyes, surprised he'd slept so deeply. Bela still slept, naked and partially wrapped around him. It took a moment for him to realize that he was naked, too, and then he realized he was dreaming and he relaxed. What a nice dream.

The walls sang the lullaby Bela had sung to him in order to dull their unwanted voices. It was a lovely lullaby, a soothing melody which comforted him, which pulled him into the deepest of sleeps.

To be trapped in this enchanted mountain where voices invaded his mind should be a nightmare, a terror, but at this moment he did not feel at all terrified. He'd had nightmares before, and this was not one of them.

Bela would not appear in any of his nightmares, he was sure. She was a woman of pleasant dreams, the participant in dreams he did not want to end. The kind where upon waking, he would try to fall asleep again quickly, so he could regain the wonder.

She lifted her head and smiled at him, and her hands danced boldly along his body. Her hair fell in chestnut waves, and she gave him that wide and wonderful smile which made him love her.

She fed him, taking freshly sliced fruit and roasted meat from a nearby plate and slipping the small pieces into his mouth. He was hungry, and it was good to eat something besides an oatcake. When he'd had his fill, he returned the favor and fed Bela, taking pieces of food from the golden plate that never seemed to diminish, no matter how much they ate. It was a dream, after all.

After they had eaten, they kissed for a while. They kissed as if they had been apart for a very long time and could not stay apart. Bela was his, and she was so giving, so unguarded. His hand slipped between her thighs, and they opened for him. She was warm and wet, slick and ready.

"Again, husband?" she whispered as her soft hand closed around his shaft.

"Again," he said, and the dream grew brighter than before.

THE walk back to the hut seemed endless, but Savyn knew the journey took them a mere two days. A day and a half, more rightly. Along the way they had stopped to sleep on the side of the road, but neither of them had slept very long. The dangers of the night and the tension between them made it impossible.

Savyn already felt guilty for being so harsh with Leyla, but it was best that the end of this relationship be decisive—even if that meant it had to be cruel. He could be ruthless where Leyla was concerned, if it meant she would make a better life without him.

He was still angry with her for taking his memories away, but he could understand. She had been making the same sort of sacrifice for him that he now made for her, and she had made it in the only way she knew how. How could he make her understand that he cared nothing for the few years between them, or the whispers of jealous and unimportant people who had nothing better to do than to gossip about the lives others? If he could see, he would try to convince her of all that, but he could not, so he would let her go, just as she had tried to release him.

Leyla was thankful when she saw the hut. She told him it was there, straight ahead, and he heard the touch of relief in her voice. Not joy—he could not remember ever hearing her speak with delight, he could not remember seeing joy in her fine, blue eyes. Had he made her happy in their times together? Had she taken away the only memories he had of joy in the woman he loved?

There had been no joy in her eyes after they'd left Childers. Every time he'd managed to catch her eye during the journey, every time he'd studied her fine face with infatuation or admiration or love, he'd seen only sadness and resignation.

Had giving him up hurt her, or was she always so cheerless?

"I'm sorry," he said as she led him through the hut's uneven doorway.

She did not pretend to be ignorant of his meaning. "There is no need to apologize. I was wrong. You have good reason to be angry."

Leyla did not ask him to forgive her; she did not plead her case or ask that they remain together after they reached the village. She simply sounded resigned to her fate. Resigned and doomed.

IT was lovely to bathe in the river. Bela held on to Merin as they splashed water all over their bare bodies, as they bathed one another and touched as only a husband and wife can.

She had become accustomed to the rainbow that was ever present in her dream, and she was no longer afraid of the river. The voices within it were quiet. They did not shout at her or torment Merin in the dream.

Bela wrapped her arms around Merin's neck. "I do love you," she said, not caring if he returned the vow or not. "So very much." He was hers entirely: heart, body, and soul.

No other man would ever take his place. No other man would ever love her this way.

He surprised her by saying the same words with just as much conviction. "I love you, Bela." His mouth was on her throat for a moment, and then he added, "Just as you are, you are the perfect woman for me. I love you."

They were in the deepest part of the water. It rushed around them in a soft eddy, but they were not afraid. It caressed rather than fighting against them. The water swirled, capturing them gently.

Merin lifted her off her feet, and she wrapped her legs around his waist. She did not think it was possible, but soon he was inside her, deep and thick. Of course this was a dream, and anything was possible in a dream. They could likely fly above the water and make love on air. She laughed as she rode, holding on to Merin with her arms and with her thighs, seeking and giving pleasure. The water added a new sensation to the experience, washing over both of them as they sought and found a shared release.

And then they did begin to float, rising out of the water still connected in body and by the braid which was again brightly colored and unmarred by time. The rainbow caught them and returned them to the side of the river, where they grasped one another and Merin told her again that he loved her.

Bela suffered her first rush of unease. She longed for Merin to tell her that he loved her, but this was just a dream. Just a fantastic, vibrant dream.

THE nap did not last long enough, and too soon Merin woke, ready to continue their journey. He woke Bela gently. Like him, she was surprised to have fallen asleep. She gave him an odd look, and when she did, he remembered a piece of a dream. A very good dream. Perhaps he'd slept

longer than he'd realized, for such a detailed dream to stay
with him this way.

He and Bela began to walk again, keeping to the rocky
bank of the buried river, following the rushing water. She
was oddly silent, but he could not blame her. It had been a
very long day.

Eventually a distant, dull roar caught Merin's attention
and gave him hope that there was an end to this journey.
His pace increased and so did Bela's, as she easily kept up
with him. The roar grew louder, more distinct, until he understood with relief and more than a little trepidation what
would be waiting at the end of this river.

Waterfall.

Light soon joined the roar, adding to his hope. The little
bit of sunlight that fought its way through the cavern made
the crystals sparkle all the more fiercely. Suddenly there
were gleams of brilliant blue and deep lavender added to
the shimmering light, then a hint of yellow sparked here
and there, as if the crystals struggled to catch the sun.

And then he saw the exit they had been searching for.
He saw light—though not a lot of it fought through the
rushing water that escaped the mountain in a gush. There
was no way to know how far the fall from the exit would
be, or if the water below was deep enough to catch them
safely.

"This is it, isn't it?" Bela said, her voice raised so he
could hear her above the roar.

"I believe so," he shouted in response. They had followed the river, as depicted in the cavern carving, and if
what they had seen was correct, this was the way to escape.
There had been no waterfall on the wall, however, no warning that this was what waited.

The water rushed strong and fast now. Their only option
was to jump in the water and let it take them where they
needed to go. There were many options when it came to the

outcome. They could drown, be smashed against rocks far below, break bones in a shallow pond . . . and then drown. Or they could fly from this mountain on a rush of enchanted water and land safely in a deep pool, and from there they could make their way to freedom. What choice was there, truly?

Bela eyed the rushing water suspiciously, obviously uncertain, obviously worried.

Sometimes worrying was the worst part.

Merin grabbed Bela and held her tight against his chest. He kissed her, deeply and quickly, then said, "Take a deep breath, love."

With only a touch of panic in her eyes she obeyed him. And they jumped.

BELA held her breath, as Merin instructed. Together they plunged into the rushing water. Voices much like Kitty's assaulted them, but they seemed to be encouraging rather than embittered or hateful. They were also quite confident in tone. One word made sense to her. *Fly.*

Great.

Merin's arms held her tight, and she held on to him as well. Bela wondered if they would be able to hang on to one another as they went over the waterfall. The water was fierce, as it had been in the carving on the cavern wall. She told herself that in that particular succession of images, they had survived. Could she trust her life to an ancient stick figure drawing? Apparently she just had.

They were pulled under, deep, and then they were pushed past glimmering rock and into a more natural light. Sunlight. As soon as they left the mountain, the voices ceased.

And she and Merin did fly.

They were ripped apart, unable to hold on to one another in the rush of water, but the braided rope remained.

They were in the waterfall, a part of the river as it escaped the mountain. A scream was ripped from Bela's throat, and her arms flailed uselessly. They should've cut the rope before jumping into the water. They should've taken a knife and severed the braided cord. If Merin had given her time to think, she would've suggested it, but he had not.

The fall was great, but not deadly. They splashed into the water below, landing in a deep pool that swirled and churned beneath the waterfall, then turned more peaceful as it gently flowed away from the mountain. The cord which connected them was stretched to the limit, but not for long. They had been apart and then they came together again, as was right.

Bela sputtered as she broke the surface, and Merin did the same. Then he laughed. He *laughed.*

"Have you lost your mind?" she asked as they swam toward shore. Given the long time he'd been in the crystal-influenced water, listening to those voices, it was certainly possible.

"No," he said, sounding quite sane until he added, "That was fun."

"Fun?" she said sharply, as their feet found ground and they stood in the pond.

"Yes." He looked at her, curling hair wet and hanging past his shoulders, beard making him look primitive, handsome still, with his clothing stuck to his fine body here and there.

Before they'd jumped, he had called her "love." He'd never used an endearment for her before, and after the dreams she'd had, "love" seemed particularly appropriate.

Now was not the time to ask Merin if he loved her. They had greater concerns.

They stepped slowly to the rocky shore, walking easily through the gently rushing water in the shallows. Not far below, the valley turned green, fed by the water and the sun. Exhausted, they sat on the first suitable dry rock they could claim, breathing hard and deep. Bela was surprised to see the sun still so high in the sky. It had seemed as if more time had passed while they'd traveled through the mountain. Nothing was as it seemed in the caverns, which were as enchanted as Kitty.

After a few minutes, Bela asked, "Why didn't you cut the rope before we jumped?"

"We're in this together, Bela, for better or for worse."

"Yes, but it was dangerous. We should've cut the rope."

A muscle in his jaw clenched. "I wasn't sure you'd wish to remain married, now that we've seen what the future holds. If we sever the bonds, we'll be wed for another three years, and then we'll have to go through this all over again."

She was hurt, more than a little. Last night and this morning it had seemed to be decided. They would remain married. She would be his wife and he would be her husband. There would be children.

But that had been before the revelation that their daughter was meant to be a warrior who carried Kitty, before all the questions about how they had come to be here and the wondering about the authenticity of their emotions. Exactly how much had they been led to end up here?

"Besides," he added in a more casual tone, "we gave our word."

"You would rather die than break your word?"

He looked her in the eye. "I suppose I would."

For a long while they stared at one another. She knew these dark brown eyes so well, they were a comfort to her. What did Merin see when he looked into her eyes? Did he take comfort in her, or did he wonder if he truly knew her at all?

Merin finally turned his gaze to the west and frowned. "We were inside the mountain for hours, though I swear it seemed like longer, and now we must make our way to the other side and down again. We have to get back to the village before Nobel comes again."

"The others will be ready for him. He won't catch us unaware again."

"I would like to be there, in any case."

Bela sighed. "So would I. Our swords will be needed." She grimaced. "Drat. I will need a new sword, straightaway."

Merin turned his head to look at her, and suddenly they seemed closer. "I don't suppose I can convince you to hide yourself away with the other women while we fight Nobel and his men."

"You're right about that. I do not hide from a fight, not ever."

"Not even if you're carrying a daughter destined to be born?"

"If I am, and if she is destined to be born, then I'll survive the fight."

Merin frowned. "Why does that argument not make me feel any better?"

He hadn't said that he loved her; he saved those words for her dreams. But he did care. Would he still care about her when they were away from Kitty's influence? Had the enchanted sword ever had power to affect their emotions as well as their thoughts? And who had carved her life into a stone wall?

The same someone who had made Kitty, she supposed.

Bela sat up and glanced around the pond. This was truly an enchanted place, lush and beautiful against a backdrop of rock, verdant amid a barren land. Just as on the other side of Forbidden Mountain, there were no animals, no life beyond the plants and the water itself. In all the years this had existed, why had it not drawn life? Did the powers of the mountain drive away all life, even here? If that was true, why did she feel as if she could stay here forever and be perfectly content?

Surely the power of the crystals had driven away any who dared set foot here, just as it had on the other side of this mountain. She and Merin were welcome here, at least for now, for reasons Bela did not wish to dwell upon.

"We have a long while until darkness," she said, rising slowly to her feet. Her legs were still shaking a little as she surveyed the side of the mountain and pointed. "If we hurry, we can reach that ridge before sunset. From there it should be an easy enough trip to the other side. See the way the rock winds just so? We can walk that with no problem. Coming out on this side of the mountain might cost us only another three or four days."

Merin struggled to his feet. "Then let's hurry, but not until we gather a bit of food and drink some water. It'll be two days at the very least, more likely four, before we reach the campsite where we left our supplies."

Bela wrinkled her nose at the water Merin suggested they drink. True, the water in the pond did not speak, not that she had heard, but did that mean it was untainted? Did that mean it was safe for her to take into her body, when a child might be growing there?

She longed to fall back against the soft grass and sleep, even though she had just had a nap inside the mountain. But Nobel was coming, and Kitty was gone, and she had a deep desire to get far away from this unnatural mountain.

Chapter Fifteen

✳

THEY were husband and wife, at least for the present time, and Merin truly believed he could make a lifetime with Bela. A good lifetime. He could love her, he *did* love her, in a way he had not thought possible before coming to the village of the Turis. His love for Bela had bloomed unexpectedly, and it had grown stronger on this very mountain. He'd come close to losing her at the hands of an assassin and had been forced to imagine a world without her; that was one reason. They had consummated their marriage; that had not hurt matters at all.

But he did not entirely trust what he felt. They remained atop a mountain filled with a living crystal that had the ability to reach into his mind. Even though he could no longer hear words, even though the crystal seemed not to be invading him at the moment, how could he be sure he was not being unduly influenced? How could he know he was not being used simply to produce the child Kitty demanded?

Had the crystals sent him the sexual dreams which were

surely meant to arouse? Even now, he could see Bela's naked body awash in a rainbow, he could hear her cries of
pleasure.

When they were back in the village, away from Kitty
and the rest, and his feelings for Bela remained unchanged,
then perhaps he could consider remaining married to her.
Perhaps then he could believe that what he felt was real,
and not some kind of magic that had stolen their control.

Bela seemed to be having the same thoughts, the same
doubts. They lay upon the ground in the shadow of an overhang that protected them from the night winds, but she did
not make a move toward him, not as she had last night.

"I have always thought myself a strong woman," she
said after a long period of silence.

"You are," Merin said. "Too strong, sometimes."

"That's what my mother says." She sighed.

"But strength is not a bad thing to possess, Bela. I'm
glad you're a strong woman."

"Most of the men who have been so foolish as to attempt to woo me wanted to tame me. They seemed to think
it was their duty, or even their right."

Merin smiled. "I don't imagine any of them lasted very
long."

"Not long at all," she responded.

He took a deep breath of the cool night air, happy for his
freedom, glad to be out of the cavern and away from the
crystal voices. "I do not wish to tame you," he said honestly.

"I know," she whispered. "That is one of the things
I lo—like about you." She stuttered only a little, but he
understood. She'd spoken words of love before, but surely
she was suffering the same doubts he was about the genu-
ineness of those emotions.

"Honestly," she continued, changing the subject deftly,
"I never understood my mother's objections to my chosen

lifestyle until I saw that drawing of our daughter—if there is a daughter—standing tall with a sword in her hand. It was a rough depiction, that's true, but she looked so determined, so incredibly strong. What sort of battle requires a destined warrior and a magical sword?" Her voice rose to a pitch that spoke of near panic. "What monsters must she be called to fight? This child of ours does not yet exist, might never exist, and already I am worried for her. If she does come into this world, she would be better off a wife and mother, protected by the men around her."

"You have never wished protection for yourself," Merin said, and then he smiled. "Woe be to the man who might be so foolish as to suggest you need protection."

"I know, but I do wish it for my children. If I have children," she added quickly. "Who carved those pictures?" she asked angrily, and then she added in a sullen voice, "My breasts are not so large and they do not sag, and though your manly appendage is of a considerable size, it is not as large as your arm, a fact for which I am very grateful. And who or *what* would feel the need to be so *specific* in their depictions?"

"We may never know the answers to any of these questions," Merin said calmly.

"That's so unfair," Bela muttered.

"I suppose it is, in a way, and yet . . ."

She rolled to face him, but still did not move close. "And yet what?"

"What if we were given a glimpse of what might be?" Merin suggested. "Not what is destined to be, not a future that is unchangeable, but what could happen, if we choose. There might already be a child, but then again, that might not be so. There was more than one possible future depicted, including one we have already moved past."

They had not died in the cavern, and Merin vowed he would not allow Nobel to harm Bela. Kitty had been left behind, concealed deep in the mountain where no one would ever find her, so Nobel would never possess the magical sword he desired.

"What if there are a thousand or more possibilities before us, and whatever future comes is that which we make? If we have a daughter, and if she is very much like you, then perhaps one day she will choose to be a warrior. If that is her calling, we cannot keep her from it, no matter how much we might wish for another life for her. You would be miserable if you led the kind of life your mother wished for you."

Bela made a comical face, and Merin smiled.

"Do you disagree?"

"No."

"My mother wished a different life for me, too," Merin said. "She wanted me to become a blacksmith, like my father, but I was determined to go to Arthes and become a sentinel. She never forgave me."

"When was the last time you saw her?"

"Ten years ago. The visit was not a pleasant one, I'm afraid."

"Do you have any other family?"

Merin hesitated. "My mother remarried after my father died, and she had another child, one who seemed to be more agreeable than I had been. Savyn was apprenticing to a wheelwright when last I saw him. He was fifteen then, already a strong lad and the obedient son I had not been."

"Was your mother not impressed by your success?"

"If she was, she did not show her pride in any way. She died two years after my last visit, before the war with Ciro began, and I have not been back."

"Not even to see your brother?"

Merin shrugged to emphasize his indifference. "I left home when I was fifteen. Savyn was seven at that time, a child. My few visits since then were brief and more unpleasant than not. He does not know me and I do not know him. What would be the point of seeking out a relation-ship?"

Bela sat up. "But he's your brother!"

"Half brother," Merin said sullenly.

"He is still your blood," she said, and then she sighed and reclined upon their hard bed again. "My brothers can be maddening, but I love them dearly. Don't you dare tell them I said so!" she added, and Merin smiled.

"Maybe one day, when I have the time, I'll travel down that way and see if Savyn is still living in Childers." He had not thought of the boy in a long time. What he remem-bered most about his little brother was Savyn's easy smile, that and the fact that people said they looked alike. They both had their mother's curly hair and brown eyes, though Savyn's eyes were warmer and lighter in color and mood than Merin's had ever been.

"I'm hungry," Bela grumbled.

"You did not like the tasty leaves we found by the wa-terfall?"

"They were bitter and not at all filling," she said. "I want bread. Meat. Hot oats. Boiled tubers."

Merin's stomach growled. "We might reach the packs we left outside the cave entrance in two or three days. I'd guess." If they were lucky. "We have oatcakes and dried fruit mix there." Enough to finish the journey to the bot-tom of the mountain, at least.

"Yum," Bela muttered with a decided lack of enthusiasm.

INSTEAD of collecting their possessions and setting out for the village and freedom, Leyla and Savyn had settled once again in the hut which had become a home of sorts. Every day they found an excuse to remain. Every day they said that the following morning would be soon enough to set out.

And yet they did not leave. They existed together in uncomfortable silence, eating and sleeping together and never touching any more than was necessary. There was not, could not be, a repeat of what had happened on the forest floor.

Leyla reasoned that Savyn was not yet ready to leave this place. Since he had learned to use the stick, it only made sense that he take some time and become more comfortable with it before going on his own. He was beginning to get around more confidently, with the aid of that stick and his remaining senses. His sense of smell was keen, and he could feel an object with his fingers and know it. He could hear the rustle of her skirt or the twittering of a bird at a great distance, as he listened with great care.

Savyn could feed himself with no trouble, and he could drink from the tin cup without a single spill. He could take care of bathing himself and could see to more personal matters on his own. He said he wanted to try shaving himself, but Leyla insisted on performing that chore herself. Not only was she not ready to put a razor in his hands, it was the only time she was allowed to touch him, and that was a pleasure she was not ready to give up.

As they lay in the dark, silent and strained, Leyla tried to convince herself that this was what she'd wanted all along. Savyn was no longer tied to her; he did not feel any obligation toward her at all, so he could go on with his life. Whether he regained his sight or not, he would be well. Already he was walking more assuredly, using the stick he had found as if it were another part of himself, relying on his other senses while his eyes remained useless. He was more confident now, more ready to go out on his own. He did not need her.

So why did she cry? She shed her tears silently, stifling the need to blubber as she attempted to convince herself that this was what she wanted. A new life; Savyn free to find love, marry a woman nearer his own age, and have children. When they had been in the forest and he had been inside her, it had seemed that nothing had changed between them. She'd thought for a brief and wonderful moment that they could find a way to be together. They could start fresh, with new names, in a place where no one knew either of them. She could lie about her age, or be like Savyn and simply not care what others thought. Heaven knows she'd been told often enough that she did not look her age, and her witch's blood would give her a longer life than most—a trade-off for the burden of the ability she had never wanted. If she chose to keep the secret, no one would know she was older than Savyn, no one would know that she was—or rather had been—monied and titled by marriage, while Savyn had worked with his hands to eke out a living. They could literally start over. Together. All that had gone through her mind in a brief and wonderful moment of bliss.

And then Savyn had spoken and he'd ruined all her silly dreams, which was no more than she deserved for what she'd done. She should hurt. She should carry this pain with her forever.

Somehow, she would find a way to start over alone, and so would Savyn. He could not continue as a wheelwright or a swordmaker if his sight did not return, but he had a lovely singing voice and could play the lute very well. He had never considered music as a potential livelihood, but he could sing and play with his eyes closed, so he could sing and play blind, if necessary. Considering how well he was getting around these days, she could only imagine that there were other things he could do to get by. He had a brother in Arthes. They were not close, but surely this brother would help, given the circumstances. Once they reached the village, they had only to wait until travelers on their way to the capital city came through. She would convince these travelers to take Savyn with them; she would make sure, with her gift, that they'd take good care of him and deliver him safely to his brother.

Someone would help him; someone would love him. That someone could not be her.

"Stop it," Savyn said harshly.

"Stop what?" she asked, working very hard to keep her voice clear, just as she had kept her crying silent.

"I can smell your tears," Savyn said, his voice filled with wonder at the new ability, and even with sorrow. Perhaps even guilt.

"It has been a long day and I'm afraid," she said honestly.

"You will be fine," he said gruffly. "With your beauty, I imagine you can walk into any village or city in Columbyana and capture the heart of the richest man available. If your beauty is not enough, you can touch the man you choose and make him love you."

"I don't think love can be given that way," she said, "though apparently it can be taken away."

"Lust, then, if not love. Plant a few seeds of desire in the mind of the man you choose, and he will be yours. Most men cannot tell the difference between lust and love, so you will have all that you want."

All that she wanted was here, in this room, and she did not dare say so.

"We will share the money I found in Trinity's saddlebags," she said. "That will help us get started. After that, I thought I might find a job as a governess or a nurse. I don't have much experience caring for children, but I have always liked them well enough, and many such positions come with room and board."

"No woman will hire you," Savyn said harshly. "You are too beautiful for her to trust, if there is a man in the house."

"I won't marry without love, not again," Leyla said harshly. "I am a fully grown woman, and I will make my own way, wherever that takes me."

"You would rather be a governess than a lady?" Savyn asked, disbelief dripping from his usually pleasant voice.

"Yes. I want an honest life, even if it becomes a harsh one in the process."

"Honest," Savyn said softly. "Does that mean you will no longer use your abilities?"

"I suppose it does." She would use them to benefit Savyn, to get him safely to Arthes, but that was not the same as using the gift to get what she wanted; to make her life easier.

Savyn rolled onto his side so he faced her, even though it was pitch-black in the hut and he could not see her face. This was what he saw all the time, now. Knowing that, her heart broke.

"Since you have decided to embrace honesty," he said, his voice still bitter but perhaps less so, "and obviously neither of us is near sleep, will you tell me how we met?"

Her heart thumped. Oh, this was a horrible idea! Why would he wish to torture her with the telling of details? She did not want to remember, much less relive, what she'd given up. But how could she refuse him something so simple? "I have always known you, since I arrived in Childers. In a small town . . ."

"That's not what I mean, and you know it," he said harshly. "You took the memories from me. The least you can do is inform me how and why we were so foolish as to become lovers."

She did owe him that much, she supposed, even though the telling would hurt. She'd made so many mistakes in her life. "It started a little more than two years ago," she said. "My husband had been gone nearly three years, and I'd had a very bad day dealing with my stepson. He wanted to arrange another marriage for me. He wanted to make me a part of a business deal. I refused, and he was very unhappy with me.

"The wheel on my carriage needed repair, and you saw to it, as usual. When you were finished, I offered you something to eat, as you had worked right through suppertime and I knew you would be hungry."

"You fed me yourself, instead of calling upon one of your servants to see to the menial task?"

"I did. It was late in the day, and everyone else was busy or had retired for the evening, and I . . . I didn't want you to go just yet."

"Why not?"

He was going to make her say it. "Because you are so incredibly beautiful, and I had little beauty in my life. You always smiled at me, and your smile was genuine and without motive. And yes, I knew you looked at me the way a man looks at a woman he desires—I am not blind to such things—but there seemed to be something more. Something I had missed in my life."

"Who made the first move?"

"I'm not sure," she whispered. "We were alone in the kitchen and you smiled at me, and it was different from other times. Maybe because we were alone, maybe because I'd had such a bad day and it was so nice. The smile was . . . inviting. It made my heart leap more than a little. When I took your emptied plate from you, our hands touched and it was startling. I felt like lightning had passed through my blood. I had never . . ." she stopped. How much should she say? How much was safe?

"You never what?" he prodded.

Perhaps she owed him honesty this time. Perhaps that was all she could do to make up for what she'd done. "I had never known desire until that moment. I was no virgin, no untouched maid. I'd been sold to a husband who would not be denied his rights." Her voice was bitter as she remembered her unhappy marriage. "But desire, for me . . . it was unknown, it was new and exciting. So I kissed you. You were sitting there, and I held your plate in my hand and I bent down and pressed my lips to yours. It was an innocent enough kiss, a test of sorts. You kissed me back, and I was lost in sensations which were so new to me, which were so wonderful and exciting.

"We made love that very night. I secretly led you up the back stairway, telling myself all along that it would be only that one time, that I was curious and lonely and you were more than willing, so what was the harm? With your good looks and your strength and your manliness, I assumed you were an experienced lover, but it was your first time." If she had known he'd never lain with a woman, perhaps she would've had more control that night.

"I was already in love," Savyn said softly. "I was foolishly saving myself for you. I still don't remember the details of that night, but I can imagine how happy I must've been."

"You should not remember love," Leyla said.

"You took away the memories of our relationship," he said. "I was in love with you long before any sort of relationship began. You didn't take that away. You could not."

"I thought you said . . ." She remembered too well what he had said. He did not love her, and if he ever had, it was now gone. She'd killed it.

"I lied to hurt you," he said harshly. "To hurt you and to set you free from the burden I have become. I cannot stay angry with you, Leyla, no matter how I wish to do so. I still plan to go my own way, once we reach the village. That has not changed. It's best for you."

Leyla scooted closer to Savyn and placed her head against his chest. She could hear his heartbeat, as she had so many times before, and she took comfort in the steady sound. "Perhaps, perhaps not."

"You do not think I will do as I say?"

Hurting and scared, she still managed a smile. "I cannot tell you how many nights we said it was the last time. We both knew there was no future in our relationship, that if we ever got caught, it would be disastrous for both of us. And yet we continued to find ways to be together. One night I would vow to let you go, and the next I was meeting you in the stable, or you were sneaking up the back stairway, or I was opening my window to you. It's not so easy to give up something you want so desperately, even if you know it's not good for you or for someone else." Someone you love—she could not say that.

"More than two years, and you did not catch a child," Savyn said. "Why? Is one of us unable?"

"At first we were just lucky, I suppose, but soon after we began meeting, I started taking a potion to keep me from conceiving. It was the same potion I secretly took while my husband was living."

"You don't want babies?"

"I did not want his."

It was likely too late for her, even if she did dream of children. She was thirty-four years old and had never given birth. Yes, she had the body of a younger woman, thanks to her witch's blood, but still . . . thirty-four!

"Are you taking that potion now?" Savyn asked.

"No. I saw no need." For the past two years she had taken what she wanted from Savyn, losing herself in him, taking her only joy in life from their time together. He made her laugh, he made her scream in pleasure, he made her dream of all the wonders of life she could never have, and yet the dream continued.

"And now?" he asked.

Leyla imagined the emperor's sentinels searching for and finding what remained of the traveling party Trinity had decimated. She'd heard Hilde's screams, so she knew the other woman was dead. Would they think the body in the carriage was that of Lady Leyla Hagan? Would the world believe she was gone? The very idea made her feel suddenly and wonderfully free.

"You might not agree, you might think I'm incredibly

foolish, but I'm going to tell you what I want to happen next."

"Tell me," Savyn whispered, when she did not immediately continue.

All her life she had allowed choices to be made for her. She had bemoaned her lot in life and done nothing to change it. This was her chance, perhaps her last and only chance, to make her life what she wished it to be. Was she brave enough to say what was in her heart?

"If I could choose," she said softly, "if I could have all that I desired . . . I would want us to stay here a while longer."

"In this hut?" he asked, amazed. "Maybe I can't see it now, but I do remember well what it looks like. It's small and dirty and falling apart . . ."

"I've cleaned it very well," Leyla interrupted. "And I've moved things around a bit, separating what's useful from what's not. The hut is not as bad as it was when we first found it."

"Still, it's hardly what you are accustomed to."

She did not tell Savyn this place was not so very different from the house where she'd been born. "Not for very long, just . . . I want to take time enough for you to heal, to wait awhile and see if your sight will return, and I enjoy being alone with you. I like having you all to myself."

"I'm blind."

"You're Savyn, and that's all that matters to me." How honest could she—*should* she—be? If she was going to be straightforward with him, perhaps she could not hold back, not anymore. "I would never let myself love you before, because I knew it was foolish. I told myself we could never be together, that we could never have more than stolen moments. I told myself again and again that it was wrong to keep you from finding a love you could proclaim to the world, a love you did not have to be ashamed of. We can be together now, if we wish."

"Is that what you want?"

She was laying her heart out for a man who had reason to hate her, to squash her, to decimate her. It was more frightening than facing an assassin, more terrifying than not knowing what tomorrow would bring. "Yes, more than anything. I want us to stay here, as if we were man and wife and this was our home. I will call you my husband, if you'll let me, and we will lie together each night. We will learn, in time, if what we have is more than forbidden passion, if it's more than sex and laughter. True love survives tragedy, it lives through hardships as well as happiness. Maybe your sight will return, maybe it will not. I don't care, and if you love me at all, you'll allow me to help you. You'll allow us to try to live a normal life, together."

In the moment of silence that followed, Leyla held her breath and waited for Savyn to tell her again that he did not need or want her.

"We are not normal," he said.

"True enough. You're blind and I'm an old witch."

"What a perfect pair we make," he responded.

Leyla smiled. Savyn laughed. And then somehow she was in his arms and the night was not so black.

BELA was breathless, though she did everything in her power not to let Merin see the weakness. They had traveled from the ledge where they'd spent that first night to a ragged passageway near the top of the mountain. The passage had been rough, but they had managed. They'd found water, they'd slept when it was necessary, they'd clung to one another in the night and not spoken of their uncertainties or of the child she might be carrying. The nights had been chilly and they'd had no fire to warm them, so they'd had to rely on one another for warmth. They'd held one another, but it had gone no further. She would not make the next move, not when Merin was so obviously hesitant.

In a matter of days, they'd traveled over the summit of Forbidden Mountain and down a rugged path to recover what they had left behind when they'd entered the small cave where Kitty had been discovered years ago. The last time she and Merin had been there they had found . . . well, she did not want to think of what they had found there. It was best to leave it all behind, to forget, for now. She tried to think ahead. They were not horribly behind schedule, as they had planned to have a few days to search this part of the mountain.

She felt as if they had been on this mountain far longer than they had. Three days up, a long a day inside the mountain, then another four days to get back to the original campsite. There would be another three days getting off the mountain and to the village, which by her reckoning would give them only three days to prepare for Nobel's visit. They had been on this mountain more than long enough!

Bela was damn tired of sleeping on bare rock and eating the bitter leaves Merin had insisted on taking from the waterfall site. She had never thought to be glad to eat a cold, hard oatcake! Tonight she would sleep on a blanket, and perhaps, if they traveled to the creek and collected some wood, they could have a fire.

Their campsite was exactly as they had left it, except there was no longer an entrance to the mountain there. Rocks small and large blocked the way; the face of the mountain had changed here. Kitty was in there, deep in the rock and alone, hidden from the world for the time being.

Was it foolish to miss a sword the way one might miss a friend? Was it shallow of her to long to have the magic of the sword in her possession again? Not that she had ever possessed Kitty. Kitty might've possessed her. Yes, that was closer to the truth.

With their packs and blankets recovered, she and Merin made their way back down the mountain. There was still so much to be decided. It wasn't as though she did not want Merin, and she knew very well that he wanted her. Men were so easy to understand in that respect, especially when they slept so close at night.

But was the wanting real? When they reached the village and were without the influence of the crystals which wanted their child, would they feel this same incredible draw to one another?

They did spend that night by the creek, and there was a warming fire and fresh water. There were blankets, fire, and food—of sorts. There was little conversation and not even a hint that Merin still desired her. Exhausted, they slept deeply. The next morning they rose early and began again.

It was not long into the day before they passed the site of the attack, and though she claimed to be as tough as any man, Bela quickly turned away. There were no wild animals on this mountain. The power of the crystals kept life away, she knew that now. But buzzards had been drawn to the dead and had done their work well. The two bodies which remained on this plateau had been picked practically clean. Had the crystals called the buzzards here to clean up what was left of the invaders who had been so foolish as to come here?

Though he did not dare to do so openly, Merin protected her from the gruesome sight by always managing to place his body between her and the remains. She would not think of chastising him for being so protective. Not now, when she appreciated his efforts so much. Not now, when she understood him. He was a good man, through and through.

They were well away from the site of the battle when he suggested that they stop for a few minutes. She would not argue with him, not when she wanted nothing more than to rest, even if for a short while.

He leaned against a rock wall and studied her in that

intense way he had. Dark eyes smart, and even cunning and dangerous, looked her up and down before he asked, "Have you felt the influence of Kitty or any of her kind since we left the waterfall?"

"No," Bela said. "But just because we can't feel their influence, does that mean it isn't there?"

"Not necessarily, but I suspect we're safer with distance. Otherwise . . ."

"Otherwise there would have been chaos in the village long ago."

"Exactly."

Bela glanced up, grateful for the distance between her and the crystals. "They must scare away the miners who come too close," she said. "All through the mountain range there are Turi miners digging and panning for gems, but there's no one here. Even though the mountain is forbidden, surely some brave ones came exploring, or got lost as Clyn did. And yet, they did not stay. They knew, as the animals have known, that they are not welcomed here, not as we were welcome. The crystals scare away what they do not want on their lands. They influence all that they can."

"That makes sense," Merin said casually.

Bela narrowed her eyes. "So, it makes sense that where their influence ends is where we will begin to see people and animals again." She wrinkled her nose. "I don't think buzzards count."

Merin almost smiled. His lips twitched a little.

"What are we going to do?" she asked bluntly. She wasn't sure if Merin was still considering staying married to her, or if he planned to ride away and leave her behind. Surely he would not think of offering her to his emperor, not after all they had been through. They could cut the rope that bound them at any time, and just tell the others, when they returned to the village, that they'd changed their minds about dissolving the marriage—Merin's blasted honor about breaking his word aside. She could do the cutting, if he refused. Some would talk, yes, but did she really care? They would be married, and that was all that mattered to her.

Was it important that Merin had not touched her since he'd seen the cavern carvings? Had the destiny portrayed on those walls frightened him away from her?

"We should arrive in the village in two and a half days, if we do not tarry," he said.

"Yes," she responded, knowing full well how far they had to travel.

This time he did smile, and it was lovely. "Once we're there and Forbidden Mountain is behind us, I suggest we present ourselves to your parents, tell them we intend to remain married, and cut the cord together."

Bela almost sighed in relief, and then Merin said, "Unless . . ."

"Unless what?" she snapped.

"Unless once we get to the village, we realize that what we've been experiencing has not been real. If either of us decides marriage is not what we want, then we will remain bound until the dissolution is complete. Just a few more days, Bela."

It had been on her mind, so she had to ask. "Is that why you have not touched me since we left the mountain? Are you less than sure?"

Dark eyes smoldered. "I am very sure of what I want," Merin said, "and I do not expect to change my mind. I rarely do. However, I'm not so certain about you."

"Me?"

"You have never cared for marriage before now."

"You were not here," she said honestly.

"And you're a little twitchy without Kitty. You're uncertain and worried and maybe a little obsessed. You miss her too much."

"How do you know all that?" she asked, annoyed. Could he reach into her mind as Kitty had done?

"It's on your face, Bela. I see it well."

It was true enough that she had never been good at hiding her feelings, and Merin knew her as well as anyone else. Perhaps better than anyone else. "I don't expect to change my mind, either," she said.

"Even if marriage to me means your daughter will be a warrior?"

Her heart skipped a beat. That possibility still concerned her greatly. There could already be a daughter, conceived on that night—or that morning—before they had entered the mountain. Then again, the destined warrior might not yet exist, not even as a seed in her belly. It was just too soon to tell. "You said we could make our own destiny."

"I hope we can," he said softly.

She could see very well the life she might make with Merin. Here or in his world, in Arthes, it did not matter where. She could imagine, so well, sleeping with him each night. She could almost see their children, boys and girls with their father's strength and their mother's stubbornness. That should be terrifying, but somehow the idea was soothing and heartwarming. She wanted it so much. Would she feel the same way when they were off this blasted rock?

Yes, yes she would. There was no magic in the feelings she experienced, none other than that which they made.

"I can't imagine myself married to any other man," Bela said softly. "I can't imagine giving myself body and soul to any other." If she was going to open her heart and bleed, she might as well go all the way. "I would rather die."

"You have ruined me for other women, Bela," Merin said. "There is not another like you."

Frustration caught up with her. "So why haven't you touched me in more days than I can count?"

Again he seemed to smolder. "If we both feel the same

way once we get to the village, then trust me, you will not be safe for very long."

Bela managed a smile. "I do not wish to be safe, not from you." She leaned slightly toward him, already thinking again of keeping him as her husband and what they would be like in the years to come. Her imagination was quite vivid in that respect.

Would their emotions change when they were off Forbidden Mountain? If Merin did not feel the same when they left this place, if he did not look at her this way and speak so wonderfully of keeping her, she would let him go. Even if she was already with child, even if they had to remain husband and wife, separated by the distance of a great country, she would let him go and she would raise her child alone.

And she would never love another man. She would have dreams of Merin, and they would have to be enough. "Time to get moving," she said, leading the way down the path as quickly as was safe. She would not know what her future held until they were off this blasted rock!

Chapter Sixteen

GOING down the mountain was a bit less arduous than going up, but no less dangerous, especially on the steepest part of the journey. They stopped to sleep when darkness and exhaustion made it necessary, but they were both anxious to get to the village as soon as possible. Neither was pleased that they were behind schedule, thanks to the treacherous mountain exit that had dumped them out on the wrong side.

Near the foot of the mountain the curves flattened and the jagged rocks smoothed somewhat. When it was possible, they ran. Not that either of them could get very far from the other, with the braided rope connecting them. Merin sometimes purposely fell behind just so he could watch Bela run. No other woman moved as she did, no other would find such joy in racing down a mountainside. Yes, he loved her. That would not change. He would not allow it.

After nearly three weeks of suffering at their hands, the

once bright red, white, and black braid that stretched between them was dulled and frayed. It was gray in many places and appeared weak in others, but the rope remained strong, as a proper marriage should in times of trouble. Perhaps this marriage dissolution ceremony was not a ridiculous Turi custom after all. Perhaps it was very, very smart.

It was late in the evening when they arrived at the far edge of the village. Bela tensed, and so did Merin, as they walked toward her family home, where they would sever the rope together, making it clear they intended to remain married—unless she changed her mind before they got that far.

The small farmhouse they walked past was too quiet. No one was about. No smoke rose from the chimney, at a time of day when the farmer's wife should be cooking supper for her family. A gust of wind made the tall grasses in their path dance, and a chill walked up Merin's spine. In the distance the village sat as it always had, but it, too, was more still than it should be.

"Something is wrong," Bela said softly, mirroring his thoughts.

Merin agreed with a nod of his head. There was an air of tension even here, a good distance from the village, and he smelled battle—he smelled smoke and blood.

They ran again, trotting at an increasingly frantic pace. When they reached the far end of the muddy main thoroughfare that ran through the Turi village straight as an arrow, the scene before them said it all. Wounded men sat around the village square, being tended by the women. Five men not of this village—also wounded—were bound together and placed off to the side. No one tended to their injuries. One of the prisoners was the red-headed Nobel, who bled from a nasty wound to his left arm as well as from his slashed thigh. A blazing fire lit the center of town.

"The bastard attacked early," Bela said angrily, as they began to run again. "I should've known we could not trust him!"

"Why would he attack early?" Merin asked. "For all he knew, he was going to get what he wanted."

"Perhaps he did not trust your word and wished to take us by surprise," Bela suggested.

"Possible."

Heads turned as Bela and Merin walked toward the center of the square, where Turi soldiers, wounded and unwounded, had gathered. Most of their faces were drawn, the men exhausted by battle. Merin could see that Bela was searching anxiously for her father and her brothers.

It was Tyman who saw them, Tyman who raced away from the gathering to meet them. He was not wounded, not that Merin could see, but he was battle-weary. His eyes said too much.

"Where have you two been?" Bela's more difficult brother asked in a too-loud voice. "Blast you both, we could've used your swords when Nobel attacked. We expected you to be here."

"We were delayed," Bela said, her eyes studying the wounded men, men she knew. Merin knew that look; she was not only searching for who was wounded but to also see who was missing. "It was unavoidable. Besides, how were we to know he would attack early?"

Tyman glared at his sister with dark, accusing eyes. "Good God, you cannot even count the days." He drew his blood-encrusted sword and swung it high, then quickly and precisely brought it down onto the rope which bound Merin and Bela. The sharp blade easily sliced through the frayed fabric.

"No!" Bela protested, but it was too late. The braid swung free.

"Never fear, little sister, your sad little marriage is undone," Tyman said harshly.

"It is not!" Bela shouted. "We did not lose count of the days!"

"Your marriage was undone yesterday, as scheduled," her brother said. He glanced at Merin with rage in his eyes. This was a rage that had nothing to do with his sister, and had everything to do with an obviously difficult battle—a battle the Turis had won, but not easily. "Congratulations, General, you are a free man."

Merin knew he had not miscounted the time that had passed since leaving this village in search of knowledge about Kitty. The marriage would not be undone for another three and a half days.

And then he realized with a sick twist in his stomach what had happened. The nap they had taken in the cavern, the short period of sleep they had claimed in order to re-cover their strength after walking through the water and listening to the insistent crystal voices . . . it had not been a short nap at all. They had passed *days* on that cold rock bed.

THOUGH she and Merin were no longer bound together, they moved as if they were. It was habit, Bela supposed, and she was glad enough of it. She was not ready to be far from the man she had come to love so much.

Once Tyman had rushed back to the others—after assuring Bela that Clyn and their father were also unwounded—Merin took her arm and led her away from the crowd. "When we slept in the cavern, did you dream?" he asked sharply.

Bela's cheeks grew warm as she remembered. "Yes. What does that have to do with anything?"

"We did not miscount the days, you know we did not."

She wrinkled her nose. "It was a trick of that blasted

mountain. How could they—they, it, whatever the magic there might be," she sputtered, "make time disappear?"

"Time did not disappear," Merin said with certainty. "We slept through those days. Well, it was a sort of sleep, if I'm correct, a sleep colored by rainbows and lullabies that came from the walls around us." He squirmed a little. "I'm almost positive the dreams we had were not actual dreams at all. Somehow, they were real. Enchanted, but very real."

Her heart skipped a beat. "How can you be sure?"

"Shall we compare those dreams?" he asked.

She remembered them vividly, which was unusual after all the time that had passed. Could he be right? "There was one in the water," she said. "There was a gentle whirlpool."

"Yes, and the rainbows were everywhere, and we . . . we flew."

Bela swallowed hard. That was enough to tell her that what they'd experienced had not been dreams, yet still she continued. "A time or two it rained on us, a soft rain that came from the cavern itself."

Merin took her chin in his hand. "We cannot be sure, but I suspect the crystals or the mountain or the water or whatever it is in that place that lives kept us there until it was sure the child it desires had taken hold within you."

So, it was done, at least in part. Kitty's warrior was growing inside her at that very moment. Probably. "We can't be certain."

"No, we can't." Merin glanced at the enemy prisoners. "I have a few questions for your most recent suitor," he said, abruptly changing the subject.

"So do I," Bela said.

They made their way to Nobel, who was being guarded by four armed and angry Turi warriors. When his eyes fell on her and the severed braid that swung from her waist, he grimaced. "I should've known you would not be here as you promised," he said. "You're no more reliable than any other woman."

Bela wanted nothing more than to kick the man who had caused all this trouble, but she did not wish to get that close to him. She satisfied herself with standing back and over him. "Do you know how the Turis dispose of invaders? Of course you do. You were once Turi yourself. Perhaps you have even seen the ceremony. I saw one, long ago, and though I am not a squeamish person, I could not stomach the sight for very long." She leaned slightly closer. "The screams, however . . . I could not escape the bloodcurdling screams that continued throughout the night."

Nobel paled, as he should.

"Where is your precious Kitty?" he asked.

Nobel was faced with a horrific and slow death, and he was still concerned with the magical sword he lusted after? "She's gone."

"That can't be," Nobel whispered. "I was assured . . ." Abruptly he stopped speaking, pursing his mouth tightly closed.

Bela took a step closer. "You were assured what?" she asked, beyond curious. What had precipitated Nobel's renewed interest in her and the magical sword? What had sent him so foolishly here?

"I cannot say," he whispered.

She saw the terror in his eyes.

"I cannot offer you freedom," Bela said softly, hoping the nearby guards would not hear, "but I can deliver to you a quick death rather than the slow and painful one which has been planned for you."

"Let me go," Nobel whispered.

Bela shook her head. "I cannot do that. All I can do is kill you quickly." If he had ever seen the ceremony to dispose of attackers, he would agree to anything she asked.

After taking a few deep breaths, Nobel nodded. "Promise me."

Bela nodded. "I give my word."

Merin remained beside her and silent, though he had said he had questions of his own. Perhaps their questions were the same. His sword was ready to defend her, if necessary. Instead of being annoyed that he was so obviously protecting her, she felt oddly serene and safe.

Nobel glanced up from his seated position on the ground. With the wound to his leg he was likely not able to stand, even if he wished to. The man to his left was already dead. The other three were more seriously wounded.

"In the wintertime I found a child, a little girl, wandering in the mountains near my mines." His eyes flickered. "I felt sorry for her, at first. It was cold, and we had had a wicked snowstorm. She was a little thing, so frail-looking and pretty. I thought she was a miner's child who'd gotten lost, but then she told me she lived in the mountains. Alone." His brow furrowed. "She can do things, Bela," he whispered. "And sometimes her eyes turn from innocent blue to midnight, evil black. Sometimes her hair looks like fire—living, flickering fire—and when she looks at me in a certain way, I feel like she's tearing me apart on the inside. But other times she's so sweet, so innocent, and I know in my soul that it's my purpose to protect her."

Before he had finished, Bela knew what had brought Nobel to this point. She had heard rumors of demon-children, but until now had dismissed them as fable. Myth. The stuff of bedtime stories.

"Uryen showed me where to find gems, gems that made me rich beyond my wildest dreams." His eyes glinted. "Then she guided me to men—or else she brought them to me—who were hungry for a share of those gems. These men would do anything if I offered them enough wealth. I quickly became rich and I had my own army. Uryen became a daughter to me. She loved me like the father she never knew, I know she did."

Nobel licked his dry, cracked lips. "Then a few weeks ago she told me about the marriage. She was frantic, so scared, as she told me about the rope that bound you and the importance of making sure you two separated and remained separate." He swallowed hard; his fingers trembled. "Keeping you apart would stop you and the general from making a child, she said. "I was to make you mine, to make Kitty mine as well, and then I would give the sword to her so she could . . . destroy it. Your child will kill her, she said." He sounded almost desperate. "My little Uryen wants to destroy the sword and you to protect herself, but she can't do it alone. She's too small, and does not yet have her full powers. She needs me."

One of Bela's first responses was relief. There was no traitor in the village. Jocylen had not betrayed her, not even unknowingly. All Nobel's information had come from a demon-child. She'd much rather face a demon than a traitorous friend.

"What did this Uryen promise you for your service?" Merin asked. "Surely you did not do all this without a promised reward."

Nobel smiled. "Uryen promised me immortality and riches beyond my imagination. Gems would grow at my feet, and I would never grow old. She will be my daughter now and she will be my wife when the time comes, when she's grown and her powers are strong. I could have everything. Anything I want, I have only to ask. All I had to do was separate you two and take the sword." He looked momentarily puzzled. "It didn't seem too arduous a task. She did not want a war with the Turis. She said it was a war she could not yet win. But if I married Bela and took her and Kitty away . . ."

"And yet you did battle with the Turis anyway," Bela said sharply.

Nobel looked at her accusingly. "You were not here, as you promised!" he said accusingly. "What was I to do?"

"Where is this Uryen?" Merin asked.

Nobel laughed and paled. "Gone, I suspect, deep in the mountains, waiting for another man to find and protect her. She will know that I've lost this battle, she will know that I've failed." He shook his head. "She knows everything—almost everything. One day she will know all, but now she sees only what is closest to her. Yes, she will know I have failed her. She hates me now, I suppose. It's better that I die here than to return to her defeated."

He looked up at Bela. "That is all. Now, kill me as you said you would." His eyes filled with tears. Perhaps he, too, had once heard the screams of tortured invaders. "Please."

Was he afraid of the Turi torture or Uryen's wrath?

Before Bela could act, Merin lunged forward and his sword pierced Nobel's heart. Nobel looked relieved, almost peaceful, before Merin withdrew his sword and the prisoner slumped to the ground, dead.

The attacker's death, too quick and painless, drew attention. Soon they were surrounded by angry Turi warriors, including her father and her brothers.

"What have you done?" Clyn shouted.

"I've killed the man who dared to attempt to take my wife," Merin said calmly. "Is that not my right?"

"She's not your wife any longer," Tyman shouted.

Merin glanced at her. "I plan to remedy that as soon as possible, if she will have me."

Bela held her breath. Did he still want her? Away from the influence of the crystals, her own feelings had not changed. She loved him. She would go anywhere with Merin. She would follow him to Arthes or to find his brother, or to the farthest reaches of the earth, where their daughter would be safe.

Her father stepped forward. "You have just gone through a difficult dissolution ceremony, and yet now you wish to claim her?"

"Yes," Merin said calmly. "But this is not the place to have the discussion." His eyes met hers. "I won't talk of the future while I hold a bloody sword in my hands and a dead man lies at my feet. It's hardly proper."

Bela's father nodded to Clyn, who collected Bela with strong, insistent hands and led her away. She was not ready to leave, and she made her reluctance known. Not that it made any difference to Clyn. He lifted her from her feet with one strong arm and carried her toward home.

When she realized that fighting her elder brother was useless, she calmed down and said, "Put me down. This is completely undignified."

Clyn asked, as he did *not* put her down, "Since when have you cared about dignity?"

"Just do it."

He stopped walking. "You won't run?"

"No."

"Swear."

Bela sighed. "I give you my word."

Clyn placed her on her feet. "Good. I'm too tired to carry you, anyway. My sword arm is aching."

Bela did not look back as they headed toward home. "Did we lose many in the fight?"

"Two dead, many wounded but none seriously." He nodded in pride, and then gave her the names of the dead: a farmer and a young man who worked on a ranch near the village. "We were ready for him this time."

"I wish I had been here."

Clyn looked down at her. "Why weren't you?"

"It's complicated. I'd just as soon tell the tale to all of you at once." She still wasn't sure how much to tell, and she wanted Merin with her when she faced her family.

"That's good enough, I suppose," Clyn said. "So, General Merin intends to court you?"

"God above, I hope not," Bela muttered.

"What?" Clyn asked sharply. "I thought . . ."

"I just want to be married." She sighed. "Courtship is silly. In this case it's unnecessary." She thought of all that Jocelyn and Rab had gone through in the days before their wedding. "Why is my life always so complicated?"

At that, Clyn laughed out loud, and Bela was very glad to see her home waiting before her.

MERIN wasn't sure how much he should tell Bela's family about what had happened in the cavern. What most concerned them was the lost time, and he could not very well tell them how they'd passed those days. When the time came, Merin offered his suggestion that the crystals had somehow lulled them into an extraordinarily long sleep. They had seen what Kitty could do, and no one suggested such an idea was ludicrous.

Speaking was difficult with Bela present. She wore a dress, of all things, and had a circlet of gold in her hair. The green dress and the circlet were both plain but looked incredibly elegant on her. Everything about her was perfection, from the gentle wave of her hair to the toes that peeked through her sandals. Good heavens, he was *smitten* with her, and her very presence was distracting. That was so unlike him. *Nothing* distracted him.

He and Bela suggested that the mountain where Kitty had been abandoned remain truly forbidden to the Turis, and the chieftain heartily agreed. It wasn't as if the people were drawn to that part of the mountain range in any case. It was too barren—too lonely and uninviting.

And now they knew why. The crystals kept other life away from their home. Knowing their power, realizing now what they could do, it was surely a gift to the Turis and others who might travel this way that they were not welcome there.

When explanations were done, Merin quickly turned to the business at hand. "When can Bela and I be married?"

The chieftain sighed and shook his head. "The marriage was just undone. Can't you two make up your minds?"

"We had planned to cut the bonds here, together," Bela said, "before the union was undone, but the lost days ruined that plan." She locked eyes with Merin. "I have made up my mind, Papa. I know what I want."

He shook his head and gave in to a smile. "You always do."

"Properly done, the courtship should last at least fourteen days . . ." Bela's mother began.

"No," Merin said briskly, "that is unacceptable."

"Three days is the very least amount of time . . ."

"Last time we shared a few words, a kiss, and a clumsy dance," Merin interrupted impatiently. "Will that not suffice again? Now?"

"Now?" Bela's mother asked shrilly.

"Why not now?" he asked.

Tyman and Clyn were amused by the proceedings. The chieftain was hard to read, as usual. Bela rose up on her toes, as impatient as Merin to have this done. A few lost days, and all was ruined.

"The daughter of the chieftain should be wooed," Gayene said calmly. "The people of the village should see that she's desired as a woman, that you find her worthy of your time and attention."

"I must return to Arthes." Where he'd have to explain to the emperor that he'd decided to claim this potential bride for himself. That would not go over well, he imagined.

"Will a mere three days make all that much difference?" Tyman asked.

Merin looked to Bela, waiting for her to join him in his argument. She was oddly quiet. "Have you changed your mind?" he asked. If she did not want him he would leave tonight.

"I have not changed my mind, not at all," she said.

"But?" he said, seeing the uncertainty on her face.

"But I find I am not at all opposed to being courted. For three days," she added quickly. "Not fourteen, that would be much too long. And I think I would like a more proper wedding this time, since it is necessary that we remarry in any case. Something to remember. Something we can tell our children about."

Merin smiled. "You have a woman's heart after all," he said gently.

"I suppose I do."

He bowed crisply to his former and future wife. "If you wish to be courted, I will court you properly. If you wish to have an appropriate wedding, we will have one. But three days is as long as I'm prepared to wait."

She grinned. If waiting three days would make her smile this way, then he would gladly suffer the wait.

Bela offered her hand, and he took it. "It's late," she said. "We can go home now. I'm so ready to fall asleep in that awful sagging bed, after too many nights sleeping on rock."

"Oh, no." Tyman and Clyn both stood, and so did Gayene, who spoke with authority. "You two are no longer wed, so it would be most improper for you to share that little cottage."

Bela's mouth dropped open. "But many couples live together in the days before they're wed."

Gayene's chin snapped up. "Common folk do, but it would be improper for the daughter of the chieftain to live with a man before marriage."

"We've lived together for weeks!"

"You were married," Gayene reminded her daughter. "As of yesterday, that is no longer the case."

"Then forget the courtship," Bela said as she stepped toward Merin. "We'll just say the words here and now, and you can't stop us."

Merin took Bela's hand and leaned down to kiss her knuckles. She deserved better than a quick ceremony followed by a proper bedding. She deserved to be shown how much he wanted her, how much he desired her as his wife. "We'll wait," he whispered. "Three days."

"But . . ." Bela began.

"I will woo you, Bela," Merin said confidently. "I will win you the way a man is supposed to win a wife. You will not doubt that I am sure of what I want when we are married in a ceremony that takes place before the entire village."

"But three *days*," she whined. Somewhere in the background, one of her brothers growled.

Merin did not take his eyes from Bela's face. "Three very long days, and then a lifetime together. I will gladly wait those days for you." And by the time they were married, she would have no doubt that he loved her without reservation.

BELA waited until the rest of the household was asleep, which seemed to be a very long time. The two prisoners who had not died of their battle wounds had stopped screaming an hour or so ago, but she did not doubt that they still lived—and would, for a while longer. She could almost feel sorry for them, if they had not made the ultimate mistake of aligning themselves with Nobel Andyrs and a daughter of the Isen Demon.

Her mind would not be still. All night she had thought

of the child she was meant to bear, of the demon-girl that child was meant to kill. She considered the fate of the world if destiny did not play out as it should. A mother should not have to concern herself with the fate of the world, not where her child was concerned, but what was she to do? Whether she liked the idea or not, her daughter would be a warrior. With a father like Merin to teach her and a devoted mother to guide her, she would be the finest of warriors.

Escape by the front entrance would be impossible, since there was still much activity in the village square. Bela decided she would sneak around the back of the houses to reach the small cottage where Merin waited. Would he be surprised to see her, or was he expecting her visit?

She could not wait to touch him, to make love to him again. They'd always had the red; they'd survived the black; now she knew what the white truly meant. Pure love. Love that could survive anything.

Wearing her usual garb—Tyman's hand-me-downs— Bela opened the single, large window in her bedchamber and put one booted foot outside.

The voice that came out of the darkness surprised her. "I don't think so."

Instead of withdrawing into the room, she leaned out to see her brother—he whose clothing she currently wore— leaning against the house as if he were waiting for her escape.

"What are you doing here?" she asked sharply.

Tyman grinned. "Waiting for this very moment, little sister. Retreat to your room and get some sleep. Morning will be here before you know it."

"But Merin . . ."

"Merin is not your husband at this moment. If he abuses your affections, I might have to kill him, and that would be unfortunate."

Halfway in and halfway out, Bela made herself as comfortable as possible. "Unfortunate? I thought you didn't like him."

Tyman shrugged. "I did not like General Merin when I thought he'd hurt you. In truth, he is the only man I have ever met who is worthy of you, even if he is not Turi."

Escape thwarted, Bela resigned herself to sleeping alone tonight. Knowing her brothers, she suspected that if Tyman left his post to sleep for a while, Clyn would take his place.

"Who is watching over Merin?" she asked testily, crossing her arms over her chest in defiance.

Tyman's lips twitched. "As long as one of you is under guard, all should be well."

That was true enough.

"We're practically wed," she snapped. "We have been married before, and in three days will be married again."

"When those three days pass, it will no longer be necessary for me to watch your bedroom window."

"Merin and I have already had sex, if that's what you're so worried about."

Tyman made a gagging sound, then added, "I do not wish to hear this."

Bela smiled. "Many times. Many times in many different ways. He's quite talented and . . ."

"Am I going to have to gag you for three full days?"

Bela relaxed. "No, of course not. What's wrong, Tyman? Are you ignorant in the ways of love? Does hearing about my sexual experiences make you blush?"

"I am not ignorant," he said in a low voice. "That does not mean I wish to hear my *sister* talk about how talented her soon-to-be husband is in bed."

"Actual beds are not at all necessary," Bela said, "though they are quite nice, especially when . . ."

Tyman came to the window, forcibly assisted Bela back

into her room, and then shut the window behind her with a decisive thud and evident relief.

Bela knelt there for a while, her head resting on the windowsill as she watched her brother pace. She finally fell asleep there, oddly peaceful and wonderfully content.

Chapter Seventeen

"**TOMORROW** we'll have to go to town to buy food," Leyla said as she served up most of what was left for their breakfast. She sounded nervous about the prospect, and Savyn knew that if she had her way, they would remain here forever, hidden away from the world.

"Just as well," he said. "I'm tired of dried meat and hard biscuits."

"And berries," she added.

"And berries." On her last trip to gather the sweet morsels, two days ago, Leyla had insisted that he go with her. She did not quite trust him, not yet. He had told her that he loved her, but she was still afraid of losing him. That would not happen. Not ever.

It had been during that berry-hunting trip that Savyn had had the first sign that his sight was returning. The headache had been less on that morning, and his head had felt not quite so overly full. When they'd walked away from the hut, hand in hand, he had sensed as much as seen a shifting in the light. That shifting light had been enough to give him hope that perhaps his sight would return, but he had not been sure, so he'd said nothing.

Now he watched Leyla. He watched her! The fine lines of her features and the details of her ragged and stained gown were blurry still, but she was solid and beautiful before him as she arranged their food on a battered tin plate she had found on a dusty shelf.

"I'm not very hungry," he said.

"You need to eat, to keep up your strength."

"I'm not a child who needs to be told when to eat," he said. "And there are other things I would prefer to do right now."

Savyn would forever regret his harsh words to Leyla as they lay on the forest floor, but he had done all he could to make amends in days past. He'd felt her body quiver and squeeze his, he'd listened to her sighs of satisfaction. He'd told her time and again that he loved her, and she'd spoken the words to him in return.

There had even been moments in recent days when he'd been certain all would be well, whether he regained his sight or not. Every day it had become a bit easier to walk, to eat, to orient himself, to function. If he had no other choice, he could learn to live without his sight, and he could even be content. He knew that now, because he had been content here, where they had nothing but each other.

It was Leyla who brought about this turn in his thinking. She was all he truly needed.

But in all those days he had not been able to see her face, not as he could now. His vision was not perfect, and might never be, but he could *see* her.

Savyn walked directly to Leyla, took her arm, and led her into the morning sunlight that broke through the holes in the roof. He smiled as the radiance hit her face and she blinked against the brightness.

Leyla deserved better than a rough bed on the floor of a hut no self-respecting hermit would live in. She should have a better haven than an abandoned hut that was literally falling apart, a single tin plate, a scarcity of food. One day he would see that she had the fine home she deserved, but he could not discount all that had happened in this hut. She had been happy here. So had he.

In the past few days she had spoken often of starting over as man and wife in some other place. More than once Leyla had mentioned changing their names and hiding from the dangers and the censure of the world. He had not told her that would never happen, but neither had he agreed.

Now he reached out and cupped her face in his hands, running his thumbs along her soft lips, as he had done quite often, then leaning in and down to kiss her. She opened to him with that kiss. She held nothing back. He ended the kiss too soon for her and backed away so he could see her face. "You are so beautiful," he whispered.

He saw the pain in her eyes, the slight frown of her wonderful mouth. "There's more to what we have than beauty, Savyn."

"Yes, there is," he said, "but I will never get tired of looking at you. Your eyes are the most perfect shade of blue, and the curve of your cheek is perfection, and your mouth is not only soft and kissable but a lovely shade of red, like a ripe plum."

She blinked and looked into his eyes. "You can . . ."

"See you?" he finished. "Yes, I can. Not as well as I'd like, not yet, but . . ."

Leyla threw her arms around his neck and squealed before he could finish. Then she cried a little, before laughing some more.

"Do you know what I missed most when I could not see?" He did not give her a chance to answer. "I missed seeing you. Your smile, your eyes, the swell of your breasts . . ."

"Savyn!"

"It's true. Even when I did not remember what we had once been to one another, when we were traveling and I did not dare to tell you how I felt . . . just to look upon you gave me great joy and peace." He stepped away and looked her up and down. In the sunlight he could see her very well. "Your fine dress is stained with mud."

"I tried to clean it, but the mud went too deep," she explained.

"Soon we will buy you another," he said, allowing his fingers to trace the swell of her breasts. He wanted to take this stained garment off her body and see every inch of her skin, and he would. Soon. All these nights when they'd made this hut their home, he had loved her in the dark. To be with her in that way had been fine, very fine, but he wanted more. "I wish to see all of you, bare and smiling." He unfastened a small button and slipped his fingers inside to touch her skin.

She tried to help him, tried to quickly undress herself, but he stopped her by gently pushing her hands aside. "No, I will do this myself, as I can now discern every blasted button, hook, and eye."

Leyla stood in the sunlight and allowed him to undress her, as he wished. She was more beautiful than any fantasy, and he did his best to commit every line to memory. When he pushed one faded blue sleeve down her arm, a fading but still ugly bruise marred her shoulder. Trinity had done that. The assassin should be condemned to hell for hurting one so tender as Leyla. Savyn kissed the damaged shoulder, allowing his mouth to linger there for a moment before he continued with the slow disrobing.

But for that ugly bruise, she was perfection. She was his. He ran his rough hands along her pale, soft skin, and there was no rush to get to the end of this exploration. When she stood before him completely naked, he kissed her breasts, tasting the small, dark nipples and feeling them grow hard against his tongue. He lifted his head to watch the dawning ecstasy on her sunlit face as he slipped his fingers between her legs and aroused her.

She was as beautiful as she had been in his fantasies. More so, if that was possible. Every soft curve, every inch of flesh, was perfection. And her face . . . Leyla was not just beautiful, she revealed her emotions and her desires in her open expressions. How could he ever have doubted that she loved him as much as he loved her?

He did not want to take her out of the sunlight, not even to lay her on their makeshift, hard bed. She undressed him there in the warm shaft of sunlight, and then he lay on the floor right there and she straddled him anxiously.

Lost inside her, he watched the press of his hard body to her pale softness, he watched the growing need on her face, and then he watched as she quivered and lurched above him. A sob was caught in her throat as she moved her hips to invite him deeper, harder, and then he shattered with her.

They were still joined, still awash in the sun, when he said, "Promise me that you will never use your magical abilities on me again."

"I swear," she whispered.

They would make new memories, and he would cherish them all. "Tomorrow we will go to the village up the road, where we will buy food and two horses and a proper dress."

"Why horses?" she asked, her expression one of concern. "We can catch a ride with a traveler, or walk to the next village, or just stay there, if it suits us. The money we have will have to last us for a while, so we should be very careful how it is spent. I've been thinking of names . . ."

Savyn pulled Leyla to him and silenced her with a kiss, a kiss she willingly accepted.

"And while we are there in the village," he said, ignoring her objections, "we will say the words that will make us man and wife."

Her face was close to his as she whispered, "I do not need words."

"I do," Savyn said. "And what of our children?"

Even though her face was now in shadow, he could see well enough to note the wrinkle that appeared between her eyebrows. "I had not given much thought to children," she confessed.

"You should, as often as we have attempted to make one." A terrible thought occurred to him. "Don't you want children?"

"If they are yours, yes," she said without hesitation.

"Then they should have their father's name, should they not?"

"Whatever name we . . ."

Savyn shook his head. "They will have the name Leone, and none other, and they will know that their father is Savyn and their mother is Leyla. I will not hide, and our children will not live with deception. I know you think the only way we can be together is to change our names and lie about our ages and hide away for the rest of our lives in a hut much like this one."

"It would not be so bad," she whispered.

"It would be a lie. Besides, you know the name of the woman who attempted to have you killed. The emperor should know."

"What do you propose?" she asked, more worried than annoyed. "Is it safe to go to Arthes? What if the emperor still wants me to participate in his silly bridal contest?"

"By the time we arrive in Arthes, you will be *my* wife, and with any luck you'll be carrying our first child."

"Then why should we go there at all?"

"We will inform the emperor or an official in his command that our party was attacked by someone who intended to kill you, and you will tell him what Trinity told you before he left. I will find my brother, if he is still living in Arthes, and perhaps he can help me find a proper and well-respected swordmaker who will take me on as a worker until I can save enough to start my own business. Tearlach is a general in the emperor's command, so he would be the one to help us get word to Emperor Jahn, I suppose." He kissed her again. "And I will tell the whole world that I love you, Lady Leyla. Leyla Leone." He smiled. "We will not disappear. We will not run in fear, not from those who would dare to hurt you, and certainly not from those who might not approve of us, for one reason or another. I love you and you love me. There is no need for us to hide ourselves away."

Leyla took a deep, stilling breath, and he waited for her argument even as he appreciated the swelling of her chest against his. Recently she had been so set on hiding away for the remainder of their days. But instead of arguing, she whispered a very agreeable "Yes, dear," before once again turning her thoughts to finer matters.

TRINITY sat with his back against a tree near the road, knees to his chest, stomach empty and growling a protest. He had no money, and he could no longer bring himself to hurt or even threaten innocents to have what he wanted and needed. Whenever he tried, he was beset by guilt, and the faces of those he'd killed in the past became clearer and closer. Their voices grew louder as they harangued him.

It was easier to starve.

The face of a hefty and balding merchant he had killed more than fifty years ago swam before him. "You could work for a living."

"Doing what?" Trinity asked.

"You're a strong man," the merchant said. "There's always work to be found on a farm or a ranch. Perhaps you could go south toward the sea and find work with a fisherman."

"I hate the smell of fish," Trinity whispered.

"Beg, then," the merchant said. "Beg or starve, if you will not search for honest work."

Honest work. He had done what anyone would consider honest work for the last two hundred years or so. He'd brought death to those whose time had come. He'd settled disputes in the only way he knew how, violently and decisively, for those who paid him. Since his profession paid so well, if he lived frugally he could take care of his needs for a long time with the proceeds from one job.

This most recent job would've seen him through at least two years, but the first half of his pay was in his saddlebags, and the other half would not be collected, as he had not been able to complete the job.

He had not been told the woman to be dispatched was a witch. She should've told him! Now he was ruined, unable to so much as strike an innocent.

Lady Rikka was not innocent, not at all. She had hired him to kill the witch, so did that mean he could kill her without pain or suffering? Did that mean he could make her pay for sending him to the witch unprepared? The thought had brought Trinity his only moments of peace in the days since the witch had cursed him. Yes, he only knew an edge of sanity when he thought of killing the woman who had sent him to his fate.

Trinity slipped deeper into the woods when he heard the clopping of a horse's hooves. He didn't want anyone to see him this way, not even a stranger. From his hiding place in the forest he watched the road, waiting for the horse and whoever rode upon it to pass. When the animal came into view, his heart almost burst through his chest.

"Gano," he cried as he jumped up and ran toward the road and his horse. His fine, loyal, magnificent stallion. He pushed past limbs and bushes, not caring that his cheek was scratched along the way. It stung and bled, but not for long. "You found me." Trinity threw his arms around the animal's neck and held on, taking comfort from the feel of the warmth against his cheek, reveling in the comforting heat and the familiarity. He thought he might cry again, but managed to push the tears away.

It was a sign. Just as he'd been thinking again of making his way to Lady Rikka and committing one last murder—a woman who was anything but innocent—his companion and transport arrived.

He searched the saddlebags for money or food but found none. The witch had taken it all, but she had not been able to keep Gano. Somehow Gano had escaped and found his rightful owner.

Trinity hefted himself into the saddle. He had not been fond of the idea of hard work to earn food and shelter for himself, but he would gladly work to earn food and shelter for Gano. He patted the horse's neck and sighed in relief. "It might take us a while to get to her, but together we will make Lady Rikka pay for what she's done to us. She'll pay, in more ways than one." And then he and Gano would head for the mountains, where once again Trinity would hide from immortality and loneliness and a world that could not accept him.

As Trinity rode down the road, nearly a hundred souls followed, chattering to him endlessly about the pain and suffering he had brought them. He wondered for the span of a few miles if Lady Rikka would haunt him as the others did, but soon decided it did not matter. What was one more voice among so many?

BELA had never known three days could be so long. She did get to see Merin, but they were always chaperoned by some diligent member of her family. He'd managed to steal a kiss or two, but those kisses had been too quick and too few. She wanted more.

But he did woo her quite properly, which was nice. He brought flowers, the exact wildflowers she preferred, and he was always at her door at sunset to walk her about town—with Tyman or Clyn trailing behind them to make sure they didn't have too much fun.

Tonight the wait would finally be over, and they would say the words which would make them man and wife. Again. Forever, this time, and without trickery or deception of any kind.

But like it or not, she still had doubts. What if Merin loved her only because the crystals of Forbidden Mountain directed him to do so? What if they married, and halfway to Arthes the love he'd thought was real faded away and he was horrified to find himself married to her?

Late in the afternoon, Bela found herself knocking on Rafal Fiers's door. The seer's small and solid cottage was located on the eastern edge of the village, where he had a perfect and unobstructed view of the mountain where she and Merin had lost days. Was that a coincidence? If anyone could answer her questions, it would be Rafal.

He answered her knock quickly, as if he had been expecting her. Maybe he had been, knowing Rafal and his tricks. He didn't even raise an eyebrow as he invited her inside. Bela wrinkled her nose. The cottage smelled of bitter herbs and sulfurous concoctions.

"Shouldn't you be getting ready for your wedding ceremony?" he asked.

"I have plenty of time," Bela said. "Do you know why I'm here?"

"Perhaps." He gestured to a small wooden chair, but Bela shook her head and told the seer she'd prefer to stand. She was much too anxious to sit!

The small man raised his bushy eyebrows, and Bela obediently—if impatiently—took the chair. Rafal placed himself in front of her, for once looking down upon her rather than tilting his head back and looking up.

"A woman in your delicate condition should not exert herself overmuch. Sit and rest when you can, Mother."

Bela swallowed hard. She had suspected that it might be true, especially after she and Merin had compared notes on their "dreams," but she had not known with any certainty, not until now. "So, it is done."

Rafal smiled. He did not do so often, and the expression was strange. "Yes, it is done."

All Bela's fears rushed to the surface, and at this moment those fears were not only about whether or not Merin loved her. "How can I keep her safe? How can I protect her? It is absolutely terrifying that a demon-child wishes to take the life of this daughter who has not yet been born."

"*Half* demon," Rafal said with a shake of a bony finger. "And you will not have to worry about that one for many years to come. She has retreated into the mountains, where she will remain for a long while." He wrinkled his nose and spat on the floor, as if he had smelled something bad as he spoke about the child who had gotten Nobel to do her bidding. "Her time to stop what was meant to be has passed, and she knows it well, just as I do."

That was a relief, one that washed through Bela as strongly as the mountain river. She swallowed, and forced herself to ask the other question which had been on her mind for the past few days. "Does Merin really love me, or is what he feels a trick of the crystal?"

Yes, Rafal could smile. "If the crystal was able to make Merin experience an uncommon affection for you, it might've done so until the child was conceived. Now that it is done, there is no reason for them to attempt something so . . . impossible."

"Impossible?"

"For as long as magic has existed, which is a very long time, many wizards and witches and others of their type have attempted to create a true love potion. All have failed. Lust can be created, and has been, but love is of the heart and soul, and cannot be created magically."

Bela was glad to hear this, but was not surprised. And still, she could only be relieved. Merin did love her; his love was real. Her own love was so real and unshakable, she did not know how it could be created from nothing. "So, the crystals could've made him want me, but there was no way for them to make him *love* me."

"None. The same is true for you, Bela. The affections you have found are real. No sword, no crystal, no enchanted cavern can make such power grow where there is none."

Everything Rafal told her was what she wanted to hear. That in itself was suspicious. How could she be certain he was telling the truth? "Are you sure my daughter will be safe?" *Their* daughter, hers and Merin's, a woman destined to do battle. The seed already planted inside her, growing.

Rafal's eyes seemed to glaze over, and his smile faded sharply. "I have told you once. Do you not believe me?"

"It's not that . . ." Though it was exactly that . . . "You seem to know so much, but you never liked the fact that Kitty chose me. Now it's clear that she could not have chosen anyone else." Could he explain *that*?

"I always thought it would be best if the sword remained secreted until your daughter was ready, but those more powerful than I did not agree. She was made for your daughter, not for you, and there is so much power in that weapon . . . yes, I was concerned. You can be quite imprudent at times."

She could not argue with that. "You might've warned me what was coming," Bela accused.

"No, I could not. You would not have believed me."

She twisted her lips. "Well, I believe you now."

"Good. Then hear this." Rafal's voice grew deeper, flatter. "The daughter you carry is more than his seed and your womb, she is more than human. She was conceived in the waters of the mountain and has a touch of that water in her blood and in her eyes. Your daughter, our warrior, she will be nigh indestructible. You need not worry about her." His eyes and his voice changed, turning more normal, and he shrugged. "No more than any mother worries about her daughter."

"*Our* warrior?" Bela asked, standing so that she could look down on the seer. "What do you mean, *our* warrior, and how do you know about the water?" She had come here for answers, that was true, but Rafal knew too much! Surely some moments were meant to be private!

"You could not leave the mountain until they knew the child had taken hold," Rafal said. "We have waited for her for too many years."

We? Bela felt the blood rush from her face. "Kitty. The carvings. You?" She glanced down at the old man's battered and gnarled hands, and she could imagine, too well, a younger Rafal standing in the cavern, etching her life onto a stone wall; she could see younger hands carving stone and forging steel.

"I did not work alone," Rafal said, "but I did my part." Again, he gave her that unexpected smile. "Do not worry, Bela. All will be well."

"Truly?"

"Truly. Now, go get married. Your husband is waiting anxiously, I suspect."

A bonfire shone bright on a perfect spring night. Summer approached, and the coming season could be felt in the warmth of this night. Music played and people danced. Bela smiled, and she was gorgeous in her red, white, and black dress. Merin loved her in that dress. Even more, he could not wait to get her out of it. He had spent three long days without her constantly beside him. In a way he could not explain, they remained connected, as surely as they had when they'd been physically bound.

He did not doubt that, destiny aside, their love was real. As real as it gets.

Bela was whispering something to her friend Jocylen, but her eyes cut to him often. And she smiled. What a smile his wife possessed. It could grab the heart of any man; it could brighten the darkest night.

"Turi custom is not so silly now, eh?"

Merin turned to look down at the village seer, the oddly grinning Rafal Fiers. "Perhaps not."

"I knew you would come around," the little man said. "What was meant to be, cannot be denied."

"What are you talking about?" Merin asked sharply.

"You are awash in destiny, General Merin. The warrior girl-child you have made will be born amid the snows of winter, and with her will come a time of peace followed by a time of turmoil. Such is the way of life. When the time is right, she will find the enchanted sword . . . or it will find her, no matter where you make your home, no matter how you try to hide. She will play an important part in the war against the demon-daughters, a war which cannot be won without one born, one created, and one . . ." He wrinkled his nose. "One hatched."

"Hatched?" Merin asked, horrified. "What does that mean?"

"I'm not sure. Not yet," Fiers added.

He did not ask about the one who would be created. That was almost as alarming as one to be hatched—but not quite.

Merin was not surprised to hear that the child already existed within Bela. He had suspected as much when they'd discovered the lost time, but it was more than that. He felt as if he already knew of the girl's existence in this world, as if she were already here—and his.

He would not fight this destiny—as if it could be fought. When the time was right, his daughter would learn to wield a sword. As a child, she would know every trick Merin had learned in his lifetime, and more. She would fight with grace and ease and remarkable skill. He would see to it.

"You know more than you have shared with me," Merin accused.

"I know more than I have shared with anyone, General. Knowledge alone is not enough. The gifting of that knowledge must be made at the correct time, or else it is useless."

It was true enough, he supposed. Merin knew that if he had been told upon arrival that he and Bela were destined to create a warrior daughter who would use Kitty against the daughters of a demon he had fought very hard to destroy, he probably would've run in the night. Now it was too late for that. Much too late.

"Did you know all along that I would love her this way?" Merin asked. "When you bound us together and did your little dance, did you know?"

Fiers only smiled and walked away, just as Bela skipped toward Merin. "Another dance, husband," she said as she threw herself at him.

"One," he said, catching her and moving in time with the melody that was played so sweetly.

She stuck out her lower lip. "Only one?"

"One, and then we are going to say good night and go to bed, where I will slip that dress from your body and make love to you until dawn breaks and neither of us is capable of movement."

"Oh," she said, quickly replacing her pout with a sensual smile. "I do like the sound of that."

"So do I."

He took her in his arms and began to move.

"We have not had much time to talk tonight," Bela whispered as he held her close.

"I'm not planning on much talking as the evening progresses, either," he said honestly.

"Still, you should know . . ." She leaned back and looked him in the eye. "I had a long talk with Rafal Fiers this afternoon."

Interesting.

"I got pregnant during those lost days. In the water, he said."

"I suspected as much."

"She's going to be very different, our daughter. Very . . . strong."

"I don't doubt it." He pulled Bela's head to his shoulder. "I talked with the old man myself. I suspect we should compare these conversations and see if we can make some sense of what lies ahead of us."

"I suspect we should."

The music did not end, but Merin stopped dancing. He tipped Bela's face up and looked into her warm green eyes. "But that conversation can wait until morning. Tonight is just for us."

Bela smiled, too wide, too bright. He loved that smile.

With villagers and family watching, Merin lifted Bela off her feet and carried her toward their little cottage which was home for one more night, or perhaps two. In the distance, a gentle glow throbbed briefly from Forbidden

Mountain, as if the crystals there were celebrating in their own manner, as if they were saying good luck or well done or . . . finally!

There was no time to waste, but Merin would not be rushed from his marriage ceremony to the road, not so quickly, not without a proper wedding night or two. Maybe he and Bela would reach Arthes by the first night of the Summer Festival, and maybe they would not. At this moment he did not care.

Emperor Jahn would not be pleased when Merin arrived with one of the potential brides as his wife—and their child. Still, Jahn should get over the disappointment quickly. Bela was not the type of woman he preferred, and he would have five others to choose from. He could choose one of those suitable women; he could not have Bela. The scandal might cost Merin his position in the palace, but he did not care. He suspected that within five years, teaching and training his daughter would claim a goodly portion of his days.

At that time they would probably be back here, in this Turi village, within call of the mountain where his daughter's weapon waited. Maybe they would live in this very cottage for a while, he thought, as he kicked the door closed behind him. They could not stay here for very long, though. This cottage was just right for two, but not suitable for a family.

"I believe now," Bela said as Merin set her on her feet and began to carefully remove the dress she had worn when she offered him a sip of wine, accepted a bouquet of wild-flowers, kissed, and danced. Simple as the ceremony had been, it resonated in him, in a soul-deep way. The ritual spoke of give and take, of passion and joy.

"You believe in what?" he asked.

"The white," Bela said. "The pureness of love that exists to fight against the black, and to mingle with the red. I did not believe such a love was possible, until you showed me it was real. It is real," she said earnestly. "It's real and important."

"Yes, it is," Merin agreed, and then, instead of telling his wife how he felt, he showed her, until dawn broke the eastern sky and together they slept the deep and peaceful sleep of the truly spent, and the truly loved.

Epilogue

✸

THEY'D had to travel hard, at times, in order to arrive at the palace before the first night of the Summer Festival. Merin had insisted time and again that if she did not feel up to riding at a steady pace, or if she needed to stop and rest for a day or two, he would simply be late. Pregnancy, at least in these early stages, agreed with Bela. She felt fine. She was energized and gloriously happy, and had never felt healthier. Besides, she knew how Merin hated to be late!

The palace was impressive, and had been from that first, distant glance. She'd never seen anything quite like it. It was monstrously tall and solid and massive, and once inside, she had continued to be amazed. There were green-clad sentinels at every turn. The few rooms she had been able to peek into were nicely and even extravagantly furnished. The men who were not uniformed sentinels were dressed in finery such as she had never seen, and the women . . . the women wore gowns so fancy she did not see how they could move or even *breathe*, and they all seemed to wear ornate hairstyles and heavy jewels. They were pretty and decidedly odd, and not one of them looked comfortable.

The small chamber they had been directed to was on the second floor and seemed to be equipped for meetings of an official sort. There were matching crimson-backed chairs and a long table, and there were many framed paintings on the walls, a mixture of landscapes and portraits. The room was well lit with oil lamps, and smelled of scented oils.

Merin had promised that in his personal chambers a real bed awaited them. A real bed! She could not wait. For that reason she had not minded rushing to get here.

Since the deadline was this very night, however, there was first the emperor to contend with. Merin also wanted to tell someone that an attempt had been made on her life, and by whom. Bela was almost convinced that Nobel's little demon-child might've had something to do with the attack, but Merin would not rest until he knew with certainty.

They had been waiting only a few minutes before a thin, distraught man in a crimson robe rushed into the room. He was pale as snow and his hands shook. His lips were thin and hard. All was not well in his world, that much was evident.

"Thank the heavens you are here!" the man said when he laid eyes on Merin. "We feared for your life, General. Did you not meet the sentinels we sent in search of you and your party?"

"We did not," Merin answered. "We took a number of less traveled routes in order to get here as quickly as possible, as there were . . . delays along the way. I would guess that's why we did not see them."

The thin man turned his gaze to Bela. In a sweeping and disapproving glance he took in her manly attire and her muddy boots, and her less than well-kept braid. She smiled widely.

"Is this . . . her?"

"Bela, this is Minister Calvyno," Merin said in a serene and commanding voice. "He's Minister of Foreign Affairs."

"Pleased to meet you," Bela said.

Merin's eyebrows rose slightly at her polite response. As if she would embarrass him here in this place where he was of such importance!

Calvyno released a long breath. "You have arrived just in time. We must hurry. I'm sure we can find her a proper gown and arrange for a bath and a lady to dress her hair . . ."

Merin did not give the man time to finish. "Minister Calvyno, this is my wife, Belavalari Merin."

Impossibly, Calvyno went paler than before. He seemed unsteady as he searched for and found the nearest chair. "This cannot be," he mumbled as he dropped into the seat. "This is unforgivable and outrageous!"

Merin remained calm. "I don't understand your concerns, Minister. There are other candidates more suitable . . ."

"There are not!" The minister lifted his head to glare at Merin. "You have no idea what has been happening here since you left, General. The emperor is livid. I have never seen him in such a state! He reminds me more than a little bit of his father, these days. I never thought I would see this, not in him."

"Tell me," Merin instructed, in a voice that left no room for argument.

Still sitting, Calvyno spoke, his voice quick. "Princess Edlyn was murdered, and for a time it was believed that Prince Alix took her life."

"No," Merin said softly. "He would not."

"No, of course not. Prince Alix was here in the palace a short time ago, and while here he was married." He took a deep breath. "His wife spends most of her time . . . blue." He pondered this curious statement for a moment.

"What of the others?" Merin prompted, no doubt thinking of the attempt on Bela's life. Perhaps the demon-child had truly not had a hand in the assassination attempt on Forbidden Mountain.

"Lady Verity survived an attack and made it here safely, only to decline the emperor's offer and make off with a sentinel." He shook his head. "Shocking. Lady Morgana refused . . . *refused* . . . to so much as present herself to the emperor. Her stepfather is mortified by her outrageous actions. I hear he threw her out of the house with nothing but the clothes on her back. I can't say that I blame him."

Bela snorted. "A woman should be allowed to . . ."

Calvyno lifted his head and glared at her, and she decided to end her protest there, for Merin's sake more than her own.

The Minister continued. "Just a few days ago, what remains of Lady Leyla Hagan's party was discovered, ravaged, all there dead."

"There should be one more bride," Merin said.

Calvyno straightened his spine. "Yes, there is. Lady Danya has been residing in the palace for some weeks now. She's quite anxious to be empress. It looks as if she will get her wish when the emperor lines up what should be six potential brides and finds himself with one. He doesn't even like her much."

"Someone tried to kill Bela," Merin said solemnly. "Before he died, the man who made the attempt said he'd been hired by Lady Rikka."

Calvyno's eyes brightened for a moment. "Lady Rikka! Yes, I suppose she would have reason to see the emperor and his brother unhappy, but to kill so many blameless women . . . it is not at all logical. Why would she go to such lengths?"

"What about the one candidate who remains?" Merin asked. "Was an attempt made on her life?"

"No, but she arrived here much earlier than was necessary. Perhaps Lady Danya was safely in the palace before former Empress Rikka could make her plans."

Bela thought that perhaps Lady Danya had a hand in it all, though killing the competition, with the help of an old, embittered empress, wasn't exactly a subtle way to get what she wanted. She kept her opinions to herself, for now.

There was a brief knock on the door, and then it flew open and an older sentinel stuck his head inside. "Minister Calvyno, there is a young couple here who claim they must speak to General Merin immediately. It is a matter of life and death, they say."

Calvyno waved his hand dismissively. "Send them away. We have more important matters to attend to."

"But the man says he is General Merin's brother."

"Savyn?" Merin asked, stunned.

"That is the name he gave, General. Savyn Leone and his wife, Leyla."

Calvyno paled again. Bela was certain that if he lost any more color, he would disappear entirely. "What are the odds that *this* Leyla . . ." the old man said, his words drifting off to nothing, much as his color had.

Merin took Bela's arm, and together they headed for the door. Minister Calvyno looked as if he might remain in his chair for a while longer, but with a burst of energy he pushed himself up and followed in their footsteps.

"If this is the correct Leyla, and she is indeed married to your brother, I have to see it with my own eyes," he mumbled. "Where does a former Minister of Foreign Affairs search for new employment, I wonder."

Merin gave into a small smile and squeezed Bela's arm possessively. "We'll meet with the emperor shortly, love. It's shaping up to be quite a memorable evening. But first, let's go meet my little brother and his wife."

Bela had lived in the shadow of magic all her life. She had touched enchantment, she had bathed in it . . . she had found a love she'd thought impossible. Was it a coincidence that Merin's long-lost brother was here, now, on this very night? No, she knew too much of magic to believe in coincidence. Tearlach Merin was now surrounded by his family, as was right and proper. This strange palace was home, for now, and it would be a good home for as long as they were meant to be here.

She could not help but smile. She and the child she carried were a very large part of that family. They were his home. "Let's," she whispered.

Turn the page for a preview of the next romance

from Linda Winstead Jones

Bride by Command

Coming March 2009

from Berkley Sensation!

Prologue

※

The Columbyanan Palace in the Sixth Year of the
Reign of Emperor Nechtyn Jahn Calcus Sadwyn Beckyt
First Night of the Spring Festival

WHEN he had dismissed the last of his advisors, Jahn
gave a tired sigh and sat heavily in the padded crimson
chair which dominated one corner of his spacious and ornate bed chamber. There were times when he found peace
in this private room he called his own. The bed was large
and comfortable; the furnishings were finer than anything
he had known before coming to Arthes; there was a fire
whenever he wanted or needed one; and there was no
skimping when it came to the scented oils which burned
here and there, lighting the dimmer corners and adding a
sweet scent to the air. Here there were no demands made of
him. Those demanding moments took place in the ball-
room or his suite of offices. This chamber, decorated in
imperial crimson and made as comfortable as any man
could wish for, was meant for pleasure and rest and peace.

But tonight Jahn could find no peace. What had he
done? In a fit of pique he had set in motion a ridiculous
contest which would end in his inevitable and unwelcome
marriage. Perhaps he would have a bit of fun along the

way, as he watched those around him scramble to make this concept work, but would it be worth the trouble? He could just as easily have instructed any one of his ministers to choose a bride for him. They all had very strong ideas about which woman would make the best empress. Every woman suggested was talented or intelligent or beautiful or came from a fine bloodline which would strengthen his ties with a country or a tribe. It wasn't as if love or physical attraction would play any part in his decision, no matter how the game was played.

Being emperor had its advantages, and he was not ignorant of them. His word was law. Literally. If he wanted something, anything, all he had to do was ask and it was delivered to him. Loose women, his favorite type, cared only for pleasing him. He had his own army at his command. His days of indulging in physical labor and answering the command of another were over.

And yet he could not have the simple luxury of falling in love before marriage. He could not choose to remain unwed, even if such a lifestyle suited him. This extraordinary palace was often more of a prison than a home, and there were days when he could almost feel the walls closing in on him, as they did now. Marriage and fatherhood would only imprison him more surely.

He was trapped.

Still sitting, Jahn began to unfasten his long, cumbersome robe. He was damned tired of crimson, especially on this night when he had set the wheels of change in motion. One word and the sentinels who were positioned outside his door would fetch one or two of Jahn's favorite ladies, and they would make him forget that he was as much a prisoner as a ruler. They would make him forget everything. Melusina, perhaps, or Anrid. Just the thought of them made him grin. Melusina had a wonderful laugh that always made him smile, and Anrid possessed large, white breasts so soft he could happily fondle them for hours.

Once he was married, he would give them up—he supposed. He *could* keep all the women he desired. He *could* continue to live as if he were not a husband, as if he had no bonds, no boundaries. His marriage could, if he so chose, be approached as if it were for nothing more than politics and for the sake of producing a child, and once the empress caught a babe, he could banish her to some remote corner of the palace, bringing her out for holidays and social affairs and such, while he resumed his lascivious lifestyle.

But he would not. Jahn was determined that he would not become his father. No matter what his weaknesses might be, he was a good ruler who put the needs of the people first, always. He had not been trained all his life for this position; he had not been born and bred with politics in his mind and his heart. But he knew how to make people like him when it was necessary, and he was good at surrounding himself with capable people who did their jobs well and in the process made him look as if *he* were capable.

And unlike his father, once he was wed, he would be faithful—even if it killed him.

Knowing his carefree days were numbered, Jahn found the energy to leap from his chair and rush to the door, the blasted crimson robe halfway undone. He opened that door swiftly to reveal four sentinels whose duty was to keep their emperor safe. Jahn's eyes fell on Blane, a quiet and sensible and slightly rotund man who had been with him from the beginning.

"Melusina," he said sharply.

Blane nodded once and turned away.

"And Anrid," Jahn called after him. If his days were numbered, he might as well enjoy them all to the utmost.

LADY Morgana Ramsden had crept from her soft bed, escaped through her bedchamber window, and walked a relatively short distance from her fine home to hide in the shadows of the forest and watch the servants and villagers dance around the bonfire and celebrate the season of life, of fertility. Morgana had heard whispers that for some it was also a season of sexual awakening, of virile men and welcoming women—a celebration of pleasure given and taken, of life begun. Knowing how protective her stepfather was, it was no wonder she was not allowed to attend such a common celebration, that she had been forbidden even to observe the festivities from afar. What her stepfather didn't know wouldn't hurt him.

Morgana led a blessed life for the most part, a much easier life than those of the plainly dressed girls who danced around the fire and laughed out loud and flirted with brawny men. She watched in awe as a young woman with wild, dark hair all but pressed her large round bosom in the face of a momentarily startled man and then danced away laughing. The man recovered from his surprise quickly and followed, and he laughed, too. Any one of those girls would likely do anything to be in Morgana's position, and yet she often envied them their laughter and freedom.

She was so intent on watching the revelers she did not realize Tomas Glyn was behind her until he laid a hand on her shoulder. Instinctively Morgana gasped, threw off his hand, and spun about. Her fair hair whipped across her face, and even though she was relieved to see it was a lifelong family friend who had surprised her, she remained angry.

"You should not sneak up on a girl that way," she admonished. "You startled me. I would not wish to hurt you."

Tomas smiled widely. "You? Hurt me? Impossible."

"I might've been armed with a dagger or a small sword."

"Are you?" he asked, his tone friendly.

"No, of course not, but I *might've* been."

He moved a step closer. "A fine lady of your position should not be out here all alone. It is not fitting."

The back of her neck tingled; she did not like the way he looked at her. "I am not alone now."

"True enough." Tomas looked past her to watch the revelry she had so recently envied. The peasants were far enough away that they could not hear whispers from the forest over their laughter and song. "Look at them. Aren't they pathetic? Dancing around the fire and singing as if some god or goddess will bless them simply because they threw a party to see in the new season. I suppose they must take whatever small pleasures they can find, poor creatures."

Morgana did not think the villagers pathetic, not at all, but neither did she wish to argue. "You won't tell my stepfather that you saw me, will you?" she asked. "He has forbidden me to wander away from home on my own, and he would be livid if he knew I'd sneaked out at night. I shouldn't have disobeyed him, I know, but I did so want to see the celebration." In years past she had considered stealing away to watch one festivity or another, but this was the first time she'd dared to actually leave the house.

Tomas's eyes narrowed in obvious disapproval. "You should not defy Almund. He's been very good to you."

"Yes, he has."

Tomas could not accept that agreement and move on. He had to elaborate. "Almund gave you his name, raised you as his own, and even now, he allows you to have more freedom than any woman should."

Morgana's chin came up. They had had this conversation before, too many times. "I suppose you are speaking of my unwillingness to marry?"

"Yes," Tomas said softly.

Before her death seven years earlier Morgana's mother, the lovely Awel Ramsden, had made her husband, Almund, promise that he would not force their only child to take a husband she did not love. Awel had been frantically insistent, in fact. Caught up in the emotion of the moment, a grieving husband had agreed to his wife's last request, and so far had stuck with that promise, even though he was openly weary of Morgana's constant refusals of offers. What Almund Ramsden did not know was that his wife had also begged her daughter not to give in to marriage until she discovered a love she could trust. Awel's first marriage, her short-lived union with Morgana's long-deceased father, had been an arranged one. Though Awel had never offered Morgana details, she had made it clear that to marry without love was a terrible mistake.

Real love was worth waiting for, Awel Ramsden had insisted fervently not long before she took her last breath.

Morgana was taken by surprise when Tomas reached out and caressed her hair. He'd offered himself as husband more than once, and she'd always refused, just as she refused all others. Unlike her stepfather and the other men who no longer called upon her, Tomas displayed quite a lot of patience. He was persistent to a fault.

"Marry me," he said, not for the first time.

"No."

"I know you're uncertain about me, but if it's love you want, as so many women seem to do, then be assured that love will come, in time," he said. "Even if it does not, we can be great friends for a lifetime. Are the best of marriages not between friends?"

"My answer remains no." She did not know if the kind of love her mother had spoken of existed for her—it certainly had not shown itself thus far—but she did understand that she didn't love Tomas and never would.

In the darkness she could not see his face well. Shadows from the forest which surrounded her home and the village not far beyond hid his expression from her. But she saw too well the tightening of his lips, the tick of his jaw. "Are you too good for me, Lady Morgana, is that it? Are you too pretty? Too rich? Too pure?"

"No! That's not it at all."

"Then what is your problem? Why do you constantly refuse me when I have done everything to win you to my side?" Tomas's frustration was clear in his voice and in the alarming balling of his fists.

Morgana instinctively stepped back, wondering if Tomas would catch her if she tried to escape. Of course he would. His legs were longer than hers and he was not impeded by a heavy, cumbersome skirt.

He looked into her eyes, and something in his expression softened. "There's nothing to be afraid of," he said, and he reached out to boldly caress her breast with the tips of his fingers, much in the same casual way he had caressed her hair moments earlier. When Morgana stepped away once more, when she tried to move away from his touch, Tomas grabbed the fabric of her dark blue gown, chosen for this night so she could blend into the shadows, and forcefully pulled her to him. Stitches popped, fabric ripped, and Morgana felt a growing chill inside her, as if a seed of fear took root in her heart.

"Stop," she whispered.

"I'll show you there's nothing to be afraid of," Tomas said, and then he grabbed her chin and with unkind fingers forced her face up. He planted his mouth over hers for what she supposed was meant to be a kiss which would sway her. As if his forcefulness would make her desire to take him as a husband! Morgana pursed her lips and tried to push him away, but he was too strong. The chill grew colder and larger. It reached deep, like shards of ice, as Tomas forced his tongue into her mouth.

She had never felt so cold, and the chill at the center of her being scared her almost as much as Tomas's insistent touch. "Stop right now or you will be sorry," Morgana said when she was able to turn her mouth from his and take a deep, ragged breath.

"I don't think so," Tomas said with confidence. "Until now I have been very tolerant of your quirks and demands. I have asked nicely, and I've waited for you to come to your senses. I'm not going to wait anymore. Almund has spoiled you, but I will not. I see now that tolerance is not what you need from a man. Perhaps you have simply been waiting for a man to take what he requires from you. You need a man to command you, a man to own you. I'm man enough to take what I want, Morgana. When I saw you slip out of your window, I knew this would be the night."

The chill inside Morgana grew and seemed to move throughout her body, traveling through the blood in her veins. She was struck by the certainty that this chill was not normal. Something was very wrong. "You followed me?"

"You're mine," Tomas said in a threatening voice. "Stop fighting what is meant to be."

Like the others who had pursued her, what was "meant to be" was a partnership with the Ramsden family fortune and lands. One day her stepfather would be gone and the house and the land would all be hers. It was an elegant, finely crafted house and there was a lot of land. Tomas was greedy like all the rest, not a friend at all. "Stop this while you can," Morgana said softly.

Maybe Tomas heard something he did not like in her voice, because for a moment he did stop. He went very still, but unfortunately that stillness did not last. He foolishly continued, clumsily lifting her skirt and poking at her with his fingers.

"Do you like that?" he asked.

"No," Morgana whispered, trying to contain the frostiness that made her feel as if her heart was literally made of ice. Her fingers tingled, and it seemed that icy water flowed through her veins as cold as a winter's snow. Tomas's hand slipped between her legs and he grabbed. It hurt; his rough touch terrified her. She tried to slip from his grasp; she slapped his hands and pushed against him, hoping to free herself from his hold on her and *run*, taking the chance that she could lose him in the dark shadows, but he held her tightly.

"You will like me well enough before I'm done. Relax, and you will like it very well."

Unable to escape, Morgana attempted to contain the iciness inside her, to push it down. She didn't understand the growing coldness which was coursing through her, but she knew instinctively that it was bad. No good could come of it. But the excitement of the moment, the danger, the rush of vulnerability and anger had awakened a dark power she did not wish to possess. There was no turning back. Still, she tried. She reached for calmness, for peace, and found only coldness. She reached deep inside herself for control and found only chaos. Never in her life had she experienced pure panic, a complete loss of control and peace, not until now.

"You will marry me, Morgana," Tomas said. "After tonight, you will have no choice. No other suitable man will have you once everyone knows we've become lovers beneath the moon of the First Night of the Spring Festival."

"There is no love in this, Tomas. Please stop."

He slapped her once and threw her to the ground and then quickly dropped down to press his heavy body atop her. That was a terrible mistake. With his violence he made it impossible for her to contain the horror he had awakened. What Morgana had so hoped to control was now unleashed, and there was no turning back. Tears stung her eyes, trailing down her cheeks and turning to ice that clung to her skin. Her body went rigid and a scream rose in her chest. She fought to contain that scream.

"You truly are cold," Tomas said as he reached down to

unfasten his trousers so he could take by force what he considered to be his. "Cold to the bone. Cold skin, cold eyes . . . cold heart, I suspect. Stop fighting, Morgana. Relax. Do you not know that this is the season of carnal initiation? Never fear, woman. What I'm about to teach you will warm you up quite well."

What she had attempted to still was unleashed, and Morgana screamed. The sound which tore from her throat was foreign and frightening, even to her own ears. Surely only a wounded animal would screech so.

Tomas backed away from her, falling to the side and rolling away, coming up on his knees. "What the hell was that?"

He was no longer on top of her, no longer an immediate danger, but it was too late for her to stop what had begun as a simple chill. The unearthly coldness that had been building inside Morgana escaped from her body in one pulse, coloring a circle around her in blue and white light, and transforming everything within that circle—everything but Morgana herself—to crystal clear glass.

The grass, the fallen leaves, the trees, and Tomas, all clear and lifeless. Moonlight glimmered on what had once been life and was now cold, hard death. Lying on the ground in the midst of it all, Morgana reached out and touched what had once been a long blade of grass growing in the forest. It looked sharp but crumbled beneath her fingers, turning to dust without even marking her skin.

This should not be possible. It was wrong, unnatural, and wicked. What was she? What had she become? Was this destruction the result of a curse? Whatever the reason for her ghastly act, Morgana knew she had to escape before anyone found her here. She longed for the safety and warmth of home; she craved the heat of a fire in the hearth and a warm blanket and a locked door which would keep men like Tomas away from her.

As she stood, rising to her feet as carefully as possible,

crystal grass and leaves beneath her feet broke into tiny pieces. The crystal was as fragile as the thinnest piece of glass but did not pierce her slippers to cut her feet. No, instead it simply crumbled into dust, more fragile than any ice or stone could ever be. The substance everything in the path of her rage had become was unknown to her; it was not stone nor was it crystal.

For a moment she stared at what was left of Tomas. The statue before her looked like the man she knew, but he had been sculpted of ice, down to the shape of his lips and the crease in his jacket and his halfway unfastened trousers. Moonlight gleamed on his frozen face; he looked so scared, as if in his last moment of life he'd realized what was happening, what he'd awakened, what a monster she was.

Morgana felt a surge of hope. If she had the power to transform everything in her path to this strange substance, perhaps she also had the power to undo it. A deep chill had preceded the burst of power. Perhaps warmth would turn Tomas to a man again. She reached out and touched his cold, hard face gently, hoping to give him some of the warmth which had returned to her. She leaned forward and blew a warm breath upon him, hoping all the while that he would become a man again.

Then she would run.

But Tomas did not transform; he remained a crystal statue in the shadows of the forest. A sob escaped Morgana's throat. Tomas was a bad person, a greedy man who was willing to take what he wanted if it was not offered to him, but that didn't mean he deserved to die this way. Was he entirely cold? Was there any life left in the form before her?

If only she had stayed in her room tonight, as her stepfather had commanded, Tomas would still be alive. Too soon Morgana heard the villagers approaching, their voices carrying sharply. She looked toward the bonfire to see that at least half of the men there were headed her way. They had been lured by her screech or the flash of light, and they could not find her here with what was left of Tomas. If they found her here in the midst of destruction, they would know she was to blame—they would know she was cursed.

"I'm sorry," Morgana whispered, and then she ran, crystal crunching easily beneath her feet until she left the circle of destruction she had created. Long before she reached her bedroom window, she heard the first villager's scream.